Bio-Weapon

(Doom Star 2)

by
Vaughn Heppner

ISBN-13: 978-1496145710
ISBN-10: 1496145712
BISAC: Fiction / Science Fiction / Military

Neutraloids

1.

"We're hunting dogs, Omi, nothing more."

The Korean ex-gang member shook his bullet-shaped head, clearly not liking that kind of talk.

Marten Kluge rolled back his sleeve to show the meaty part of his forearm and a bluish-purple barcode tattoo.

"Branded like cattle," Marten said.

"In case you die," Omi said. "So they know your blood-type when they resurrect you."

"You believe that?" Marten was a lean, ropy-muscled man with bristly blond hair. He wore a brown jumpsuit, the shock trooper, training uniform. It had patch of a skull on his right shoulder and another on his left pectoral pocket.

Omi wore a similar shock trooper jumpsuit. Both uniforms showed sweat stains and both men had circles under their eyes. Their grueling training surpassed anything they'd ever known, and they'd known plenty of bad.

"They also use the barcode to track you," Omi said. "We're little blips in the station computer."

Marten's expression didn't change as they strode down an empty corridor, a utilitarian steel hall with emergency float rails on the sides. This was sleep-time, but Marten had convinced Omi to slip from the barracks so he could show him something.

"Watch," Marten said. He unlatched a secret wall panel and withdrew a recorder.

Omi frowned before leaning near. The recorder was small, square and compact, voice activated. It was something HB officers used when watching their drills.

"Is it stolen?"

A wild light flashed in Marten's eyes. Then it was gone, giving him the sleepy obedient look most of them wore around the Highborn. "Admitting a theft gets you five in the pain booth."

Omi glanced about the deserted corridor.

"It's clean," Marten said. "No listening devices."

"How do you know?"

"Because I searched until I found them."

Omi lifted a single eyebrow.

"I borrowed a bug and set it in a different corridor, one the HBs use. Then I piped it here." Marten tapped the recorder.

"Dangerous."

A hard smile was Marten's only reply.

"You might as well play it," Omi said.

Marten set the recorder on the steel floor. Then he sat cross-legged and looked up. Omi raised an eyebrow, a trademark gesture he'd perfected in the slums. Finally, he shrugged and sat on the other side of the recorder.

Marten reached out. *Click.*

There wasn't anything at first. Omi leaned closer, so did Marten.

"I thought—"

"Shhh," Marten said. He glanced at the recorder as the sounds started.

There were footfalls in a corridor, someone wearing boots.

"It's hard to hear at first," Marten said, an edge to his voice.

Omi closed his eyes. The sounds of boots striking metal grew louder. He imagined huge Highborn. They always radiated a weird vitality and had eyes like pit bulls about to pounce. Their skin was pearl-white, their lips razor thin, almost nonexistent. Any Highborn could take out a five-man maniple.

2

An HB, he was... Omi didn't hate their superiority the way Marten did, but he couldn't say he liked it either.

A hard voice, authoritative, full of vigor, spoke. But the garbled words were still too far from the hidden mike.

"I can't hear him," Omi said.

"Shhh," Marten said, scowling.

Then out of the recorder: "...can't agree, Praetor."

"The Praetor?" Omi asked, fear twisting his belly.

"Listen!" Marten said. "It's him and Training Master Lycon."

LYCON: Yes, gelding has its virtues. It would make them docile, tractable and more prone to obedience. But what about their fighting spirit?

PRAETOR: Of premen?

LYCON: Not just premen, but trained shock troopers.

PRAETOR: There's no difference. Their sex drive compels them to wild, unpredictable behavior. In space, we must know exactly how they will react. This thing called fighting spirit... I've never really seen premen with it. Let us rely on fierce hate conditioning, combat drugs and hypnotic commands.

LYCON: They are premen and they are inferior to us. But they are still capable of fighting spirit. The shock troops have been trained to a fine pitch. Why ruin it with gelding?

The voices in the recorder had grown stronger. Now they reached apogee and grew fainter again, their footfalls ringing in the background.

PRAETOR: Perhaps as you say, well-trained, some of them even simulate an apparent viciousness.

LYCON: All heel to my command, I assure you.

PRAETOR: Yes, you are to be commended on your work, Training Master. It's just that..."

Both Marten and Omi leaned over the recorder listening, the tops of their heads almost touching. The words and even the footfalls faded into nothing.

The two shock troopers straightened, Marten taking the recorder and snapping it off.

"Gelding?" asked Omi.

Marten nodded sharply, and said, "Cutting off our balls."

"They... They can't be serious."

Marten snorted. Then he walked to the secret wall panel and sealed the recorder in it.

"The Praetor was talking to Lycon, our Training Master?" Omi asked.

"Yes," Marten said.

Omi blinked several times. "You're talking castration. Would they use a pair of scissors?" Omi shook his head. "The Highborn have done a lot dirty tricks to use, but cutting off our jewels like a neutered dog, that's too much."

"What if I said we could leave here?" Marten asked.

"We're stranded in the Sun Works Factory. We're orbiting Mercury."

Marten gestured farther down the corridor.

"Forbidden territory," Omi said. "Yeah. Show me."

2.

Both Marten and Omi had found themselves aboard the Mercury Sun Works Factory through a complicated set of circumstances.

On 10 May 2350, the *Genghis Khan* and the *Julius Caesar* had entered the edge of Earth's stratosphere. The two Doom Stars had annihilated the vast Social Unity sea and air armadas that had gone into action to help the beleaguered Japanese. Social Unity had sent up half of Earth's space interceptors and launched swarms of merculite missiles against the Doom Stars. Then they'd fired the newly developed proton beams, more deadly than the old military lasers. It had taken five HB asteroids plunging earthward to take out the five SU beam installations.

Unfortunately, powering the energy-hungry proton beams had taken the full output of five major cities' deep-core mines. Such mines tapped the thermal power of the planet's core.

To house Earth's 40 billion citizens took cities that burrowed kilometers downward. Like bees, humanity survived in vast, underground hives. The asteroids had destroyed Greater Hong Kong, Manila, Beijing, Taipei and Vladivostok, and had thus slain a billion unfortunates.

Even so, Social Unity's Military Arm came within a hair's breath of destroying the *Genghis Khan*. As the Doom Stars were the bedrock of Highborn power, they absolutely had to repair the *Genghis Khan*. In the Solar System, only one place had the capacity to do so: the naval yards where they had been built. The Mercury Sun Works Factory.

5

The losses of *Genghis Khan* personnel had sharply brought home to the Highborn their greatest weakness. They only numbered a couple of million, versus billons of Homo sapiens. So Highborn Command had pondered the idea of putting a complement of shock troopers aboard each ship. To the Highborn, the shock troopers were "premen"—mere Homo sapiens. The initial shock trooper test-run took place at the Sun Works Factory. The Highborn had combed the Free Earth Corps divisions used in the Japan Campaign. FEC was filled with humans the Highborn had convinced to fight for them instead of fighting for Social Unity. Marten and Omi had been in Japan because the Highborn had captured them in Sydney, Australian Sector and each had "volunteered" for military duty. Both had won decorations for bravery, the reason the Highborn had chosen them as shock troopers.

***

Marten and Omi headed into forbidden territory. Marten knew the way. He'd been here before, and in a certain sense he'd come home. Back in the days when Social Unity ran everything, his parents had been engineers on the Sun Works Factory. Long ago, there had been a labor strike, an attempt at unionization. Political Harmony Corps had brutally suppressed it. His parents and others had then escaped into the vast ring-factory.

Marten opened a hatch and stepped through. Omi followed.

Black and yellow lines painted on the ceiling, wall and floor warned them to stay out. Newly placed red posters with skulls and crossbones made it clear.

"Don't worry," Marten said. "I've already been here several times."

They hurried. Sleep-time would soon be over and their maniple would return to training.

"This way," Marten said. He wheeled a valve, grunted as he swung a heavy hatch open with a hiss of pressure equalizing and poked his shoulders through. The corridor was smaller here.

"It's cold," Omi said. "What's that sound?"

"A pinpoint leak. The lowered pressure makes it colder.

"Are you sure we're safe?"

6

"Here we are," Marten said.

He led Omi to a small deck, with a bubble-dome where the wall should have been. A hiss came from four meters up the dome's side.

Omi squinted at the bubble-dome's tiny fracture. "It's not dangerous, right?"

"Not yet," Marten said. He pointed outside at Mercury.

The ring-factory rotated around the planet just as Saturn's rings did around Saturn. The factory's rotation supplied pseudo-gravity. They presently faced away from the Sun, but the radiation and glare would have killed and blinded them except for the dampening devices and heavy sun-filters.

The dead, pockmarked planet filled over three-quarters of the view. Mercury wasn't big as planets went. If the Earth were a baseball, Mercury would be a golf ball. It had a magnetic field one percent of Earth's. A person weighing 100 pounds on Terra would weigh thirty-eight pounds on Mercury. The solar body it most resembled was the Earth's Moon. Just like the Lunar Planet, thousands of craters littered Mercury. Dominating the view below was the Caloris Basin, a mare or sea like those on the Moon. Instead of salt water, however, well-baked dust filled the mares. The Caloris Basin was 1300 kilometers in diameter, on a planet only 4880 kilometers in diameter.

Marten pointed at the Sun Works Factory as it curved away from them—they were inside the fantastic structure. The curving space satellite seemed to go on forever, until it disappeared behind the planet. On the outer side of the factory, unseen from the viewing deck because the outside part faced the Sun, were huge solar panels that soaked up the fierce energy and fed it into waiting furnaces. Catapulted from Mercury came load after load of various ores.

"Look at that," Omi said.

Far to their left sat the damaged Doom Star *Genghis Khan*. It was a huge warship kilometers spherical. Blue and red lights winked around it, sometimes dipping into it. They were repair pods. Some were automated robots and some were human-occupied modules.

7

Omi turned to Marten. "So how is standing here going to help us from getting gelded?"

"Look over there."

Omi squinted and shook his head.

"There," Marten said, pointing more emphatically. "See?"

"That pod?"

"Correct."

A small, one-man pod floated about a hundred meters from the habitat's inner surface. No lights winked from it. It sat there, seemingly dead, a simple ball with several arms controlled from within. There were welder arms, clamps and work lasers. Anyone sitting inside the pod could punch in a flight code. Particles of hydrogen would spray out the burner.

"What about it?" Omi asked.

"Remember how I told you I grew up here?"

Omi nodded.

"Well," Marten said, "I bet most of my equipment—my family's equipment—should still be intact. It was well hidden."

"So?"

"So my family built an ultra-stealth pod to escape to the Jupiter Confederation."

"PHC found it, you said, over four and half years ago."

"I'm pretty sure they found it back then. But that doesn't matter because I could build another one."

"Impossible."

Marten managed a smile. "You're right. Let's stay and get gelded."

Omi paled. "How do you plan on going about this, a...?"

"I need a vacc suit," Marten said. "So I can go outside and enter the pod."

"Then?"

"Then it gets hard," admitted Marten.

"But not impossible, right?"

Marten checked his chronometer. "Time to head back."

Omi glanced at the hissing spot in the plexiglass bubble, and then he turned with Marten for the barracks.

3.

On the experimental Social Unity Beamship *Bangladesh*, Admiral Rica Sioux sank into her acceleration couch. She wore a silver vacc suit, the faceplate dark and the conditioner-unit humming. Around her and suited as well languished the officers of the armored command capsule.

Despite the *Bangladesh's* heavy shielding, months in near-Sun orbit had leaked enough radiation so Admiral Sioux had ordered the command crew together with the Security detail into the vacc suits. There had barely been enough suits for higher command and security, a grim oversight from requisitioning. The rest of ship's company had bitterly complained about the lack of vacc suits for them. After the first cases of radiation sickness, Security had overheard talk of mutiny. Finally, in order to regain a sort of normalcy, the Admiral had ordered drumhead executions of the ringleaders—in this instance, randomly selected personnel.

The experimental spacecraft, the only one of its kind, had already set two hazardous duty records: one for its nearness to the Sun, two for the duration of its stay. Their greatest danger was an unexpected solar flare. One such flare, over 60,000 kilometers long, had already shot out of the Sun's photosphere and looped over the *Bangladesh*, only to fall back into the cauldron of nuclear fire. The ship's heavy magnetic shielding, the same as in Earth's deep-core mines, kept the x-rays, ultraviolet and visible radiation and high-speed protons and electrons from penetrating the ship and killing everyone aboard. Not even the vacc suits would have protected them

9

from that. Unfortunately, the rare occurrence of a giant solar flare had signaled the commencement of Admiral Sioux's troubles. The image of their beamship sailing under the flare's magnetic loop of hot gas had horrified the crew. If a flare should ever hit them—even with the beamship's magnetic shields at full power they would be instantly annihilated.

The ship had been in near-Sun orbit since the start of hostilities. Their ship was probably the only one in the Solar System that could have done it. The magnetic shields that protected them this near the nuclear furnace took fantastic amounts of energy to maintain—too much to make the M-shields useful in combat. The collection of power here was simple but deadly for the personnel aboard. Special solar panels soaked up the incredible mega wattage pouring out of the Sun. Unfortunately, they couldn't collect when the magnetic shields were up. So they switched off the M-shield and used the heavy particle shields—millions of tons of matter—to keep the worst radiation at bay while the solar collectors collected a full charge. Then—and none too soon—up went the magnetic shields. Most of the radiation exposure, naturally, occurred between these switches.

Admiral Sioux had chosen the near-Sun orbit to hide out of basic necessity. Social Unity Military Command well knew the combat capabilities of the enemy Doom Stars. No combination of the Social Unity Fleet could face one, and at the rebellion's commencement, the Highborn had captured all five. So to save the Fleet, SUMC had ordered an immediate dispersion of ships into the nether regions of space. The scattering kept the Fleet in being, and just as importantly, it forced the enemy to split his Doom Stars, if he wanted to picket each of the four inner planets.

This near the Sun was the perfect hiding spot, at least since the destruction of the robot radar probes that had long ago been set at far-Sun orbit. Neither radar nor optics could spot the *Bangladesh* if the viewer looked directly at the Sun. The Sun's harsh radio signals blanketed the beamship, while the Star's light—seeing the *Bangladesh* in near-Sun orbit would be like trying to pinpoint a candle's flame with a forest fire right behind it. The trick, of course, would be to look "down" and

10

get a side view, with space as the background and not the nuclear ball of fire. It was the military reason for the three robot radar probes at equidistant locations around the Sun, and why the Admiral had destroyed the probes.

Admiral Sioux shifted on her couch, trying to relax her left shoulder. The horrible acceleration threatened to cramp her muscles. Nor could she lift her arm and massage her shoulder. Simply breathing, forcing her chest up in order to drag down another breath, was becoming hard.

She took short, small breaths and her thigh cramped. Despite that, she grinned hideously. The acceleration made it so.

A week ago, they had picked up General James Hawthorne's scratchy orders. It had taken computer enhancement to make sense of the Supreme Military Commander's words. Because of the orders, she now used the Sun as a pivoting post, building up speed.*We are finally going to hit back*, she thought. After long months of inactivity, she would be allowed to hurt the enemy.

The Sun's diameter was roughly 1.4 million kilometers, or about 109 times that of the Earth. The *Bangladesh* thus circled the Sun at a greater distance than the Moon did in its orbit around the Earth. The diameter of the Moon's orbit was approximately 770,000 kilometers.

The beamship's huge engines increased power and changed the direction of their thrust, and the experimental *Bangladesh* broke free from its near-Sun orbit. It sped toward Mercury. In three weeks, the ship would pass the planet at a distance of 30 million kilometers.

A second later, the awful acceleration snapped off. The G-forces shoving Admiral Sioux into the couch quit. She expelled air, and then she clamped her teeth together, forcing herself not to vomit. The sudden weightlessness always did that to her, a weakness she despised in herself.

She unbuckled her harness and sat up. So did the others.

The *Bangladesh* still hid in the Sun's glare from anyone looking from Mercury. They coasted now and thus gave away no gravity-wave signatures. Just as importantly, they knew exactly where their target would be during the coming window

11

of opportunity. Everything depended upon surprise–complete, utter and total surprise.

Behind her darkened visor, the Admiral flashed a wicked smile.

The *Bangladesh* had been built for just such an attack. In this one particular, it broke the "rules" of modern space warfare.

She pushed off the couch and floated to the First Gunner. Together and with ship's AI, they would work out several attack patterns.

Admiral Sioux chinned on her suit's outer speakers, and said to the Command Crew, "We must not fail."

Several dark visors turned toward her.

Finally, they were going to hit back at the Highborn. No more hiding, no more cowering from the enemy. Her chest swelled with pride. "For Social Unity," she said, thrusting her arm in the Party salute.

Only the First Gunner raised his hand in return. Two others turned away, another was coughing.

Admiral Sioux squinted thoughtfully. If they lived through the attack, she would mark this into each of their profiles, this lack of zeal in face of the enemy. But there was no sense bringing it up now and ruining morale even more. Better if she didn't have to bring Security into the command capsule.

Sioux reached the First Gunner, grabbed his shoulder and settled herself into the module beside him. She logged onto the targeting computer and rubbed her gloved hands in glee. Soon everyone would see the power of the *Bangladesh*. Then, yes, then her name would blaze as the visionary who had saved Social Unity.

4.

The Sun Works Factory rotated around the dead planet. A million lights glittered from this greatest of space stations. Thousands of system-craft darted into docking bays or launched outward. They went to or returned from other parts of the factory that were half a world away. They powered down to the planet or caught the billions of tons of ores catapulted from Mercury. Many circled the mighty Doom Star *Genghis Khan*. Others endlessly patched, fixed and mended the spinning satellite. Relentless work was the only way to keep the hated enemy—entropy—at bay.

Several military shuttles docked at a kilometers-huge Zero-G Training Room that drifted between the Sun Works Factory and Mercury. Inside, Training Master Lycon put his shock troops through their paces.

Within the enormous room floated cubes and triangles the size of barns. The geometric shapes had been made to look like portions of a blasted spaceship. Far in the background and all around appeared points of light, make-believe stars. The farthest wall shone brightly, the supposed sun-reflected side of an orbital habitat.

Floating thickest in the room's midsection were nearly fifty frozen shock troops. They wore stiff orange bodysuits that periodically buzzed. The sound was the suit's generator releasing punishment-volts that jolted through the frozen victim. The enclosed helmets kept any grunting or groaning internal, although a detector within the helmet picked up the noise, causing the generator to add a few extra volts during the next charge.

The Highborn firmly believed in the virtue of suffering in silence. Premen training theory also stated that failures should be instantly punished. Furthermore, these pain procedures accustomed premen to pain endurance, another virtue. Also, the fear of training failure made the exercise "real" in the subjective sense of the punished trainee. Finally, at least so the theory went, how could an instructor train premen to overcome pressure unless pressure was vigorously applied?

On the simulated space-habitat wall watchdogged a single remaining laser pulse-cannon, this one ready to emit a low-watt beam. The pitted nozzle rotated back and forth, hunting for motion and the color orange.

The last maniple hid behind a nearby cube, out of sight of the cannon. They were all that was left of the attackers. These five knew that if one of those pulses touched their suit they would freeze, giving a practice kill to the enemy for this satellite storming drill.

One of the floating, orange-suited men peeked around the cube's corner and at the pulse-cannon. On the top of his helmet was stenciled OMI.

The other four floated behind him, holding onto rails. Their helmets read MARTEN, KANG, LANCE and VIP. Kang was a massive man and dwarfed the others. Vip was the smallest. Otherwise, their bodysuits and helmet seemed identical.

Omi jerked back as a low-watt pulse grazed the cube's corner. He held a heavy laser tube, his image glowing in the momentary red beam.

"A good leader leads through example," Vip said, peering at Marten as he spoke via comlink. Through Vip's faceplate showed the little man's hair-lip scar and a pulp nose, all mashed about his narrow face.

"That's a good maxim," said Lance. "Bet the HBs would like it."

Marten kept staring at Vip, watching the man's twitchy eyeballs, like little lead pips. They were always on the move. *Yeah, like a weasel looking for a chicken to steal.*

"What'cha grinning at?" asked Vip.

14

When Marten didn't answer, Lance said, "You've been outvoted, Marten."

Marten touched his holster. As maniple leader, his laser pistol could freeze their suits. So far, it had always trumped any of their arguments.

"Whatever we do we're gonna take hits," Marten said. "So—"

"Give me Omi's laser tube and I'll take out the pulse-cannon," Vip said.

"Trade potshots with it?" Marten asked.

"You don't think I can?"

"We have to move," Kang said.

Omi nodded. "Immobility brings death." He quoted an HB combat maxim. The genetic super-soldiers had hundreds of them, quoting them with dreadful regularity.

"Right," Marten said. "Lance, Vip, at my signal you fly left."

"We'll get hit," complained Vip.

"Correct," Marten said.

"You and Omi fly left," Vip said sullenly.

Kang hung onto a float rail with his left hand, reached out and grabbed Vip with his right and slammed him against the cube.

"Kang and I will take the wall-buster and go right," Marten said, paying no attention to those two. "Omi, you take out the pulse-cannon if you can. Everyone ready?"

Vip shook his head from where his helmet had struck the cube. His upper lip curled as he stared at Kang. Lance settled between Kang and Vip as he glared at the massive man.

"Use your thrusters," Marten said. "Make the pulse-cannon really have to swivel in order to hit us all."

"What tactical brilliance," Vip said. "By the time you brake for the wall—"

"Go!" Marten said.

Both Lance and Vip, who hung onto the float rail and had pushed up against the cube, thrust with their legs. They sailed fast in the zero gravity, Lance in the lead. Both men thumbed the switch on the handle gripped in their right fists. Oxygen belched from their jetpacks, causing them to jerk and fly faster.

15

The pulse-cannon swiveled and tracked. *Spat, spat.* Twin shots flashed past the men's feet. The cannon minutely adjusted for thruster-speed and fired again.

Washed with red light, Lance froze. His comlink cut out and sliced his groan in half. Vip fired his laser pistol, an ineffectual weapon against the cannon, but it made the HBs happy seeing aggressive gestures. Vip's beam washed over the pulse-cannon a second before it froze him.

From the other side of the cube and in the other direction, Kang and Marten jetted. Between them, they held an imitation wall-buster. The pitted pulse-cannon swiveled. Omi peeked from behind the cube as he aimed the heavy laser tube.

The pulse-cannon beeped in warning, jerking hard toward Omi, who fired. His beam missed, splashing a foot from the armored cannon.

"Aim!" crackled Kang's voice.

Another shot missed and then Omi froze, hit.

Marten and Kang sped at ramming speed toward the fast-approaching wall.

"Brake," Kang said.

Marten laughed as his jetpack continued to hiss propellant.

The pulse-cannon swiveled onto them as it pumped red flashes like tracers.

Kang let go of the wall-buster. He twisted expertly as his thick thumb jerked the handle switch. His jetpack quit. Once in position—with his back to the wall—Kang jabbed his thumb down. Air hissed and he braked. All the while, his other hand aimed his laser and fired at the hated cannon. Then Kang froze as the pulse-cannon triggered the lock on his bodysuit. Each punishment jolt brought a muffled curse from in his helmet.

Marten crashed against the simulated space habitat wall. His teeth rattled and his right ankle twisted and popped. But the wall-buster stuck to the habitat and a loud siren shrieked. At this point, the wall-buster would explode and breach the enemy habitat. That was military success for this tactical practice, as one hundred percent casualties had been within the allowable limits.

Lights immediately snapped on all over the huge gym, destroying the illusion of a battle-strewn space-field. The bodysuits unfroze and shock troopers shivered, or groaned, or laughed, or did whatever was natural to them with the stoppage of punishment pain. One by one, the premen jetted toward the exit. From there they filed aboard the shuttles, which returned them to barracks.

A few of the shock troopers congratulated Marten. Others scowled. They were angry his maniple had won the competition.

Everyone toweled off after showering. Then the winning maniple donned blue tunics, brown spylo jackets, civilian pants and boots and re-boarded a shuttle. Their victory reward was an evening in the famed Recreation Level 49, Section 218 of the Sun Works Factory, the Pleasure Palace.

Marten sat at a shuttle window, glumly peering out at the mighty space station.

The ring-factory rotated in order to simulate Earth-normal gravity for those within. The gargantuan space station was a veritable world unto itself, a world now run by the Highborn. It was their furnace and incubation for continued greatness.

The Highborn had controlled it less than a year. Grand Admiral Cassius had made it second priority at the rebellion's commencement. First priority had been capturing all five Doom Stars. The majority of the population had lived on the satellite for over ten years, formerly card-carrying Social Unitarians, and in HB parlance, premen. Next in number after the native Sun Workers were recently imported Earthmen: FEC soldiers, ex-peacekeepers and ex-SU Military Intelligence operatives. FEC was Free Earth Corps. Their single uniqueness was allegiance to the New Order. The bulk of them came from Antarctica and Australian Sector, although lately several shipments of Japanese had arrived. All had gone through HB reeducation camps. The Earthmen composed nearly one hundred percent of the space station's guards, police and monitors. The Sun Workers provided the service techs, mechanics, software specialists, recreation personnel, factory coolies and the like.

The switch from State-sponsored socialism under Social Unity to a form of quasi-capitalism under the Highborn brought many new ills. The Highborn urged success of product

17

over rigorous application of ideology. In other words, did a thing work? Monitors watched to suppress rebellion, no longer gauging every thought and action. Thus while before the Highborn a lackluster black-market had survived in the factory, now a thriving illegal drug trade together with greater theft and its accompanying rise in assault and murder rates plagued the giant space habitat.

Some said it was the price of free-market capitalism. A handful of people got richer quicker while many others died sooner. A few were spaced: shoved out the airlocks without any vacc suits. The Highborn, it was said, threw up their hands. This once again proved their superiority over the premen, who acted like beasts, like cattle. Whenever it got too bad, a few new divisions of monitors hit the streets.

Marten held nominal leadership of the 101st Maniple, Shock Troopers. He wasn't the toughest, strongest, nor quickest, and he was not the most brutal, savage or street-savvy. The HBs however had judged him to have the best tactical mind. And he had something extra: a deep inner drive.

Kang, the massive Mongol sitting across from Marten, had black tattoos on his arms and a flat-looking face. He shaved his head bald. Before the war, he'd been a Sydney slum gang leader, running a vicious lot called the Red Blades. During the Japan Campaign, he'd been a fanatical FEC First Lieutenant, personally killing hundreds of Japanese.

"Hey, Kang," called Vip, standing in the aisle. The shuttle was nearly empty, giving the 101st effective run of the passenger area.

Kang ignored the little man as he penciled a crossword puzzle. He didn't fill in the blanks with letters, but shaded heavy lined triangles.

Vip nudged Lance, the rangy Brit sitting in an isle seat. Lance counted his pathetic supply of plastic tokens—credits.

"Hey, Kang," Vip said. "How come you didn't hit the wall like Marten did?"

Kang stopped his doodling and ponderously raised his head.

"You ever hope to take maniple leadership from Marten you're gonna have to do stuff like that," Vip said.

18

Out of the corner of his eye, Marten watched the silent Mongol. Kang had killed more men in combat than the rest of them put together. They were all FEC Army heroes, having all fought in the Japan Campaign six months ago.

"You want to know why?" Kang asked.

"I asked you, didn't I?" Vip said.

Kang scratched at his crossword puzzle. Then he held it out for Vip. "I wrote out the reason."

Vip winked at Lance before stepping near to grab the journal.

For all his bulk, Kang could strike quicker than a mongoose. He dropped the crossword puzzle and latched on to Vip's wrist. Then he stood, yanked Vip against his chest and with one hand grabbed the little man by his jacket collar. He lifted Vip off his toes.

"Dance, boy," Kang said. He jerked Vip up and down like an ape with a rat. Suddenly Vip slapped the vast forearm with something that sizzled.

Kang hissed as his hand opened reflexively.

Vip jumped back into the main aisle. Metal glittered in his palm. It was a stolen agonizer, a PHC tool, probably dropped somewhere when the Highborn had killed the Social Unitarians at the start of the rebellion. The stubborn PHC people had refused to surrender.

Kang tested his hand by flexing it several times. Then he glared at Vip.

Lance took that moment to stand, pocket his plastic credits and block Kang's way out. Although as tall and broad-shouldered as Kang, the Brit with his sweeping dark hair probably weighed only half as much. But then, he was mostly gristle and whalebone, as he liked to say.

Kang's upper lip twitched.

"Vip!" Marten said. He desperately wanted to avoid a forbidden shuttle fight that would cancel the trip.

Kang, Lance and Vip glanced at him, as did Omi, who sat beside Marten.

"Give me the agonizer," Marten said.

"It's mine," Vip said.

"Yeah," Marten said. "But I don't want you carrying it during leave and getting yourself in trouble."

"If I don't have it," Vip said. "Then you'll have it, and then you'll get in trouble. Bet you hadn't thought of that."

"Gimme," Marten said, holding out his hand.

Vip weighed the tiny torture device.

Lance turned from Kang, giving his friend Vip a significant glance before he jerked his head at Marten.

Vip whined, "But I want to fix the dealer who thought he could—"

Lance cleared his throat and shook his head. "Give it up," he said.

Vip pouted a moment longer, then shrugged and tossed it to Marten. He put the agonizer in his jacket pocket.

Marten now regarded Kang, who still flexed his hand. "You ought to relax. In a few more minutes we're at the Pleasure Palace and we can all get drinks."

"Are you buying me a round?" Kang asked.

Marten calculated his slender supply of credits—a few less than Lance because he'd played poker with him last night. "Sure," he said, knowing he needed every plastic token he had. "One round."

Kang grunted. Then he picked the crossword journal off the floor and sat down. He used his pencil to trace heavy lines one tiny box at a time.

"Docking in one minute," a female pilot said over the intercom. "Please take your seats and buckle in."

Omi and Marten exchanged glances. Because the HB mania for rank and status had infected most of the shock troopers, they hadn't told the others about the gelding tape. As elite shock troopers, they outranked all Earthbound FEC fighters. In the carefully layered strata for premen, fighting forces in space or planet-side trumped everyone else. Next were police and monitors. Below them were the captains of industry and the personal techs of various Highborn.

Among the shock troops, the most coveted position was maniple leader. As soon as the Highborn created higher command slots, such as mission first commander and second and third, then no doubt the struggle among the maniple leaders for those slots would become intense.

So…who to trust? That had been Marten's question. Not Kang, who had always been first even if only in street gangs. Vip was too twitchy to know which way he'd jump. Lance…he was sneaky. It was hard to know what he really thought about anything so Marten didn't know if he could trust him.

Marten stared gloomily out the shuttle window. He had his few credits, and Omi's, he supposed, and a listening device. Otherwise, all he had was his wits to try to obtain a vacc suit. He had only this trip to do it, too, because who knew if he could win another reward trip before the snip-snip moment made it all academic. He rubbed his jacket over the spot on his forearm where the barcode was tattooed. Tagged like a beast.

The shuttle began to brake.

Marten's chest tightened. Whatever it took. Do or die. He blew out his cheeks and wished this shuttle would hurry and dock.

5.

They exited the shuttle and followed the route card that Marten had been given at the barracks. He limped because of his ankle. It was tightly wrapped and he'd been given a shot to reduce swelling, but it was tender. Soon they stood in a sterile hall and before a row of steel-colored lift doors.

"Seventeen C," Marten said, checking his card.

"This way then," said Lance.

They found the lift, Marten slid the route card through the slot and door pinged, opening. They entered. He slid the card in the destination slot, and up they went toward Level 49, the Pleasure Palace.

Most of the Sun Factory was automated and empty of people. It was a giant construct and it would have taken billions of people to fill. Unsurprisingly, most people wanted to be around other people. So there were only a few areas in the Sun Works Factory were the vast majority congregated. The Pleasure Palace was one of those places. The shock trooper training area was another, and a third was the Highborn facilities.

Each was an oasis of humanity amid an empty sea of thousands of miles of corridors and holding bays.

"You owe me a drink," Kang said as they rode the lift.

"I haven't forgotten," Marten said.

"Where do we go first?" Vip asked Lance. "The game pit or the card room?"

"You got to study the crowds first," explained Lance. "Get a feel for the luck of a place."

22

Vip nodded sagely.

Kang said, "Only losers talk about luck."

Vip laughed in a know-it-all way, while Lance looked at the ceiling and pursed his lips.

"I don't know how many times I've heard losers whine to me to give them a second chance," Kang said. "'The shipment got fouled up due to bad luck,' they'd say. 'Yeah?' I'd ask. 'Real bad luck, Kang. You watch, and my luck will turn around. No,' I'd say. 'I don't think your luck will ever change. Why not, Kang? Sure it will.' I'd shake my head, get up and stick a vibroblade in his belly. 'That's why not,' I'd tell them. I was never wrong."

"Where was that?" asked Lance, perhaps a bit too eagerly.

Kang shrugged.

Marten knew where. Back in the slums of Sydney, Australian Sector where Kang had been the gang leader of the Red Blades. Just like in the old French Foreign Legion, many in the shock troops kept their past to themselves. Neither Lance nor Vip had been with them in the Japan Campaign, back when Omi, Kang and Marten had been soldiers in the 93rd Slumlord Battalion of the 10th FEC Division.

Before anyone could say more, the lift opened and they were assaulted by noise and a waft of mingled human odors. They hurried onto the broad passageway with its glittering festival-lights. Slender imitation trees swayed in the perfumed breeze, while crowds seethed across the floor space. The people wore bright party clothes and happy drunken grins. Paygirls or men in even gaudier costumes draped on partygoers' arms.

Dotted among this mass were the obvious uniformed police and undercover monitors. Along the sides of the passageway stood souvenir shops, restaurants, pleasure parlors, and game and card rooms. Snack-shacks provided a shot of pick-me-up or pills, and sandwiches, that provided energy to arouse the sluggish.

"Back at ten?" asked Lance.

"Don't be late to the shuttle or it's a mark against all of us," Marten said.

Vip waved good-bye and then plunged into the crowd. Lance strode after him.

"Now what?" asked Omi.

"Now Marten owes me a drink," Kang said.

Marten peered at the festive masses. Tonight, here, few cared that the Highborn ruled, few cared that a vast civil war raged in the Inner Planets. This was Level 49, the party palace. "What's your poison?" Marten asked Kang.

"Smirnoff on the rocks at Smade's Tavern."

"Never heard of either," Marten said.

Kang turned his bulk toward the crowds and waded in. Marten glanced at Omi, who shrugged. They followed Kang. Like a bear or gorilla, the huge Mongol shouldered people out of the way. Many saw him coming and hurried aside. A few glared. Those found themselves sprawled on the floor. A policeman with a truncheon squinted as Kang headed straight at him. With a brutal shoulder-shove, Kang knocked the cop flying.

As Marten passed, the cop leaped up and snarled into a mike on his collar. Then he sprang after Kang.

"This could take care of our problem," Omi said.

"No," Marten said. "Kang's 101st. We've got to back him up."

"Getting motherly are you?"

The cop grabbed Kang's arm. Kang jerked his arm in annoyance and kept moving. Then the crowds thinned and two more policemen bore down on Kang. At a more leisurely pace behind them, there followed a thin man with bushy eyebrows. He wore a red tunic, with purple pantaloons and curly-toed slippers. He was older, with sparse hair, maybe in his late forties.

"Halt," said the cop behind Kang.

Kang neither halted nor acknowledged that he'd heard.

The two approaching cops glanced at one another. They drew shock rods and flicked power so the batons hummed. They braced themselves.

Kang stopped so suddenly that the cop behind crashed into him. Kang seemed barely to swivel around, but he put that cop

24

in a headlock and applied pressure so the man's face turned red.

"Let him go," warned the taller of the other two cops.

The thin man with the purple pantaloons and curly-toed slippers widened his eyes in astonishment. "Kang?" he asked.

Kang peered at the slim man with sparse hair. He had foxy features, sly and cruel. Kang snorted. "Heydrich Hansen, huh? Good old Sydney slum-trash."

The taller of the two police turned to Hansen. "You know him, sir?"

"Indeed."

"What are your wishes for him, sir?"

"Sir?" Kang asked Hansen. "Changed professions, huh?"

Hansen's smile lost some of its charm. "Why not let the policeman go, Kang. I'll buy you a few drinks—to make up for that time I was late."

Kang seemed to consider it, as if he was doing Hansen a favor.

Marten leaned near Omi, whispering, "Do you know this Hansen?"

Omi frowned, shaking his head.

The policeman in the headlock had started to turn purple. He no longer seemed to be breathing.

"Sir!" said the taller of the two policemen.

"I'll buy your friends a round, too, Kang."

"You said several rounds," Kang said.

Hansen turned rueful. "Perhaps I shouldn't say this, but these days I'm a monitor. I'm presently on the job."

Kang tapped the shock trooper patch on the breast of his jacket.

Hansen peered at it. "Ah. You and your happy band of killers are here tonight. Seems like nothing ever changes."

"No," Kang said.

"Why not consider yourself my guest tonight?" said Hansen. "For old time's sake."

Kang thought a moment longer and finally released the cop, who dropped like a sack of carrots. The cop shuddered and wheezed. He began to tremble.

The two cops with shock rods advanced warily toward their fellow peace officer.

Kang paid them no heed. He lumbered up and slapped Hansen on the back, staggering the monitor, the secret policeman for the Highborn. Marten and Omi trailed behind.

"Where were you headed?" asked Hansen.

"Smade's," Kang said.

"I should have known. It's a rat hole. Just the place a Red Blade would want to go."

Kang put a heavy paw on Hansen's shoulder and pushed him along. Then he peered over his shoulder at Marten. "You still owe me a round."

"I haven't forgotten," Marten said.

6.

Smade's Tavern was dim. An oaken bar stood in front of a mirror where an ugly bartender hid like a troll under a bridge. Waitresses went to him and sauntered back with drinks on their trays. Booths and tables littered the gloom. Serious drinkers hunched over their glasses. A few nibbled on peanuts.

The four of them sat at two mini-tables that Kang had shoved together. With his thick fingers, Kang twisted a vodka bottle's cap, breaking the paper seal. The clear liquid gurgled as he poured into a glass filled with ice cubes. He lifted the glass and stretched out his lips, slurping.

"Ah..." Kang said.

Bushy-eyed Hansen grinned like a fox.

Marten and Omi sipped spiced tea, a pot of it on the table. They had declined any liquor or party pills.

"Do you know why Hansen is so happy?" Kang asked Omi.

Hansen cleared his throat, shaking his head when Kang glanced at him.

"They didn't call Hansen *sir* back then," Kang said.

"No?" Omi said.

"A moment, please," said Hansen.

Kang frowned as he poured himself more vodka. "You interrupting my story, you little maggot?"

"You know me better than that, Kang," Hansen said. "But why rehash bad feelings? I'm not that man and you're no longer chief of the Red Blades."

"What's that supposed to mean?" Kang asked.

27

"Only that life has played one of its constant pranks and rearranged our roles," said Hansen.

"You calling me a mule, a drug runner?" Kang asked.

"No, no," said Hansen, holding up his slender hands. "Simply that once you ran a vicious—the most vicious—gang in Sydney. Who dared tread on your territory? None!"

Kang stared at Hansen.

"Now," said the thin man with a sly smile, "I run Level 49, the Pleasure Palace." He leaned forward, whispering, "Chief Monitor Bock is my only superior." Hansen leaned back and crossed his arms, grinning.

"They put a petty thief in charge of security?" asked Kang.

Hansen shook his head. "Kang, Kang, let bygones be bygones. Otherwise I'll—"

Hansen stopped because Kang dropped a hand onto his wrist. "What'll you do, you little maggot?"

Hansen licked his lips, and he minutely shook his head.

Marten, who had reached for the teapot, glanced around, trying to see whom Hansen had signaled. He spotted two big men at the bar. They wore silky shirts with billowing sleeves. One of them palmed a gun of some sort. The other slid his weapon back into a sleeve-sheath. Monitors, Marten realized. Secret policemen to back up their— Hadn't Hansen said he reported to the Chief Monitor? Did he mean the chief preman monitor of the entire Sun Works Factory? As Marten poured tea, he noticed another pair of monitors sitting several tables over. They were a man and woman team, but too hard-eyed to be partygoers, too observant and tense, and too intent on watching Kang.

"Listen up, maggot," Kang told Hansen. "I know you got a few bully-boys around here. I'm not blind. But you're in the last stages of syphilis if you think we've switched places. You still slink around sniffing people's butts. I still kill." Kang tapped the shock trooper patch on his jacket. "Even if you and your thugs could take me out—" Kang leered. "I turn up missing, you little maggot, this party-town gets trashed as the HBs search for me."

Hansen laughed, a trifle uneasily it seemed to Marten. "Oh, what does it matter? We're all friends here, aren't we?"

28

Kang breathed heavily through his nose, let go of Hansen's wrist and poured more vodka. After a stiff belt, he said, "Omi used to be a gunman for Eastman."

"Really?" said Hansen. "Eastman always broke people too soon—in my professional opinion. But then that must have given you a lot of work," he said to Omi.

Omi shrugged.

Hansen laughed more freely now. "Oh, the old days. I don't miss them, I'll tell you. The gang leader and the gunman, two toughs that nobody wants to meet in a back alley or in his home. Good old Sydney! But now you're shock troopers, hired guns fighting for the Highborn."

"So speaks the part-time drug runner and full-time informer," Kang said.

Hansen slapped the table in outrage. "Now see here, Kang. Maybe I smuggled a tot or two of black sand—I won't deny that among friends. We all lived in the slums, after all, and had to make ends meet. But this charge of, of…" He angrily shook his long head.

"Informer," Kang said. "Job training, in your case." He snorted. It was his way of laughing.

Hansen's foxy eyes narrowed and his veneer of joviality vanished, leaving him more sinister-seeming.

"Bet I can guess you how you got this far," Kang said. "You must have fast-talked the HBs when they were looking for people to trust. Yeah, sure, I bet that's how you did it. You'd learned enough about undercover work to fool them into letting you be a monitor."

"You used to hold your liquor better," grumbled Hansen.

"Don't get your panties in a bunch," Kang said. "We're all friends here, like you've been saying. A gang leader, a gunman, a drug runner and a—Marten, you didn't live in the slums."

Marten shrugged.

"Where are you from?" asked Hansen, a bit too eagerly, no doubt to stop talking about old times with Kang.

"He's from here," Kang said.

"You're from the Sun Works Factory?" asked Hansen. "That's very rare for someone here to have made it into the shock troops."

"He emigrated to Earth first," Kang said. "Didn't you, Marten?"

Hansen lifted his eyebrows, giving Marten a more careful examination. It heightened Hansen's narrow features, the weakness to his chin and the crafty way his pupils darted. He seemed like a weaker animal, one that constantly judged danger and how close it was to him. "How did it happen that you emigrated to Earth?" he asked.

"It's a long story," Marten said. He slid his chair and stood. "Nature calls."

"He's a quiet one," Marten heard Hansen saying as he limped away. "They're always the most dangerous. Remember the time..." Then Marten went to the restroom, relieved himself and as he returned, he noticed a woman in the main doorway glancing about the tavern. He might not have noticed her but she seemed so out of place and frazzled, worried, at wit's end.

She wore an engineer's gray jumpsuit with heavy magnetic boots and a tool belt still hooked around her waist. Her engineer's cap with a sun logo showed that she serviced the habitat's outer sun shield. Marten idly wondered what she was doing in Smade's, what she was doing in the Pleasure Palace at all. She had a heart-shaped face, was pretty and of medium height and regular build. Despite the jumpsuit, it was clear she was well-endowed. Alert eyes, small nose and a mobile mouth, a kissing mouth, Marten thought to himself.

Their eyes met. He nodded. She looked away, then back at him as he sat down. Her gaze slid onto his tablemates. Recognition leaped onto her face as resolve settled upon her. She strode toward them.

Hansen and Kang argued about something, so neither of them noticed her. Marten saw the two monitors by the bar glance at her, each other and then jump to their feet.

She beat them to the table. "There's a problem," the engineer said without preamble.

Hansen looked up. "Nadia Pravda, what are you doing here?"

The two big monitors slid up behind her.

"The sump exploded and we lost an entire batch of product," Nadia said. "Tell Bock that it wasn't my fault."

Hansen's eyes goggled. He glanced at Kang, then at Nadia Pravda. "Get her out of here," he said. "Teach her to be more careful about. To, ah—"

The big monitors each grabbed an arm.

Hansen glanced at Kang again, then at his men. "—Just get her out of here," he said.

"It's not my fault!" Nadia said, as they started dragging her out. "Tell Bock—"

"Silence!" said Hansen, with a sharp, authoritative bark as he stood and slapped the tabletop.

People looked up. One of the monitors holding onto Nadia peered meaningfully at Hansen, who jerked his head to one side. The big monitor nodded and the two of them hustled her out.

"Product?" Kang asked, as Hansen sat down. "Does that mean you're still in the drug trade?"

Hansen shot Kang an angry stare.

"It couldn't be black sand," Kang said. "The HBs sell it openly to whoever wants it. Ah. Sure. You're making dream dust, aren't you?"

Hansen tried to stare Kang down and when it didn't work, he slumped in his chair.

"She said Bock," Kang mused. "Could that be the same Chief Monitor Bock you told us that you report to?"

Marten hid his excitement. Hansen made illegal drugs under the noses of the Highborn. He even had an engineer involved. Even better, this Nadia Pravda, this engineer, sounded as if she was in trouble with Hansen. Marten needed a way to move under security if he was ever going to steal a vacc suit in order to spacewalk to the broken-down pod. Here was his chance to find out how Hansen did it.

"Listen, Kang," Hansen was saying, with a greasy smile on his face. Then he peered at his slender hands and ordered an eye-bender from the bar.

Marten stood. "I'm sorry, but I have to leave. This reunion, it's none of my affair." He motioned to Omi.

"Nor mine," Omi said, standing.

Hansen peered at them, his features calculating. "No," he said a moment later. "This is between Kang and me. You may go."

"Hey, maggot," Kang said. "My buddies and I do whatever we feel like. We're shock troopers, which is top of the heap around here. You're the one who's going to need permission to leave, not them."

Marten didn't hear Hansen's reply. He pushed Omi toward the door, and whispered, "Do you think Kang will be all right?"

"Hansen is too scared to try anything stupid. Kang could probably clear the bar if felt like it."

"I'm sure you're right."

Coming out of Smade's they blinked at the glittering lights. Marten looked around and pointed at the two monitors frog-marching the engineer. They weren't far ahead. She seemed resigned to her fate and wasn't resisting.

"We'd better act natural," Marten said, thrusting his hands into his jacket pockets. He sauntered along as if looking at the sights.

"You want to follow her?" Omi asked.

"This is our chance," Marten said. "But we have to hurry."

Omi blinked once and then laughed, immediately launching into the role of a tourist-type gawker. He pointed at a tall spire in the distance before grabbing Marten's arm and dragging him faster.

The two monitors frog-marched Pravda around a corner. Marten and Omi hurried after them. Marten made it around the corner in time to see them shove her behind two plastic trees near the wall. The monitors took her down a small alleyway. A hidden door behind the two fake trees slid open. Marten and Omi broke into a run. The woman finally started talking, her voice wheedling, pleading. Marten plunged between the two plastic props, through the door and into a lift, with Omi almost on top of him.

32

One of the monitors had his back turned. The other jerked his head in surprise. He had a nasty scar across his forehead. "You two aren't allowed—"

Marten punched him in the throat as the lift closed and headed down. He grabbed the man's hair and slammed the meaty face down against his up-thrusting knee. Teeth crunched and the monitor slumped onto the floor. When he tried to get up Marten kicked him. Omi took out the second one.

Nadia Pravda the engineer stared at the two of them in wonder and dread.

"They were going to kill you," Omi told her.

Marten looked at Omi in surprise.

"What?" she said.

"We heard Hansen order it," Omi lied.

Nadia's eyes got big and round. She glanced at Marten.

He shrugged.

Omi, who searched the bodies, handed Marten a small pistol. "It's a projac," he said. "Shoots drugged ice needles. Knocks a person out in seconds." Omi checked the monitor's pocket. "Hello." He pulled out a small clip for the pistol and examined the side print. He tossed it to Marten. "Know what that is?"

Marten shook his head.

"Explosive glass sliver rounds. A perfect murder weapon for use in a space hab."

"You're not monitors, are you?" Nadia asked.

Marten stared at her, uncertain how to go about this.

"I'm sure this isn't about helping me," she said, "although I do appreciate the help."

"The lift is slowing down," warned Omi.

"Look," she said. "What..." Perspiration glistened on her brow. "You two swear that they were going to kill me?"

"What do you think these are for?" Marten asked, showing her the clip.

Nadia moaned and hugged herself. "It wasn't my fault."

"That doesn't matter anymore," Omi said.

"I know that!" she said.

The lift stopped and the door slid open.

She stared at the empty corridor. Then she turned to Marten. Fear twisted her features, turning her skin pale under the shadow of her hat.

"Let's make a deal," Marten said.

"What kind of deal?" Nadia asked.

"I want to know why a solar engineer is working for drug lords," Marten said.

"Not drug lords," she said. "I work for the monitors."

"Not for all of them," Marten said, guessing. "But for the corrupt ones."

Her shoulders sagged. She nodded. "I needed the credits."

"I don't want to know your reason," Marten said. "Tell me theirs."

"This is all very interesting," Omi said. "But what are we going to do about these two? We have to move them."

"Well?" Marten asked her. "Why did they need you?"

"Because the plant is there," she shouted. "Why do you think?"

"The plant is where?" Marten asked.

"In the solar panels where I work."

Marten smiled for the first time. He bet vacc suits were in the solar panels. He needed a vacc suit to spacewalk to the broken-down pod. "Last question." He shrugged off his jacket and showed her his barcode tattoo. "Have you ever seen one of these before?"

"The monitors have them," she said. "It tracks them, I think they said."

"That's right," Marten said. "Do you know how they take themselves off the tracking screen?"

A shifty look entered her eyes. "What's it worth you to know?"

"Nadia," Marten said. "Either you tell me or there's no deal. Then you're on your own again."

She glanced at the two unconscious monitors, at Omi as he shot each of them with a second projac. The monitors jerked. The one with the forehead scar and the missing teeth opened his eyes. Then the knockout drugs took over and the eyes closed again.

"It's a little device that Hansen keeps with him," Nadia said. "I've seen him slide it over two of his guards before, when they came to… to help me. One of them said something about it making them invisible. I guess he meant invisible to the station tracker."

"Good," Marten said. "That's all I wanted to hear."

7.

Marten reentered Smade's. He needed the device that would deactivate his barcode tattoo. Nadia said Hansen kept it on his person. He hoped she was right.

Before Marten adjusted to the gloom, Kang bellowed a greeting. Marten strode in that direction and a moment later slid into his chair. Hansen had his slender hands wrapped around a frosty glass of blue liquid. He looked dejected, his thinning hair messed up at the sides as if he'd been scratching his head. The massive Kang sat at the table as if he were a king. The dim light shone off the top of his bald head, while his eyes were a little more open than usual. His pupils had started turning glassy.

"Where's Omi?" Kang asked.

"He's with a girl," Marten said. "I figured there's no sense in trying to find Lance and Vip. So…"

"They're more of you?" Hansen asked in alarm.

Kang leered. "Poor little informer, always wants to know everything, don't you?"

Hansen made a peevish gesture.

"What are you having?" Marten asked Hansen.

"Eye-bender," mumbled the monitor. "Do you want one? It'll be on me."

"Sure," Marten said.

Hansen snapped his fingers and soon a waitress set a tall frosty eye-bender before Marten. He raised his glass to Hansen. Glumly, Hansen raised his and they clicked glasses.

"To old friends," Marten said.

"I'll drink to that," Kang said, picking up his glass and clicking it against theirs.

Kang slurped vodka. Marten sipped, while Hansen took a mouthful of eye-bender and swallowed as if it were a lump of clay.

"Do you know why Hansen looks so sad?" Kang asked.

"Please," said Hansen. "Do you have to speak so loudly? Must everyone hear?"

Kang leered. "Sorry," he whispered. "Is that better?"

Hansen sighed, peered at his eye-bender and took another of his doleful swallows.

"He thinks I'll spill his secrets," Kang said.

"We're all Sydney boys," said Hansen in a dispirited way. "We have to stick together."

"That's so right," Kang said. "So very right."

Marten wondered how much vodka Kang had put away.

"But if I scratch your back, you little maggot, how are you gonna scratch mine?" asked Kang.

Hansen reached into his pockets and put a small pile of plastic credits on the table. "It's all I have."

Kang leered at Marten. "Do you think that's enough?"

"For what?" asked Marten.

"To buy the 101st's silence."

Marten studied the credits and then Hansen. "Isn't it dangerous what you're doing? This entire setup?"

"No more dangerous than your profession," said Hansen.

"Are you trying to say you're as brave as us?" growled Kang.

"The saints forbid that I dare claim that," said Hansen. He studied his eye-bender and a grin twitched. "But my profession does pay better and there are more perks."

"I'm glad to hear it," Kang said. "At least about the better pay."

Hansen winced, shook his long head and finished his eye-bender. "I must be leaving," he said.

Kang dropped his hand onto Hansen's wrist. "Going to get reinforcements are you? Maybe have them take me out somewhere quiet and work me over?"

37

"Do you think I'm insane?" asked Hansen. "The HBs would come flying to your rescue."

"That's right," Kang said. "Then you'd all be in the pain booth. And then one of you would talk, would break under the pressure. It would be over for you. You'd take a spacewalk in your skivvies."

"I know, I know," said Hansen, sweat beading on his tall forehead.

"You little maggot," Kang said. "You don't know at all. You think you've finally got me drunk, got me stupid. You really think you can outsmart me. You, a little informer—" Kang spat on the table.

Hansen closed his eyes. When he opened them, the man and woman monitor-team that had been watching them stood at the table. The woman was taller than the man and had long black hair. Although short, the man had wide shoulders and seemingly no neck, and there was something odd about his eyes. They were gray and seemed empty, devoid of emotion.

Kang leaned back, eyeing the pair. "Are they yours?" he asked Hansen.

"Is everything all right, boss?" asked the man.

Hansen pursed his lips. "Have either of you spoken to Dalt or Methlen?"

"No, boss."

Hansen glanced at Kang as he spoke to his team. "I think you two should check on them."

Kang grunted his okay.

"Yes," said Hansen. "That's what I want you to do."

"What about you, boss?"

"I'll be fine," said Hansen. "These are old friends."

"Are you certain about that?"

Hansen slapped the table. "I said I would be all right, didn't I? Now do what I ask, Ervil."

Ervil darted his dead eyes at Kang and Marten. Finally, he dipped his thick head.

"Report back when you find them," said Hansen.

"Like you say, boss." Ervil took the black-haired woman's hand and they left.

"There," said Hansen. "Satisfied?"

38

Kang poured more vodka.

"But I must tell you that if I press a switch or don't report to HQ in another half hour that monitors will descend upon me," said Hansen. "Then it's detention for both of you."

"And then your secret is out," Kang said.

"Not necessarily," said Hansen. "As I said before, Chief Monitor Bock runs the secret police."

"All the monitors help make dream dust?" asked Kang.

"No," said Hansen. "But enough."

Kang nodded and slurped more vodka. "Not a bad racket, you little maggot, not bad at all. I'm impressed."

The thin monitor sat a little straighter and he even adjusted his collar. "If you can make it in Sydney's slums then you can make it anywhere."

"That's right," Kang said.

Hansen smiled ruefully. He turned to Marten and noticed his eye-bender. "You've hardly sipped your drink."

"It's not really what I expected," Marten said. "Would you like it?" He slid it over.

Hansen peered at him, shrugged. He took the tall glass and took another of his measured swallows. Kang slurped more vodka.

Marten waited, wondering just how big a bladder each man had.

"Maybe this is all for the best," said Hansen. "I'm looking for more sellers I can trust and Bock wants to break into new areas."

Kang sneered. "Me work for you?"

"Of course not," said Hansen. "You'd work for Chief Monitor Bock. What do you think?"

Kang glanced at Marten. Marten sat impassively. Kang shook his head at Hansen, who had watched the exchange. Hansen now looked with new interest at Marten.

Marten slid his chair back. "That spiced tea before has gone right through me. What about you, Hansen?"

It took Hansen a half-beat. "Yes. I need to use the restroom."

Kang laughed. "Oh no you don't."

"Don't worry," Marten said. "I won't let him call for reinforcements."

Kang grumbled, then shrugged and waved his thick hand. "Go, go, be my guest."

Marten and Hansen rose and headed for the restroom.

"You're the leader of the 101st?" whispered Hansen.

"That's right," Marten said.

"Kang has to listen to you?"

"Yes," Marten said.

Hansen nodded ruefully. "Yes. Wise of you to let him play me out. Now it is I who am impressed."

Marten opened the restroom door and gestured for Hansen to proceed.

"I'm glad I can work with a reasonable man," said Hansen as he walked in. "Our survival depends upon logic and precision, not brute force and rage." He turned around.

Marten shot him twice as the projac made little hissing sounds.

The ice slivers penetrated Hansen's tunic and into his stomach. The thin monitor had time to widen his eyes in astonishment and pain. Then he staggered backward as the knockout drugs took hold. Marten caught him under the armpits and shuffled into a stall. He lowered the drugged monitor onto a toilet seat. He patted Hansen down, coming up with another projac pistol, several more clips, a wallet stuffed with credits, a communicator and a flat device with a barcode on the back. Marten took it and ran it over his tattoo. The device flashed a green light. Marten slid it over his tattoo again. The device flashed red. Green, off, red, on.

Marten debated killing Hansen instead of just leaving him drugged. He shook his head. With that decided, Marten stuffed his jacket with the loot. Then he adjusted Hansen's clothes, put the man's hands over his stomach and spread his feet wider. Marten locked the stall, dropped to his stomach and slid under the bottom. Disgusting, but it worked. He dusted himself and strolled into the barroom.

"Where's Hansen?" Kang said as Marten sat down. "You said you weren't going to leave him alone."

"He pulled a gun on me," Marten said. He pulled out the projac and showed Kang under the table.

"The little maggot! What was he thinking?"

Marten showed Kang his knuckles from where he's hit the monitor in the throat before. "I took Hansen out. Set him on the toilet seat and locked the stall."

Kang grunted.

"But I think we'd better get out of here," Marten said.

"Because of that little maggot? You've got to be kidding."

"He's a monitor, Kang."

"He drew a gun on you," Kang snarled. "I'll—" Kang half rose, but Marten put his hand on the Mongol's massive forearms.

"I took these off him," Marten said, slapping a handful of credits on the table, beside Hansen's earlier pile. "Take them."

Kang sat and started stuffing his pockets.

"We don't want any trouble," Marten said. "There's no telling how the Training Master will view all this—if we get thrown into detention or found to have killed monitors."

Kang grunted.

"So get drunk," Marten said, "just not here."

"What about you?"

"I should probably find Lance and Vip and tell them to be careful. Do you want to help me look for them?"

Kang snorted. Then he grabbed his latest vodka bottle by the neck, rose ponderously and headed for the door. A waitress hurried to intercept him.

Marten motioned sharply.

She looked at Kang once more and came over.

"Do you know Hansen?" Marten asked.

"He's come in here before," she said. "Wasn't he with you?"

"He's still in the restroom."

"Oh. Yes, that's right. I saw him go in."

"He's sleeping one off," Marten said. "I don't think he wants to be disturbed either."

She blinked several times. "That's kind of strange," she finally said.

"He has strange… tastes," Marten said.

41

"Oh," said the waitress. "Then why does he come to Smade's? There are other places for that sort of thing."

Marten shrugged.

"Well, it doesn't really matter to me," she said.

"A good policy," agreed Marten. "Hansen will pay the score."

The waitress glanced at Kang as he exited. "All right," she said.

"But here's a small gratuity from us," Marten said. He put several credits on her tray. "Put the customary fifteen percent tip on Hansen's bill as well."

"Thank you, sir."

Marten patted her arm and hurried out.

8.

Nadia Pravda gasped as the three of them loped down an empty utility corridor. Sweat dripped from her waxen face as her breathing turned harsher. Her heavy magnetic boots clumped at each stride and her tool belt jingled as the tiny clamps struck one another.

Omi and Marten jogged effortlessly. They were both in peak condition and knew that time ran against them.

"Sl—Slow down," wheezed Nadia.

Marten glanced back and then at Omi. "Hey," he said. Omi raised an eyebrow. Marten nodded at Nadia. The two of them each took an arm and helped her run.

Marten couldn't believe he was doing this again. Four and half years ago, he'd hidden in the Sun Works Factory like a rat. His parents had been alive and the monolith of Social Unity had ruled the four Inner Planets.

It had all started seven years ago when Political Harmony Corps had brutally suppressed the unionization attempt of the Sun Works Engineers. If he'd asked, Marten was sure Nadia could have told him a grim tale about that time. Social Unity, it was said back then, provided for all, was all. The State and its people were one, thus unionization was an absurdity, a non sequitur. Thus, the engineer's strike had been *dispersed*—a word that failed to convey the savage fighting, the interrogations and the police murders of the ringleaders and their lieutenants. A few Unionists had slipped into hiding among the millions of kilometers of passageways and empty maintenance corridors. Most of them were caught and killed after some agonizing torture. Marten, his father and mother, with several others, had kept one step ahead of the hunters and built an ultra-stealth pod in an abandoned, high radiation area. The long-range goal had been to slip from the Inner Planets and to the Jupiter Confederation or anywhere beyond the reach of the Social Unity fanatics.

PHC had caught his mother and father and killed them. He'd used emergency computer codes and a special credcard that his mother had forged in order to board a shuttle to Earth and then to Australian Sector.

He knew the hidden passageways of the Sun Works Factory, or some of them, at least. But that was a lifetime ago. The Highborn invasion, joining Free Earth Corps in Australia, the brutal Japan Campaign and then transferred to the shock troopers—What if seven years ago his parents had surrendered like everyone else? Would he and Nadia be friends now? It might have happened.

Despite her sorry state, she was pretty and had a beautiful, heart-shaped face.

Omi cleared his throat. Marten gave him a swift glance and then quit staring at Nadia. There was no time to stop and look at the scenery, not and get that vacc suit he hoped was where they made dust. Once he found a vacc suit, he could spacewalk to the forgotten pod.

"Could we stop, please," Nadia wheezed.

They ignored her. After a while, they turned a corner. The maintenance passage seemed to go on forever.

"Please," she wheezed, "my sides are going to explode."

"For a minute," Marten said.

She slumped to the floor and then slid against a wall as she gasped. She tore off her cap and shook out damp, shoulder-length hair. It made her prettier.

Marten and Omi squatted on their heels, waiting.

She took a rag and mopped her face. She seemed on the verge of speaking and then simply kept on breathing hard.

"Is it much farther?" Marten asked. He studied her, her features and the pretty way her lips quivered.

"Using this route," she wheezed. "It's another two kilometers."

44

They waited, and her breathing started evening out.

"We'd better go," Omi said, sounding impatient.

"Wait," she said. "My side finally isn't hurting."

Omi glanced at Marten.

"We'll give her another minute," Marten said.

Omi stared stonily at the floor.

"They won't let us in," she said.

"That's not what you said before," Marten said.

"Do you know how security-conscious they are?"

"I can imagine."

"Then you should know that I'm not cleared."

"You worked the sump," he said.

"That's different. That's manufacturing. We're heading to distribution, where they store the product. They're crazy about protection." She put her cap on. "Maybe we should call the whole thing off."

"Right," Marten said. "Then Hansen's people find you and shove you out an airlock."

"I've been thinking about that," she said. "You two must have heard it wrong. Hansen can't afford to kill me. He worked too hard finding someone with my training and position. He needs me."

"We need you too," Omi said, without warmth.

She licked her lips. "I can understand that. How about I simply tell you how to get in?"

"No," Marten said, standing, motioning her to get up.

She didn't move. "I'm going to insist on doing this another way. You see—"

Omi jerked her to her feet. Marten took the other arm and they started jogging, forcing her to run.

"You're killing me, doing this," she said. "They'll hunt me down and make an example."

"You were already dead," Omi said.

"No, I refuse to believe that. Hansen needs me. This is murder what you're doing."

Marten stopped so suddenly that Omi didn't quite realize it in time. They pulled Nadia two ways. She yelled. Omi let go. Marten swung her around to face him. "What *we're* doing is murder? What do you think dream dust does to people?"

"Huh?" she said, frowning, looking perplexed.

"People waste away is what happens!" Marten said. "They snort dust, dream their fantasies and forget to eat and drink and even sleep. It kills them if they have enough dust."

"Hey," she said, "they don't have to buy it."

"They don't have to buy it!" Marten said, outraged. "Woe to them! You have rushed for profit into Balaam's error."

"Come again," said Nadia. She glanced at Omi, but he looked as confused as she did. Then she became suspicious. "Are you saying you don't want the dream dust?"

Omi shook his head and turned away.

"You really don't want the dust," Nadia said in surprise. "Then what do you want? Why are you even here?"

"Listen to me," Marten said. "We're going in and taking the dust."

She laughed. "No, I don't think you can take it. So that means I'm out of here." She turned to go.

Marten put his projac under her chin.

She looked deep into his eyes, and smiled. "No, you can't shoot me either."

"I can," Omi said softly.

"Yes," she said after a moment. "I believe you could. But would he let you?"

Marten exhaled sharply. "Nadia, I'm desperate. I don't like making a profit out of other people's misery—in fact, I won't. But I'll kill to stay alive."

"And to make staying alive worth it," Omi added.

Marten nodded.

"What's that supposed to mean?" asked Nadia.

"Never mind," Marten said.

"Let me get this straight," she said. "I'm supposed to help you rob the monitors. From that moment on, I'm on the run. But none of this is to make any credits. No, it's to do…what?" She lifted her eyebrows.

Marten wished he could keep his mouth shut when it counted. But whatever else happened, he had to have a vacc suit.

Omi said, "We're undercover operatives who watch the monitors."

She frowned. "That doesn't make sense. You wouldn't have needed the barcode eraser from Hansen."

"Wrong," Omi said. "We had to make it look as if—"

"If you two want my help you'll have to tell me what's really going on. No more smoke," she said.

Omi glared at Marten, slicing one of his fingers across his muscled throat.

Marten said, "Look—"

"Were they really going to kill me?" she asked.

"Maybe," Marten said, "maybe just beat you up or just talk to you sternly."

"But you didn't hear Hansen order my death?" she asked.

"I didn't. No."

Omi groaned, shaking his head.

"Look," Marten told him. "If we have someone on the outside helping us we can finish faster."

"Finish what faster?" she asked.

"Let me ask you a question," Marten said. "Do you want to live here?"

"In the Sun Works Factory?" she asked.

"No," Marten said, "in the Inner Planets."

"You mean if I could leave to somewhere else, would I?" she asked.

"Yes."

She considered it. "I've never thought about it before."

"We want to leave," Marten said.

She laughed.

"I'm serious."

She frowned. "How could you leave? Not by highjacking a shuttle."

Marten glanced at Omi before saying, "I have a way. It's dangerous. I won't deny that. You could come if you wanted, or you could stay. Either way I'll help you to help us."

"How can you help me?" she asked.

"By giving you lots of money, for one thing."

"But I'd have the monitors hunting for me," she said. "What's to keep me from going to Hansen and baring all in order to get back into his good graces?"

"Well…" Marten said, trying to think of something.

47

"If we get caught," Omi said, "we'll talk and bring everyone down with us. The Highborn hate dream dust. Your only hope is that we don't get caught."

"Or that the monitors kill you," she said.

Marten grinned. "That won't be so easy for them."

"No," she said, "I suppose not." She thought about it while chewing her lower lip. "There is the possibility that Dalt and Methlen were dragging me to that corridor to have me killed, right?"

"Who?" asked Marten.

"Dalt and Methlen," she said. "The monitors you two took out."

"I'd say without a doubt they were going to kill you," Omi said.

She heaved a mournful sigh. "Either way it's dangerous. But…" She eyed Marten. He smiled. She smiled back, before frowning and looking away. "I don't really trust Hansen. I keep getting the feeling they plan on covering their tracks soon."

"You'll help us?" Marten asked.

"At least to hit this place," she said.

"We'd better hurry," Omi said.

"One thing," Marten said.

"What?"

"Do they have any vacc suits there?"

She shrugged. "Two or three are usually lying around. Why?"

"I'll tell you after we're done," Marten said.

9.

Nadia was nervous. *Stay calm, stay calm,* she told herself. Fortunately, she remembered the code-knock. She wore her cap low so they wouldn't see the fear in her eyes or that her face was pale. The door opened and Omi and Marten followed her in.

Their projacs hissed. Men and women standing at tables chopping and packaging dust fell. One monitor to the side wore body armor. Omi shot him in the face. Marten bounded across the room, diving as a man popped up over a heavy box.

"Hey!" shouted Omi.

The monitor swiveled a las-rifle at the Korean shock trooper. Marten rolled around the box and pumped shots into the man's side.

Then silence filled the large room, which was a former engineer tool shed. Marten and Omi checked every corner, then every person, to make sure that they were out. The man Omi shot in the face was dead.

"You switched clips," Nadia whispered, staring at the corpse.

"No," Omi said, kneeling beside him. "A sliver went through his eye and must have lodged in his brain."

Marten overturned boxes. Then he shouted with triumph, showing Omi a vacc suit.

"Is it good?" asked Omi.

Marten checked it over. "It's good." He laughed and turned to Nadia. "Help us stuff dust into these suits."

49

She continued to stare at the dead man, a monitor, wondering what that meant for her future.

"Help us," Omi said, who already grabbed plastic bags full of dust and shoved them down a vacc suit.

They worked in silence, until the two suits were full. They lifted the suits and put them in a box marked "Sealant, Industrial." Marten rolled out a trolley and hefted the box onto it. "Let's go," he said.

"I don't get it," she said, bewildered at their speed and professionalism. "If you're not going to sell the dream dust, why take it? Why not burn it?"

"I want them to think we hit them for the dust," Marten said. "Now do you see this box?"

She nodded.

"You're going to make sure it ends up at Dock 10, Bay EE. Think you can do that?"

"What if someone opens it?" she asked.

"That's my worry."

"What if I take the dust?" she said.

"Then Omi comes hunting for you."

Nadia studied the muscle-bound Korean, and told Marten, "He would never be able to find me."

"Hansen could," Marten said.

"He can anyway," she said.

"Maybe not," Marten said. "I know of a few hideaways I bet no one else does. You could go there."

"Then I lose my job," she said.

Marten went to a table and scooped up hundreds of plastic credits, shoving them into a sack. He brought her the sack. "Do you think you can last on those awhile?"

"Why don't you come with me?" she said, hefting the sack, liking its weight.

"Not yet," Marten said.

"These won't last me forever," she said.

"But for several weeks they should."

"You can get us out of the Sun Works Factory in several weeks?"

"Are you a gambler?" he asked.

50

She stared at him. "I listened to Hansen's recruitment speech. So I guess I am."

"I can get us out of here in several weeks," Marten said. "At least now I can, and with your help."

She peered at the box on the trolley. Finally, she thought she understood. "You want the vacc suits. None of this is about dream dust." She squinted. Could she trust him? He looked trustworthy. But what did that mean? She reexamined the dead monitor, and all those lying in drugged sleep. In a fight, she'd never seen anything like these two. "I'll give you the three weeks," she whispered. "But if you're wrong..."

"I'm not wrong," Marten said. He pushed the trolley toward the door and Omi followed.

10.

They left Nadia and reentered the Pleasure Palace, Level 49.

"Our luck can't hold," Omi said.

"We're not using luck," Marten said. "Speed and surprise, and savagery, those are our tools. The only luck we had was running into Hansen. Everything else we've taken."

Marten studied the crowds, the costumes, and the gaiety, the drunkenness and drugged hyperactivity. Women laughed as men pawed them. Musicians danced as they piped a merry tune or strummed guitars. Comedians with senso-masks acted out plays and scenes on various corners. Jugglers juggled holocubes imaged to show naked women or flickering suns or black holes that swirled with ultimate destruction. Over it all, festive lights sparkled with colors.

It was strange walking through the Pleasure Palace, knowing that around them were thousands of miles of empty corridors, holding bays and ore bins. For a moment, Marten felt like it wasn't real. With an effort of will, he shook off the feeling.

"Take off your jacket," Marten said to Omi, as he shrugged off his and slung it over his arm. He eyed Omi and shook his head. "Follow me."

In the distance rose the main spire. Smade's Tavern was on the other side of it. That meant... Marten turned in a circle and finally noticed the square lift building. Some people poured out of it while others staggered in or had friends carry them through the archways. The Pleasure Palace never stopped, though different shifts came and went. Marten saw an unusual number of unobtrusive but observant janitors sweeping up, polishing and hauling litter. He stepped behind a large man in a flowing robe as one of them glanced his way.

"Over here," he told Omi, pulling him by the arm. Janitor seemed like a perfect disguise for a monitor. "Hey," he said, "this is just what we need." He darted into a costume shop.

"We gotta find the others," Omi said. "We don't have time for shopping."

A slim man in an ancient-style toga greeted them with raised hands. He wore a wreath around his head and glitter about his dark eyes. "Ah, and how may I help you gentlemen today?"

"We'd like something… baggy," Marten said.

"Baggy?" asked the man.

Marten glanced about. "Like that."

"Ah, splendid indeed, sir. Pirates on the High Seas. Rogues and ruffians!" The salesman led them to the mannequin of a Blackbeard-style pirate. "I suggest complete sets, sir. Let the pirate persona overwhelm and invest you. Here we are. Hat, shirt, breeches and boots, and accessories, too. An eye-patch would be perfect for you, sir," he told Omi. "And cutlasses all around and imitation wheellock pistols, I'm sure. And—"

"We'll take the hats," Marten said, "and these shirts." He pursed his lips. "Do you have tote bags?"

"Indeed, sir. But I suggest lockers. Why carry around your old clothes when you can safely store your belongings in our—"

"Three tote bags," Marten said. Then his eyes lit up as he scanned another rack. "Throw in two red kerchiefs, yes, like those over there, and add a tube of glitter like you're wearing."

"A fine start, sir. Now—"

"Do you have a changing room?" asked Marten.

"Certainly."

"What's all this cost?"

"A trifling sum, I assure you, sir. Enough so that this jacket here and a brace of pistols for your partner—"

"No, this is good," Marten said. "Tally it please while we change."

53

"Very well, sir," said the salesman, acting a bit crestfallen.

Marten and Omi entered the dressing rooms and came out wearing the silky red shirts with billowing sleeves and floppy black pirate hats. Their shock trooper jackets and shirts were stuffed in the tote bags hidden and slung around their torsos. Each of them kept his projac tucked in the waist of his pants. The kerchiefs, tube of glitter and other needed items Marten carried in a third tote bag.

"Twenty-six credits, sir," the man said at the counter.

Marten paid the sum with stolen plastic chips, then he and Omi sauntered onto the street.

"Flimsy disguises," grumbled Omi.

"But better than strutting around in here-I-am shock trooper jackets."

They started checking card rooms and game pits as they searched for Lance and Vip. They choked on narcotic stimstick smoke in the first, Billy the Kid's Card Room. Men and women sat hunched around Western Period wooden tables. Many drank. Others popped pills. The lights were dim and there was a constant sound of shuffling cards and "draw, hit me," tinkling chips and scraping chairs as angry people left and eager gamblers took their place. The pounding piano provided backdrop noise.

Sharper's Place was quieter and more serious. Red stimstick smoke drifted lazily in the dim lighting. Men and women inhaled their narcotic cigarettes to life and peeked at the cards close to their vests. Roulette wheels spun and several Blackjack tables did brisk business.

"Ahoy, matey," said a drunken masked man to Omi. A moment later, Marten chopped a thief's wrist as he tried to lift their credits.

As they stepped outside of the second dive, Omi spat. "I'm sick of those places, and I'm starting to feel lightheaded."

"We have to keep searching," Marten answered grimly.

They marched into Razor's Den, one of the fish tank places. Bloodthirsty, cheering bettors surrounded the nearest octagon-shaped pool. The pond had been sunken into the floor and contained tiny pens along the sides. Each held a six-inch, colorful fish that seemed to be three quarters teeth. They all swam in furious circles, lashing their tail fins, each stamped with a tiny colored tag. As the throng cheered lustily, others crouched and studied the little monsters. People argued, or shoved credits into a slot and ripped out the paper ticket vomited in return. Finally, the first match ended. Then the doors in the little cages opened and out darted the fighting fish into the main tank. A furious, twisting battle engaged, each one's teeth biting, tearing and savaging the other fish. In a few moments, one emerged victorious, and the winning bettors rushed to the cashier to collect.

"That's what we are," Omi said. "Little fish fighting for our masters."

The comment startled Marten. He didn't expect something like that from Omi. He nodded though, and they continued the search.

As they exited Razor's Den, Marten heard a new sound, one he'd been dreading. He put his finger in his ear and stood very still.

"What is it?" Omi asked.

Marten held up a hand for silence. Then he swallowed audibly. "It just got worse," he said.

Omi waited.

"I planted my listening device on Hansen."

"When?"

"When I put him to sleep on the toilet seat. But someone just shot him with wake-up stims. Shhh." Marten shut his eyes, listening. "Hansen has ordered a hunt."

"For us?"

"Let's go."

They half-ran into Galaxy Gold and then out, rushed through Sly Man's Pit and finally found Lance and Vip in the Barracuda Barn. A large shark tank had been built into the south wall. Three-meter monsters fought, made savage through electrodes implanted within their tiny brains. People cheered so loudly that Marten had to shout in Lance's ear. Lance gave him a wondering look. Marten motioned him and Vip toward the door.

"Here, put these on," Marten said, opening the tote bag and handing each a red kerchief. "And take off your jackets."

"Whatever for?" asked Lance.

"For a disguise," Marten said.

Vip fingered Omi's red silk shirt. "That must have cost."

"You're right," said Lance. To Marten: "Where did you get the money?"

Marten glanced both ways and lifted his shirt to show them the projac tucked in his waistband.

"Are you insane?" asked Lance. "No wonder the monitors are after you."

"What?" Vip said. "They are? How come, Marten? What did you do?"

"It's a long story," Marten said.

"This doesn't make sense," said Lance.

"Maybe not," Marten said. "But the monitors will kill us now."

"Whoa," said Lance. "Slow down. They'll do what? Kill you? Is that what you said?"

"There's no time to explain," Marten said.

"I don't want to get killed," Vip said.

"You won't," Omi said. He patted his waist.

"You have a weapon too?" said Lance.

Marten put a finger in his ear, adjusting the tiny receiver. He cursed quietly and removed the receiver, a little black speck on the tip of his index finger.

"Hansen find it?" Omi asked.

Marten nodded.

Lance grabbed him by the arm. "Guns, bugs and credits. Did the Training Master put you up to this?"

Omi snorted.

"Either we find Kang and get to the shuttle now or the monitors will kill us," Marten said. "At this point it's them or us."

"Yeah?" said Lance. "So why don't they pick you up at the barracks? All the monitors have to do is show cause, fill out a request and the Training Master will hand you over."

Marten shook his head. "We stumbled onto a drug ring. These are corrupt monitors."

"So report them," said Lance.

Marten shoved the majority of his credits at Lance. "We robbed them."

Lance squinted suspiciously. "That isn't like you, maniple leader. What's really going on?"

"Do you want your cut or not?" asked Marten.

Lance shoved the credits back. "Sorry, not my style."

"Okay," Marten said, almost trusting Lance enough to tell him the truth. But there wasn't time. "You can report us and you're safe. Or you can come with us. But you have to decide now. If you do nothing they'll think you're with us and kill you too."

Lance studied the two of them. "What do you think, Vip?"

The small man said, "They're 101st. The others are corrupt monitors."

"Right," said Lance. "We're in," he told Marten.

Ten minutes later, they found Kang in a dark bar where he sang quietly to himself. Marten dosed him with some anti-drunk that he'd picked up at a pill shop. They dragged Kang outside and hurried down the street, brushing through the crowds.

"Shouldn't we move more slowly?" asked Lance. "Try to catch them napping?"

"Speed and surprise," Marten said.

"And savagery," added Omi.

"Right," Marten said. "That's all we've got."

"It probably doesn't hurt then that we're shock troopers," said Lance wryly.

They neared the lift building as Kang started blinking. He'd been in a near trance, eyes staring as he moved like a sleepwalker. "What's going on?" he muttered.

"Hansen is double-crossing us," Omi said.

"The little maggot?" Kang said.

"What—" Lance started to say.

"Sir!" said a policeman, stepping in front of Marten.

Omi used Vip to shield the projac from the crowd and shot the cop with two sleep needles. They pushed the falling policeman aside and hurried through an archway covered with imitation vines.

"Stop them!" shouted a man on the street, a janitor who dropped his broom and pulled out a communicator and gun.

"Run!" shouted Marten.

The five-man team knocked people flying. Kang bellowed in delight. Vip giggled. Omi, Lance and Marten concentrated with grim intensity. They skidded, almost tripping as they hit the lifts. Marten dug out his card. Omi twisted around and snapped shots at three monitors running at them. Two fell. The last one, shorter than the other two and with wide shoulders—it was Ervil from Smade's—threw himself prone and fired back. Vip grunted and slammed against the lift as the door opened. Lance dragged him in and they all hugged the floor. The door slid shut as needles prickled the back wall.

"I'm hit," Vip said, touching his thigh. Then his eyes drooped shut.

"This is too much," said Lance. "Either way the HBs are gonna know about it."

"Maybe not," Marten said.

"In any case," said Lance, "the monitors will be waiting for us."

"Hansen can't have that many crooked monitors," Marten said. "Besides, he just woke up and must be trying to pull them all together."

"Yeah, right" said Lance. He checked Vip and turned back to Marten. "Where did you get the bug?"

"What bug?" Kang said.

"He stole it from Hansen," Omi said.

"We're slowing down," Marten said.

They braced themselves, projacs drawn as they knelt on either side of the door. It opened—the hall was empty.

"Go, Kang," whispered Marten. "Take Vip. Use him as a shield."

"Hey," said Lance. "That's—"

Kang charged with the unconscious Vip in his arms. Two big men in black suits stepped from around a corner, firing. It was Dalt and Methlen, the original duo from Smade's. One had a bloody mouth and he was missing two front teeth. Someone must have found the sleeping duo, reported it and medics had probably given them wake-up and stims.

58

Omi and Marten returned fire. One of the monitors slid to the floor. The other, who was missing his teeth, must have been wearing a vest.

Kang roared as he charged.

The last monitor snarled, lifted his projac—

Marten dove out of the lift for a better angle, firing, hitting the man's arm. The man dropped his weapon. Then Kang was on him.

"Go," Marten said, jumping off the floor.

"Is he hit again?" Lance asked Kang as they sprinted down the corridor.

"He's still breathing. Here." Kang tossed him Vip, then the four ran even harder. Behind them, lift doors opened and angry men shouted. Pounding feet told of a hotly contested chase.

"Kang!" shouted Hansen, probably using an amplifier. "This isn't the end of it, Kang!"

Kang laughed. "We can take them," he said.

"Go, go," Marten said.

They raced toward the docking tube, Marten in the lead. He forgot what Lycon had told them about shuttle procedure. He didn't know if the tube doors would only open when their leave was over or whether they could come back early and get in.

"Here we go," Marten said, pitching his projac to Kang. Marten hit the tube door with a grunt, fumbled with the slot and slid the card through. "Open," he pleaded.

"Here they come," Omi said.

"Try it again!" snarled Lance.

Marten slid the card again, and again. He cursed, turned the card around and slid it through again. The door opened.

They piled through, Marten last of all. He glanced back. Three monitors with guns raced into view, one of them short wide-shouldered Ervil together with his taller, dark-haired companion. Hansen, his thin hair disheveled and his face flushed and sweaty, came up behind them.

"Stop!" shouted Hansen.

The door closed and Marten raced up the boarding tube to catch up with the others. Finally, he passed the airlock and boarded the military shuttle.

"What are you going to do about your weapons?" whispered Lance. "We can't take them to the barracks."

"Wait," Marten said, taking his projac back from Kang.

A minute went by, two, three and four more.

"We made it," Omi said. "We're safe—for now."

Marten heaved off his knee where he'd hidden beside the airlock. He slid into a seat and grinned. "I'll tell you what we're going to do." He raised his projac. "We'll break them apart and flush them down the toilet once we take off."

Lance shook his head. "Sure hope it works."

"Yeah," Marten said. "Me too."

11.

Earth—Joho Mountains, China Sector

Taking a billion civilian casualties hardly seemed like a victory, especially when added to the loss of the Japanese home islands, the evaporation of 700,000 trained soldiers and the destruction of Earth's naval and air fleets. In return, they had only bled the Highborn by several thousand personnel, a couple hundred orbital fighters and a nearly crippled Doom Star, the *Genghis Khan*. Still, to date, it was the best Social Unity had been able to achieve against their genetic superiors, and the tactics that had allowed it were the brainchild of General James Hawthorne.

The Earth government's propaganda mills proclaimed him the Savior of Social Unity, and the Directorate of Inner Planets, led by Madam Director Blanche-Aster, granted him vast powers for the further prosecution of the war.

That had been six months ago. Now General Hawthorne paced in his office in China Sector as he spoke via comlink with Director Blanche-Aster. The tall, gaunt Supreme Commander with his wispy blond hair and aristocratic bearing had worn a long path in his carpet. He thought best while pacing, a nervous habit. He wore a green uniform with red piping along the crease of his trousers.

"I can't help you there, General," said Madam Director Blanche-Aster. The holo-screen was blank. She had been operated on yesterday, and had said she didn't feel like having people stare at her, gauging her health.

"Political Harmony Corps is chipping away at my authority," said Hawthorne. "Six months ago PHC worked hand in glove with me. Now they've thrown up a blizzard of red tape and ill will in my face."

"You've scared them, General. You've shown them a Social Unity world where they wield diminished power."

"Nonsense!"

"General Hawthorne," she said. "For the last time, I can't help you there. You must accept the reemergence of PHC hostility and concentrate on military matters. I hesitate to tell you this, but the other directors—Director Gannel has gained a following. I must tread carefully when arbitrating between you and PHC. There's nothing more I can say."

Hawthorne swung his long arms behind his back. So it had come to this. It was going to make everything that much harder.

"About the *Bangladesh*," said Blanche-Aster. "The attack must not fail."

"No military endeavor is without risks."

"But you assured me we would catch the Highborn by surprise."

"I still believe we shall," said Hawthorne. "Yet a good commander has contingency plans. I cannot simply point my finger and say: 'Here I will win.'"

"Don't be fatuous, General."

"That wasn't my intention."

"We must win somewhere," said Blanche-Aster. "We must hurt the Highborn. Make them bleed."

"The Sun Works Factory is such a place," Hawthorne said. "It is their supply base and headquarters. It is their vulnerable point. The *Bangladesh* is the best tool we have to hit them, to hurt them, to surprise them—which is probably the only way we could do this."

"Then... Do you think we will catch them by surprise?" asked Blanche-Aster.

"I wouldn't have ordered the attack unless I thought so."

"So it isn't a gamble?" she asked.

"Director. War is always a gamble. It is the nature of the beast. We have weapons and will, they have weapons and will. Each side reacts to the other."

"Yes, yes, but—"

"I urge you to hold on. To wait patiently."

"How can I wait?" asked Blanche-Aster. "How do you propose I sit patiently while Director Gannel rouses the others with his militant speeches? General, I don't think you understand the precariousness of our position."

"Social Unity is strong," said Hawthorne. "We are all bound together as one: humanity against the Supremacists. In time our sheer numbers will tell against the genetic freaks."

There was a pause before Blanche-Aster said, "I was speaking about our positions, General, yours and mine as Supreme War Leader and Madam Director. We could be replaced. Neither of our posts is as secure as only six months ago. The *Bangladesh* must be victorious."

"I see," said Hawthorne.

"I sincerely hope you do, General. PHC wants your head. Director Gannel is after my chair. Only victory somewhere will secure our posts. Now, my doctor has arrived. I must go."

"Thank you for your time, Director."

"Yes. Good-bye."

He closed the link.

General Hawthorne continued to pace. The *Bangladesh* even now sped toward Mercury, toward its destiny with the Sun Works Factory. Would they catch the Highborn by surprise? He wondered what the space hab's defenses were like. How did the stationmaster spend his time? If the stationmaster should guess how the attack would be made...

General Hawthorne exhaled sharply. Much rested upon this attack. It was a wild gamble. He knew that. But the Highborn were winning the war and they had to hurt them somehow. He hoped the *Bangladesh* was the answer, or at the very least, that it would buy him some time until the Cyborgs from Neptune arrived.

12.

Training Master Lycon of the Shock Troops hurried to his appointment with the Praetor of the Sun Works Factory. Like all Highborn, the Training Master's mind seethed with plans and programs, and he never seemed to have enough hours in the day to see them through. Unlike a preman, however, what he did have was endless energy, boundless enthusiasm and a grinding work ethic.

He hoped the Praetor didn't bring up that wild idea again of castrating his shock troopers. What a preposterous scheme!

Lycon strode down a street-sized corridor bustling with harried-looking aides and monitors. They were all premen, the hardest-working and most ambitious of them. Their higher rank and very close access to their genetic superiors proved it.

The overhead lights blazed like miniature suns, while stunted and potted pines lent a forest-like feel to the corridor. The holo-walls had been imaged to look like old log buildings. Quaint, to say the least; the effect was ruined by the modern uniforms everyone wore. The aides provided technical and mechanical help: shipping masters in their silk executive suits, chief industrialists in rough-cut jackets and heavy boots. They wished to show their nearness to the workers they had so recently risen from. There were white-coated computer specialists and solar engineers in their ubiquitous jumpsuits. Then there were the Monitors—just a fancy name for secret policemen. They were the Highborn's eyes and ears among the premen masses.

Lycon wore a smart blue uniform with crisscrossing white belts across his torso and another around his waist. A gold Magnetic Star, First Class decorated his chest and a well-worn sidearm rode his hip. Finally finished speaking, he turned off the recorder in his hand. He loathed losing ideas, and thus he spoke into the recorder in order to capture the purest essence of them the moment they arrived.

He was seven feet tall, powerful, with lightning-like reflexes, and pearl-white skin. Older than most Highborn, his white hair was cut so close to his scalp it seemed like fur. His dark eyes were intense beyond any normal man's, not unusual among Highborn, while his features were severely angular, as if a woodsman had taken an axe to hew him cheeks and a forehead.

"Training Master Lycon?"

Surprised out of his reverie, Lycon glanced about to see who had addressed him. Aides hurried by, their eyes downcast. It was inconceivable that any of them had hailed him. These premen knew better. Then he noticed an older, heavier man in a black uniform and hat. The fool peered up at him, stared at him, in fact, and seemed on the verge of addressing him.

"Sir," said the man.

Taken aback, Lycon could only raise his hand.

The black-uniformed man paused.

Lycon didn't recognize him, and he prided himself on being able to distinguish premen. To most Highborn, premen looked alike: dull, gaping stupidity stamped on their features, slow of wit and speech and sluggish almost beyond conception. His work among the shock troopers had allowed Lycon to penetrate the subtle differences, the ones the sub-species found so fascinating among themselves. Still, he didn't recognize this monitor.

The man blinked anxiously—a much older man, fat instead of merely heavy. The man blinked as if he would gush out with a torrent of words.

Many, actually, *most* Highborn would have slapped such an impertinent fellow hard enough across the face to knock him down, perhaps even hard enough to break his neck. But Lycon was more tolerant than most Highborn. Perhaps it was because he was beta. His eyes tightened. He loathed that word, *beta*. He hated any indication that he was less than a superior.

"Yes?" asked Lycon, in a warning voice as deep as a bear's.

The old man dipped his head, although he continued to stare upward. "The Praetor asks you to join him in the Gymnasium."

"Who are you?" said Lycon.

"Chief Monitor Bock, Training Master. I would also like a word with you, if I may."

"You dare to address me without proper protocol?"

A minute widening of the man's brown eyes indicated fear. Then he lowered his head and stared at the floor. "Forgive me, Highborn. I meant no offense."

Lycon grunted. Strict discipline was his guidepost in dealing with premen. He knew the Praetor thought likewise. This… it was more than impertinence. Chief Monitor was the highest rank premen secret policemen could achieve. So…

Lycon's angular features stiffened. He turned and strode toward the lift to the Gymnasium, leaving Bock far behind.

Lot 6, beta, an original, they all were derogatory terms used to describe a so-called inferior Highborn—used by others to describe him! Used, at least, behind his back.

He touched his Magnetic Star as his intense eyes narrowed. Beta, eh? Well, he knew that the road to rank went fastest by combat exploits. He would ride his shock troopers roughshod over every obstacle. A hard smile played on his lips. He would use his supposed inferiority to surpass his superiors. His beta-ness had allowed him to see a truth that the others missed.

No, they didn't all miss it. Grand Admiral Cassius understood. But he was a rarity among the Top Ranked. This truth was perhaps his only trump card, his lone ace to play in his quest for greatness. It had gotten him the Magnetic Star in the Japan Campaign. It had earned him this berth in the Sun Works Factory, as the Training Master of the shock troops.

"Training Master!"

Lycon scowled and turned. Who could have addressed him? All he saw were premen. Then he saw the Chief Monitor huffing to catch up. The overweight, older man surely couldn't have dared to shout at him, could he?

"Training Master," gasped Chief Monitor Bock. "Training Master please, I would like a word with you."

"You shouted at me?"

"Sir, I have information about your shock troopers that you need to know!"

"So you did shout at me. You actually admit it?"

The Chief Monitor bobbed his head.

Rage washed over Lycon. That the Praetor should use a preman to relay a message was bad enough. That this preman dared speak first was double impertinence. No, it was an insult. The Praetor wanted to rub his nose in his Lot-6-ness. Why else did the Praetor want to meet in the Gymnasium? Why else had the Chief Monitor dared act as he had?

Lycon turned from the Chief Monitor as he struggled to control his rage. *Remember that the Praetor is Fourth, and very dangerous. You must watch yourself.* He nodded. Although his sponsor was the Grand Admiral, the Admiral was a long way from the Sun Works Factory.

"Wait, Training Master," Chief Monitor Bock panted. "Your 101st has committed a terrible breach of discipline."

Lycon rubbed his forehead. *The Praetor is Fourth and the Chief Monitor is his preman.*

Then Chief Monitor Bock put his hand on Lycon's arm. "Training Master, please, I would like a word with—"

With an inarticulate roar, Lycon spun around and chopped with the flat of his hand. He caught the flabby Chief Monitor in the neck. Bones snapped. The preman flopped onto the deck, jerking, choking and trying to form words. His eyes goggled and then his body relaxed in its final throes. Blood seeped past its lips.

Lycon blinked at the heap of dead flesh. He frowned, looked up and saw the still sea of premen staring at him. His eyes narrowed. The crowd dropped their gaze. He strode to the nearest premen and grabbed him by the arm.

The man mewled in fear.

"What is your rank?" asked Lycon.

"Shipping Master, Second Class, Highborn."

"Do you have security clearance?"

"Yes, Highborn."

"Good." Lycon took out his recorder, flicking it. "Tell me what you just witnessed."

"Highborn, I saw the Chief Monitor grab your arm."

"He touched me without my leave then, is that correct?"

"Yes, Highborn."

The crowd began to slink away.

"Halt!" ordered Lycon.

Everyone froze.

One preman after another spoke into his recorder. They stated that the Chief Monitor had dared grab a Highborn, a death offense. Lycon had simply acted as any Highborn would, defending his honor and person.

Though I am beta, not even the Praetor's Chief Monitor may dare lay hands on me.

Finally satisfied with his recordings, Lycon let them leave. Then he marched to the lift, wondering how to broach this to the Praetor. He peered at the old-style Western saloon door. A beep told of a successful retina scan. The door slid open and he entered the computerized box. The pioneer motif ended here, thankfully. He was sick of it.

"Gymnasium," he said.

The door closed and the lift purred as it headed up.

Lycon wondered if the Praetor… No, no, better to keep such suspicions hidden deep inside. The walls had ears. How soon, he wondered, until some tech invented a device that monitored thoughts?

The lift slowed, and Lycon's premonitions grew. He must tread very softly. The Praetor would make a terrible enemy. Yet he hoped the Praetor wasn't going to make the common and mistaken assumption that a beta always rolled over for a superior.

13.

Lycon stood next to the Praetor. He still hadn't told him about the Chief Monitor. They peered down a walkway railing at a sandpit, where twelve-year-old boys wrestled. Surrounding the boys stood the coaches, Highborn with silver whistles glittering on their tunics.

The boys were huge and muscular, sweating as they grappled for a throw-hold. They wore loincloths and sported angry red welts, purple bruises and scars. Each, seething with Highborn vigor, clamped his mouth and breathed heavily through his nose. Each moved fast, lunging, grunting, twisting, grinning at successful throws and growling if he left his feet. None asked for quarter. None offered any.

"They fight well," said the Praetor.

Lycon nodded.

The Praetor towered over Lycon by an easy two feet. His shoulders were broader, his chest deeper and the angles of his face sharper. He wore a loose-fitting brown uniform with green bars on the sleeves. His hands were massive and strong. Like Lycon, his dark hair was cut to his scalp. But his eyes were strangely pink, eerie and unearthly, filled with unholy zeal.

The harsh breathing, the meaty slaps as boys grappled and clutched for holds and the sound of feet kicking sand filled this area.

The training of Highborn had changed since Lycon's birth.

He rankled at the thought of birth…

It was a taboo subject among the Highborn. None of them had ever been in a fleshly womb. Eugenicists had carefully bioengineered them in labs. Many long years ago, the rulers of Social Unity, of the four Inner Planets, had decided that the good of humanity mandated that the Solar System be governed rationally. Capitalist exploitation and imperialist designs had no place in the scheme of social harmony. Equality of resources meant that the Outer Planets had to share their wealth and technology with the masses in the Inner Planets. But evil men would want to keep their inequities. Selfishness yet ruled in too many hearts. So the rulers of Social Unity had come to the sad, reluctant conclusion that they needed an army and space fleet to subjugate the Outer Planets for the good of humanity. However, the social synthesis policies and submissiveness of their mass of humanity—and the fact that anyone with a backbone had all been killed in the slime pits—meant that soldierly qualities were lacking in the Inner Planets. At least so the rulers believed.

"Let us make super-soldiers," they said to one another.

The Directorate thus gathered biologists, eugenicists, and other technicians and began the secret program of bioengineered man. The results were cloned thousands of times over. And so the super-soldiers were born.

Well, not *born* exactly, not like regular humans. Test tube babies they would have been called, in past centuries.

Lab-grown, called vat-clones or "tankers," the fetuses grew by the hundreds in carefully controlled machines. "Birth" occurred six months after fertilization. The batch obtained its identification number and feeders and comforters took care of the squalling little specimens. Den mother and fathers rotated too often for the growing pre-soldiers to get attached. In truth, the less said about the first seven years the better. After the seventh year, they entered barracks and school and began their soldiering trade.

Somewhere along the line—before an invasion fleet had been sent to the Jupiter Confederation, the closest target—the super-soldiers had decided that they themselves should rule the Inner Planets. Most commentators believed that the decision to rebel had happened after they were given command of Doom Stars and after they had shown their mettle at the Second Battle of Deep Mars Orbit. Soon thereafter, they bit the hand that fed them. They tried to kill those who had given them birth.

Birth. It was a touchy word with the super-soldiers. And didn't they need a better name than "super-soldiers" or "space marines?" They wanted to be called something that would distinguish them from, from…premen, normals, *Homo sapiens* (spoken with a lilting sneer).

What about Highborn?

Yes!

High-BORN.

Ironic.

Perfect.

"Look at the boy over there," said the Praetor, who stood with his shoulders arrogantly thrust back and his head as erect and predatory as an eagle.

Lycon nodded. He saw the one: a long-armed lad with a bloody nose. He locked an opponent in a full Nelson. The boy's hands were pressed against the back of his opponent's head, while his arms were wrapped under his opponent's armpits.

Whistles blew as instructors noticed the two.

"Will he kill him?" asked the Praetor.

Lycon was shocked to realize that he would.

The winning boy's teeth were visible as his lips curled in a savage snarl. His forearm muscles were stark and trembling, his neck was seemingly made of cords and cables as he strained with all his might. The other boy's head bent lower and lower, but he refused to cry out or ask for quarter.

Lycon resisted the urge to leap over the barrier and into the sandpit. He disapproved of killing one so young. Revival at this age strangely tainted them. He recalled a Lot 6 specimen by the name of Sigmir. He shook his head. If he jumped down and stopped the lad from killing the weaker boy, he knew he would lose face in the Praetor's eyes. He couldn't afford that, not today.

"Well?" asked the Praetor. "Will he kill him or not?"

The instructors shrilly blew their whistles as they rushed toward the two boys.

The crack of a breaking neck was loud and sinister. The killer didn't seem to react to what he'd done. He just coldly let go and watched the corpse drop onto the sand.

The instructors knocked the killer aside as they knelt beside the dead boy, his head tilted at an impossible angle. Pneumospray hypos appeared in their hands and hissed as the instructors pumped Suspend into the corpse.

"Will they be in time?" asked the Praetor.

"It seems so," said Lycon.

"Yes," said the Praetor. "The boy should make a clean revival."

In this year 2350, the dead didn't always stay down. Resurrection techniques revived many if Suspend froze their brains and various organs in time.

"What will happen to the other boy?" asked Lycon.

"The killer?" said the Praetor.

Lycon waited. Over-talkativeness was a bad trait.

"He will be punished," said the Praetor, "and marked as a ranker, a climber."

Lycon had known it would be so. Teach them to obey, but use a natural killer where he belonged: leading combat troops. The Praetor ran the Gymnasium strictly according to regulations.

"Come with me," said the Praetor.

They strolled along the walkway, passing other sandpits: knife-training areas, boxing matches and battle-stick duels. Lycon kept debating with himself when he should tell the Praetor about today's little incident.

"You are an infantry specialist," the Praetor said. "What is your analysis of our future?"

"They are well-trained."

"And strong, yes?

"Big and strong," said Lycon.

"True Highborn," the Praetor said.

Lycon nodded, not trusting himself to speak, wondering if the Praetor meant more by the remark.

They came to the end of the walkway. To the left, stairs led down to a staging area. The Praetor ignored the stairs. He kept heading toward the wall.

"Praetor," said Lycon.

The Praetor turned.

"Did you instruct your Chief Monitor to relay a message to me today?"

"You query me, Training Master?"

"Your Chief Monitor spoke to me. I'm simply curious if he was ordered by you to do so."

"He had no orders from me," the Praetor said.

"It was from him that I learned to come to the Gymnasium."

The Praetor appeared surprised. "I left a note on my door. Perhaps he read it and took it upon himself to deliver the message."

"Ah," said Lycon.

"He spoke with you?"

"The Chief Monitor hailed me."

"Without correct address?" the Praetor asked.

Lycon nodded.

"He will be punished."

Lycon rubbed his jaw. "He touched me. He grabbed my arm to stop me."

The Praetor blinked. "You can verify this?"

Lycon hid his anger at being asked such a question. "I struck him for this outrage. Unfortunately, my blow killed."

"You killed my Chief Monitor?"

Lycon pulled out his recorder. "If you would care to replay this…"

The Praetor accepted the slender recorder and listened to the premen. "You acted correctly," he said later, returning the recorder.

"It was not my wish to kill him," said Lycon.

"Next time I won't select a fool for a Chief Monitor. I hold no ill will, Training Master."

Lycon dipped his head.

"Now, come with me." The Praetor strode toward the wall.

Lycon was puzzled but said nothing. He was relieved the Praetor had taken the Chief Monitor's death so well. Some Highborn became attached to their premen.

The Praetor strode to the wall, glanced about—no one seemed to be watching—and spoke sharply. A section of wall slid open. The Praetor hurried through and Lycon followed.

Behind them, the wall section slid shut. Lights snapped on. They stood in a small changing room, complete with lockers and benches. The Praetor marched to the farthest bench and opened a locker, taking out leather garments.

"Yours are in the next one," said the Praetor.

Lycon hesitated.

The Praetor, perhaps alert for this, asked, "Is something wrong, Training Master?"

"I don't understand the meaning of this."

"Exercise."

"I have plenty of it while training the shock troops."

"I'm certain of that, Training Master. But I have so many chores and tasks that often I'm forced to skip physical activity. Also, you're an infantry specialist. So I wanted your opinion, and how better than to actually engage in it."

"It, Praetor?"

"Oh, do leave me my surprises, Training Master. It's finally ready and you're the first besides me to run through it."

Highborn prided themselves on decisiveness. Lycon was no different. "Yes, of course," Lycon said.

He disrobed, folding his blue uniform. Beside him, the Praetor did likewise. Both were highly muscled and perfectly toned. There was no flab on the Praetor, despite his protests of lack of exercise. Lycon was thinner and leaner, although compared to a preman he was massive and thick. Both donned skin-suits and went barefoot.

"You'll have to leave your sidearm behind," the Praetor said.

Lycon set his big gun on top of his uniform. Then he put them in a locker.

"Take this," said the Praetor.

Lycon accepted gauntlets with small iron knobs on the knuckles. He watched the Praetor slip on his own pair.

"Are we to spar?" asked Lycon.

The Praetor's weird pink eyes seemed to glitter. "Does such a prospect worry an infantry specialist?"

74

"Only a fool ignores disparities in capability." Lycon said. "I do not like to think of myself as a fool."

"Well said, Training Master. No, it is not my wish to spar today. Rather, we hunt."

"What do we hunt?"

"That is an interesting question," the Praetor said. "I haven't yet thought of what to call them. Perhaps after today you can name them for me."

Lycon liked this less and less. He followed the Praetor out the locker room and through another sliding wall.

14.

They entered a huge room unlike any other in the Sun Works Factory, a former zoological area. It seemed endless. Sand, tall cacti and sagebrush were everywhere, with rolling dunes and rust-colored boulders. Overhead, an undeterminable distance away, shined what seemed to be a sun. Breezes blew. Birds called.

"Observe," said the Praetor, pointing.

Lycon frowned. A vulture wheeled overhead. "Is it real?"

"A holo-image, but very convincing. Yes?"

"Are there any real animals here?"

"Most certainly."

"The ones we are to hunt?" asked Lycon.

The Praetor said, "Perhaps hunt isn't the correct word. Perhaps it is we who are the prey." He slapped the wall. "We can't get out this way. We have to cross the dunes to the other side."

Lycon dared put a hand on the Praetor's forearm. "Am I to believe that you would allow yourself to be hunted, the Praetor of the Sun Works Factory, the Fourth Highest among us?"

The Praetor stared haughtily at the hand.

Lycon removed it.

The Praetor considered the dunes as he expanded his massive chest. He exuded power and rank and something the Highborn referred to as excellence. "Yes. I allow myself to be hunted."

"Why?

"To prove a point."

"Which is?"

"Walk with me," the Praetor said, with a harder tone.

Lycon moved on the balls of his feet, listening, watching and ready for some insane beast, a wolf-tiger hybrid or some other monstrosity, to leap out and attack.

The Praetor also watched, his head swiveling, his pink eyes alert and alive.

"It would help if I knew what to look for," Lycon said.

"I will pose a question. How can two million Highborn hope to conquer the Solar System?"

Was this a complaint against the Grand Admiral's strategy? Lycon didn't think so, but...

"Earth alone holds forty billion premen," the Praetor said.

"Our conquest of the Inner Planets moves strictly according to the Grand Admiral's scheme," said Lycon

"Ah," the Praetor said. "Therein lies your reluctance, eh? Rest assured that I am not asking in a seditious manner. No. Think of it as a...as a philosophical question."

"I'm not sure I understand."

The Praetor froze. His nostrils widened. Tension coiled with extreme urgency. Although motionless, he seemed gripped with throttled frenzy.

Lycon also tested the air, but he could detect nothing unusual. A whispery wind stirred grit against a nearby boulder. Before them rose a dune dotted with sagebrush.

The Praetor minutely twisted his head. Then he set out moving in a half crouch. Lycon followed, wary, troubled and alert. They crested the dune.

Before them spread a tiny valley. Boulders were tumbled here and there. Giant cacti held aloft their spiky branches. The breeze rattled grit in shifting patterns over the hardpan.

Tension oozed from the Praetor, although his pink eyes seemed to shine as he regarded Lycon. "Two million, Training Master. Just a mere two million Highborn to conquer billions of premen. Oh, we have replacements, as you've just seen. But a handful, really, a hundred thousand each year. Say we do conquer the Solar System. How can we control them?"

Lycon grew even more wary. "You are Fourth, Praetor. I am certain such questions engage your energies. As for me, I train the shock troopers."

"Which is exactly why I pose you the question. Come. This way."

The Praetor started down the hill. His eyes roved everywhere. He paused once to test the wind. Lycon followed. At a boulder the Praetor stopped. He touched the towering rock. "Take a look around."

Lycon scrambled up the boulder. He peered at every shadow. Then he jumped down and shook his head.

The Praetor appeared puzzled, and a twitch of annoyance crossed his features. He strode several steps before he froze. He turned back. A strange ecstasy now softened his features. When he spoke, it was with husky overtones.

"I've read your paper, Training Master."

Lycon tested the wind. He smelled nothing unusual. Were the Praetor's senses so much sharper than his? He disliked the idea.

"*Janissaries in 2350*," the Praetor said.

"Oh."

"Please, no false modesty. We both know the Grand Admiral fawns on historical anecdotes."

"I might phrase it differently."

"Finally!" the Praetor said. "We see the Janissary Lieutenant-Aga speaking, not simply the meek Training Master of Shock Troopers."

Lycon debated with himself. The Grand Admiral had sponsored him. Grand Admiral held his loyalties, while the Praetor had perhaps already mocked him with Chief Monitor Bock, perhaps mocked him even now.

"You have addressed a profound problem," Lycon said. "Two million of us, billions of them. There may be many answers. One of them, I believe, has been supplied by history."

"By your Janissaries?"

Lycon nodded.

The Janissaries had been an extraordinary invention of the Ottoman Turks of the Middle Ages. *Yeni-Tzeri* or "New Soldiers," had become the *corps d'elite* of the conquering

78

Ottomans. "Send in the Janissaries" became a cry to terrify the world. An empire had been carved with them. Yet not one soldier in the Janissaries had been Turkish. All had been the children of Christian parents who had lived within the Muslim Ottoman Empire.

Every five years the Muslim Sultan levied the Christians parents with a general conscription. Seven-year-old sons—of the Christians only—were inspected. Those of promising physique and intelligence were taken, never to return home or see their parents again. In the Muslim capital, they were given further tests. Those who seemed destined to strength and endurance went to special camps. Harsh training, enforced abstinence, countless privations and strict discipline turned them into hard professional soldiers. They were forbidden to marry or have families. Rather, pride in their order was taught. Pride in their privileges and battle skills.

Christian by birth, spartan by upbringing and fanatical Muslims by conversion, the Janissaries combined the arrogant militarism of the West with the religious fanaticism of the East. With scimitar, arquebus and round shield they had expanded the empire for their Ottoman overlords. More than simple slave-soldiers and much greater than mere mercenaries, the Janissaries had been unique.

"You've modeled your shock troopers on them," the Praetor said.

Lycon agreed.

The Praetor sneered. "Slave soldiers, Training Master, that's all they really are. The same as the Free Earth Corps fools who enlisted under the Grand Admiral's banner."

"You speak of Mamelukes, Praetor."

"I said slave soldiers."

"So the Mamelukes were, at least originally. Enslaved horse-archers sold in the Egyptian slave marts. They became the first warriors to defeat the conquering Mongols."

"Ah. You spout historical anecdotes. Illusions propped up by official lies that we dare call truth."

"You are wrong to spurn facts, Praetor. History is simply race experience. A wise man studies past errors so he can avoid the obvious pitfalls before him."

The Praetor's weird pink eyes narrowed.

"Slave soldiers or Mamelukes can, under the right conditions, prove to be excellent warriors," Lycon said. "As I would argue our FEC Armies are now worthwhile. But the Janissariy, that is another type of soldier. Ideas, even more than force or simple rewards, motivated them."

The Praetor exploded with passion. "Do you believe your shock troopers to be loyal?"

"I stake my reputation on it," said Lycon.

"So we must put all our trust in you then?"

"Praetor, each shock trooper is a proven soldier, a FEC Army hero from the Japan Campaign. Each of them has already fought hard in our cause."

"So you base such assumptions on bits of tin?" asked the Praetor.

"I base it on past actions and performances."

The Praetor ran massive fingers through his hair. Blood flushed his features. He turned away and in a half crouch slid toward a new boulder.

"Battling on a planet is one thing, Training Master. War in space... we must be doubly and triply certain of premen loyalty there."

"If we can't trust the shock troops, who can we trust?" Lycon asked.

The Praetor stopped, and straightened. A strange smile played on his lips. "You state my own worry. Two million of us, as you've said, billions and more billions of them. If they ever learned to fight, even a little bit... How can we defeat them all, and then rule them?"

"Increase the number of Highborn," Lycon said.

"Are you certain that's wise?"

"I don't understand," Lycon said carefully.

"Come now, Training Master. You, a beta, don't understand?"

Lycon stiffened.

"Oh, I'm sorry. I meant no offense. But surely it's clear to you that our bio-geneticists will keep improving us."

Lycon kept his features immobile. "You are Fourth, Praetor, and are surely privy to policies and questions that if spoken or thought of by someone like me would be considered treasonous."

"Meaning?"

"That I am under-qualified to consider such things."

The Praetor tapped his muscled thigh. "Then... I should throw out your paper?"

"Might that not be hasty, Praetor? Why not let the shock troopers prove themselves. Actions, after all, speak louder than boasts."

The Praetor twisted his lips. "So if your shock troopers proved treasonous..."

"Do you have any evidence of treason?"

"Not yet."

Lycon glanced upward, considering the holo-clouds. He couldn't understand the Praetor's dislike of the shock troops. Yet clearly, it was there, as well as threats.

"I have a counter-proposal for you, Training Master."

"You merely need order me," said Lycon.

"I do not want automatons. I want believers."

"Believers in what?" asked Lycon.

"Your Janissary idea has certain promise. To take and convert is right. But ideas—we cannot trust premen to hold to mere ideas. Look how easily we've shifted these socialists and turned them into capitalists."

"The upper crust has shifted," Lycon said.

"They are the only ones that matter. In any case, take and convert, change, in other words."

"My shock troopers—"

The Praetor waved that aside. "Sometimes they will fight as trained, for even the FEC soldiers fought. But what if I produced men who will always fight and do exactly what I train them to do?"

"Why not use both our ideas?" asked Lycon.

The Praetor's nostrils twitched. He grinned. "Let me show you why not." He moved sideways toward the nearest boulder.

And now Lycon noticed a new odor. It was subtle and musty.

The Praetor hissed. Lycon hurried beside him. "Look," whispered the Praetor, as he knelt beside the boulder. Lycon saw the footprint, man-sized, preman. He frowned at the Praetor, who rose and scanned the small valley. "Ah. There." Lycon followed the Praetor's gesture. He caught a glimpse of deep blue. The color stood out in this stark landscape.

"They're hiding," whispered Lycon.

"No. They're flanking us."

Lycon stared at the Praetor, who kept watching the dunes. "How many of them are there?" asked Lycon.

"Six."

Lycon frowned. "Why all this caution, Praetor? Do the premen have weapons?"

"Indeed."

Lycon dropped to a crouch and scanned all around. "Lasers or carbines?" he snapped.

"Knives."

"Knives?" asked Lycon, wondering why he'd been worried.

"Meter-long knives"

"Six premen with knives?" Lycon asked, as he rose from his crouch.

"Too few do you think?"

"Praetor…" Lycon frowned more deeply than before.

"No, I am not so soft that six premen frighten me. But these aren't premen."

"What are they then?"

"You tell me," the Praetor said. "Here they come."

Lycon saw five blue-colored men march down the dune toward them. Despite the strange color, they were normal-sized. Their eyes bulged, although not with fear but intense hatred. Their taut muscles quivered. They wore loincloths and wielded glittering meter-long knives. Swords, really. They exuded a strong odor.

"Are they combat-trained?" Lycon asked.

"No."

"Why do you consider them so fearsome?"

"Tell me, Training Master. Do they look afraid?"

Lycon observed no fear. Strange, unless…

"Do they cower as most premen would against two such as us?" asked the Praetor, the way a father might ask another about his son.

"Are they familiar with Highborn?" asked Lycon.

A harsh laugh and a nod told him the answer.

"You said there were six of them," said Lycon. "I count five."

A startling cry, from behind, surprised him. Lycon spun around. A blue man sliding toward them sprang at him. The man moved fast. His knife flashed. Lycon twisted minutely. His gauntlet smashed the thing's face. Lycon picked up the blade. He turned and raced to help the Praetor, who set himself against five sprinting, snarling, bestial—not premen. Something else. Others.

Only a Highborn could have followed their swift moves. These men had uncanny reflexes. They circled the Praetor, and together lunged at him. A knife slashed skin. Blood spurted. The Praetor roared, kicked and punched. Two blue men flew backward. Knives stabbed again. One blade now stuck from the Praetor's thigh like a growth. Then Lycon jumped among them, a whirlwind of thrusts and blocks. Seven seconds more and it was over. Six blue corpses lay bleeding and broken on the sand.

Lycon turned toward the Praetor, who jerked the knife from his thigh. He ripped a strip of buckskin from his garment and tied it around his wounded leg.

"How bad?" asked Lycon.

"Lucky for us I didn't give them poison."

It was only then that Lycon realized he had a cut under his ribs. It was shallow, but there it was. That was amazing.

"You said they weren't combat trained," Lycon said.

"They weren't," said the Praetor.

"Why were they so fast and clever?"

"Faster than any normal preman, yes?"

"Unless a soldier took a dose of Tempo," Lycon said. But even then he wouldn't be so fast."

The Praetor limped to the nearest blue corpse. "Let me show you this."

Lycon went to the other side.

83

The Praetor ripped away the loincloth.

Lycon saw it immediately. The man's genitals had been removed.

"Gelded," the Praetor said.

Lycon stared up sharply. "Surely the removal of his sex organs didn't grant him such speed."

"Each was given a new internal organ. The organ seeps Tempo and other drugs directly into their bloodstream."

"What?" said Lycon. *Direct tampering?*

"Naturally, they must eat certain foods for the new organ to manufacture these drugs. But the toxins in their skin cause them to crave these foods."

"Toxins?"

"They are tattooed into the skin."

Lycon studied the altered men. Part of him considered this monstrous. Another part—"They're... Neutraloids," he said. "You've neutered them, but made them..." Lycon shook his head in wonder.

"What did you call them?"

"Neutraloids."

The Praetor clapped his hands. "I accept the name. They are Neutraloids. And these are what we must have in space with us."

"Instead of the shock troopers?"

"Can you think of any reason why not?"

Lycon pondered the six corpses. Gelded. Implanted with a new organ. Tattooed over their entire body, and that a deep blue color. "Yes, Praetor, I can think of several reasons."

"Please enumerate them."

"Perhaps once I have pondered—"

The Praetor limped beside Lycon. "I picked you, Training Master, because you're unbiased. You hope to ride your shock troopers. I've read your paper and understood that immediately. Yet here I've shown you a new and better way to rise."

"Certainly they fought savagely," said Lycon.

"Which is exactly what we need."

"But why are they castrated?"

"Why is that bad?" asked the Praetor.

84

"It will ruin the morale of other premen. Those who have already experienced sexual pleasure will not want it taken away. Nor their symbols of manhood."

"Ah. I see your point. Already you've been helpful. Good, good. Now, I propose that only space soldiers be converted. Leave the FEC Armies alone for now. But in space, our very special preserve, here we use only the Neutraloids and none of the other lesser species. Of course we keep the making of Neutraloids secret from the FEC masses."

"It won't stay secret for long," Lycon said.

"The trick will be in doing it for long enough."

"Not that I agree with you," Lycon said, "but I understand your reasoning. My second objection is the new gland."

"Meaningless. Only the space soldiers will be so converted. The others will not have to fear it."

"It isn't the reaction of the premen I was thinking about. Rather, the cost, time and effort to plant these organs into these... these Neutraloids."

"Hmm. Any other objections?"

"They attacked us."

"They had been ordered to do."

"Will they obey orders not to?" asked Lycon.

The Praetor frowned, hesitated and then admitted, "Their worldview has become distorted. They are pessimists. Hate dominates their thinking and a certain feeling of futility. A right combination of drugs will correct that."

Lycon nodded thoughtfully.

"Any other objections?"

"Praetor, as I see it you mean drugs to replace ideas as the motive force."

"Drugs are more trustworthy."

"I'm not so certain. In any case, they're more expensive. With ideas we've brought millions of Social Unitarians to our side."

"Fear did that," the Praetor said.

"Fear helped," agreed Lycon.

The Praetor expanded his chest. He seemed to consider his words. "Are you with me?"

"I am not against you."

"Let me rephrase. The shock troops will make perfect test subjects. This week we should begin to convert them into Neutraloids."

"But the shock troops are trained and ready to deploy," Lycon said.

"Let me be frank, Training Master. I do not trust premen in space. On planets and at this point in our conquest we need them. In space and in our spacecraft, we must have utterly loyal soldiers. Space is the high ground. We dare not take chances there."

"I tell you that shock troops are loyal."

The Praetor stared at Lycon. "For your sake you'd better be right."

15.

"We can't do it," whispered Omi. "Not with those new spy-sticks the Training Master put in."

The rest of the 101st lay asleep in their bunks, Kang already snoring. Several days had passed since their return from the Pleasure Palace. Yesterday the entire shock troop regiment had been marched onto the training field. Lycon had stepped onto a stand and addressed them in his deep voice. He told them about the spy-sticks, about rumors of disloyalty and that nothing would stand in his way of making their names shine among the Highborn. They, the shock troopers, could climb in rank and privilege as long as they remained loyal. Disloyalty, traitorous actions after they had been given so much—no, the Training Master couldn't envision that from any of them.

"Why doesn't he tell us about the upcoming gelding?" Marten had whispered to Omi.

The Training Master had warned them that when they were away from the barracks they should be careful. Not everyone in the Sun Works Factory wanted them to succeed and gain rank. However, even given that, such things shouldn't concern them. Excellence alone was what every one of them should strive for.

"We can't do it," Omi whispered from his bunk.

Marten rolled out.

"They just put in spy-sticks," Omi hissed. "The watchers will be alert."

"I have a timetable to keep."

"Because of Nadia? Because you want to see her again?"

Marten eased into the slick-suit he'd secreted under his bunk. It was a smooth piece of body-fabric that clung to every muscle. He picked up the barcode eraser and ran it over his tattoo.

"Madness," whispered Omi.

Marten leaned near. "It's better if I do this alone."

Omi stared at him in the darkness, then rolled over and pulled the blanket over his head.

Marten crept out of the 101st's sleep zone and through the 910th and 52nd's. He checked both ways, slid open a window whose tripwire he'd spliced and rerouted yesterday. Crawling through, he shut the window and removed a floor-piece outside. His body ached and he craved sleep. Shock trooper training was brutally intense. He slipped a stim-pill and waited. Chemical strength soon flooded him. He was going to pay for it one of these days, but hopefully on the long trip to the Jupiter Confederation and not as a gelded neuter here.

He took the sucker climbing equipment from the hidden floor space, the elbow, kneepads and gloves, and like a fly—*pop, pop, pop* as quietly as he could—climbed the tall barracks building. The brown-colored cube rose over a track and field area where the Highborn ran them like dogs day and night. He couldn't cross the area on foot with the new spy-sticks in place.

He reached the top of the barracks, his muscles quivering from the exertion, and rested for a moment. Then he shucked off the climbing equipment and crawled to the barracks' flagpole. He shimmied to the top, unclipped a line from his belt, swung the hook twice then threw it. With a soft click, it latched to the ceiling vent. He tested it, closed his eyes as he muttered a prayer, and then hoisted himself to the vent. The fit between the grilles was tight, but he crawled through, coiled his line and hooked it to his belt. Then he put his back against one side of the shaft and his feet against the other and climbed like a crab. By the time he reached the joint where the shaft leveled, he dripped with sweat.

Ten minutes of effort later, he dropped from a vent in a maintenance area. He donned a previously hidden maintenance uniform, opened a door-lock and jogged down a utility corridor. Five kilometers later, he opened another hatch and walked briskly past other maintenance personnel with their mops, buckets and spray kits. Soon he passed dockworkers and shuttle mechanics. He entered a huge hanger buzzing with lifts moving shuttle engines and yellow-suited mechanics working on the engines or shuttles. Foremen shouted. Welding equipment created bright arc-glares. Marten hurried through, nodded at a man who yelled at him and pointed at Marten's bare head. Everyone else wore hardhats. Marten stepped through a door and walked down the carpeted corridor. He passed men and women drinking coffee in a cafeteria and opened a door with a restricted sign.

He jogged again and entered a different hanger. This one was empty, with a dusty floor and feeling of disuse. He hurried down rows of fifty-foot shelves made of girders and steel sheets. Finally, he reached his destination. Up four shelves sat two boxes. One should be marked "Industrial Sealant."

He lacked a forklift, so he climbed the shelves. At the box, he balanced himself and crowbarred the lid, looked in and smiled.

"I knew you'd do it," he whispered.

Marten removed the plastic bags, stuffed the vacc-suit and helmet into a duffel bag and returned to the floor. He checked his chronometer. Lycon might call an emergency drill in another hour. That would be cutting it tight if he tried to make it back in time. But the Training Master might not call one. He'd hope for luck.

Marten exited the empty hanger, strode to a new utility corridor and set off on the six-kilometer jog. Halfway there he palmed another stim, knowing the price his body would soon demand, or even worse that he would give himself a heart attack. Maybe that was the price of freedom, or attempting freedom.

"Don't think, Marten. Do."

He wondered if Nadia would keep her appointment. He hoped so. Then the stim kicked in and he increased the pace.

16.

Nadia Pravda nervously paced before a plexiglass bubble dome that hissed from a crack four meters up. She was a fool. She should phone Hansen and explain that none of this was her fault. She was sick of hiding in crawl spaces, wondering if Marten could build a spacecraft to take her out of here.

She laughed at the impossibility of the idea. Yet she recalled his performance at the Pleasure Palace. He had taken out the two monitors and then everyone in the drug room. Stunning. She shivered as she remembered the tumbling bodies and that dead monitor the thickly muscled Korean shot through the eye. Omi had checked each person, shooting several just to make sure they were soundly asleep. He'd seemed ruthless. But Marten, he seemed to be more than ruthless. Something drove him.

She made a face. The smart thing would be to call in and tell her foreman she'd been sick, so sick that she hadn't even been able to reach the com system. He would know she was lying. That's why she might need a call from Hansen. Then she should have her job back. Yes, and then she would owe Hansen two favors, one for not killing her and another for getting her job back.

But why had the sump exploded that day?

Nadia eyed the hissing crack and checked her watch. Marten was late. Fear twisted her resolve. What if he didn't show? What if he had been caught? What if even now monitors raced here to, to—Nadia hugged herself. Would they really shove her out an airlock naked? That's what they'd threatened to do if she double-crossed them.

Nadia began to pace. Being alone for days, hiding in that crawl space was driving her mad. Why—

Her head snapped up. Her eyes grew round and she couldn't breathe.

She heard a valve turn. A door creaked. Someone was coming.

Please, please let it be Marten.

A man turned the corner, a white-faced, sweating man who stumbled toward her. He looked exhausted and sick. Then Nadia breathed again as she realized it was Marten. And despite her resolve over the past several days not to, she felt a stirring within her.

17.

Marten staggered, caught himself and leaned against the wall as he wheezed. He shivered and wondered if he was sick.

"Marten?"

He willed himself upright. Nadia looked better than he remembered. Her hair was combed, her face clean and not disheveled. She seemed worried for him. He liked that, and smiled.

"You look awful," she said.

He used his sleeve to wipe his forehead.

"And you're shivering," she said.

He felt cold, that's true.

"Are you sure you can do this?" she asked.

"How have you been?"

"You're kidding, right? I'm hunted. I've lost my job. If I get caught I'm dead. Oh, I've been fine. You?"

"Did you bring water?"

She stared at him before handing him a flask.

He drained it despite the queasiness in his stomach. He needed fluids. "Do you have any more?"

"You're a camel," she asked, handing him a second flask.

He drained that one too, although he almost threw up. The sweat on his face started to dry. He shivered, feeling colder than before.

"I don't think you can do this," she said.

"I'm not dead."

"Is that supposed to be funny?"

"When I'm dead I'll quit. Until then it's simply mind over matter."

"Oh, you're one of those. You can think things into existence. Like bullets in the belly wouldn't stop you, not if you will-powered them away."

He grinned. "It's good to see you too, Nadia." He opened the duffel bag, pulled out the vacc suit and started donning it. She already wore hers.

"Do you really think we can do this?" she asked.

"Did you bring the line and the magnetic anchor?"

"It was all where you said it should be. How did you get it? That's what I kept wondering."

"It was stashed several years ago," he said.

Interest flickered on her face. "Who put it there?"

"Me."

"You lived here before the war?" she asked in surprise.

"My parents were Unionists. PHC got them both."

"I'm sorry. I didn't know."

He shrugged. "That was several years ago."

She stepped closer and touched his face. "You were a Nonconformist?"

"The square peg," he said bitterly.

"When you say that, your eyes…" She nodded. "Maybe we *can* do this."

"Ready?" he asked, with the vacc helmet in his hands.

"Do you have stims?" she asked.

"If I take another one, my heart will explode. But I still have a lot of will power."

She shook her head. "If you can joke about it, it can't be that bad."

"Right," he said, putting on the helmet and snapping the seals. He still felt nauseous and shaky, but this was the time to do it. He hefted the magnetic anchor, a long flexible coil-line and the tool kit she'd brought that his mother had once made. All this was backup equipment from a time he would rather forget. He sighed. He'd better remember if he wanted off the Sun Works.

A valve hissed and oxygen flooded his vacc suit. Nadia was ready, so he moved to the hatch.

A few minutes later, they exited the airlock and switched on their boots. With a metallic clang, clang, clang they walked outside the Sun Works, the magnetic attraction keeping them on the shadowy side of the station. The plexiglass dome was to their right, but now they were looking into the hab, not out. From their subjective sense, Mercury loomed above, while all around in the distance moved a myriad of lights that indicated repair pods, shuttles and various spacecraft, hundreds, maybe thousands of them in an ever moving, shifting pattern.

Marten pointed. Nadia nodded. They didn't have radios or comlinks. This was going to be done with hand signals. She came up beside him. He couldn't see into her helmet. Like his, the visor was polarized against sun-glare. She grabbed his free hand. He smiled, but all he saw was her dark visor.

Hand in hand, they moved exactly one hundred meters. He checked his bearings, stopped and pointed at the dead pod floating above. It had a small engine with a dome built around a pilot's seat and that had three arms, a clamping arm, a laser-welder arm and a riveting-arm. The pod had the same velocity-spin as the habitat and therefore stayed at exactly the same relative position.

But it was nearly a hundred meters out of reach.

Marten attached the anchor to the Sun Works and snapped the line to it. The other end of the line he snapped to his belt. He switched off his magnetic boots, judged the distance and leaped at the dead pod. He floated from Nadia. He looked back and waved. She waved back. Then he watched the nearing pod. Closer, closer, he stretched and tried to catch it. Then he relaxed and sighed as he floated past the pod by several arms lengths. He started reeling himself back to the magnetic anchor, looping the line as he went. Nadia reeled him from her end. Soon he was back on the Sun Works.

He studied the pod, gauged his earlier failure and remembered that both the satellite and the pod moved as he sailed through space. He leaped again, floated toward it, closer, closer—his fingertips brushed across the pod's skin, sliding, sliding. Then his fingers curled around a float rail. He hung on. His momentum pulled him and his forearm strained. He used his other hand and pulled himself to the pod, and switched on his boots.

Marten whooped with delight ad his boots clamped on, the sound loud in his helmet, and he no longer shivered. He began to explore.

The pod wasn't locked, which was a big break. He wedged himself into the tiny cabin. The controls looked fine. He tried turning it on. Dead. Nothing. Okay, he hadn't expected it to work. He used tools from the kit and pulled out a panel. A blown fuse box. He hoped that was all that was wrong with the pod.

He moved outside, attached the line and hand over hand hauled himself to Nadia. Together, very gently, they tugged the pod toward them. Its mass was several tons, so they didn't want to build up momentum. Instead, they waited fifteen minutes until it arrived. Then they used gentle pressure to stop it and they dragged it with them and secured it near the airlock. That was all they could do for now, so they entered the airlock, waited for it to pressurize and soon stepped into the observation pit.

He took off his helmet.

"You did it," she said, hugging him.

They laughed. He peered into her eyes and that was a mistake. She was beautiful and he kissed her.

She arched her head, staring at him in surprise.

A mixture of impulses surged through him. He ignored the ones that said slow down, this might not be wise. He put his hand behind her head and kissed her again. She responded, and then both his arms were around her.

"Marten," she whispered.

He pulled back, blinking, finally thinking about what he was doing. "I have to go," he said.

"Not now."

"I'm late already."

"But..."

"Don't worry. Tomorrow—"

She kissed him. "Are you really sure you want to go?"

"I don't *want* to go."

"Let's hide together like the Nonconformists."

It wasn't a bad idea. "What about my friends? I won't be able to slip into the barracks and get them if the Highborn are hunting for me. Especially now. The Training Master is worried about something."

"Is Hansen—?"

"There's no time to explain. I need a class 5a fuse box and a cylinder of hydrogen propellant. The way you'll get them— I'd better write it down so you won't forget."

She disengaged, stared into his eyes and turned away. "I don't know if can do this."

He put a hand on her shoulder. "We'll have the trip to the Jupiter Confederation together."

"With all your friends along?" she asked.

"Nadia!"

She turned and forced a smile. "What do I need to do?"

She wrote as he removed his vacc suit, telling her. He then stored the suit in a locker by the airlock.

"Tomorrow, same time," he said.

She nodded, but brooded.

He shouldn't have kissed her. He turned to go, came back, hugged her and kissed her again. They lingered.

"I'll come back," he whispered.

"You'd better."

He touched her face, pulled free and hurried for the barracks.

18.

Hansen's stomach cramped, so he popped another pill and suppressed a groan. He hurried down the same street where Chief Monitor Bock had been slain. Pain creased Hansen's sly features. The doctors said he shouldn't feel the stitches in his abdominal region where Marten Kluge had shot him. Where the ice slivers had melted and drugged him. But he didn't trust the doctors. He felt those stitches all right.

Hansen mopped his face with his sleeve. He would have scowled, but that increased the pain, the eternal cramp. Ah! It tightened. Hansen leaned against a holo-pine on the wall, breathing heavily.

Here in this very street Chief Monitor Bock had spoken with Training Master Lycon. Hansen had talked to a monitor who had witnessed everything. He had warned Bock against bringing the charges to the Training Master. Highborn were notoriously touchy about their areas of authority. Stubborn Bock, outraged at how the shock troopers had stolen from him and killed one of his top operatives in the cutting room. Bock had claimed he had them. Shootings in public, assaulting policemen, Bock had ranted. Well, Bock was dead, slain by the Training Master. It was amazing really. The files said that Lycon was a paragon of Highborn virtue. Yet he had killed the Chief Monitor in order to protect Marten Kluge and his allies. It was very strange and unusual. Despite his warning to Bock, Hansen still couldn't fathom it.

And now he'd been summoned to see the Praetor.

Hansen mopped his face and dared touch his stomach. Pain flared. He groaned. The Praetor—why did the lord of the Sun Works Factory want to speak with him?

He popped another painkiller, straightened his uniform and hurried down the street.

Had the Training Master known about the dust? Is that why he'd killed Bock? Hansen dreaded the pain booth and even more, he dreaded the, the... He groaned. He didn't even want to envision the punishment worse than the pain booth, no, not for a moment. The Highborn were unbelievably cruel and savage. Oh, why had he ever agreed to help Bock make and sell dream dust? They had money, lots and lots of money, that's true. They were almost millionaires now—well, Bock *had been* a near millionaire—but that was meaningless before the wrath of the Highborn.

"Why, Bock?" whispered Hansen to himself. "Why tell the Training Master?"

He swallowed, straightened his uniform once more and knocked on the Praetor's door.

A stern-eyed woman with ponderous breasts ushered him down a hall where others strode this way and that. She brought him to a steel chair and told him to sit. He did, and he fidgeted, sweated and gritted his teeth whenever a cramp came.

"Monitor?"

Hansen almost yelped in terror. Instead, he sat straighter and nodded.

"This way, please," said a husky, uniformed man.

Hansen followed him down another plain hall. The man pointed at an open office door. Hansen peered in, gulped and tiptoed into a spartan room. The huge Praetor in his stiff uniform, with his back to him, sat behind a mammoth desk with a model of a Doom Star the only thing on it. The dull blue walls were bare. Nothing hung on them, no paintings, mementos or plaques, nothing. The Praetor spoke softly into a wall-phone. It sounded like the rumblings of a tiger. Suddenly, the huge Praetor turned and stared at him with those eerie pink eyes. The eyes tightened, and menace, a near hysterical rage barely held under control swept into the room.

98

Hansen was horrified to realize that he was staring at the Praetor. He immediately looked at the floor, at his feet. He almost apologized, but then he would have spoken first, a taboo breaking of the worst sort. The Praetor's presence, his vitality and excellence seemed to expand and roll over him. Hansen felt smaller and smaller, and his knees quaked and the worst cramp of all roiled in his gut.

"Monitor Hansen."

"Yes, Highborn."

"You have heard of Chief Monitor Bock's death?"

"Yes, Highborn." Hansen oozed sweat and fear.

The Praetor paused. "Are you ill, Monitor? You sway and your pulse races. I detect abnormal fear."

"I'll be fine, Highborn. May, may I speak?"

"Speak."

"I'm awed to be here, Highborn. I truly am not worthy. Perhaps that is the 'abnormal fear' you sense."

"Hmm. Perhaps. Training Master Lycon slew the Chief Monitor."

Hansen remained silent, as he hadn't been directly addressed.

"Did you know the Chief Monitor well?"

"Yes, Highborn," Hansen whispered.

"Speak up, preman."

"Yes, Highborn," Hansen almost shouted.

"Would you like to avenge his death?"

Hansen looked up in surprise. The Praetor stared strangely at him. Hansen dropped his gaze and peered at the spotless floor.

"When I ask a question, preman, I want an answer."

"Highborn, I-I would never dream of doing anything against one of the Master Race."

"Have you ever seen the Training Master?"

"No, Highborn."

"He is not a true Highborn. He is an original, a beta."

Hansen said nothing. He didn't understand what was going on.

"A beta slew my Chief Monitor. Now I lack. I have studied the files and I find that Chief Monitor Bock relied heavily upon you. You will be the new Chief Monitor."

"Thank you, Highborn," Hansen said, his mind racing.

"Your first order of business will be to watch the shock troops. I want you to find out anything out of the ordinary. By doing this, by finding treasonous action, you will break the Training Master for me and gain your revenge. Do you understand?"

"Yes, Highborn." Hansen wondered if this was a trap. Was this the moment he should spill the information about the dream dust? Could he put it all on Bock's shoulders? Then he could tell the Praetor about Marten Kluge and give the Highborn the traitorous action he apparently craved. Hansen opened his mouth.

"That is all. You may go."

Hansen hesitated. Then it registered he'd been dismissed. That meant the Praetor didn't know about the dust. That meant that he, Heydrich Hansen, had control of it. He spun on his heels and marched out the room. He didn't realize it for a while, but his stomach no longer cramped or hurt.

Now he would have his revenge on Marten Kluge and then… Ha! Then Kang would die screaming, pleading for life.

"We'll see who is the maggot," whispered Hansen, hurrying to his new office and wondering where Bock had stashed his hidden credits.

19.

Two days later an exhausted Marten Kluge slipped from barracks to work on the repair pod. He'd lost several pounds and the skin under his eyes sagged and had an unhealthy tinge. He had a rattle in his throat whenever he breathed too deeply. No, matter. Work until you drop, sleep in the grave. If they gelded him, he'd rue every second he'd rested.

While wearing the bulky vacc suit he took out the old fuse box and installed one rebuilt by his mother over five years ago. He checked and double-checked the wiring of the flight panel. Sweat kept dripping into his eyes, stinging them, making him blink. He made mistakes and had to go over procedures he should have gotten right the first time. Everything seemed to take twice as long as it should, and Nadia kept getting in the way. He'd point there. She'd go there and watch him. Then he'd float beside her, bump into her and point outside. Finally, she tapped his shoulder and signaled that she was returning to the hab. He gave her the okay signal, and it seemed that she whirled around a bit too suddenly. He shrugged. He didn't have time to keep her happy.

He double-checked fuel. Luckily, the pod still had propellant in the tanks. With the extra Nadia had brought each day, the tanks were a third full. That wasn't great, but at least he had some.

Then came the moment Marten feared. Everything checked, so he carefully put away each tool and secured the kit to his belt. He settled into the pilot seat. The controls for the three outer arms—the clamp, laser-welder and riveter—were to his left. The flight dials and switches were to his right. A glance around showed him the shadowy inner side of the habitat, with lights shining from observation decks. Cratered Mercury dominated his right. The background stars where dulled by the thousands of spacecrafts' running lights and exhaust plumes. He studied the flight board. His gloved index finger hovered over the ignition switch. If the pod didn't work... He crossed his fingers, said a prayer and flipped the switch. The little repair pod shuddered, quivered and then the hydrogen burner purred into life.

Marten sagged into the cramped pilot's seat. If it hadn't worked—maybe then he wouldn't have to slip out the barracks anymore and he could rest. Rest and sleep and rest and... he shook his head, poked outside the pod and made a thumb's up sign to Nadia, who watched from the observation dome.

Several minutes later she space-walked outside and detached the anchor from the hab and clamped it to the pod.

He squeezed over and she wedged beside him.

They clinked helmets together.

"Ready?" he asked.

"Let's go."

They didn't have radios or comlinks, but they could speak by shouting and letting the contact of their helmets carry the sound waves.

Marten engaged the thrusters; they spewed a fine spray of hydrogen particles. Below them in a subjective sense, the Sun Works Factory's inner skin passed underneath the pod. Their pod had no running lights, although their tracker worked.

It was a gamble, but better than being gelded.

He glanced at Nadia as she pressed against him. This was much better than being gelded! He squeezed her arm. She faced him and he imagined her smiling. It made him smile. Then he concentrated on flying.

The kilometers went by. He checked the fuel. He slowed and read the huge numbers painted on the habitat skin and dared take them into an area that four and half years ago he'd never flown in for security reasons. He had realized several days ago that he couldn't build a ship like his parents. It was either this or highjack a shuttle, which would be desperation indeed.

He braked, slowed and stopped. They secured the pod with the anchor and floated onto the habitat, switching on their magnetic boots. His heart thudded as they clanged across the surface. So many memories... his eyes turned watery. Clang. Clang. Clang.

Marten stopped at an ordinary-looking hatch. By careful observation, one could see the welded lines of a much bigger opening. This hatch was akin to a portal in a castle gate. As soon as he pressed the 4, it all came back. 4-8-8-2-A-1-1-2-3. He felt the hatch shudder. If someone had punched in the wrong code, well, he was certain that his Dad's rigging would still kill the unwary or overcurious, if it was still operative.

The hatch swung open. Marten couldn't breathe. He didn't dare believe that, that... He grabbed the float rail and drew himself into a dark shaft, with Nadia behind him. Here. He reached for a flashlight that long ago... yes. His heart pounded harder as he wrapped his hand around the flashlight. He turned and groped for Nadia's hand, clenching it tightly. Then he turned on the flashlight and washed the beam into the darkness. His eyes goggled. It was going to work. They really could get off the Sun Works Factory.

A huge shape made out of stealth material sat before him. He blinked and remembered the countless hours his Dad and he had worked to make the ultra-stealth pod. And here it was. PHC had never found it. It had no fuel, however. But...

Nadia clinked her helmet against his.

"Is that it?" she asked.

"Yes."

"That means we can escape?"

"As soon as we fill her with hydrogen."

The flood of emotions became too much and Marten began laughing and whooping in delight and shedding tears in remembrance of his parents.

20.

"Chief Monitor," said a young woman in a dark, secret policeman's uniform.

Hansen looked up from behind his messy desk. There were a thousand details to this job and finding Bock's hidden wealth had taken all his extra time. He'd had no idea that Bock was so secretive. He scratched his cheek. The woman before him—ah, by her shoulder tabs she was a class three operative. She was pretty in a slattern sort of way. No doubt, she had once been Sydney slum-trash just like him. She held onto photos and grinned as if she had something important.

"Yes," he said.

She slid a photo onto the litter of papers.

He peered at—he smiled. There was Marten Kluge as he hurried down a utility corridor. Marten wore a white maintenance uniform. Well, well, well. He reached for the photo, but the woman placed a second one on top of the first.

He hunched forward, glanced up sharply and picked up the second photo. He couldn't be certain, but the woman in the photo looked like Nadia Pravda. She wore a vacc suit.

"I brought them right away," the class three operative said.

Hansen leaned back. This woman was ambitious. A climber, in Highborn terms.

"I knew you'd want to see them," she said, smiling, making promises with her eyes.

Yes, a climber indeed. "These photos were taken during your night duty?" he asked.

"Yes, Chief Monitor." She cocked a hip and her smile grew.

"I take it that only you have seen these?"

"Yes, Chief Monitor. I knew you'd be interested. The man is a shock trooper. The computer matched him. Marten Kluge is his name."

"Very good work," said Hansen. "Does your superior know?"

"Hmm…I hope I did the right then by bringing them directly to you."

Hansen gave her his patented fox-with-a-chicken-in-his-mouth grin. "Would you wait outside, please? And tell no one else about this."

"Yes, Chief Monitor."

She exited. Hansen studied the photos and then called on the intercom for his best cleanup man. The Praetor wanted the shock troopers, and he would give them to him. But first, he planned a little revenge of his own, a few more key deaths, some returned product and mouths that would never talk. Too bad the class three operative who had given him this would have to die. *Loose lips sink ships.* Well, no one was going to sink him.

The door opened and a short, wide-shouldered monitor entered. His gray eyes were dead, lifeless, without any emotion.

"I have a little assignment for you, Ervil," Hansen began.

21.

Behind her dark visor, Admiral Rica Sioux chewed her lip.

A little over a week of weightlessness had given her chest pains. She refused medication, as that would be a sign of weakness. And if the others saw weakness as they neared the Sun Works Factory—*no, at least admit it to yourself. They neared the Highborn.* No one had ever defeated the genetic super-soldiers. Who was she to think the *Bangladesh* could?

She squeezed her eyelids together. The waiting wearied her. She felt a tap on her shoulder and turned.

The First Gunner raised his gloved thumb.

What did he want now?

He tapped the command-pad on his arm. His visor slid open, revealing a dark, bearded, unwashed face. Hollow marks ringed his brown eyes. He was from Pakistan Sector, a good officer, one of the last true loyalists aboard the beamship.

Ship etiquette overruled her wants. Admiral Sioux chinned a control, and her visor slid open. She was old, with a terribly wrinkled face, as only her Native American ancestors seemed to have ever had. Her longevity treatments had started late, and she'd never had time for skin tucks. So her face showed all of her one hundred and twenty-one years of age.

Admiral Sioux scrunched the flat, triangular-shaped nose that dominated her face. The command capsule stank of unwashed bodies and stale sweat. She peered around the small circular room, with its sunken pits and VR-module screens. Only half the posts were filled. Some of the officers lay strapped on the acceleration couches in the center of the capsule. They were apparently asleep as their visors pointed up at the low ceiling.

"Admiral," said the First Gunner. "I think you should look at this."

"Do you smell that?" she said.

"What? Oh, yes, yes, of course. If you'll please look at this, Admiral."

"Maybe I should order them out of their suits. We're past the radiation leakage." She knew she should have already thought of that.

"Admiral Sioux."

Maybe this enforced inactivity, or maybe the dreadful waiting...

"Admiral!"

She scowled, not liking the First Gunner's tone.

"Admiral," he said, pointing at his VR-imager.

She studied the readings and frowned. "Radar pulses?" she asked.

"Enemy."

A sharp pain stabbed her chest. She wanted to vomit. So she clenched her teeth together.

Of course, the Highborn would launch new robot probes. And just as certain, a few of the SU Cruisers in this region were supposed to have tracked and destroyed them. SUMC had assured her of that.

"As per your orders, Admiral, the beamship's ECM warfare pods are inactive."

She chewed her lip, thinking. The *Bangladesh* traveled roughly 90,000 kilometers an hour, or 25.4 kilometers per second. She'd ordered the heavy particle shields aimed at Mercury and to the sides of their craft. 600-meter thick shields of rock and metal would give a radar signature of an asteroid. The question became, when the Highborn checked their radar would they think of the *Bangladesh* as a rogue asteroid or a newly discovered comet?

No, definitely not.

"Admiral—"

"Let me think!" she said. Her rheumy old eyes glittered, a window to the reason why at her age she still captained a ship. Not just any ship, either, but an experimental super-ship.

In a little less than two weeks, Mercury would reach perihelion, its closest distance to the Sun: 46 million kilometers. During much of those two weeks the fiery Sun looming behind the *Bangladesh* would make it impossible for optic visuals of them *from* Mercury. The harsh radio waves from the Sun would make it just as impossible for radar location.

Admiral Sioux was certain the Highborn didn't have a combat beam that could reach this far, at least not accurately. She grinned tightly. Space warfare had its own unique set of problems.

Light traveled at roughly 300,000 kilometers per second. So a laser beam fired from the Sun to Mercury at perihelion (46 million kilometers) would take nearly 2.6 minutes to reach the target. Yet how did one spot the target? If by radar, the beam had to travel to the target, bounce off it and then return. That took 5.2 minutes. If by optics...it had better be damn good optics, and there had better be enough light to see by, too.

What if the target shifted or jinked just a little? Then by the time the beam reached its target, the beam would sail harmlessly past, that's what.

Admiral Rica Sioux studied the radar signal being bounced off her precious beamship. They had traveled from the Sun for over a week. She needed approximately eleven more days to bring her to what the SUMC tacticians on Earth considered her practical, outer-range limit. When Mercury reached perihelion, its closest orbital distance to the Sun, the *Bangladesh* would fly past the planet at 30 million kilometers range. The beamship angled toward the flyby point at 25.4 kilometers per second, while Mercury sped along its orbital path at roughly 50 kilometers per second. In eleven days therefore, and for a week after, Mercury would be in the *Bangladesh's* range. Or more precisely, the very stable Sun Works Factory circling Mercury would be in range.

Admiral Sioux grinned, and some of the chest pain went away.

108

By their very nature, spaceships could be moved, shifted and jinked. But space habitats, especially world-spanning ones like the Sun Works Factory, their orbital location was known to a mathematical nicety.

In eleven days, the target would be a little over 30 million kilometers away. Her ultra-powerful proton beam, the same type used in Earth's May 10 Defense, would fire and travel at 300,000 kilometers per second. It would reach the target about 100 seconds later.

Of course, the proton beam could reach farther than that. That fact made it important to know if any friends were behind what one attacked. In this case, that wasn't going to be a problem. The reason 30 million kilometers was the practical range-limit was that the proton beam spread over distance (its dissipation range) and that the *Bangladesh* lacked a more accurate targeting system.

Thus, as a matter of reality, because spaceships jinked, shifted and changed headings, lasers were close-in weapons, usually used at a distance no greater than 100,000 kilometers. She recalled her training teacher and his comparison reference. The average distance of the Moon from the Earth was 385,000 kilometers. Under 100,000 kilometers, the time lag of the speed of light became much less of a tactical military problem.

Long-range missiles, although infinitely slower than beam weapons, became the tools of choice in distance-duels because of their self-adjusting abilities. A missile was launched toward a cone of probability: to where the enemy ship would most likely be at the time of the missile's arrival. Then the nearness to the target would allow more accurate readings and the missile could readjust. Sometimes there were laser-firing missiles, and sometimes—

Admiral Sioux shook her head and furrowed her brow. The entire point of a 30-million-kilometer flyby was that by the time they first fired their beam, the Highborn would be unable to launch any missiles from Mercury that could reach them before the missile's fuel exhausted itself. The *Bangladesh's* head start would make missiles catching them a near impossibility. Or rather the ship's much greater velocity, as it shot past the planet, would do that. But if the Highborn knew where they were now… This radar ping might turn the entire mission into a close run thing.

"Do we kill the radar probe?" whispered the First Gunner.

"Ship's AI has backtracked the pulse?" asked Admiral Sioux.

The First Gunner pointed at his screen.

"If we kill it," she said, "the HBs will have no doubt that we're hostile."

"In my opinion, Admiral…" The First Gunner trailed off as she peered at him.

"Yes? For the record, First Gunner?"

He swallowed, perspiration slicking his brow.

"You don't want to stick out your professional neck, is that it, mister?"

The First Gunner licked his lips and said, "They already know we're a ship, Admiral."

"I agree," she said. "Destroy the radar probe."

His hands flew over the controls.

Admiral Sioux shouted to propulsion. "Warm up the engines. We're going to jink." She peered at her screen. Then she turned sharply. "Everyone out of their vacc suits, and let's take showers, people. This place smells like a gym."

22.

Marten strolled down a corridor, one they were allowed to use during a break period such as this. He checked for spy-sticks, to see if they'd put in a new one. He'd deactivated the one already in place. Satisfied, he pried open a secret wall panel and took out his recorder. Nadia had secured another bug in place of the one he'd used on Hansen. The bug was linked to this device.

He clicked on the recorder.

NADIA: It's fueled and ready to go. All I need is the entrance code and you and your friends. Then... Well, you know what I mean. I love you. Please hurry. Out.

He hefted the recorder, smiling, and then shook his head. After all this time, it was really going to happen. His features hardened. He wasn't aboard yet. So he erased the message and replaced the recorder.

He checked his chronometer: forty-five minutes until the end of break. With a rueful smile, he strode to a hatch at the end of the corridor. It was specially coded, but he'd cracked that several weeks ago. It was with surprise that he now saw it open. He didn't know of anyone else who used it.

Hansen stepped through, together with Ervil and two other backup men. The backup men were big and tough looking. One of them had a nasty scar across his forehead and two obviously false teeth. They aimed projacs at Marten, grinning the entire time.

"Marten Kluge," said Hansen. "This is a surprise. Well, a surprise for you, I would imagine. I've been itching to speak with you again. So have Dalt and Methlen. They've reminded me more than once than they owe you several beatings."

"This is a restricted area," Marten said.

"Is it now?" asked Hansen. He glanced about. "Who enforces the restriction?"

"There are spy-sticks recording every move," Marten said.

"How can that be?" asked Hansen. "You removed them. Or should I say you short-circuited them?"

Marten glanced at the projacs. If he made a break—

Ervil stepped near, reaching. Marten struck the wide hand. Ervil moved with the economical speed of a close-combat expert and used his other hand to grab. He caught Marten's sleeve and jerked Marten toward him. Marten lowered his head and butted Ervil's nose.

A whistle blasted.

Hansen hissed.

Ervil released Marten's sleeve and stepped back. Marten jumped away, warily eyeing the projacs. Ervil held his bloody nose and eyed Marten with those strange, dead eyes.

A whistle blasted again, and a beta Highborn marched into the hall.

"Hurry to the auditorium!" the Highborn shouted at Marten.

Marten backed away from Hansen.

"I know what you're up to, Kluge," Hansen said, just loud enough for Marten to hear. "Unless I get my product back I'll blow the whistle on your little game."

"You premen," the Highborn said, "you aren't shock troopers. Identify yourselves."

"Chief Monitor Hansen, Highborn."

"Why are you in shock trooper territory?"

"We came at the Praetor's express orders, Highborn. We enforce the curfew."

Marten paused.

"Yes," said Hansen quietly. "I'm the new Chief Monitor."

"Training Master Lycon enforces the curfew," the Highborn shouted.

"I beg your pardon, Highborn. In my zeal I have perhaps overstepped myself."

"Hurry, shock trooper," the Highborn told Marten. "The entire corps will be addressed in fifteen minutes. It is an A-One priority message."

"Do you request further investigation of our actions, Highborn?" Hansen asked.

"No, but leave at once."

"Yes, Highborn."

Hansen sneered at Marten before motioning his men.

23.

The shock troopers stared silently, eyes forward. Each black beret was perfectly aslant and their black boots the regulation twelve inches apart as they sat in the auditorium seats. Two white-coated techs stood by the front screen. Ten beta Highborn stood against the walls, heavy blasters holstered on their belts. Training Master Lycon wore his blue dress uniform with a gold Magnetic Star First Class on his chest.

"Men," said Lycon, in his bear-deep voice.

The shock troopers swiped away their berets in a single, fluid motion.

Lycon inclined his head and cleared his throat. "Men, the moment has arrived to put theory to the test, to see if practice matches reality. You have trained these many months and you are now more capable than any human before you could have dreamed possible. Most of you are already combat veterans. Clearly, you are the best of the best that Homo sapiens have to offer. But," he held up a single finger. "How will you react in real space combat? Does our faith in you always have to rely upon possibilities and probabilities? No, it does not. The enemy—"

Training Master Lycon closed his eyes. His lip-less mouth twitched. Then he regarded them, peering at his shock troopers.

"I shall be frank. There are those on the Grand Admiral's Command Staff who feel that it is unworthy of us to allow... to allow the Homo sapiens among us. They do not mean on the planets. The FEC Armies are useful allies. But in space, where the Highborn reign supreme, do the... the Homo sapiens truly belong here as well?"

"Certainly we shall soon find out," Lycon said. "This great test, this *honor*. It is difficult to express the glory put upon you. As your trainer I am keenly anxious." He smiled. "Yes. Sometimes Highborn can know the flutter of uncertainty. Have you soldiers been able to absorb my theories, my lessons so painstakingly taught you? In that sense, I am anxious about the outcome of your coming combat. Naturally, only the best maniples will be chosen for this assignment, although I understand that if you could fight among yourselves for this privilege, that no doubt not one of you would be left standing.

"Now. I have but a single question. What is the essence of true glory?"

The Training Master scanned the throng. Not a shock trooper moved. "Come now, this is rare moment. I have given you leave to speak. Surely, one of you... ah, very good."

An arm stretched.

"Marten Kluge, Leader of the 101st Maniple. Speak."

A sinking, dreadful feeling made Marten reckless. "Training Master," he said, too loudly perhaps, "HB glory is gained through extreme risk."

A profound silence descended upon the auditorium.

Marten glanced about and then snapped his head forward to stare in regulation pose at Lycon. "Um. Please forgive me, Training Master. Not HB, I meant Highborn."

Lycon's eyes seemed to glitter.

A cold sweat broke over Marten. Beside him, Omi dug the toe of his boot into his leg. Otherwise, no one moved or looked at the doomed maniple leader.

"Because I have selected you and your maniple as first team, Marten, this... this breach of protocol will be deemed as not to have occurred."

Shock troopers widened their eyes in disbelief. Such a gesture was unprecedented.

"Lights," said Lycon.

One of the techs touched his wrist. The auditorium went dark.

Click.

On screen blazed the Sun, with swirling dark sunspots and spewing solar flares.

Dwarfed by the image of the Sun, Lycon stood beside the screen, clicker in hand, as he spoke.

"The Highborn Battlefleets have swept the four inner planets clean of orbital enemy. However, for good or for ill, the various naval units as well as single ships of the SU Space Fleets fled precipitously. Some have gone to the Jupiter Confederation, and there been confiscated and incorporated into the Jupiter navy. Others hide in the void between the planets. A few skulked near Venus to play a misguided guerrilla role. Those perished. But one ship in particular has been hiding near here, very near the Sun.

"This ship has now dared leave its sanctuary and try a sneaking run past us to points unknown. They cleverly destroyed most of our robot radar probes near the Sun. But one probe arriving on station a mere few hours ago spotted them. Before the probe was destroyed we learned the ship's configuration."

Click.

A strange sort of spacecraft filled the screen. It was massive, oblong-shaped, with heavy particle shields making it look like a smooth asteroid with engine nozzles in the rear. When the 600-meter shields rolled away—like a visor on a helmet—big laser tubes and missile launch systems would be visible.

"The ship's mass conforms to the *Zhukov*-class Battleship you see on the screen, but with several interesting peculiarities that are of little matter to you. Further analysis of this ship has led the Grand Admiral's Command Staff to a single clue, a name."

Click.

X-Ship *Bangladesh*.

"An experimental spacecraft of battleship size," said Lycon, "the *Bangladesh*. Again, it is meaningless to you, but of great interest to the Grand Admiral. Apparently, SU Military Intelligence has been able to keep this ship's capabilities secret. Our greatest interest lies in the ship's ability to orbit near enough to the Sun to hide from our detectors. That is a feat of value and the reason why the Grand Admiral wants this ship intact."

Click.

The Sun Works Factory circling Mercury leaped onto the screen.

"If it keeps its present heading, the *Bangladesh* will fly by Mercury at about 30 million kilometers, when Mercury reaches perihelion."

Click.

The edge of the Sun filled one end of the screen, Mercury the other.

Click.

A bright dot appeared a bit over a third of the way from the Sun to Mercury.

"The *Bangladesh's* present location."

Click.

A dotted line went from the *Bangladesh* to past Mercury.

"As is well known, effective beam range is one hundred thousand kilometers. During a recent wargame, however, the Doom Star *Napoleon Bonaparte* struck with lasers at ranges exceeding a million kilometers. The proviso was that a stable target, like the Sun Works Factory, was selected. Perhaps Social Unity could do likewise, although High Command gives this a low probability. A million kilometers would be a revolution in space beam warfare. Let us then note once more that this X-ship approaches Mercury no nearer than 30 million kilometers."

The Training Master let that hang. Then he smiled, the way a tiger might as it appraised a baby deer.

"Men, Social Unity is getting desperate. Command believes this new ship to be a missile carrier of unique capacity. To try to sneak past us as near as 30 million kilometers—no, the SU Fleet is much more cautious than that. The nearness can only signal one thing. This must be another attempt to duel via missile. They hoped to slip this X-ship very near the Sun Works Factory and launch a surprise attack. Normally a quick spread of our missiles would take care of such folly. However, this is no ordinary ship. This is perhaps the most secret and

117

modern weapon developed by the former lords of the Inner Planets."

Training Master Lycon fixed the shock troopers with an eagle-like stare.

"Grand Admiral Cassius wants this X-ship."

Click.

A squat sort of hybrid vessel, a kind of ship-missile hybrid, filled the screen.

"Behold. The Storm-Assault Missile," Lycon said.

Clothes rustled in the darkness as shock troopers squirmed. They'd heard about this missile, none of it to their liking.

Click.

On screen, a swarm of the missiles flew in perfect formation. In front were EMP Blasters and X-ray Pulse Bombs. Behind them came ECM drones, used to jam enemy radar and optics, and finally followed twenty of the Storm-Assault Missiles.

"There are those on the Grand Admiral's Command Staff who don't believe that... that Homo sapiens are capable of combat-precision feats. I argued otherwise. Highborn of exalted rank were swayed by my impassioned pleas, to let this be a test of the shock troopers. Men."

Lycon's eyes shone with brilliance, perhaps even pride.

"The honor of the shock troops rides upon this performance, this chance granted me. Your mission will be to fly out to the *Bangladesh*, storm aboard and capture it before the X-ship escapes out of range."

24.

Marten stared at his feet. From the auditorium, they'd marched in formation straight to the shuttles. All shock trooper-Highborn with their weapons had marched with them. He'd had no chance to break and run. He'd had no way to slip out and scurry into hiding. What would Nadia think when he didn't show up? How could he warn her about Hansen? Marten peered past the pilot's window. He saw orbital fighters flying with them. Even if he overpowered the pilot and took control of this craft, it was all senseless.

A void within stole his strength. He was so tired. He was only vaguely aware of people speaking.

"What?" Vip said. "Are you crazy?"

"It's perfectly safe," the young tech said. He had slick black hair and wore an air of bored superiority. He kept pursing his thin lips and tapping his chin as he made his pronouncements. He slouched in his crash-seat as if he didn't care what they thought about what he said.

"I ain't no vampire," Vip said, his eyeballs jittering. "Weeks of sleep, no, sorry, that ain't for me."

"Oh, don't worry about that," the tech said. "You'll be awake most of the time."

"What?" Vip asked.

"Drugged, though." The tech tap-tapped his chin. "Some of the testers said it felt like being buried alive."

Vip's eyeballs slewed around.

They rode in a tiny shuttle, a teardrop-shaped van. The pilot was crammed low up front so they could barely see the top of her helmet. The maniple sat on a U-shaped padded couch and faced the tech in his white coat. He explained the particulars of the Storm-Assault Missile they shuttled to.

"But you're not mere test subjects," the tech said, grinning, "you're the military elite. You could probably do this whole, three-week trip while standing on your heads. This'll be nothing for you guys."

With the twitch now in his voice, Vip asked, "What do mean, buried alive?"

The tech pursed his lips.

Marten, although sunk in gloom, shook his head at the young tech. Vip more than any of them was freaking out about the particulars of the SA missile.

"A smothering sensation," the tech said, ignoring Marten. "Like being several kilometers deep in the ocean."

Vip moaned.

"What's the matter with you?" Marten said.

"Me?" asked the tech. "Just answering questions as ordered."

"Did you see me shake my head?" asked Marten.

"I can't help it if you have a nervous tic," the tech said. "I thought it was better to pretend I didn't notice."

Kang raised his head. He'd been resting his chin on his massive chest. Omi also peered at the tech.

"You could put me under though, couldn't you?" asked Vip. "As a favor? Just shoot me full of Suspend or something, timed until we're almost there."

The tech shrugged.

"I'm talking to you," Marten said, now fully alert to his surroundings and deeply angry.

The young tech frowned, maybe realizing how close he was to these shock troopers. With a sudden move he swiveled his crash-seat and said to the pilot, "How much longer, Kim?"

"Ten minutes," said the pilot, the Sun Works Factory passing outside her view-screen.

The tech swiveled back. His bored grin had returned, as if the pilot's proven nearness had reinforced his confidence. He told Vip, "Really, it's best not to think about it."

"How am I supposed to do that?" asked Vip, his left cheek twitching.

"Sure wish I knew," said the tech. He pursed his lips. Tap-tap to the chin. "Maybe if you pretended you're a worm. You know, digging your way to the bottom of the Earth. Then the buried feeling will seem natural." He chuckled as Vip paled, jerked around and stared dull-eyed at the shuttle's low bulkhead.

Marten put his left hand on the tech's knee. In his right hand, under the tech's nose, he held a knife, a wicked little blade.

The tech with the dark, slicked-back hair stopped chuckling. His lifted his eyebrows, trying to appear nonchalant, as if he had angry shock troopers pull knives on him all the time.

"I'm talking to you," whispered Marten.

"It's the pain booth for sure if I report this," said the tech.

Marten stared dead-eyed.

"He's right, Marten," said Lance, sounding worried.

"What about this?" Omi asked. "The little prick isn't alive to report it?"

"That would make it harder," Kang rumbled.

"Not if the HBs resurrected him," Lance said.

"Maybe," Kang said. "But there isn't any Suspend aboard. So he'd stay down."

"Look here," said the tech.

Marten pressed the razor-point against the smooth skin.

"Do you see what you did?" Omi asked the tech. "Now he's mad."

"Hey, you're right," said Lance. He turned to the tech. "That was pretty stupid of you." Then, in a perfect imitation of the tech, Lance pursed his lips and tapped his chin. "Maybe if you unbuckled yourself and bent down and kissed Marten's boots. That might mollify him."

The tech opened his mouth.

"Shhh," Marten said. With the knife, he rotated the tech's head so he faced Vip. "Lance," Marten said.

Lance gently shook Vip, who still stared at the low bulkhead. The little shock trooper hummed to himself.

121

"Vip," Marten said.

When he didn't respond, Lance shook him again.

"What?" Vip asked.

"I want you to listen to a promise I going to make this—he's a vulture, Vip. He thinks it's funny that you're—"

"I'm not scared," Vip said.

"I know that," Marten said, as he stared at the ever-increasingly-worried tech. "It's no big deal, Vip. But listen anyway, okay?"

"Okay."

Marten pushed the knifepoint just a little more, making the tech cry out and arch his head in order to escape the deadly blade.

"What's going on back there?" the pilot asked.

"Nothing," Kang said.

"Are you okay, Ito?" asked the pilot.

A pinprick of blood welled on the tech's check.

"He's fine," Marten said. "Aren't you, Ito?"

"Fine!" said the tech, his head arched back but unwilling to turn and face the pilot.

The pilot shifted in her seat to look over her shoulder, but she was jammed down low and couldn't see past the tech's back.

"Worry about flying," Kang told her.

Maybe the menace in his voice convinced her, maybe the fact that they were about to dock. Besides, what would the shock troopers dare do to a Highborn's tech?

Marten stared at the young man. "If you die in this coming assault, Vip, then one of us will come back and kill this vulture who thought it funny to try to scare you."

"Really?" Vip said.

"I swear it."

"So do I," Omi said.

"Me, too," said Lance.

Kang grunted, gracing the pale tech with a brutal, sinister study.

"Think about that while we're traveling," Marten said, but whether he meant it for Vip or the tech he didn't say.

"Docking in four minutes," the pilot said, sounding very professional now, as if shuttling was all she cared about.

Marten released the tech's knee and wiped the blade on the tech's suit. He then slipped the knife into its armpit sheath.

The tech reached a trembling hand to his cheek. He stared at the minute red dot on his fingertip. Disbelief made round circles of his eyes. For a second it seemed he would speak, then he whirled around, facing the pilot, even as Kang and Lance starting talking about the tech's probable deviant sexual preferences.

***

The subdued tech led them through the airlock and into the Storm-Assault Missile. The first room contained five penetrator torpedoes. Like huge cartridges, they lay side by side, near the single firing tube. Beside each torpedo was a shock trooper battlesuit. There were five names stenciled on the helmets: MARTEN, OMI, KANG, LANCE and VIP. They were big, exoskeleton-powered suits, with oxygen tanks in back, HUD helmets and articulated armor. The shock trooper skull-patch was on the right sleeve of each battlesuit and the left pectoral. Their lasers, breach-bombs and torches were already packed in the torpedoes.

Marten and the others eyed the suits and the torps. They were accustomed to them, well-practiced in their use.

"It won't be a space hab we're storming," Omi said.

"A freaking ship in the void," said Lance.

Kang cracked his knuckles. "Won't make any difference. Either we get in or we don't."

"No," Omi said. "There's no pickup ship if we don't get in."

"We'll get in," Marten said. He refused to think about Nadia or how close he'd come to escaping. He would get another chance if he could survive. That's all that mattered now. And killing Hansen later if the Chief Monitor harmed Nadia.

"The void," whispered Vip, shivering.

The tech cleared his throat. He floated by the partition hatch. "Training Master Lycon wants everyone in by oh-eight-hundred."

123

"Gonna wet your pants if we're late?" asked Lance.

"You're really starting to get on my nerves, you little creep," Kang said. "Marten, where's your knife?"

Marten patted his armpit sheath.

"What'cha got in mind?" asked Lance.

"It's an old Mongol custom," Kang said. "Blood sacrifice. I practiced it back in Sydney."

Marten believed it.

"Blood sacrifice appeases the spirits and helps gain victory," Kang said.

Omi lifted his left eyebrow, and nodded sagely.

The young tech licked his lips as he kept searching their faces for a smile, or for some indication that they were joking. "Y-You need my help getting into the G-suits," he finally said.

Lance snorted. "We know how to climb into suits."

"Not these," said the tech. "T-They're…"

A clang sounded from the outer hatch. Air hissed into the lock. Everyone turned. The inner hatch popped open. Into the cramped room floated Training Master Lycon. He wore a vacc suit, working off its bubble helmet as he entered.

The five men of the maniple straightened even as they lowered their eyes in regulation pose.

Training Master Lycon swept his gaze over them, settling onto Marten. There seemed something especially ferocious in his glance. Maybe he'd talked with the pilot.

"Tech," he said.

The tech floated near the Highborn. He also carefully kept his eyes cast downward.

"Is everything in order?"

"Yes, Training Master."

"The maniple has been thoroughly briefed?"

"Yes, Training Master."

"Do you believe they understand the procedure?"

"Yes, Training Master."

"Then you have nothing else to report, is that correct?"

The tech hesitated as his shoulders tensed.

"Time is critical," said Lycon.

The tech swallowed audibly. "Yes, Training Master. I-I mean no, nothing else to report."

124

Lycon nodded. Then he studied the five shock troopers, finally settling on Marten. "Maniple Leader."

"Yes, sir."

"Excellence in training does not negate all sins. You are therefore under disciplinary punishment. Kang."

"Yes, sir."

"You are maniple leader for the duration of the mission."

"Yes, sir."

"If Marten commits any breach of discipline, shoot him."

"Yes, sir."

"Unless you perform some outstanding feat of value, Marten, noted and reported by your maniple leader, on your return you will receive twenty minutes in the pain booth."

"Yes, sir."

Lycon swept his fierce gaze over the team. He abruptly settled the vacc helmet over his head and left through the hatch.

After it clanged, Lance turned to Marten. "That's tough luck."

Marten shrugged.

The tech had his grin back. "Okay, let's go," he said. "Into the G-suits."

"Don't think this nulls my promise," Marten told him.

The young tech appeared shocked. "Threatening me is a breach of discipline." He turned and pointed to Kang. "That means you have to shoot him."

"Shut up," growled Kang.

"But—"

Kang floated over, grabbed the tech's finger and twisted so he yelped

"None of that," Marten said. "You heard the Training Master, we have to harness up."

Kang turned, with a frown on his flat face. "I'm giving the orders now."

Marten hesitated only a moment. "Right. I'm sorry, Maniple Leader."

"Noted," Kang said. "Okay, you heard the Training Master, we have to harness up." He smiled mirthlessly at Marten.

Since Marten was nearest to the hatch, he opened it and was the first into the other room. There were only two habitable rooms on the entire SA Missile.

Even more cramped than the first room, this one had five acceleration couches side by side. On the couches lay the G-suits, heavy, ponderous things, with thick tubes attached to the top of the helmets and out the heels and other various locations. For as long as the trip took, they would be in those things.

Shedding their garments until they were naked, assisted by the tech, the maniple worked past the eel-like mass of tubes and slid into the very slick fabric within the suits.

"It's freezing," said Lance.

"It feels like oil," Omi said.

"The inside of each suit conforms to your body shape," said the tech, for once sounding professional.

After they were secure, he latched them closed, checking the seals and dropping their visors. He came to Marten last.

"You know what?" whispered the tech.

Marten lay snug like a caterpillar in its cocoon, and about as immobile. He peered at the tech smiling down at him. The boy had bad breath.

"You getting brave now?" asked Marten.

"I could poke out your eyes," said the tech, showing Marten the penlight laser-spotter in his hand. "But you know why I'm not going too?"

"'Cause the sight of blood scares you?"

"No, Mr. Tough-Guy, because every way you look at this, you're doomed. The Highborn are firing their spreads into five different cones of probability, and even then, they're not really sure they'll get this X-ship. Think about that. Five different vectors they're firing into, using a hundred Storm-Assault Missiles like this one. And you can bet that if you miss your target that you're never coming home. You'll just go on sailing forever, sooner or later dying from lack of oxygen."

Marten remained silent because he couldn't think of anything to say.

The tech nodded and looked at the others.

Marten knew the look. He was building up courage, probably to shout this information to everyone.

Marten said, "Remember, though, we *might* make it back."

"What?"

"One out of five isn't zero."

The tech stared. "You're even dumber than you look if you think those are good odds. Besides, even if you get there you have to break into the battleship."

"Yeah, bad odds," Marten said. "But do you want to bet your life on it?"

The tech's eyes shifted away. He pushed off Marten's suit and floated out the room. As the hatch slammed shut, hypos from the suit's medikit pricked each of them. A cool, numbing sensation spread over Marten. Then his helmet grew opaque and VR-images blossomed onto the HUD section of the visor. It showed him a view of the outside of the missile, from a camera there.

A bloated, queasy feeling suddenly overwhelmed him. Then his helmet's intercom buzzed.

"I feel like throwing up," Vip said.

"Just try to relax," said Lance.

"Yeah," Marten said.

By the sounds, valves in the room opened and a gloppy solution that made sludge seem thin oozed in. It pressed against the G-suits and the oily inner surface of the suit's interior seemed to sink into Marten's skin. As the tech had predicated, Marten felt as if he was being smothered. Three atmospheric pressures pressed against each of their G-suits. The drugs helped their bodies to resist the force.

The fragility of the human body meant that a person could only take about eight Gs before passing out from lack of oxygen to the brain. Highborn could take about twice as much, which was another of their superiorities over premen. With these suits, however, the shock troopers could survive the twenty-five G acceleration that the missile needed in order to catch up to the *Bangladesh* after the beamship passed Mercury. The suits would also stimulate their muscles throughout the trip so they wouldn't atrophy.

"This is gonna be a load of fun," said Lance dryly.

With his chin pressing the various switches in his suit, Marten checked the VR files. Battle plans, entertainment

127

dramas, porn, it was all here. He switched to the missile's cone camera, watching them being carried out of the hanger and toward the gargantuan boost ship.

Highborn glory: Succeed or die.

The quiet, desperate rage that he'd been struggling to contain blossomed into something darker and more urgent. Not only were they ripping him away from all that he'd ever worked for, but they were cheap missile fodder, a mere biological component webbed into a warhead—*becoming* the warhead. They were a bio-weapon of a different sort. They were dogs to kick around and abuse, and geld if they became too intractable. No. This was worse than madness. It was inhuman debasement, a shredding of all dignity. Escape was no longer good enough. If he made to the Outer Planets he vowed to warn them of the hell that was coming and do everything he could to help stop it.

25.

Both Highborn Grand Admiral Cassius and Social Unity's Supreme Commander, General James Hawthorne, considered themselves keen students of military history. Each searched the past for clues, looking for what to avoid or what to do.

Throughout his life, the Grand Admiral had only known victory. Beginning as a young clone-cadet in the Moscow War Academy, to the stunning and brilliant Second Battle of Deep Mars Orbit in 2339, he'd shown dash, iron will and a fanatical, almost otherworldly genius. In the Second Battle of Deep Mars Orbit, he had crushed the combined Fleets of the Mars Rebels and the Jupiter Confederation's Expeditionary Force sent to help the Martians. Genius had marked even his planning and execution of the Highborn Rebellion in 2349.

Most Highborn likened him to the ancient world-conqueror, Alexander the Great, while the Social Unitarians thought he more resembled the worst of civilization's scourges, Genghis Khan.

The Grand Admiral planned to outdo both ancient warlords. After conquering the four inner planets and crushing Social Unity, he dreamt of continuing with the Jupiter System. He would crush its Galilean moon-kingdoms of Io, Europa, Ganymede and Callisto, together with the rest of the gas giant's snowballs awash in wealth and high technology. The strange space-habitat states orbiting Jupiter would also be plucked like ripe fruit. Then he would lunge at the Saturn System, at Uranus. He dreamed of the subjection of the entire Solar System, all the way to the distant science outposts on Charon.

The crux of his reasoning settled upon the fact that he was a Highborn, a true lord of Order and genetically superior to the masses of Homo sapiens spread helter-skelter throughout the system. After all, the two examples from the past had been mere premen. Still, both premen had overcome fantastic odds and preformed outstanding feats of daring and strategic brilliance. In some senses, they could be emulated. But instead of their earthbound glories, future ages would marvel at his conquests, at his stunning judgments and genius. Or so he mused in his quieter moments of reflection.

As he lay in his study aboard the Doom Star *Julius Caesar*, which orbited the Earth's Moon, he pondered a different problem: namely, the X-Ship *Bangladesh*. He pondered it as he laid his nine-foot frame on the couch. He had tossed his boots aside. His feet crossed at the ankles and perched on the couch's armrest. He kept twitching his VR-gloved hand, images flashing across the lens of his VR-goggles.

The people and point in history he settled upon were the Japanese of the early to middle Twentieth Century. They had been militarists, men who understood about honor and the will to fight. What most intrigued the Grand Admiral were the last days of 1941 and the next several months of 1942. It began with a naval battle called Pearl Harbor. He twitched his fingers, studying the plan, the risks and the brilliant execution of this Nipponese Admiral Yamamoto. After the incredible victory in Hawaii, the Japanese Fleets had scored one stunning win after another from the Philippines to the Indian Ocean. Finally, with their island empire won in a few swift months, the Japanese gathered their naval vessels into a vast armada to finish off the Americans at Midway.

The Grand Admiral read fast and he frowned at what he read. At Pearl Harbor, the Japanese had planned in minute detail and with painstaking thoroughness. They had trained to a pitch of excellence of nearly Highborn quality. But the Midway Operation, it had been a sloppy affair born of conceit. Ah, the old historian had a phrase for it: victory disease. The Japanese of World War Two had won so handily and so quickly that they soon believed that their superiority was inborn, innate and would always be that way.

Much like many of his men were now behaving and thinking.

Victory disease... becoming sloppy...

The Grand Admiral read about the staggering Japanese defeat off the Midway Islands. Prime carriers destroyed one, two, three. It was most amazing. The mighty Admiral Yamamoto forced to flee from the very foes he had come to annihilate.

Grand Admiral Cassius sat up and tore off his VR-goggles.

The premen weren't stupid. They were inferior, yes, but still with the ability to bite. Hadn't he almost lost the *Genghis Khan* to them on May 10?

This X-ship, the *Bangladesh*, it could very well be dangerous. And it approached the one location the Highborn could not afford destroyed.

The Grand Admiral pulled on his boots and strode out the door.

26.

The Grand Admiral's laser-beamed orders took immediate effect, even as the massive booster ships built up speed orbiting Mercury. Each booster ship appeared to be little more than an asteroid with a flock of missiles perched on its forward surface. X-ray Pulse Bombs, EMP Blasters, ECM drones and the SA Missiles were all ready to launch. Meanwhile, massive engines fed on hydrogen and left a white exhaust behind the booster ship. It looked like a comet's tail. Faster and faster went the booster ships, automated vessels, increasing velocity in as short a time as possible.

The Grand Admiral's orders brought a burst of activity to the Sun Works Factory. A horde of repair pods zoomed from the Doom Star *Genghis Khan*. The giant warship's engines were warmed up. Soon the mighty spacecraft pulled out of the cradle that had been so carefully built around it. The Grand Admiral had ordered the *Genghis Khan* to take station behind Mercury, in relation to the approaching *Bangladesh*. There it would stay until they discovered what the X in the X-ship actually meant.

The majority of the repair pods flew into storage and shut down, while the millions of tons of warheads, laser juice and other combustibles and military explosives went into their special emergency compartments on the Sun Works. The Grand Admiral didn't want the SU military catching the Sun Works Factory the way the American pilots at the Battle of Midway had caught the four Japanese carriers *Akagi, Kaga, Hiryu* and *Soryu*. He didn't know how the *Bangladesh* could

132

possibly do any damage to the Sun Works, but—why were they flying by at 30 million kilometers distance? Why not much farther out or much nearer in? There was a reason for the 30-million-kilometer range, and he didn't know what it was. He felt certain about the SU capabilities—but he would not allow himself to become arrogant. *Pride goes before a fall.* It was an ancient proverb, well proven by history. And in yet another way, he would show the Highborn superior to the premen. He would actually learn from history.

As the Sun Works Factory went into emergency war-drill, the five booster ships reached boost velocity.

The first asteroid-ship changed the direction of its thrust and shot from Mercury's orbit. A white hydrogen tail billowed behind it. It sped toward the first cone of probability. Then the first missiles were catapulted off the boost ship. The Law of Motion was immutable. For every action, there is a reaction. So the catapulting of these missiles slowed the forward motion of the boost ship by the amount of their mass, which was the reason why these boost ships had been built so massively. When the final set of missiles were slung off the asteroid, the hunk of rock turned into a ship.

As those missiles launched, the second boost ship altered orbit. It sped toward a different cone of probability.

***

"Do you feel that?" Vip asked, sounding worried.

"We're launching," Marten said. His VR-goggles were set on the missile's viewer.

Then his suit's gauges wobbled. It felt as if he was being flattened with the acceleration. He found it hard to breathe.

"This is horrible," Lance said in a choking voice.

"The tachyon drive has kicked in," Marten said. He squeezed his eyes shut and concentrated on breathing. Would his internal organs rupture?

"Are we accelerating at twenty-five Gs?"

Marten didn't know who said that. "Yeah," he said. He wondered if he could ever get used to this feeling.

"How long is this trip gonna last?" Vip asked, with a tremor in his voice.

"Watch a video," Marten suggested.

"I don't know how."

Marten had to concentrate before he explained it one more time. He wondered if he was going to die like this, squeezed in a suit and buried in goop, or would they reach the *Bangladesh* and start the automated drain procedure?

Maybe it was time for him to watch a video himelf. Anything to get his mind off this crushing pressure and off Nadia and the ultra-stealth pod waiting in the Sun Works Factory for somebody to use.

Bionics

1.

Earth—Joho Mountains, China Sector

General James Hawthorne paced in his office as he spoke with Commodore Tivoli, who ran Military Intelligence.

Tivoli was a small woman with compact shoulders and hard wrinkles in the corners of her hazel eyes. She played a dangerous and constant game with PHC. In the scheme of Social Unity, three prime movers composed the State: the Military, the Party, and the Political Harmony Corps, the State's secret police.

Ever since May 10, 2350—six long months ago—the infighting had turned nastier than usual. The enemy asteroid impacts had hurled billions of tons of fine particles and debris into the air. The previous pollution together with the new additives had created a heavy, greasy cloud of reflective dust. Temperatures dropped rapidly because the sun's rays were reflected away from Earth. The rapid change created hurricane-strength winds that whipped across the planet in ever-increasing power. That, combined with more than a billion deaths, had created an intolerable strain on Earth's social fabric. News of the disaster had spread over the planet.

Six months ago Greater Hong Kong had vanished, and Beijing, Manila, Taipei and Vladivostok. The million-ton meteors dropped on them had left vast smoking craters.

The numbed inhabitants of Earth wondered how it could have happened. Their holosets had daily informed them that the Supremacists were on the run, soon to be defeated. Yes, Antarctica had fallen because of a treacherous sneak attack by the specially bioengineered soldiers. The neighboring islands of Tasmania and New Zealand had also been snatched up by the self-styled *Highborn*. Perhaps the loss of Australian Sector soon thereafter shook a few alarmists, but a stint in the slime pits had cured those.

But on May 10, enemy Doom Stars had actually entered the stratosphere. That could only mean the Social Unity Space Fleets had been defeated. No person on Earth, no matter how deep in the mantle he lived, was safe from more million-ton meteors raining down from the heavens.

With that realization, forty billion people knew gut-wrenching fear. Most lived in the vast underground cities, human hives that often burrowed more than fifty-five levels down. Social Unity gave them harmony, guidance and solace, and had turned them into a sheeplike, submissive horde. They believed in humanity's manifest destiny, and worked for the good of the whole. Now the truth dawned. They'd been given propaganda swill.

A billion people dead in an instant, slain by asteroids maneuvered into Earth orbit and then rocketed down. It meant they were all defenseless.

On the holosets six months ago, the Social Unity familiars urged caution, that the latest disaster had been studied and was now well in hand. "Be assured that it couldn't happen again." The mere idea of a repeat attack was ridiculous and anyone who suggested otherwise should be reported to the nearest hall leader. In memory of those so tragically lost on May 10, a planet-wide hum-a-long would commence in one hour. Anyone not participating would be given ten demerits to his profile.

It should have worked. The people had been well trained and loved the hum-a-longs.

Instead, in one hour, as if they were a psychically connected mass organism, the hordes of Social Unity went mad with rage and grief. In the seventy major megalopolises, riots broke out. Billions smashed stores and looted. In some places, the peacekeepers fought back. Sometimes they were stripped of shock batons and beaten; elsewhere they joined the looting. The South American masses turned vicious. There the hordes wielded bricks and recklessly slew the police. In North America the opposite occurred. The peacekeepers went berserk and slaughtered thousands of rioters, thereby gaining temporary control.

Naturally, from their newly conquered Pacific Basin Stronghold, the Highborn got wind of what occurred.

"Send in the FEC Armies," urged several ground commanders. The FEC Armies: Free Earth Corps, composed of captured and reeducated Social Unitarians from Antarctica and Australian Sector.

"Nonsense," said other Highborn. "This is a trap, crudely fashioned by the premen to get us to split our forces and be overwhelmed in detail."

As the precious days slipped by, the SU peacekeepers regrouped, reinforced by army units and PHC shock squads. They waited for orders from the Directorate. The six surviving members of the Directorate were too busy jockeying for power in the absence of the late Lord Director Enkov. Into the vacuum stepped General James Hawthorne, the man who had almost destroyed the enemy Doom Star *Genghis Khan*. He steeled himself to issue savage orders. Control must be regained or the war was lost.

Then Highborn electronics broke into the world-wide datanet. If the premen had truly lost their grip, and this wasn't a Social Unity trick, the HB psychologists said a propaganda broadcast would push the masses over the edge. So Highborn Command beamed images of the former fighting that had gone on in the Japanese home islands, unedited shots of what had really happened on the battlefield before May 10 and the crushing asteroid attack.

Grown weary by several days of rioting and returning to their cramped apartments, where there was little to do other

137

than watch the holosets, almost the entire populace of Earth witnessed the Japanese Kamikaze assaults: men, women and children hurling themselves at the nine-foot tall, battle-armored Highborn and uselessly dying. The billions in front of their sets were already emotionally drained, fatigued and beginning to wonder what their wild behavior would cost them. They wept as they watched the merciless super-soldiers, the giants in their black battle-armor, butchering inept amateurs. They seethed with a gut-wrenching hatred as space-borne lasers devoured transport after sea-transport trying to reach Japan Sector and help their brothers in need. 700,000 SU soldiers died in less than two hours. Thousands of SU fighters, bombers and space interceptors exploded on screen. The last of Earth's navies were annihilated before their eyes in the blast furnace of 10 May 2350.

"Resistance is illogical. Surrender therefore and serve the New Order."

Grand Admiral Cassius himself spoke on the holoset. For most of humanity this was their first close-in shot of a Highborn, a bioengineered soldier, originally fashioned to fight *for* Social Unity, not against it. The giant Grand Admiral had pearl-white skin, with harsh features angled in a most inhuman manner. His lips were razor thin and his hair, cut down almost to his scalp, was like a panther's pelt. He had fierce black eyes, and an intense, almost pathological energy. He smiled, and to those billions it seemed that he mocked them.

"Come, let us end this useless war. Submit and live. Resist—"

The pirated link was cut at that precise moment, not in canny timing, but because the SU technicians had finally found the Highborn frequency.

Several hours later General Hawthorne gave the order. All over the planet the peacekeepers with army escorts and PHC shock squads reentered the riot zones and then onto the residential levels. They had prepared for bitter battle. Instead, they found a subdued and repentant populace. A chilling glance at Earth's conquerors had sobered the billions out of their madness. After all, better the government you knew than one that thought itself your genetic superior.

138

It should have been the moment of greatest unity. The army and PHC had worked together to save the State. Instead, the head of PHC and certain directors grew alarmed at the military's newly gained powers. They feared General Hawthorne, and they hated the fact that they had so desperately needed him.

That had been six long months ago. Today... General Hawthorne paced in his office.

"General," said Commodore Tivoli, "I wish you would look at these figures."

"What's that?" said the General, taking the proffered report and scanning it.

"MI has lost too many operatives lately."

"Eh?" asked the General, as he sped-read the report.

"I think PHC is behind those losses," Commodore Tivoli said. "They're assassinating my operatives in a secret war against you, against the military."

"Hmm."

"They're some of my best men, General. Keen agents. Slaughtered like pigs. PHC is poking out our eyes and making sure that we're blind in intelligence matters."

The General shook the report. "These aren't the proton beam figures I asked for."

"It's a list of all the slain MI operatives in the last three months."

"I can see what it is, Commodore." Hawthorne handed her the report. "That's your department, your worry. If you need more personnel just ask."

"It isn't that, General. PHC—"

"We're late," interrupted the General, checking his chronometer.

Commodore Tivoli frowned. "I believe this is critical."

"Can't it wait until after the meeting?"

"I—yes, sir."

General Hawthorne put on his military cap and viewed himself in a mirror, tilting the hat, giving himself a bit of a rakish appearance.

"Sir, have you thought about my other suggestion?"

"Which one?" asked Hawthorne.

139

Tivoli said, "That any officer or soldier entering your presence should first surrender his sidearm."

"Ridiculous."

"But I have reports—"

"No, no," said Hawthorne, waving his bony hand. "The officers would view it as a distrusting gesture. It would alienate too many."

"But it would make things much easier for your security detail, for keeping you alive from assassination."

"That's why I have the best."

Commodore Tivoli's frown deepened.

The General knew she had problems, worries, but so did he. He had to keep on conjuring up victories, at least until the cyborgs from Neptune arrived. His throat tightened. Few knew about that secret project, not even the Commodore. What would she think if she did know?

Hawthorne shook his head. It ached all the time. Problems everywhere, burdens dumped onto him. All the domes of Mars had rebelled again. Terraformed Venus was under orbital blockade. Mercury. He didn't even want to think about the armaments the Sun Works Factory churned out for the enemy.

Why couldn't the Highborn just gloat for a while over their victory? Instead, they continued to move with their customary speed and brilliance. In six months of blitzkrieg invasions, they had snatched the rest of Earth's islands. The Philippines, the Indonesian chain, Ceylon, Madagascar, the Azores, England, Ireland, Iceland, Greenland, Cuba and Haiti and the Hawaiian Islands, all had fallen.

During the ensuing months since May 10, he had struggled to correct the strategy of the late Lord Director. But despite his best efforts, many blamed him for the loss of the islands. To his detractors he pointed out his lack of oceanic vessels, and that he'd saved three-quarter million trained troops, desperately needed troops that now bolstered the Eurasian Continent.

The Directorate had fired back and told him that his statement was illogical. If he could slip troops out, surely he could have put enough in to hold somewhere.

"That is imprecise," he'd written back. "Enemy laser stations ring the planet. Any of our military craft flying higher than fifty meters are targeted and vaporized. Meanwhile, Highborn orbital fighters routinely buzz any merchant marine we have left. If military men or material are spotted or analyzed to be aboard ship, the vessel is sunk."

"How, then, did you extract the troops?" returned the query.

"Ah. Now you begin to understand the magnitude of my accomplishment."

Several on the Directorate had bristled at his tone. He should have used more tact. He knew that now. But he had become so tired.

"General?"

"Hmm?"

The Commodore tapped her chronometer. "It's time for your staff meeting."

"The proton beam report?"

"Yes, sir."

He nodded. Despite heavy PHC interference, he'd begun a crash proton beam-building program. Everyone feared to use them. They said the Highborn would simply drop more asteroids and take them out again. He disagreed. They needed many proton weapons and enough merculite missile batteries to support them. Fortress Earth was his new strategy.

"What about my meeting with Yezhov?" he asked.

"I hadn't heard about that," she said. "When was it supposed to take place?"

"Tomorrow, I think."

She shook her head. "I doubt it will happen now. The Chief of PHC is in New Baghdad. There have been riots in the capital."

Hawthorne swung open the door.

The Commodore followed, saying, "I still suggest that you should order anyone entering your presence—"

"Please, Commodore, save it until after the meeting."

2.

Surprise was complete.

The Supreme Commander of Social Unity Armed Forces stood with his staff around a holo-image of Earth. The dark headquarters deep in the Joho Mountains of China Sector provided a safe haven from the space-borne invaders. There the officers studied the red dots circling the softly glowing, blue-green image of the planet. The dots indicated enemy space-laser platforms, orbital-fighter stations and two enemy Doom Stars, one of which orbited the Moon. Grimly, they pointed out to one another the much fewer yellow dots on the Earth: the proton beam installations and the merculite missile batteries.

As the officers discussed various strategies and the coming run of the *Bangladesh*, the door opened, flooding the darkened room with light. Air Marshal Ulrich, a bull-shouldered German, wearing his immaculate blue uniform, stepped within. A strange look twisted his florid features. Sweat glistened his face and soaked his too-tight collar.

The whispers died as one member of the staff after another glanced up.

The Air Marshal used his heel to close the door. Then, in a jerky motion, he unsnapped his holster flap and drew a heavy .55 magnum revolver.

"Ulrich! What's the—"

A deafening BOOM cut the question short. The slug tore through the holo-image of Earth and hit Space Commander Shell, a short, hawkish man standing on the other side. Shell flew backward, his chest a gaping cavity. BOOM. Colonel-

General Green, formerly of Replacement Army East, lost his head. BOOM, BOOM. Admiral O'Connor ceased to exist and Commodore Tivoli slammed against the back wall, her right shoulder gone.

Stunned, with his eyes bulging and his ears ringing, the Supreme Commander of Social Unity Armed Forces watched Ulrich stalk around the table that contained the electronics that projected the holoimage above it. General James Hawthorne found that he was shaking, and that his limbs refused to obey him. His heart pounded and suddenly he gave an agonizing gasp. Something wet soaked his left sleeve and a horrible groan awoke him to the fact that he was about to die.

Air Marshal Ulrich, with sweat pouring off his face, lifted the heavy hand cannon.

"Please, Ulrich—no!"

BOOM.

General Hawthorne flinched. Then he blinked in amazement. He felt no pain. It finally penetrated that the groaning had stopped. He twisted leftward. Commodore Tivoli no longer had a face. Ulrich had put her out of her misery.

The Air Marshal now drew a deep breath.

Seeming to move in slow motion, General Hawthorne turned toward him. He wished he could think of something profound to say, or something coolly indifferent. Instead, he had to fight not to throw himself onto his knees and beg for his life.

A grimace twisted the Air Marshal's lips. He re-targeted the smoking .55, while his other hand fumbled in his jacket pocket, finally drawing a rag. He mopped his brow and wiped sweat from his chunky neck.

"Ulrich—"

"They want you alive," interrupted the Air Marshal, his voice compressed. He wiped spittle from his lips.

Hawthorne's knees almost buckled, he was so grateful that Ulrich didn't plan to butcher him. Then his mind kicked back into focus.

The Air Marshal squinted and minutely shook his head. "No, James. Don't try it. They said to kill you if it looks like it won't work."

143

"Who are *they*?"

"Turn around."

"The Highborn?"

"Turn around!"

Although in his fifties, Hawthorne shifted onto the balls of his feet. He hoped Ulrich would wave with that sickeningly heavy pistol for him to turn around. He was grateful now for the agonizing hours he took each week keeping fit.

Ulrich had short, blunt fingers, an even thicker thumb. He used it to cock the hammer. "I understand, General. In fact, maybe it's better this way, more mercifully that they don't get their hands on you."

Panic caused Hawthorne's heart to thud in his chest. He turned around, his throat suddenly raw. He was too much of a soldier not to look at his dead friends. Space Commander Shell lay grotesquely. Commodore Tivoli—

From behind, Ulrich stepped closer. Fabric rustled. Hawthorne willed himself to move, to use his elbow and slam it into Ulrich and spin around for a death-fight. But before the thought could become action, the heavy gun-barrel poked his back.

"It's harder to be a hero than you think," said Ulrich, his breath hot on Hawthorne's ear. Then something cool touched the back of his neck.

Ulrich shuffled sideways, out of range. "Face me," he said.

Hawthorne reached for the back of his neck. He heard the *click*. Next thing he knew he was falling. He didn't feel anything until his left cheek struck the floor. Pain exploded. He wanted to rub his cheek, but his arms wouldn't move.

Click. His shoulder throbbed where it had hit the floor, but at least he could move again, and feel.

"Don't touch your neck," said Ulrich. "Now, get up slowly."

Hawthorne did. "What is it?" he said. "What did you put on me?"

"A neural inhibitor. I press my switch and it cuts off your nerve impulses from the neck down. Adhesive bonding keeps it in place."

Hawthorne noted the thumb-sized switch in Ulrich's free hand.

"Oh, one more thing. I have a second button. If I press it a mini-bomb detonates and your head detaches from your body."

"What?"

"You'll walk in front of me all the way out of here, General. If anything happens to me along the way—boom. No more head."

"Then my security team kills you."

Ulrich nodded as he wiped sweat from his face.

"Are you really willing to die?" asked Hawthorne.

Ulrich stuffed the rag in his jacket pocket.

Hawthorne indicated the dead officers. "Shooting them like pigs is one thing. Dying—"

"I'm ready to die, General, I assure you of that."

"It's worth that much to you, what they're offering?"

"James…" Pain flickered in Ulrich's eyes. He shook his head. He checked his watch, and said, "Take off your jacket. There's blood on the sleeve."

Hawthorne hesitated. Then he slipped off his green jacket, tossing it aside. He wore a white shirt with a green tie and green trousers with red piping along the creases.

Ulrich eyed him critically. "We walk all the way out. Your security team will not join us because you will forbid it. Further, you will give the needed codes and commands to insure our safe arrival outside. James." Ulrich peered closely at his former commanding officer. "I will not hesitate to kill you, even if it means my death. If you doubt my seriousness, look at your friends lying around you."

"They were your friends, too, Air Marshal."

"Look at them!"

Hawthorne did. He shivered.

"Ready?"

Hawthorne opened his mouth to say more, and he shut it.

"Good. Walk ahead of me."

Hawthorne squared his bony shoulders and stepped forward. Ulrich trained the revolver on him and dropped his other hand into his jacket pocket. As Hawthorne passed, Ulrich's hand jerked up. It held a coin-sized capsule. He

145

pressed it against Hawthorne's forearm. A jet of air shot the tiny pneumospray hypo, pumping a drug into the General's bloodstream.

"What?"

Ulrich shoved Hawthorne, hard. Caught by surprise, he staggered sideways and struck the wall, then straightened angrily.

"Wait," said Ulrich.

Hawthorne checked himself from lunging. After a moment, he rubbed his forearm. "What did you put into me?"

Ulrich smiled bitterly.

A cool, numbing feeling clouded the General's thinking. He wanted to stay enraged. Air Marshal Ulrich, a professional colleague for more than twenty years... How could he have trusted such a monster? But the rage slipped away. It was getting harder to think.

"You're ready," said Ulrich. "Let's go."

"But..."

"Go!"

Hawthorne adjusted his tie and moved to the door, opening it. He glanced back. The beefy Air Marshal slid his hand cannon into its holster, clicking the flap shut. Noticing the appraisal, Ulrich held up the black switch, his thumb ready to press.

"Go," he repeated.

Hawthorne stepped into the outer office. The consoles were empty, the entire room devoid of personnel. No doubt, Ulrich had ordered everyone out before he'd entered the inner sanctum.

Then it became difficult to concentrate as they strode through the vast underground bunker, a massive complex. Faces merged, worried and wondering, but comforted by Ulrich's explanation that the General needed to relax topside, grab some fresh air and stretch his legs for a brisk walk under the sun. In time, and as the drug lost its edge, Hawthorne found himself riding a seldom-used conveyer. He rubbed his forehead.

"Try not to dwell on it," said Ulrich.

Hawthorne faced the traitor, who had a shiny face and a foul, damp odor. Sweat stains soaked the armpits of Ulrich's blue uniform.

"In another few minute it's over, General. Then you'll never have to look at me again."

Hawthorne realized that he sneered at Ulrich. He turned toward the approaching entrance. He'd been given an obedience drug, but he hadn't been completely obedient. There was one word he should have given to cancel secret surveillance. He had implemented this particular procedure after the late Lord Director's assassination. He was certain the Air Marshal didn't know about it.

"Step off," said Ulrich.

Hawthorne hopped off the conveyer. Ulrich followed. Hawthorne strode to the door and punched in the security code. A green light flashed and the thick titanium door slid aside. They climbed the stairs and went out the last door, to a blustery park rich with evergreen odors. Pinecones littered the needled ground. A gravel path led to a hanger in the distance. Evergreens swayed all around, and surrounding the trees rose snow-capped mountains.

"Head away from the building," said Ulrich. "South."

Their shoes crunched over needles. The wind howled. Dark swirling clouds raced overhead. Higher than the stratosphere orbited the enemy's space platforms. The Highborn besieged Earth.

Ulrich made an angry sound, and said, "What's *he* doing here?"

General Hawthorne turned.

From behind a tree strode a strange kind of man. The common term was semi-prosthetic or bionic. Specialists had torn the man down and rebuilt him with synthetic muscles, titanium-reinforced bones and sheath-protected nerves. The bionic captain wore a loose military tunic and slacks. He had heavy features, giving him the look of a Twentieth Century gangster who broke bones for a living. He wore a peaked cap low over his eyes, while a barely audible whine emanated from him. Special glands had been grafted into him and if the need arose would pump drugs into his bloodstream and dull any pain he might receive or stimulate him to even greater strength and speed.

Ulrich stepped near the General. "It's your head unless you get rid of him."

Hawthorne could barely speak, but he managed to stutter, "C-Captain."

The bionic captain strode up and saluted sharply. "Is everything all right, sir?"

Hawthorne glanced at Ulrich, who sweated even more than before, although it was cold here.

"We... we needed air," said Hawthorne.

"Very good, sir." The bionic captain turned toward the Air Marshal.

Ulrich peered past him, and his eyes widened in fear.

Both Hawthorne and the bionic captain turned.

Out of the woods loped six men. They wore the red body armor of Political Harmony Corps, with black helmets, boots and silver packs. Wires from the packs ran to the slim laser pistols clutched in their gloved fists.

The bionic captain moved like liquid death. He leaped and shoved Hawthorne down. Then he drew his sidearm and went to one knee, snapping off rapid-fire shots.

Hawthorne spit pine needles out of his mouth.

The captain fired a huge gyroc pistol, the heavy slugs igniting in mid-flight, assisted by internal rockets. The armor-piercing bullets penetrated the intruders' protective shells and exploded. Three of the PHC squad already lay dead. Two fired lasers. One beam hissed over the General, the heat hot on his cheek. The other beam touched the bionic captain's non-firing arm, frying flesh and bio-metal. The captain grunted, but drugs clamped down on the pain and kept him lucid. He fired twice more and two more red suits went down.

Hawthorne froze, and he realized Ulrich had pressed the inhibitor switch. But his mouth wasn't frozen. "Behind you!" shouted Hawthorne.

BOOM.

General Hawthorne closed his eyes in sick defeat. Then he heard a familiar grunt. Ulrich. The Air Marshal pitched onto the needles beside him. The last PHC killer died under a hail of gyroc rounds.

Click.

General Hawthorne slowly rose. A moment later, the captain had his hand on his elbow. Blood dripped from the bionic shoulder.

"Are you all right?" asked Hawthorne.

"Never mind me, sir." The captain scanned the forest. "Let's get you below."

"Yes," said Hawthorne. He glanced at Ulrich, at the crushed windpipe. The bionic captain was brutally strong. He wondered then what the cyborgs were like, if they were that much superior even to the bionic men?

As the captain hustled him to the door, he realized that it had almost ended for him. His stupidity bade him recall an ancient piece of prose.

Thucydides, the historian of the Peloponnesian War between the ancient Greek city-states of Athens and Sparta, had written it. It had concerned the various factions of various feuding city-state allies. Thucydides had written about people plotting and jockeying for political power within those states.

As a rule, those who were least remarkable for intelligence showed the greater powers of survival. Such people recognized their own deficiencies and the superior intelligence of their opponents. Fearing that they might lose a debate or find themselves outmaneuvered in intrigue by their quick-witted enemies, they boldly launched straight into action. Their opponents, overconfident in the belief that they would see what was happening in advance, and not thinking it necessary to seize by force what they could secure by policy, were the more easily destroyed because they were off their guard.

Hawthorne was on his guard now against PHC plots. He just hoped it wasn't too late.

3.

Nadia lowered the headphones and stared at the bulkhead. She hid in a tiny crawl space, her home away from home. She had a folding lounge chair that served as her bed, several boxes of concentrates, a wall stacked with twenty-liter jugs of water and a hoard of tech equipment and tools. All this left her about ten square meters of floor space. Her vacc suit and helmet lay on a box and an oxygen recharger stood beside the porta-pot. The only way out was the airlock. Marten had said that this had been one of his parents' former bolt holes.

Nadia shook her head in denial of the latest catastrophe. It simply couldn't be happening. They had come so close, too close for this to happen. When Marten hadn't shown—she had waited a half-hour over the limit. Then she'd fled and come here to hide and wait and try again. And he hadn't shown the next day, at the new location. That's when she became frightened.

Now...

She dropped the headphones onto the floor. Marten was gone. Everyone in the Sun Works was in a panic. Repair pods to the docks, shuttles scurrying all over, the Doom Star *Genghis Khan* hiding behind Mercury. Those five boost ships now made sense, and all those missiles lifting from the boost ships. Marten had been in one of those. That's what the military code said, the one she'd just been listening to. The shock troops were on bearing as targeted.

Nadia sat motionless on the lounge chair, her mind blank. Finally, she forced herself to suck from a food-tube and sip

150

water. "Marten," she whispered. Tears trickled. She would never see him again. She sank into the lounge chair and cried. Later she wiped away the tears. Then she fiddled with the various pieces of equipment. Maybe he would return home from a successful mission, but she couldn't believe that, didn't dare trust it to happen. She had to think and be hardheaded.

The answer finally came. She could see no other way around it.

Nadia donned the vacc suit and boots, entered the airlock and made the long walk to the observation dome where they had first found the pod. She entered the hab and warily studied the bare area. Then she pulled a bug detector from her pocket, scanning her surroundings. Spy-sticks watched the corridor. Well, that couldn't be helped. Hopefully the operator wouldn't understand what he saw. She wasn't a shock trooper, and that's what Marten had told her they watched for.

She put the vacc suit in the locker and hurried down the corridor. A tangler was strapped to her thigh. It was the one Marten had said he'd used over four and half years ago. It had been exactly where he'd said he had hidden it. She hoped she wouldn't have to use it.

4.

Hansen chortled with glee. He had her. He sat in his office and watched a screen with Nadia Pravda as its subject. He had rerouted certain spy-sticks so they only played at his desk screen. He watched Nadia stride down a utility corridor to an empty hanger door. He wasn't sure what she was doing in there. As he waited, he typed on a special keyboard newly installed in the desk. He loved being Chief Monitor. He loved all these gadgets. Watching people when they didn't know they were being watched, he couldn't compare the feeling to anything he'd known before. It was power.

He switched back to the hanger door. What was she doing in there? Too bad, he hadn't been able to get clearance for spy-sticks in the hangers. He shrugged, waited and then checked his credit account. Oh, lovely. He bobbed his head. Dust sales had skyrocketed since he'd taken over.

A red light blinked.

He switched back to the hanger door, watching Nadia close it, glance both ways and hurry down the corridor with a heavy duffel bag slung over her shoulder.

Hansen leaned forward to examine the bag. It seemed to be full of the missing plastic bags of dust. "Beautiful," he whispered. At last, he would recover the stolen product. He needed it more than ever in order to fill the demand. Patience *did* pay off.

He turned to his intercom to summon his special team: Ervil, Dalt and Methlen. But instead, his door opened and two Trustees entered unannounced. They were beefy, sneering men

152

in brown plastic armor, the personal servants of Highborn. The Trustees as a group displayed big bushy sideburns. These two seemed too young to have grown them. Theirs were probably glued on fakes. They stood in the doorway, arrogantly looking around his cluttered office and then at him.

As he swiveled around to better see them, Hansen innocently switched off the screen and pressed another button that caused the keyboard to disappear deep into his desk.

"The least you could do is knock," he said.

"You're to come with us," said the Trustee with narrowly placed, beady eyes.

Hansen sat back, trying to think, wondering why Trustees had been sent. They were notoriously difficult to deal with. He said, "Do you realize that Chief Monitor means I keep tabs on everything that occurs on the Sun Works Factory?"

"That don't mean nothing to us."

"No?" asked Hansen. "You're innocent of all wrongdoing?"

"We're Trustees. We're immune."

"Certainly," said Hansen. "Until the moment you step out of line. And who do you think catches others doing that?"

The two Trustees glanced at one another. One of them laughed. The beady-eyed Trustee smiled nastily at Hansen.

"You're trying to suborn a Trustee?"

"Never!" said Hansen. "I'm simply curious as to your errand. Do you think you can barge in unannounced? I only ask that you give me a few moments to collect myself."

"No time, Chief Monitor," said the beady-eyed Trustee, snapping his thick fingers. "Hustle your butt over here double-time, boy."

Hansen blustered. "I'd like to come now, but I'm engaged in sensitive business. So, if you will tell me who sent you?"

The Trustees nodded to one another and strode into the office.

Hansen leaned forward and tried to click the foot alarm under his desk. A Trustee grabbed one of his skinny arms and jerked Hansen bodily out of the chair. The other Trustee grabbed the other arm. They hustled him out the office, through his secretaries' rooms and past the desks of surprised monitors.

153

His special team—led by Ervil with his heavily bandaged nose—rose from their chairs.

"We're under the Praetor's orders," the beady-eyed Trustee said.

Dalt and Methlen sank back into their chairs. The shorter Ervil dared take a step toward them.

"We can come back for you later," the beady-eyed Trustee said. "If you wanna be stupid about this, that is."

Ervil hesitated and then moved aside.

5.

Nadia heaved a sigh of relief as she donned the vacc suit and reentered the observation dome airlock. It had been a gamble going after the dream dust. But she was going to need it. She was on her own again. To live one needed credits. That was an unpleasant fact. And the universal currency was drugs in demand. It was better than gold or platinum, something that even the common man wanted.

She made the long walk to her hideaway. Back inside she felt more claustrophobic than ever. She was glad she'd spent all this time studying astrophysics. Putting away the dust, she began rummaging through the pile of electronic equipment. What a packrat's hoard. Finally, she sat, crossed her legs and went through the computer catalog. Ah, that's what it looked like.

She searched until she found the code-breaker. Then she began to gather supplies.

6.

Hansen screamed. Only his head stuck out of the metal box. The rest of his naked body was strapped and secured within the pain booth as neurowhips lashed his nerve endings. He bellowed until his voice became hoarse. His beet-colored, flushed head, with sweat pouring out him, made it seem as if he was about to pop.

Female techs with earplugs impassively watched him. They wore long white lab coats and stood behind a panel, adjusting the pain intensity and making certain the Chief Monitor served no more or less than the selected time.

Hansen screamed, wheezed and started pleading, even though he knew they couldn't hear him. He writhed, but the straps held him tightly, although he tore several muscles and tendons in his efforts.

Finally, a tech twirled a dial. The pain stopped.

Hansen gasped in relief, his eyeballs seeming to sink back into his head. For the first time in seven minutes, his body relaxed, although it continued to twitch and jerk. Tears that had streamed from his eyes began to dry on his skin.

The Praetor opened the only door into the soundproofed room. He wore his brown uniform, and with those intense pink eyes, he glared at Hansen.

The two techs removed their earplugs and came to rigid attention.

"Release him," said the Praetor.

The techs moved like robots. They unlocked the pain booth, drew back the twin doors and began removing the

156

sweat-soaked leather straps. Hansen shivered at their cold touch, they wore rubber gloves. He was naked and humiliated. Small, weak and helpless: he hated the feeling. They helped him stand, their cold, gloved hands on his skinny arms.

"Bring him here," the Praetor said.

On shaky, trembling legs, Hansen wobbled near. He would have collapsed without the two techs.

"Chief Monitor," said the Praetor.

Hansen looked up, way up at the giant Highborn. He felt like a child, a naughty boy brought before his angry father. He wondered if he was about to die.

"You have failed in your task," the Praetor said. "The shock troops have left and I may no longer prove their disloyalty. While incompetence is the chief feature of premen, you surpass the common ruck. I wonder now why the former Chief Monitor trusted you with so many tasks."

Hansen bowed his head. He wanted to confess and tell the Praetor that Marten Kluge had been a very busy shock trooper indeed. Why, Kluge had even had confederates. But Hansen knew that he had no wits now. Pain and this wretched treatment were meant to intimidate him, and it did, very much. Thus, he didn't trust himself. As a policeman, he'd learned that unless criminals were very, very careful they always implicated themselves as they tried to explain. He didn't have the wits to be careful, but at least he had enough to know that. He hung his head a little lower.

"The matter must rest for now," the Praetor said. "But I do not want you to feel that I tolerate incompetence. I loathe it. I abhor and despise it. Seven minutes in the pain booth is hardly enough for this failure. Yet you premen are so weak that more might damage you beyond repair. In fact, my psychologists tell me that you are weaker in this regard than most of your ilk."

Hansen let his head droop as far as it could go.

"A pathetic weakling, a wretched fool, a blunderer and a dolt. That is whom I have chosen as my Chief Monitor. My instincts tell me to throttle you on the spot. Instead, I have selected a new Chief Monitor."

Hansen lifted his head halfway up.

"Ah, you don't like that, do you?"

Hansen swallowed. He had too many loose ends. A new chief monitor might discover his... indiscretions. The new chief monitor would also have access to his desk and could replay all those spy-stick files and see Marten Kluge. This was a disaster.

"Yet I will not utterly demote you," the Praetor said. "Moral Enforcer will be your new title."

"Highborn?"

"I assign you a new task. It is a problem that has mushroomed. I speak of dream dust usage. The Sun Works Police Chief tells me that the merchants are very subtle. You must find and stamp out these sellers. Then you must discover where they manufacture this foul substance and destroy the sites. If you should fail me in this small task, Moral Enforcer, then these past seven minutes will seem like paradise in comparison."

Without another word, the Praetor left.

Hansen sagged and his knees buckled. Fortunately, the two techs kept him from falling.

"Time to leave, sir," said the taller of the two techs.

Hansen nodded and let them guide him to the dressing room.

7.

Nadia Pravda rode the pod to the secret hanger. She meant to leave the Sun Works Factory forever. Her heart raced and she dreaded the lack of running lights of the formerly thousands of busy space vehicles. Near space seemed so empty around the Ring-factory now. Would the station tracker pinpoint her and wonder about her unscheduled flight? She dared it because she couldn't hide in the crawl space any longer.

Her natural caution caused her to park and anchor the pod a kilometer from her destination. She towed a huge bundle of supplies and clang, clang, clanged her way along the habitat's inner ring. Later she punched in the door code and went through the smaller hatch. She used the flashlight Marten had used the first time and then clanged to the stealth pod. Soon she reached the craft's hatch, a smooth, black, oval-shaped door. She put the code-breaker over the lock and pressed a button. Lights flashed as the code-breaker went to work.

Time passed. Nadia grew impatient. After two hours, she switched oxygen tanks. Still the code-breaker winked its lights. She began to feel uneasy. She rechecked the code-breaker. Like the dumb little brute that it was it flash, flash, flashed, coming up with codes and testing each. She clicked the flashlight on and shined it around the hanger.

Bad mistake, she realized.

Two men in vacc suits floated toward her.

She yelped in terror and clawed for her tangler. Dark clots flew at her. She ducked and swayed, but one hit her vacc suit and tangled her with strong, wiry strands. She struggled, but that only tightened them.

The vacc-suited duo floated closer. Their visors were dark so she couldn't see who they were. At least they weren't big enough to be Highborn.

The code-breaker flashed green as the duo reached her. One of them switched off her magnetic boots and picked her up. No! This wasn't fair! Her stomach twisted and heaved. The other one opened the hatch and floated inside. Then, to her amazement, the second one entered the pod and took her along. She was in the ultra-stealth pod after long last, but not in the manner she had envisioned.

As the one man held her, the other explored the main cabin. He studied the board and pressed several switches. Lights came on and soon the oxygen bulb showed that the air was breathable.

The first man removed his helmet. It was Hansen. He had circles around his eyes and his mouth twitched. He seemed to be in pain. His eyes bored into her after the other man took off her helmet. Then the second man removed his. It was Ervil, with a big white bandage over his nose. He stared at her in a cold manner, as if she were an insect. He frightened her, he always had.

"What is this ship?" asked Hansen, wincing every time he moved.

"You mean you don't know?"

"Tell me," he said, trying to sound patient but doing a poor job of it.

"It's a ship, like you said."

Ervil grabbed a fistful of her vacc suit—to steady her, she realized a moment later—and slapped her across the face.

"Yes," said Hansen. "I can see that it's a ship. And you don't need to hit her, Ervil."

Ervil shrugged.

The setback was too stunning for tears. It left her flat, almost emotionless. She said, "Marten called it an ultra-stealth pod. It will, or should I say that it was supposed to have taken us to the Jupiter Confederation."

Hansen's foxy eyebrows rose. "You two have been busy. Why did you want to journey to Jupiter?"

"Who wants to live under the Highborn?" she said. "But Marten also hates Social Unity, so Jupiter, is the closest system after Mars."

"Word is the Martians rebelled against Social Unity when the Highborn first destroyed Geneva," said Hansen. "And now the Highborn no longer garrison it with a Doom Star, not after May 10. Why not flee to Mars?"

She shook her head. "It's in Inner Planets. Sooner or later it will be dragged into the war."

Hansen glanced around, wincing as he did. He asked her, "Could this pod actually make to the Jupiter System?"

She couldn't shrug with the tangle strands wrapping her. "The short answer is yes," she said.

"What are you thinking, boss?" asked Ervil.

"Have you ever spent any time in a pain booth?" Hansen asked Ervil.

The short, wide-shouldered monitor shook his head.

"It's unpleasant, an experience I don't plan on repeating," said Hansen. "It has also opened my eyes to reality. You can never please a Highborn."

"You don't think the Praetor would be pleased if you turned this up?" asked Ervil. "He might even make you Chief Monitor again."

"He plans to stamp out all dream dust production," said Hansen. "And to find the manufacturers and... I don't know his plans for them, but that's us, you and me—and you," he told Nadia.

Ervil touched the bandage swathed across his nose. His dead, emotionless eyes revealed nothing.

"I have a question," said Nadia.

"Ask," Hansen said.

"How did you find me?"

"Ah. When you last entered the habitat, to get your dream dust, I presume, a spy-stick shot an automated tracker onto your vacc suit."

Nadia closed her eyes. She had forgotten to sweep her suit for bugs. Stupid. When she opened her eyes, she said, "So what do you plan to do?"

"Can you pilot this ship?" asked Hansen.

"Yes."

Hansen blew out his cheeks in relief. "Then here and now I forgive you your errors."

"What about him?" she asked.

Hansen regarded Ervil. "We're finished in the Sun Works Factory."

"You got too greedy, boss, that was the problem."

Hansen stiffened. Maybe he wasn't used to that sort of talk from his clean-up man. "Maybe so," he said. "But I propose that we start fresh in the Jupiter System. She brought dream dust. So did I. That will be our stake in the new world."

Ervil didn't move and his gray eyes seemed to grow dull. "How long will the trip take?"

"Six months," she said. "Maybe longer."

Ervil shook his head. "You'll go stir crazy, boss. And two men with one woman, that's bad."

"We need her to pilot the ship," Hansen said.

Ervil turned his lifeless eyes on Nadia. He shrugged. "What about Dalt and Methlen?"

"They'll have to fend for themselves," Hansen said. "Five seems like too many people for this craft."

Ervil grunted.

"Now untangle her," said Hansen.

"Maybe it would be smarter to keep her tangled," Ervil said. "She could tell you what to do and you pilot the ship. That way we don't take no chances."

Hansen seemed to consider it.

"Piloting is much trickier than that," Nadia said. "I'd have to actually be at the controls."

"She double-crossed you once already, boss. I don't trust her."

"We'll watch her closely," Hansen said.

"Take turns, huh?" said Ervil.

"Now, now, none of that," Hansen said. "Don't needlessly frighten her."

162

"We can't leave right away," Nadia said, who was terrified of these two. Why had she ever gotten involved with drugs in the first place?

"Why can't we leave?" asked Hansen.

"Things are too quiet," she said. "We have to wait until the pods come back online."

Hansen pursed his lips. "I destroyed my files, so we have a little time. The sooner we can leave the better."

"Dalt and Methlen might be angry that you left them behind," said Ervil. "They might talk too much once the Highborn catch them."

"We'll have to count on their staying out of sight for a while," said Hansen. He turned to Nadia. "Do we have a deal?"

She had no choice and she knew it. But she didn't like the look in Hansen's eyes, nor in Ervil's. What would six months be like cooped up with these two? "It's a deal," she said.

"Good," said Hansen, taking the bottle off Ervil's belt. He sprayed her tangle strands and they wilted and fell to the floor. "Let's get ready to leave."

8.

Admiral Rica Sioux wore a spotless tan uniform, with a glittering row of medals. A snug, tan military cap hid her hair. She swiveled in the command chair, with a comlink embedded in her right ear and a VR-monocle over her left eye.

Everyone else on the command capsule wore a stiff, tan uniform of the Social Unity Space Fleet. Most were webbed into their modules, with VR-goggles and twitch-gloves. A clean odor filled the capsule, while brisk movement and sharply spoken words added to the military bearing. The transformation in the past eleven days had taken hold throughout the entire ship.

Admiral Sioux shifted anxiously. Short, swift, gratifying days with command briefings, inspections and practice drills had changed a sluggish, orbital-sick crew into eager warriors. Not even the flock of blips picked up by tracking had been able to check this impulse.

It was too bad about the early radar probe and the subsequent missile launches. Enemy jamming kept them in the dark about the exact nature of the incoming missiles. To warm up their own ECM pods to try to defeat the enemy sensors would give away their exact position. No. Long-distance beam shots out of the dark were the *Bangladesh's* MO. The spread of enemy missiles proved the Highborn hadn't spotted them again… unless they had done so optically. In any case, it would take over a week for the missiles to get close enough to fire any missile-borne lasers—if they even packed lasers.

Unless—she tapped her armrest—*unless the very spread of missiles was a bluff!* Admiral Sioux frowned, creasing her face full of wrinkles. *Maybe the Highborn had spread the missiles to try to fool me. Maybe they track us with a hidden, secret ship of their own.*

Admiral Sioux sipped from a sealed cup. It was a special medicated drink that smelled like coffee. This way only the medical officer knew that she was taking drugs to help calm her nerves.

Why did she have to worry so much? She hated it.

The First Gunner broke into her reverie, saying, "Entering firing range… now."

Admiral Sioux savored the moment. Now! The *Bangladesh* was intact. Despite her fears, the Highborn could surely have no idea about what was to commence. 30 million kilometers was a short distance in space terms, but in terms of Solar System ranged warfare, it was a revolution.

"Rotate the particle shield aft thirty degrees," she said.

"Aft thirty degrees," said the Shield Tech.

Outside the massive beamship, the huge 600-meter thick shield of rock and metal lifted as if a man lifted a visor on a helmet.

"Focus the projectors," said Admiral Sioux.

"Projectors focused. Projectors in firing position," said the First Gunner, his supple fingers flying over his control board.

A vast section slid open on the inner armored skin of the *Bangladesh*. A squat nozzle poked out, a green light winking in its orifice.

"Engage power," Admiral Sioux said.

"Proton Beam power on," the Power Chief said.

"Target acquired," the First Gunner said.

Admiral Rica Sioux smiled thinly. She and ship's AI had already chosen the targets ten days ago. They would follow a strict procedure aboard the *Bangladesh*. If the Highborn did something unforeseen, only then would they change procedure.

"Admiral?" the First Gunner asked.

She sighed. A good officer, the Pakistani First Gunner, but he was a little too anxious. Why couldn't he allow her to enjoy the moment? After one hundred and twenty-one years of life,

165

she had learned that savoring a coming moment was often more enjoyable than the actual moment itself.

"This day," she said to the command crew, "we teach the Imperialist warmongers that you can contain the People momentarily, but you can't keep them down forever."

One fool actually started clapping, although he quickly looked around, saw that no one else clapped and sheepishly turned back to his screen.

"Hear, hear," said the Second-in-Command.

There, much better, and with an actual touch of the antiquated navy. The Admiral liked that. She closed her eyes and refrained from fiddling with her cap, as much as she wanted to adjust it because her head itched abominably. That would seem like a nervous gesture, though. She opened her eyes, trying to memorize every detail.

"Fire," she said.

The First Gunner pressed the button.

Ship's AI took over. Within the *Bangladesh*, power flooded from the storage cells and the ship's Fusion Drive pumped in more. That power charged through the proton generators. Needles and gauges jumped and quivered, and then out of the single cannon poured the incredibly powerful proton beam.

It sped at almost 300,000 kilometers per second for Mercury, for the Sun Works Factory that churned out armaments for the Supremacists. For 1.7034 minutes, the tip of the beam flew through the vacuum of space. Meanwhile, Mercury traveled along its orbital path around the Sun, and around the pitted planet rotated the vast ring habitat, its exact tilt known even to the lonely scientists far out on Charon. The proton beam charged almost as fast as anything could possibly travel in the galaxy. It was a little less than the speed of light, amazingly fast to terrestrials, but when set against the vast distances of space, a mere crawl.

On the Sun Works Factory technicians and secretaries, Highborn officers and premen underlings, repairmen, computer specialists, welders, deck crew, cooks and maintenance all went about their normal activities. None knew what sped toward them. Nothing could have given them warning. If radar could have bounced off the proton beam, the return radar blip would have traveled only a little faster than the attacking protons. Like a literal bolt out of the blue, the proton beam flew onward.

Approximately 1.7 minutes after leaving the proton cannon, the beam lanced past the solar collectors that girded the outer shell of the Sun Works Factory. For all the precision of the *Bangladesh's* targeting system, the first shot missed its target by 100 meters. The proton beam shot past the solar collectors, flashed over the rest of the spinning station and speared at Mercury. There the beam churned the already molten surface.

Shuttle pilots and pod-crew near the beam stared at it in dread fascination. Highborn command officers swore. In seconds, alarms rang everywhere.

Then the beam shifted, as it had been shifted 1.7 minutes ago aboard the *Bangladesh*. Ship's AI had predicted the possibility of a miss. Because of that possibility, ship's AI had suggested that the Admiral re-target the beam every six seconds.

Thus six seconds after the harsh proton beam flashed past the Sun Works Factory and hit Mercury, it readjusted and smashed into the solar collectors that protected the outer skin of the station. They had never been built to take such punishment. An old-style military laser would have destroyed it and little more. For a laser beam didn't stay on target, on the same spot, for more than a nanosecond. But this was the improved proton beam, Social Unity's single trump card against the Highborn. It punched through the solar collector and through the heavy shielding behind it. It stabbed into the Sun Works Factory itself, into the orbital fighter construction yard that had been built in this part of the Factory.

The proton beam touched welder equipment and ignited engines. Blasts added to the destruction, awful, fierce annihilation. For six seconds the proton beam wreaked havoc on the vital orbital construction yard. It punched through that part of the ring-factory, slicing it like a gigantic knife. Gouts of purple plasma erupted into space. Burned bodies floated into the vacuum, some of those the crisped corpses of Highborn. Titanic ammunition blasts combined with the beam and ruptured the Sun Works, a devastating first strike. In nearby areas, the blasts ruptured hatches and ignited more fires. Shocked technicians, pilots and service personal died by fire, by vacuum and sometimes by toxic fumes.

Then the proton beam shifted again.

The first attack lasted three minutes, the beam shifting every six seconds. It was three minutes of hellish terror for everyone on the nearest side of the Sun Works Factory. In the hit locations, it was three minutes of incredible destruction. It was three minutes of brutal death. Maybe for the first time in the war, the Highborn knew they could be hurt.

Aboard the *Bangladesh*, the command crew and proton-beam technicians held their breath. Or it seemed to them they did. The three minutes went by in a flash. Then:

"Power low," the Power Chief said.

Admiral Sioux watched the seconds tick by in her VR-monocle. *Three, two, one*: "Shut down the proton beam."

"Proton beam shutting down," said the First Gunner.

"Engage engines," ordered the Admiral.

Everyone abandoned the modules and floated to the acceleration couches in the center of the capsule, buckling in. Soon the mighty engines burned. The *Bangladesh* thrust to a different heading, just in case the Highborn tried anything unexpected.

In another half-hour, they would fire again. For the next several days, they were going to pound the Sun Works Factory and see if they could teach the Highborn a thing or two about space warfare.

Admiral Rica Sioux loved it.

9.

The attack came as a dreadful shock to the Highborn. It two places, space and molten debris floated where once had been the solid ring-factory. In other places, torn skin and blasted wreckage told of the fierce annihilating power of the proton beam. More than one Highborn swore awful oaths. Many premen sat at screens, studying the orange plasma clouds, the tumbling bodies and the gaping holes in the station. Perhaps for the first time, they doubted an automatic Highborn victory. The superiors could be hurt.

Repair pods flew to the scene of the worst destruction, as well as damage control teams in Zero-G Worksuits. All over the Sun Works Factory, hanger doors opened and working orbitals zoomed out to emergency zones. Meanwhile, behind Mercury, the *Genghis Khan* powered up to fight as it was. The Doom Star *Gustavus Adolphus* halted refit as personnel raced onboard. At this point, the Highborn expected anything to happen.

The Praetor of the Sun Works Factory ordered all premen to barracks. This would be the perfect moment for SU sympathizers to strike, or so suggested several Highborn in charge of various security areas. Debates raged on what to do next. Vectors and velocities of all known Social Unity spacecraft were carefully computed.

"I want to know when each of them can reach Mercury!" the Praetor shouted.

"Do you believe this a prelude to a mass premen space attack?" Lycon asked.

169

"What do you call this?" snarled the Praetor, before striding out to collect the latest damage reports.

"They will attack again," messaged the Grand Admiral from the *Julius Caesar* in orbit around the Moon. "Implement *total* defense measures."

Several minutes after receiving it, a communications officer handed the memo to the Praetor. He scanned it. Then he asked his staff, "What does he think we've been doing?"

"You're one step ahead of him, sir," said a staff member.

The Praetor grunted.

Unlike the lower species, the Highborn prided themselves on quick reactions. Shock often produced confused sluggishness. Surprise left many bewildered. Not the Highborn, however, and certainly not the Praetor.

The *Genghis Khan* and a hundred shuttles roared to the outer portion of the Sun Works Factory. They pumped aerogel with lead additives between the probable location of the *Bangladesh* and the space hab. The aerogel was a dull cloud. Behind it, other shuttles shot packets of prismatic crystals. It was reflective chaff, useful against lasers. Maybe it would help a little against the dreaded proton beam. The cloud of protective materials moved at the same relative speed as the planet and ring hab, thus seeming to remain stationary. The volume of space needing protection was knowable and measurable. The problem was that it was also vast.

Just as bad, the next attack commenced before the aerogel and reactive shielding had begun to take form. Yet wherever the proton beam struck the aerogel with lead additives, it lost some power because it had to burn through. But the clouds weren't thick enough yet to stop the beam. And most of the places the beams slashed were unshielded by these aerosols.

Just like the first attack, the second wreaked awful destruction. More bodies tumbled into vacuum. Purple, orange and red plasma roiled into space. The proton beam sliced through another two sections of the ring-factory. Months of factory work burned, exploded or drifted into the void. Debris began a slow tumble away from Mercury, shot outward by the station's centrifugal force.

170

There was, however, an incredible amount of mass to attack. The sheer volume of the Sun Works Factory made its total destruction a matter of weeks of such beaming. Long before that happened, effective use of the factory would cease. The Highborn were as close to panic as they could be.

Three minutes later this attack stopped just as the first one had.

"Faster!" the Praetor shouted. "More aerogel, more crystals, get my station shielded!"

10.

Hansen and Ervil watched her too closely. Hansen boasted endlessly during his watches. She found out he'd been a skinny boy in Sydney, Australian Sector when his parents had been kicked out of Social Unity for graft. They had been forced to move into the sprawling slums and eke out an existence there. According to Hansen, most of the slum dwellers were third and fourth generation and knew its filthy, brutal ways. People like Kang and Omi fit perfectly. But sensitive lads like him…

Nadia learned that around the city's lower deep-core shaft radiated the slums, from City Level 41 to 49. Peacekeeper raids seldom helped keep order. Social workers rarely ventured into the slums even if guaranteed army patrols. Hall and block leaders kept a low profile there. Ward officers seldom set foot in their own territory. Desperate people lived in the slums, uneducated, violent people with bizarre modes of thought and behavior. Gangs roved at night, youth gangs being particular bloodthirsty. Drug lords hired people as mules, bodyguards and gunmen.

Hansen told her that his only hope for survival had been to sharpen his wits. Subterfuge and cunning, that's how a skinny young boy had dodged the worst horrors.

She supposed that's how a skinny older man had tried to dodge them on the Sun Works Factory.

Ervil's watches were worse. He stared at her with those dead eyes. He didn't say anything. Sometimes he did isometric exercises with a pull bar. When he did this, he took off his shirt. A layer of smooth fat hid his muscles and the stench of his sweat wasn't pleasant. She once checked the amount of pull he used. Strange Ervil was strong, probably one of those naturals that could live in any slum, at least according to Hansen's theories.

They didn't even trust her to use the bathroom alone. Each took turns watching, making her keep the door open. That's when she decided. There was no way she'd survive a six-month trip cooped up with these two.

So when Ervil was asleep one shift she began working on Hansen. She found ways to nudge him. She laughed at his jokes. She kept her eyes bright and showed interest when he repeatedly told the same stories. She soon realized he considered himself the slyest man in the solar system. He had big plans. It dawned on her that his ambition had helped him trick the Highborn into thinking he'd been a PHC agent. He knew undercover procedures because he had informed on everyone in Sydney. The way he told it, he had taught some of the agents a thing or two when sent on sting operations. And he had thoroughly learned the drug trade.

Then came a day she forced herself to let her eyes linger on him. When he turned and noticed, she looked away with a guilty start.

"What's wrong?" he asked.

She shook her head.

He moved closer. Ervil snored in the sleep compartment.

"Do you miss Marten?" he asked.

"Him?" she asked, facing Hansen. "Marten was a monomaniac. All he thought about was how to get to Jupiter." A wry look came over her. "He didn't have time for much else."

"At least his single-mindedness was good for the three of us," Hansen said with a laugh.

She laughed, too.

He let his hand fall on top of hers.

She looked up, her eyes wide. "What if Ervil catches us?" she whispered.

"Ervil does what I tell him."

"I don't understand that," she said. "He's so strong and nothing scares him."

"He's strong," admitted Hansen. He tapped his forehead. "But this is where strength really counts."

"You're so right."

He grinned and touched her cheek. She melted against his hand before she jerked away.

"I'm too scared," she whispered.

"Of me?"

"Ervil! In six months, he'll get jealous. What if he kills you?"

"Nonsense."

"Then I'll be all alone with him." She shuddered. "I don't think he practices normal sex."

Hansen slid closer and gripped her shoulders. He kissed her. She kissed back. Suddenly noise came out the sleep compartment: Ervil moving around. Hansen dropped his hands and acted normally. Nadia could have done likewise, but as the compartment door slid open, she leaped up as her hand flew to her mouth.

"Did you sleep well?" Hansen asked, covering for her.

Ervil blinked at them.

Nadia fidgeted.

On Hansen's next watch, she told him Ervil had questioned her about what had happened when he was asleep. Hansen seemed doubtful. She dropped the subject. Half a day later Hansen said he couldn't believe Ervil would ask such a thing.

"You don't see the way he watches me when you're asleep," she said. "I think he's planning to trick you."

Hansen snorted. But when the proton beam first struck the Sun Works Factory Nadia noticed he'd taken to wearing his projac at all times. Later, when the pods and shuttles flooded out to build the space shield, and she said now was the moment to leave, that's when her work bore fruit.

"We should leave for the Jupiter System today," she said, moving to the pilot seat.

"Hold it," said Ervil, putting a hand on her shoulder.

"Let her go," said Hansen.

Something in his boss's voice must have warned Ervil. The short man spun around fast and slid to the left, as if to dodge shots. Hansen, his hand on his holstered projac, now clawed to

174

get it out. Ervil roared, "You're double-crossing me?" He charged Hansen, who pumped ice slivers into him. The momentum took Ervil into Hansen. Both men crumbled to the floor. Hansen thrashed to disentangle himself. The short, wide-shouldered Ervil lay limply. Hansen finally leaped up, aiming his weapon at Nadia.

She, uncertain about the outcome, had simply played the part of a terrified woman, standing with her mouth and eyes wide.

The suspicion left Hansen. He laughed sharply as he lowered the projac. "Brains over brawn," he said. "Now to do it right." He pulled a clip out of his pocket.

"You're not going to kill him."

Hansen shrugged, switching clips.

"Why not use Suspend?" she said.

"We don't have any."

"I have some," she said.

He raised his head. "Only the military has access to Suspend."

"Marten pilfered some. I brought it with my supplies."

"Why shouldn't I just kill him?" asked Hansen. "It's much simpler and makes sure there aren't any complications."

"He was your friend once," she said. "That counts for something." She searched his eyes, giving him the doe-eyed look of an innocent.

"Certainly," he said after a moment. "Yes, yes, of course. I'm not heartless."

"Why don't you put him in his vacc suit and I'll get the Suspend. But we'll have to hurry. This is the perfect moment to leave."

Hansen nodded, holstering his weapon.

She strode to her belongings and took out a pneumospray hypo filled with a dose of Suspend. She waited as Hansen wrestled heavy Ervil into his suit. Then, as Hansen closed the magnetic seal, she stepped behind him and pressed the hypo to Hansen's neck.

Air hissed. Hansen jerked upright, whirled and grabbed her. Suspend took almost a full minute to take effect, so she kneed him hard in the groin. He doubled over, gasping. She clutched

175

her hands together and struck him across the back of the head. He slumped onto the deck, the Suspend making him sluggish, and soon he was out.

"Night-night," she whispered.

She pumped a second dose of Suspend into Ervil. Then she worked Hansen's vacc suit onto him, donned one herself and dragged them into the hanger. The Suspend would keep them alive for several weeks in their suits. Their biological functions were now slower than animals in hibernation. She set them beyond the pod's hydrogen burn range and returned to the ship.

It would be a lonely voyage to Jupiter, but better lonely than with those two scum.

Thus, as the thousands of pods and shuttles ferried aerogel and prismatic crystals from the *Genghis Khan* and to the growing space shield, a small and secret hanger in the Sun Works Factory opened. Out of it nosed the stealth pod. Using low power Nadia eased it from Mercury.

An automated tracker spotted it, studied it and decided that one of the pods had malfunctioned. Later a Highborn examined the tape and agreed with the analysis.

Several hours later Nadia dared give a little more thrust. Then the ultra-stealth pod began to coast once more.

11.

Endless monotony left Marten exhausted. The crushing pressure of three atmospheres gave him nightmares of choking to death. So as much as he needed and craved it, he hated sleeping. Just as bad were the mind-numbing dramas on his Head-Up-Display, crudely rehashed Social Unity propaganda.

Apparently, the Highborn didn't see the need for new dramas slanted to their philosophy, or maybe they simply hadn't gotten around to filming them yet. Whatever the case, someone must have told them that SU propcorp played on everyone's holos.

By law and technology no one living within Social Unity could switch off their set. The inane shows provided Inner Planets with its mass mentality. From Mercury to Mars people quoted the most popular slogans.

All the Highborn had done was take some of the old shows and 'fix' the endings.

SU morality shows, which made up about 90% of the holoset fare, came in two flavors. One, a wily villain out for himself succumbed to the mass suggestion of his hall-mates or hall leader and renounced his villainy. Or two, a self-serving villain died hideously as socially aware folk tried to save him or as a socially conscious peacekeeper blew him away in order to save others from his self-centered madness. The HB video-tech had simply chopped the ending and computer-generated new ones. Now the villain working for himself turned out to have been the smart one. Everyone else had been a jerk. The villain lived on while an insane hall leader ordered the hall-mates into slime pits where horrible funguses rotted them to death. That had hit a little too close to reality for Marten. He enjoyed it more where the hall-mates were beaten to death by out-of-control peacekeepers. At the very end of the show the former villain hurried to join the HBs in order to keep his newly won rank of self-made man, first step.

After the third show, Marten decided that old or new, they were all swill. So to keep from going stir-crazy he kept his HUD on the stars, the view routed from the missile's nose-cone camera.

Space, and a million stars, was beautiful. If only there were things like starships so he could travel to distant worlds. Or maybe if he could just get out of this suit and somehow head to the Neptune System. Instead, he raced closer toward a suicide ship-assault. Or worse, there would be no assault because the missile missed. Then they would die slowly, buried in glop, and for a million years, five dead men would serenely sail through the interstellar voids.

BUMP.

"Did you feel that?" asked Vip, via comlink. He sounded scared.

"I felt it," Marten said.

"Were we hit?"

"No, the outer pressure would've dropped and we would have exploded, turned into red smears in the bulkhead. Until the drugs wear off, we're like deep-sea creatures, kept intact by the three atmospheric pressures holding us in."

Marten's headphones crackled. A Highborn cleared his throat.

"Men."

It was Training Master Lycon, speaking via laser-link, no doubt, all the way from Mercury.

"As you may have surmised, each missile has just changed vectors, some of them rather sharply. With greater incoming data, we have determined that each had enough fuel to re-target. You will now engage the *Bangladesh en masse*. I repeat: it will be a mass assault. Battle-files of Assault Formation 42 have been beamed into your AIs for your study and implementation. Vladimir of 83rd Maniple is promoted to

178

Hauptsturmfuhrer of the 42-type Assault. Second-in-Command will be Wu of 192nd Maniple. Third in Command will be Kang of 101st Maniple. Remember, men, excellence brings rank. That is all."

The crackling in the headphones quit, and for a moment, there was silence as each absorbed the news. Then:

"Congratulations, Kang," Marten said.

A grunt was the reply.

"That should have been you who was promoted, Marten," said Lance. "What a sham. Mad Vlad in charge and our own murderer as the third runner up."

"Kang knows his business," Marten said.

"He's a psychotic killer," said Lance.

"Isn't that what Marten just said?" asked Omi.

"What?" asked Lance. "Are you saying we're all psychotic?"

No one answered.

"Oh, right," said Lance. "We've all killed people. We all survived Japan Sector. What a hellhole that was. What I'm saying is that Kang loves it. The thrill of pulling a trigger and watching the bullets rip into flesh, releasing the spirit."

"I didn't know you're religious," Vip said.

"How do you figure religious out of that?" asked Marten.

"The spirit part," Vip said.

"Oh," Marten said. "So, Lance, are you religious?"

"Of course. The whole thing is self-evident."

"What do you mean?" asked Vip.

"Look, there's God and the devil, right?" said Lance.

"Right," Marten said, when no one else answered.

"Well, look around you," said Lance. "The devil is supposed to be the Lord of Evil, and I see a lot of evil around this solar system. It proves beyond a doubt that the devil is alive and well."

"Okay," Vip said. "But that doesn't mean God is real."

"Oh yes it does," said Lance. "Because how did the devil get here unless God made him? For evil to be around there has to be God."

"God made evil?" Marten asked.

179

"No!" said Lance. "Without God there's no conception of evil. You don't know something unless you see its opposite. And since we've seen so much evil, well, that proves God is real."

"I'm not psychotic," Kang said.

Lance guffawed.

"Am I psychotic, Omi?"

"No," Omi said.

"Oh, right," said Lance, "he has to say that 'cause he knows you'll kill him if he doesn't."

"Maybe you're not psychotic, Kang" Vip said. "But you're a bastard. I'd rather have Marten as maniple leader."

"None of that," Marten said. "Kang is in charge."

"But you know that you're a better tactician than Kang," said Lance. "You're better than Mad Vlad, too. Hauptsturmfuhrer. I thought the Highborn always made logical choices, especially in matters of combat. This time they screwed up."

"I've been thinking about that," Marten said.

"I don't want to have to shoot you, Marten," Kang said.

"No, not about you being maniple leader," Marten said. "You're welcome to it."

"Are you saying that you don't want to be maniple leader?" asked Kang. He sounded dubious.

"Forget about that, will you?" Marten said. "I'm talking about the Highborn."

Omi spoke quietly. "These comlines might be bugged, Marten."

After Marten stopped laughing, he said, "That's good. We're traveling at twenty-five-Gs into oblivion and you're worried that the HBs might be tapping us. Screw them."

"That's insubordination," Kang said.

"So what?"

"So once we're out of here the discipline codes state that—"

"Kang," Marten said. "What if we don't get out of here?"

Silence.

Finally Vip said, "Don't talk defeatist."

"Why don't you switch your HUD to the stars instead of all that porn you've been watching," Marten said.

"Yeah, so," Vip said a few seconds later.

"Aren't the stars beautiful?"

"Marten's cracking up," Vip said.

"No," Marten said. "I'm facing the fact that this might be it. And that's thanks to the HBs. So like I said before: Screw them."

"You have a point," said Lance.

"No he doesn't," Kang said. "You live by the rules given you. You survive."

"Screw the rules," Marten said. "You live by being who you are."

"Or you die if that's too far out of whack with everyone else," said Lance.

"Maybe," Marten said. "Or maybe you find somewhere else to go, somewhere sane."

"Like where?" asked Lance.

"The Outer Planets."

"Enough of that," Kang said. "While I'm leader, you'll can that kind of talk."

"Doesn't it bother you being shot at the *Bangladesh?*" asked Marten. "The fact that you're nothing more than a biological bullet?"

"Ain't nothing I can do about that," Kang said.

"Isn't there?"

A heavy sigh. "Your problem, Marten, is that you're a dreamer. The world chews up dreamers and spits them out."

"Or we change the world," Marten said.

"One time out of a thousand," Kang said. "The way I count, those are poor odds."

"Okay," Marten said. "You want to let them hook you to the harness like a horse, you go ahead. You want to let them stuff you into a missile and fire you into a frozen void, you do that."

"You're letting them do it to you too," Kang said.

"What I'm saying," Marten said, "is that maybe we should rethink that."

"Rethink it how?" asked Lance.

"Maybe by declaring our independence," Marten said.

Silence.

"If I'm psychotic," Kang said, "you're a complete nut."

"Omi, tell them about the gelding."

Quietly, Omi did just that. When he was done, there was more silence.

"Yeah," said Lance. "A rotten deal if I ever heard of one. But this independence... I don't get it."

"I'll shoot the lot of you," Kang said. "You get *that*, don't you?"

"All I'm saying is that we have to be ready to seize our chance," Marten said. "If we see it—I'm going for it."

"First we have to get onto the beamship," Omi said. "Tell me how we're going to do that."

"Well," Marten said, "by first hoping that our masters have outsmarted the enemy, and that our missile reaches the *Bangladesh*, and then that the beamship doesn't kill us. Then we can worry about whether we fight our way aboard or not."

They thought about that.

"I'll shoot anybody that does something stupid," Kang said. "And if you're thinking about fragging your maniple leader, then I'll shoot you even sooner."

Marten sighed. "Look at the stars for a while, will you? And then think about your life, what it means, what it is worth and what it's all about. Maybe while you're at it you can think about Lance's God, too."

"Or the devil," Vip said.

"Sure," Marten said. "Why not? It seems like he's making the rules these days."

12.

At first, General Hawthorne was dazed. The chief members of his staff were dead, blown away by Air Marshal Ulrich. A PHC-squad in Joho Park had come to whisk him away to who knew where and for what nefarious reason. And that neural inhibitor on his neck—the bionic captain had noticed it while they descended the stairs. He'd peeled it off, and later had said that he'd felt its vibration. Reflexively the captain had clutched the neural inhibitor in his hand, and watched his hand explode a second later.

The captain was in surgery even now, as they grafted a new and better bionic hand onto him.

General Hawthorne had been dazed by the audacity of the attack, the bloody-handedness and slyness of it. It smacked of Chief Yezhov.

Right away, he noticed the rest of Bunker Command turning restive, wary, as if he had an incurable disease. Oh, at first, they made protesting noises about the immorality of the attack, but it seemed more as a matter of form than genuine passion. They soon checked themselves, and seemed to calculate their words, as if they were being recorded for posterity. Or maybe for some PHC officer later who tested their loyalty to Social Unity.

An unasked question seemed to hover on everyone's lips. If PHC could reach the General and his staff, whom couldn't they touch?

Fortunately, his dazedness didn't last.

A march to his private office, throwing open the bottom drawer and lifting the bottle of vodka there had begun the healing. He poured himself a stiff jolt and tossed it down. His eyes bulged as the warmth blossomed in his gut. He poured himself another. He blinked several times, the dazed, unreal feeling draining from him. In its place came a cold clarity.

He set the tumbler and bottle on the desk. He went to his private closet, rummaging in the back until he found his old belt and holster. He strapped it on, looping the one belt over his right shoulder and hooking it to the belt around his waist. He slapped the holster. In it was a small gun, but brutal, a short-barrel .44 that shot exploding slugs.

He marched to the command center. People grew quiet. A few noticed the holster, although no one commented. He stalked about until they went back to work. Then he eavesdropped, trying to gauge how far they would step out for him, for him personally.

With his new clarity, he was shocked to realize that it wasn't very far at all. Maybe six months ago right after the asteroid attacks they would have. Today... some muttered about PHC's latest purge. It was called the Anti-Rightist Purification. *Rightist* in SU jargon usually meant capitalists when referring to Outer Planets people or the military when talking about Inner Planets. It came to him that he'd been so concerned about his proton beams and merculite missiles that he'd forgotten to worry about the home front. About people.

Theoretically, of course, all power in Inner Planets stemmed from the Directorate, the nine that guided the people through the principles of Social Unity. Also in theory, each director was equal. In fact, some were more equal than others. Since the dictatorial days of the late Lord Director Enkov, Blanche-Aster had taken the mantle of leadership. In deference to her position, she bore the title: *Madam* Blanche-Aster. She deemed the title inoffensive but still original to her and signifying the manner of her guidance. "I am the mother of humanity," she was fond of saying. "And as a mother I wish to be gentle but firm, unwavering as I uphold Social Unity."

She backed him, and she had forced the rest of the Directorate to do likewise.

184

A call two hours later showed him yet another crack in his position. Fortunately, he took the call in a side room, a communications center.

"General Hawthorne?"

"Yes, Director."

The man in the wavering holo-image sat in a chair. He was a big man, a Venusian, and he wore an old-fashioned bond lord uniform. He had a square face and a blunt nose, with sagging jowls that wobbled as he spoke. He was seventy-five and he was therefore the youngest and most physically active of the Directorate.

Director Gannel swept a beefy hand in a theatrical gesture. Heavy brass rings encircled each finger. He loved to strike poses as he spoke. It was an old habit from his hall leader days in the thorium mines.

Director Gannel had arrived several months ago from Venus. His was a daring tale of braving the Highborn space blockade of his terraformed planet and slipping onto an "open" farm hab orbiting Earth. From there he'd taken a grain transport down to Australia Sector and slipped aboard one of Earth's last submarines and to India. In the readjustments that had occurred after the late Lord Director's death, Gannel had skillfully maneuvered his way into a director's chair.

"Then the rumors aren't true," said Gannel.

"Rumors?" asked Hawthorne.

His jowls wobbled as Gannel smiled, showing big white teeth so obviously false that they made him look like a vampire.

You want to suck my blood, you obscene old plotter.

"Why, General, it's been said that you were shot."

"How very interesting," said Hawthorne. "And who was the supposed shooter?"

"Why, I don't know," said Director Gannel.

"You do seem surprised to see me alive."

The holo-image shimmered. HB jamming and the incredibly bad storms since the asteroid attacks had adversely affected communications. Soon the image settled down.

"Yes! I am surprised," Gannel said. "Surprised that anyone would be fool enough to joke with me. To tell me you were dead."

"Well, then, Director, if that's all. It's been a pleasure, of course, speaking with you."

"Wait a minute, General. Now that I have you online there's something, well, I hope I haven't heard two wrong rumors in one day. But there's talk that you plan to prematurely order the *Bangladesh* to break off its attack."

And who leaked that? Hawthorne wondered. *Oh, of course, the Air Marshal.*

"Yes, Director. It's time to cut and run."

In his communications studio in New Baghdad, the big Venusian hunched forward, his brawler's fists clenched, showing off the heavy brass rings. "Now look here, General, that's just the sort of talk I'm sick of hearing."

"Of a successful hit and run?"

"You know that isn't what I mean. This entire... I'm going to use a word I hope you don't find offensive, General: Cowardice."

"Why would I find a charge of cowardice offensive?"

"I'm not calling you that, of course."

"Ah, splendid."

"But what else can one say to this suggestion of running away when we're finally hurting these bastards?"

"I see. Then maybe you should consider this, Director. Three irreplaceable spacecraft didn't cut and run in the Venus System. They stuck around to trade fire with the enemy. Those three missile ships were destroyed."

"Of course they were!" said Gannel. "These piecemeal attacks of yours, General, are suicide."

"Strategy drives the tactics, Director. Our present strategy is the death of a thousand cuts, to bleed the enemy to death one Highborn at a time. There are only two million of them. Thus, one hits hard and runs, to fight another day. What one doesn't do is trade blows with the Highborn or get greedy and go for more than is reasonable. Because their one great advantage is the ability to win any sustained engagement, usually in spectacular fashion."

"Don't lecture me. I know all about strategy and tactics. How do you think I achieved my rank?"

"I can't say I know. We're dealing with Highborn. Not Venusian rabble."

The cold calculating stare of Director Gannel seemed to measure Hawthorne. "I'm going to be frank, General. We don't like this splitting of the Fleet, this nipping at our enemy's heels. Our battleships should be kept together and used to strike at one precise point, to break the grip of the Highborn one at a time at each of the four planets."

"After we've sufficiently hemorrhaged them, yes, I quite agree."

"We don't have that kind of time, General. We must strike now! We must crush this rebellion before the Highborn gain allies from the Outer Planets."

"It is we who should be seeking allies," said Hawthorne.

"No!"

"Director—"

"You'd better listen to me, General. The Directorate is weary of your defeatist talk. Boldness! We want boldness in our planning."

Hawthorne pursed his lips. With his cold clarity, he analyzed the situation. He nodded. "Very well."

"Furthermore—what did you say?"

"I agree."

"You agree to what?"

"Boldness."

"If this is some verbal trick, General."

"No. You're right. This is a time for boldness."

Director Gannel leaned back. "Uh, yes, yes, good. Very good, General. I'm glad to hear you say that. You are a man of reason after all. I just hope… Well. I'm glad we could have this talk."

"As am I, Director Gannel."

Gannel glanced at something in his room that was out of sight of his holo-projector. "I must beg your pardon, General, my agenda forces me to cut the conversation short."

"Good bye, Director," said Hawthorne.

The communications ended as the holo-image collapsed into a tiny dot of light and winked out.

It left General Hawthorne silent and thoughtful. He finally rose and began to pace around the holoset. What had Commodore Tivoli told him before her untimely death? There was rioting in New Baghdad, in the capital.

He whirled around and strode for the door.

13.

No one would remember later who ordered the autopsy. But Air Marshal Ulrich's corpse lay on an operating table deep in Bunker Command's Medical Facility. Doctor Varro, the two technicians and a nurse had discovered an odd reading from Ulrich's skull. An x-ray showed tiny filaments running through the frontal lobes and a strange little device embedded near the pituitary gland.

"Can you make any sense out of it?" asked Doctor Varro. She showed them the x-ray.

The two technicians shook their heads.

"Nurse?"

"It's ghastly. Sticking things in a man's brain. Who did it?"

"Yes," said Doctor Varro, a slender woman, who had helped create over twenty bionic men. "Who indeed?"

"Should we run more tests?" asked the more cautious technician.

Doctor Varro studied the x-ray. What was that little device beside the pituitary gland? Her green eyes shone with curiosity. "Get the cranial saw," she said.

The nurse picked it up, a small circular saw, and handed it to Doctor Varro.

The more cautious technician grabbed the x-ray off the tray and peered at it again. He didn't like it, not one bit.

The cranial saw whirred into life. Doctor Varro leaned over the skull.

"Excuse me," said the more cautious technician. He hurried out of the operating room, heading for the lavatory.

Thus, only he survived the explosion that obliterated the corpse's skull and killed Doctor Varro, the other technician and the nurse. For the next two-and-a-half hours, the more cautious technician retold his story to the MI operatives grilling him on what exactly had happened. *Don't leave out any facts. Do you understand?*

He did understand, and he didn't leave out any facts. Not even the one that he practiced meditation and firmly believed in gut level instincts. Didn't they trust their own?

They did, so they drugged him, and were surprised to find out he was telling the truth. So much for the instinctual theory.

14.

General Hawthorne paced. The reports lay thick on his desk. A spontaneous riot, they called it. Several directors had fled the city. Their location was presently unknown. Nor had he been able to get through to the Madam Director, who was said to be under siege in the Directorate Complex, on New Baghdad's ninth level. Her communications were tied up, or else it was very good jamming.

His door swished open and his wife, Martha Hawthorne, rushed in,. She peered at him, her eyes worried and she came into his arms.

"James," she whispered.

They kissed and he released her, looking into her face. She was small and in her mid-forties. Still a beautiful woman with dark, shoulder-length hair and deep dark eyes, she wore a modest executive outfit. Their only daughter went to school in Montreal, Quebec Sector. Martha ran financing for Data Corp., but she'd joined him at Bunker Command ever since May 10.

They spoke tenderly, and he unburdened himself. In time, she sat at his desk, scanning the reports. She picked one up, her eyes narrowing.

"Did you see this, James?"

He stopped his incessant pacing to frown at her.

"Cybertanks in the capital," she said.

"In New Baghdad?"

She nodded.

"That seals it then."

"James," she said. "You must tread carefully. You know that PHC is already purging the army units you brought over from England Sector."

"They tried to kidnap me, Martha. Turning Air Marshal Ulrich to do their filthy deeds! They even put electrodes in his brain."

"But they failed to take you, my dear."

"Only because of Captain Mune. The rest of the military—" He shook his head. "They're paralyzed with fear and uncertainty."

She set down the cybertank report and took to worrying a fingernail with her teeth. Despite his love for her, he disliked watching her do that. It annoyed him, but he'd learned to keep quiet about it. He resumed pacing.

"The bionic men are different," she said.

"Quite."

"No. I don't mean the obvious difference of their bionics. They're... Everyone hates them."

He shrugged.

"They hate their strength, their power and bravery." Her eyes widened. "They hate their individuality."

"What do you mean?"

"The bionic men are different, James. They're not SU. Consider: Each has been carefully crafted into a devastating fighting man. He's unique, a one of a kind. Other people fear them because of that. Because most people are... aren't unique. Thus, the bionic men avoid the masses, staying among their own. And as if to heighten their differences, the late Lord-Director gathered them into a single unit and gave them vast discretionary powers."

"Police powers," said the General.

"No, more of an imperial guard power. They were loyal to him, guarded his interests when he wasn't there."

"Hmm," said the General, recalling the horrible asteroid attack on May 10, how Captain Mune had stopped him from launching the nukes that might have broken up the incoming asteroids enough so that the proton beams could have annihilated the separate and much smaller chunks. But the late Lord Director had given a no-nuke launching order without his

192

express permission. They hadn't been able to contact him, and Captain Mune's men, bionic warriors, had watched then in the Command Center to insure complete obedience to the Lord Director and his dictates.

The General grimaced. "I take your point."

"Do you?"

"I can't do without Captain Mune now."

"No, dear, you're missing the point. They're loyal to you, to you personally. They know they're hated. And they know you're the one who saved them from the tribunal. They're no longer Social Unitarians in thought, if they ever were to begin with."

The General considered that.

After the late Lord Director's death, and when Madam Blanche-Aster took over, there had been a tribunal. Someone had to take the official blame for the billion deaths. The bionic guards at the Command Center that day had seemed like the perfect choice. Hawthorne had lobbied hard otherwise, and for good reason.

Before Lord Director Enkov had died, Captain Mune had taken the General to the Director's HQ. There the captain had shot and killed the Lord Director, because during the trip Hawthorne had convinced him that the Lord Director would sacrifice him, the captain, in order to shift the blame of the stupid no-nuke launch order. Hawthorne had been certain that he too would be scapegoated, which was why he'd spoken so persuasively that day.

When the members of the tribunal had wished to question the bionic security teams, Hawthorne had taken them under his protection. Right after May 10, when he'd quelled the planet-wide riots, his authority had been vast. He'd simply vetoed the tribunal request. He didn't want to lose his special forces to a witch-hunt, and of course, he'd wanted his role in the... *removal* of the late Lord Director kept quiet. Later he'd come to incorporate the bionic warriors into his own security arrangements.

"I don't intend to sacrifice them, dear," said the General. "I didn't do so then and I won't now."

"I'm not suggesting you sacrifice them."

193

"But you called them un-SU."

"Yes, exactly."

"Don't you realize that's tantamount to signing their death warrants?"

"James, I'm telling you that here is the answer. You need loyal troops, isn't that right? Everyone else thinks like good, card-carrying Social Unitarians. Even your elite troops do. They're all terrified of PHC."

General Hawthorne saw her point, and then he saw deeper. A chill swept through him. Did he really have the nerve? For several seconds he stood frozen, trying to consider the angles. He couldn't. This had to be a gut thing. A tight grin forced its way to his lips. *Do it*, a deep part in him whispered. *Better to try and fail than never to have tried at all.*

He strode to the desk. His wife moved aside so he could sit down. He picked up the cybertank report, reading it thoroughly. Finally, he slapped the report onto the desk and pressed his intercom button. "Get me Colonel Manteuffel. And tell him to bring the cybertank codes. All of them! What? No. Don't argue. Just do what I order."

"What are thinking, dear?"

"Um," he said, picking up another report, one that gave the positions of the army units nearest the capital.

"James," she said, touching his shoulder.

He glanced up.

"Are you..." Fear had drained the color from her cheeks.

"They struck first, Martha."

"Maybe that's what Yezhov is planning for. An overreaction on your part."

The General smiled coldly. "Maybe. But I doubt he expects a *coup d'etat* from me." A harsh laugh slipped out. He rose, and turned as the door swished open. Captain Mune, with his new hand bandaged, entered and saluted.

"Excellent timing, Captain. Come with me."

15.

The tube-train whisked toward New Baghdad at 400 kilometers an hour. It rode a cushion of polarized magnetism, a mechanical worm hidden from the HB space-laser stations. Seven cars were linked together, holding less than a battalion.

Sitting together, General James Hawthorne conferred with Colonel Manteuffel, the younger brother of slain Commodore Tivoli. The Colonel was an inch over five feet, a terrier of a man with a keen, alert bearing and a shiny bald head. He wore the black uniform of a tanker, and was the General's expert on cybertanks. On his lap lay a thin computerized briefcase full of CT codes.

The cybertanks were the latest in the dehumanization of war. Human brain tissue from criminals who had been liquidated for the good of the state or purchased from Callistoian brain thieves had been carefully teased from the main brain mass. All former personality was carefully scrubbed from the tissue, embedded in special cryo-sheets, and surrounded by programming gel. Several kilos of this processed brain tissue could replace tons of specialized control and volitional systems. Just as important, military virtues encoded into these biocomps gave them a human-like cunning and bloodthirstiness. Naturally, emergency override codes had been built into such deadly war-machines. The entirety of Social Unity cybertank codes lay in the briefcase propped on Colonel Manteuffel's knees.

Ten normals surrounded the general, volunteers from Commodore Tivoli's MI section. Each had lost a friend or

195

relative to PHC in the last few months of undercover war. They worked out schedules of arrival and wrote out movement orders for the General's troops nearest New Baghdad. The troop commanders were given no explanations for the movement orders. To them it would appear all very innocent.

As Hawthorne had said, "The most important thing is that they move. It will send the PHC assessors into their think tanks to figure out what it all means."

"And what does it mean?" asked a MI operative.

"Misdirection and time," said Hawthorne, and then on that subject he would say no more.

The rest of the seven train-cars contained bionic men, big, bulky warriors with bionic body-parts and commando-style weapons and training.

Less than a thousand men to take over the rule of forty billion, mused Hawthorne. But hopefully it was the right thousand, at the right place and at the right time. Otherwise... Maybe they'd stuff a mini-bomb into his cortex as they'd done to Ulrich, or maybe they'd just line him up against a wall to be shot.

"One hour to New Baghdad," called an MI operative.

Hawthorne rose, his cap set at a rakish angle. He grinned, exuding confidence. To add to the pose he clutched his belt with both hands. "Boldness," he said, using a parade ground voice. "Absolute assurance of victory, that's what I expect from each of you." And he continued to encourage them as the tube-train zoomed toward his destiny or destruction.

16.

The very audacity of the raid aided General Hawthorne. He had also predicated it upon the fact that none of the megalopolises, the super-cities, could remain self-contained for any appreciable amount of time. New Baghdad wasn't any different. The city's population of over 200 million needed billions of different items, the majority of which arrived via tube-train. Clothing, food and water made up the bulk of the needs, and manufactured goods. Tube-trains thus arrived around the clock and from many varying directions. PHC had taken control by manning critical rail posts and switchyards with armored shock squads. General Hawthorne's answer had become routine by the time they reached the last checkpoint.

The tube-trained stopped because cannons trained on the line would have, at PHC orders, destroyed it. The front train doors slid open and a five-man squad in red plastic body armor stormed aboard. They bore carbines or lasers. Usually a sneering, arrogant PHC major followed, a man or woman used to obedience and seeing others cringe in fear. Waiting bionic men plucked the weapons from the surprised shock squad members and then threw them to the floor. The bionic strength always won against human muscles. Another bionic man slapped the major's communicator from his hand and put a vibroblade under his chin. At a nod from the MI operative who did the talking, the bionic soldier flicked the blade. Its awful hum and vibrating power so very near the major's throat had a debilitating effect on the previous arrogance.

A door opened on the last tube-car and a ten-man bionic commando team fanned out. As on so many of these posts along the way, General Hawthorne received the all-clear signal minutes later.

Five bionic men stayed behind at the post or switchyard, with the subdued PHC major to answer any calls from higher headquarters. Whenever the PHC major spoke by comlink or holo-transmission, an ugly hand cannon was aimed between his eyes. So far, the ploy had proven effective. Thus for the last two hundred kilometers, ten of these squads, fifty bionic warriors in all, kept the link to New Baghdad open for Hawthorne to his nearest Army Command Post.

"Let's hope the next part is as easy," Colonel Manteuffel said.

"You know it won't be," Hawthorne said.

17.

"She won't budge," Director Gannel said. He hunched over a communicator in his inner sanctum. Outside his door waited his Venusian security team, people who had been with him since his thorium mining days.

"Tell her the Highborn plan another asteroid attack," answered Yezhov, Chief of PHC. "That they're targeting New Baghdad."

"I did," said Gannel. "She doesn't believe it. She asks why I don't flee then."

"Maybe you should."

Gannel laughed. "Oh, no, Yezhov. We're partners, but no more than that. I'm not putting myself in your custody."

"A little more faith on your part would greatly smooth our plans, Director."

"So would divine power. But I don't see any."

"Then we'll have to squeeze her," said Yezhov.

"Dangerous."

"Yes, at least until the new conditioning is implemented."

"True, true," said Gannel. "But…"

"What troubles you, Director?"

"Do you trust the cybertanks?"

"Of course I don't *trust* them."

"You know what I mean," said Gannel. "It's a dangerous expedient using them."

"Oh, but the mobs fear them so. Frankenstein monsters, they say. Once you're in charge you must order the Military to turn over all the cybertanks to PHC."

199

"Certainly," said Gannel, who had no intention of doing so. He already feared Yezhov more than any man. Only his lust for the chairmanship kept him working with such a devious, untrustworthy schemer.

"Yes, it's time to squeeze Blanche-Aster," said Yezhov. "We have to finish this before the mobs become used to running amok. Call her in…an hour."

"And if that doesn't work?"

"Then we may be wishing that the Highborn really do drop an asteroid."

18.

After inexplicably failing to gain control of a selected cybertank, Colonel Manteuffel tucked the compucase under his arm and sprinted down the street as if the devil himself chased him. The small officer dove behind an overturned car. Behind him, rounding the heavy building's corner where he'd just been, clanked the 100-ton cybertank he'd failed to control. Bricks and twisted girders exploded out of the building's corner. The edge of the metal monster simply shouldered through, heavy treads crunching over the debris. The 100-ton cybertank then wheeled in its uniquely ponderous way toward Manteuffel

Manteuffel crawled madly, tearing and scuffing his black tanker's uniform.

Two bionic men lunged from behind another building. They grabbed the Colonel by the arms and pulled him behind their corner. At the same instant, one of the cybertank's six warfare pods aimed its cannon. A deafening roar issued. The overturned car exploded. Explosive pellets ricocheted off the street, as two antipersonnel pods chugged a thousand rounds.

The bionic men didn't hesitate. They ran. One of them threw the small Manteuffel unceremoniously over his shoulder. Servos and bionic parts whined as they pumped their legs like pistons. Manteuffel clenched his teeth. The jar of the bionic man's shoulder thrust against his gut threatened to tear Manteuffel's stomach muscles loose. Thankfully, however, the heavy, clanking sound of the cybertank receded. They fled several blocks, zigzagging through the city, until they reached where General Hawthorne waited with the bulk of the commandos.

Dumped onto his feet, Colonel Manteuffel leaned against a nearby wall. His pale face winced horribly. When he straightened, it felt as if a knife had slashed through his gut. A MI operative thrust something in his face. Oh. Manteuffel nodded, and with a trembling hand, he accepted a bottle of medication.

"Well?" asked Hawthorne. "What happened?"

They stood in a brick-laid plaza, open-air shops surrounding them. Overhead the level's sunlamps shone at 'daytime' brightness.

Manteuffel sipped the soothing liquid.

"If you could spare us a moment, Colonel."

"It's like we thought," Manteuffel said between gasps. "The cybertanks have been tampered with."

"Yes," said Hawthorne, "I can see that. But tampered how? You told me before that if anyone tried to breach their brain-case that it would detonate."

Manteuffel grimaced. "Just like the Air Marshal."

"Now isn't the time to get sentimental, Colonel."

"Sorry, sir."

Hawthorne waved it aside. He paced as his bionic commandos waited in their teams. They were on the ninth level, very near the Directorate Building and Madam Blanche-Aster's residence. Unfortunately, cybertanks kept anyone from approaching too closely.

"How did PHC sabotage the CT codes?" asked Hawthorne.

"I'm not sure they did," Manteuffel said.

"But you just said the cybertanks have been tampered with."

"Yes, but maybe not in the manner we first envisioned it."

"Explain."

"The cybertanks are human."

Hawthorne raised his eyebrows.

Manteuffel pushed himself off the wall and lowered his voice. "Are the bionic warriors human?"

"Of course they are."

"But they're part machine."

202

Hawthorne frowned before nodding. "You're saying that the cybertanks are part machine, but also partly human?"

"Entirely machine," Manteuffel said, "except for the brain."

"But not a real brain," said Hawthorne. "The brain tissue is from various donors and set in programming gel."

"Don't be deceived, General. Each cybertank quickly gains its own personality. They begin to think of themselves as human."

"Oh very well, Colonel. Now get to the point."

"I think PHC convinced the cybertanks to go along with whatever it is they're planning."

"They're part of the coup?" asked Hawthorne.

"No. Not that far in. The Mark 2042 I spoke with believes that he's protecting the government."

"You spoke to him?" said Hawthorne. "Then why didn't the override codes work?"

"I think we'll find that a new input plug was inserted."

"Is that possible?"

"The fact that the override codes don't work seems to prove it."

Hawthorne paced. "What if we yanked the new input plug?"

Manteuffel nodded, and then he winced because the head motion made his stomach rip with pain. Through clenched teeth, he said, "Maybe pulling this new plug would allow us to use the CT codes. But how would we get in close enough to pull it?"

"You're the expert!" shouted Hawthorne. He frowned as bionic men turned toward him. "Sorry, Colonel. But that's your area of expertise. Don't you know of a way?"

Manteuffel sipped from the medical bottle. He considered his torn stomach muscles. Then he studied the bionic men. Soon he said, "Yes, I think there is a way."

19.

The Mark 2042 Cybertank prowled the area of the subterfuge attack. He seethed with rage, but not enough so that he disobeyed orders and left the perimeter given him to guard. In the background rose the monumental Directorate Building. Around it fanned broad streets, plazas, fountains and squat, pentagonal government buildings.

The Mark 2042 exulted in his might and ability to destroy. In all human history, no warrior could do what he did. He was 100 tons of lethality, 20 meters by 12 by 5. Heavy tracks and a Zeitzler 5000 Electromagnetic Engine provided him motive power. He loved the sound of his clanking tracks as he chased the primitive bio-beasts. He had six interchangeable weapons pods, giving him more firepower and flexibility than any warrior ever born or made. To protect him from missiles and cannon shells he had beehive flechette launchers, exploding shrapnel that knocked them down before they could strike. The forty beehives also made excellent antipersonnel systems. Earlier this week he'd exploded one of them into a crowd, killing five hundred at a single blow. How the others had fled after that! He'd recorded it, and replayed the video whenever he was bored. That's how he knew it was 500. Well, precisely 489 dead and wounded. He'd shot the wounded one at a time or smeared them into the pavement with his treads.

On open terrain, his great weight allowed him to fire his magnetic force cannons and heavy lasers even when he moved at top speed. The 100 tons and uncanny shock systems provided the needed stability. And to complete his uniqueness and near invulnerability was his covering of 260mm-thick composite armor.

No one in New Baghdad could take him, and he knew it. The great threat of air attacks and worse, space lasers, ha, they couldn't touch him down here on the ninth city level. Oh no. If everything worked out right, it was city duty from here on in.

He shot off fifty tracers to punctuate his thought.

Tremble, worms. Hear me roar and flee like the vermin you are.

His radar and visuals had picked up movement and weaponry. He knew that several bio-beasts with strange mechanical readings prowled his precinct. What the Mark 2042 didn't know was that he'd fallen prey to one of man's oldest vices: arrogance.

Suddenly, three of the unusual bio-beasts rolled onto the street, heavy rocket launchers aimed at him. The whoosh of rocket ignition sped the missiles on their way.

How pathetic, a rookie's assault.

The Mark 2042 chugged shrapnel from a single beehive. He meant it as a shrug. The missiles blew apart. Then he revved the mighty Zeitzler 5000 and let his treads rip, tearing chunks of pavement as he gave chase.

But these three were different from other bio-beasts. Their legs pumped fast, and they moved faster. Each time he fired at them, they dodged around another corner.

Well, watch this.

He swiveled his 100-ton bulk and charged into a building. Masonry exploded. He plowed, his treads churning over desks, chairs and waiting sofas. Glass shattered and walls disappeared. Bricks rained on him.

I am unstoppable.

He burst through the rear wall and onto the next street.

The three bio-beasts had nowhere to hide. He had them dead in his sights. Usually bio-beasts gaped in horror right about now, or they started crying. He got a kick out of that. But these three were different. It's why he'd gone through the building. They dropped to their bellies and aimed their rocket launchers.

Now that's a sweet try, rookies. But I'm the big boy.

A thousand antipersonnel shells disintegrated them.

Hey, where'd you go?

As a joke, pretending he was looking for them, he clanked atop their gory shreds and then wheeled, smearing them into the pavement.

Then his sensors pinged with a new attack.

Twenty of them popped up from twenty different locations, firing lasers and rocket launchers. He shrugged off their feeble efforts, but it was nice to see they were trying. Then his probability indicator flashed a warning.

Why were they all ready for him here? Why was this particular spot seemingly point-zero?

Are you rookies trying to trap me?

Twenty of these tougher, strange-reading bio-beasts dropped from the ceiling. They dropped from the sunlamps way up there. Oh, this was going to be rich. He knew bio-beasts, what their water-sack bodies could take and what they couldn't. From that high up...

I have to get this on video.

They would go splat, gushing organs and blood everywhere.

The probability indicator flashed another warning.

Pipe down and let me have some fun, will you?

Radar and visuals showed that the twenty falling bio-beasts lacked weapons or breaching bombs.

It's raining men. Hallelujah!

Slam, slam, slam, they dropped atop him. But they didn't go splat.

Warning!—that from the probability indicator.

Servos in the bio-beasts whined. The Mark 2042 could hear them. A few of them had broken limbs or hands, but now they started crawling over him.

Die!

All forty beehives exploded shrapnel, lifting and killing fifteen of them.

Now let's try the new grid, shall we.

An electrical grid had been installed onto him twelve days ago. He charged it with power. ZAP!

Two of them actually screamed.

It was a dance of death.

But one of them still crawled.

A pesky rookie, aren't you?

A camera showed him the bio-beast's screwed up face. That was beautiful. This one was really trying, fighting through the pain and everything.

Warning!

He understood. The beast crawled for the crevice where the red suits had put the new server.

ZAP!

The bio-beast bellowed, but he kept crawling. And then he dropped into that crevice.

"DON'T TOUCH THAT!" The Mark 2042 cranked his speakers to full volume.

The bio-beast didn't listen.

Suddenly the Mark 2042 felt disoriented, dizzy, and not so certain about everything.

"Cybertank 2042," said someone via comlink.

"Yes?"

"Prepare for transmission."

"I... 2042 ready," said the Mark 2042.

20.

Colonel Manteuffel typed in the CT code and pressed transmit. Then he studied the return reading before looking up at General Hawthorne.

"He's ours."

"Yes, after twenty-three good men died," Hawthorne said.

"We can use the Mark 2042 to approach the other cybertanks."

"But we could still lose more men," said Hawthorne. "I wasn't counting on those electrical surges."

"PHC must have put that in," said Manteuffel. "It's clever. You have to give them that."

Hawthorne stared at the small Colonel. Finally, he forced a smile as he patted the man's shoulder. "Well done, Manteuffel. Now let's convert the other cybertanks."

21.

The old woman in the wheelchair heard gunfire.

She peered over the balcony railing and at the squat buildings below. Fruitless apple trees lined the empty streets. Well, empty of people, at least. Dropped placards and crumpled papers lay everywhere, but that no longer concerned her. She counted five cybertanks. Giant watchdogs, they surrounded her building. An hour ago, she had considered them protection from the protesting mobs that had been chased away by PHC shock squads. After listening to General Hawthorne, she wondered if the cybertanks were the final move in an intricate PHC plot to overthrow the government.

She was one hundred and sixty-two, kept alive by longevity treatments and her special chair. She sat in the bulky, gleaming-white unit. A withered old crone, her detractors called her. The medical unit in back of the wheelchair gurgled softly. Tubes from it snaked into her. Fluids surged through the tubes. Her unnaturally smooth face seemed brittle, although it was dotted by several stubborn liver spots that none of the skin specialists had been able to remove. She wore a white turban to cover her baldness, while a red plaid blanket hid her useless legs. A jutting, narrow nose and bright eyes, dangerously vibrant, belied any idea that she was senile.

Madam Director Blanche-Aster wasn't native to New Baghdad, the famed city of seventy-seven levels. According to Chief Yezhov of Political Harmony Corps, the rioting had been spontaneous and sudden, catching everyone by surprise. PHC most of all. She cocked her head. There it was again. Gunfire!

Dropping her trembling hand onto the chair's controls, she wheeled around, off the balcony and into her office. The space was minimalist, containing nothing but a few large off-white cubes randomly placed on the floor as *objects d'art,* and her chrome desk that was keyed to her voice.

General James Hawthorne sat on one of the cubes. He was flanked by Captain Mune standing. She shivered. She didn't like the bionic men. It was unnatural doing that to a person. Then she looked at her wheelchair. The irony did not escape her.

The General, against all the rules of someone in her presence, wore a holster and sidearm. His granite face gave little away. But she was practiced in body kinetics and read the tension in him.

"It's most incredible," she said. "Air Marshal Ulrich. How were they able to turn him?"

"Does it matter?" asked Hawthorne.

"But Yezhov is a madman if he thinks he can just send an assassin and shoot me."

"How many directors are in the city?" asked Hawthorne.

"What? Oh, um, Director Gannel, for one."

"The Venusian?" Hawthorne asked.

"What difference does that make?"

"He's Yezhov's puppet."

"You're shooting in the dark, making unsubstantiated accusations."

"Director Gannel has flooded my headquarters with demands that I launch an immediate, all-out Fleet attack against one of the systems."

"The majority of the Directorate backs him on that," said Blanche-Aster.

"And it backs him on the continued beam-assault against the Sun Works Factory. When now is the moment to break off the attack."

"No," said Blanche-Aster, "you simply don't understand, General. After many bitter months we're finally hurting them, making them bleed. You must continue to do so for as long as possible. It does wonders for morale."

General Hawthorne rose. "Our initial assessment—by long-range radar scan—showed great damage to the Sun Works Factory. But now our radar is jammed and any visuals are hidden because of a vast aerosol cloud. We must never forget that the Highborn react with uncanny speed. The longer we attack, the less damage we will actually do."

"That's speculation, not hard fact."

"It's an *assessment* from having watched and studied their reactions on many occasions."

A chime sounded. She raised a withered hand. "Enter."

The door swished open and her chief bodyguard stepped in. She was young and hard-eyed, with a buzz haircut and with a long, supple body armored in silvery mesh. When they had first arrived, the bionic men had relieved the bodyguard of her weapons. The General maintained that he didn't want any hasty mistakes.

"Yezhov has arrived in the building," the bodyguard said.

Blanche-Aster pursed her ancient lips. "Which directors are still in the city?"

"From our last reports, Madam, only Director Gannel remains here."

"That's it?" asked Blanche-Aster.

"Yes, Madam."

Blanche-Aster's eyes seemed to glitter. She had a narrow, hatchet-thin face, remarkably similar to her bodyguard's. She peered out the window, then back at General Hawthorne and then to her bodyguard. "Has Yezhov seen Director Gannel?"

"None of my operatives think so, Madam. But that was before…" The bodyguard glanced at Captain Mune.

Blanche-Aster gave her a minute nod, then turned to Hawthorne. "Despite your predications, Yezhov has come when summoned."

"I'm very surprised, to say the least," said Hawthorne.

"Surprised, General? Don't you mean elated?"

A hard smile edged onto Hawthorne's lips.

"If you and your guard will be kind enough to step into the other room I'll let Yezhov in," Blanche-Aster said.

"Madam Director, I wish to remind you that my…that you have a new security arrangement, which I hope you'll keep in mind," Hawthorne said. "Depending on developments today, perhaps your security teams will be rearmed. I also wish to remind you that the cybertanks are again under Military control."

"This is all highly unusual, General."

"So is the fact that your bodyguards are clones of yourself," said Hawthorne.

Blanche-Aster and her bodyguard traded glances, before she told Hawthorne, "I'm sure you've discovered that finding loyal people is difficult."

General Hawthorne nodded curtly. Then he put his right hand on his holster as he marched into concealment in the next room. Captain Mune followed, although he never took his eyes off the Director's clone.

As soon as the door closed, Madam Blanche-Aster said to her bodyguard, "Let him in."

The door slid open and Yezhov, the Chief of Political Harmony Corps, walked in. He wore a scarlet uniform, with black boots and a black plastic helmet held in place by a black chinstrap. Naturally, he'd surrendered his sidearm before entering the building. The bionic men had stayed out of sight, and the cybertanks had been instructed to act as if they still followed PHC's orders.

Yezhov's skin was pale, with washed-out blue eyes and a ridiculous little mustache, twin dots under his nose. There was nothing else remarkable about his appearance: short and thin, a potbelly and an almost nonexistent chin. Long ago as a youth, he'd failed the Military's physical. Next, the Peacekeeper Academy had flunked him. Choice number three had been Political Harmony Corps. Forty years of dedicated service had finally paid off.

"Madam Director," he said, in a normal, unremarkable voice. He managed a small smile by stretching the corners of his lips.

"Good of you to come, Yezhov."

"I am at your service, Madam."

"Why? To try and convince me to leave the city?"

"Madam knows best, of course."

"Which city would you suggest?"

He pulled his eyebrows together, as if considering it for the first time. "Perhaps not any city, Madam. Highborn espionage has become most cunning lately."

"Meaning?"

"We've begun to suspect that the attack on Beijing wasn't solely to take out the proton beam station."

"That's very interesting," said Blanche-Aster. "How did you arrive at that conclusion?"

He shifted uncomfortably but said nothing.

She said, "The three directors who died there on May 10 influenced your thinking, no doubt."

"Certainly that's part of it."

"But more importantly because such talk scares the other directors into doing whatever you suggest."

"Madam?"

"Come now, Yezhov, let's not lie to each other. This is your moment, is it not?"

"I'm afraid I don't understand."

"I've heard your theories before. You've likened Social Unity to a triangle. How did you explain it? The Party is one point of the angle, the Military the other and finally PHC, our benevolent secret police, complete the geometry. Each is used to keep the masses docile. The Party supplies the propaganda, the slogans that beguile. The Military insures that no one physically harms Social Unity, while PHC watches the people and weeds out the insubordinate. Yet the Military is like a bear, you've been known to say. It is a beast that will devour the other two. For the Military, if unrestrained, could rule alone. Therefore, the Party and the Secret Police hold the leashes that keep the Military from eating them. As long as the two hold on tightly, each is safe. Yet now the Military has been sorely wounded by the Highborn. May 10 and the late Lord Director's foolish policies saw to that."

Yezhov licked his lips.

"I have no intention of leaving the city," Blanche-Aster said.

"What if the Highborn drop an asteroid here?"

"Why would they?"

"To decapitate Social Unity, to kill you and the other directors. I'm afraid that I must insist that you leave, for the good of the State."

"Their targets before were the proton beam stations."

"We can't be certain of Highborn logic, Madam. They don't think like us, after all."

"I'll grant you that. But the changing weather patterns will no doubt cause them to rethink this particular tactic."

"The winds are a temporary inconvenience," Yezhov said. "They're meaningless."

"Some of my meteorologists suggest it is already the beginning of nuclear winter."

"I'm unfamiliar with the term."

"As I'm unfamiliar with giving in to fear. Until Director Gannel flees New Baghdad, I also will remain in the seat of power."

"But the rioters, Madam, what if they storm the Directorate and injure you?"

"You will restrain them long before, of that I have no doubt. However, if it turns out that you cannot, well, Social Unity will quickly find someone who can."

A hint of anger colored his checks. "If you think the Public Security Bureaus have teams who will face the mobs—"

"My dear man: Face the mobs? What a quaint term for the sheep that have lifted their heads and bleated a little louder than usual."

"Madam, I wish you would reconsider."

"Let us talk about General Hawthorne."

Yezhov blinked slowly. For the first time he glanced about the room, noticing the bodyguard. The clone gave him a faint nod. He ignored her and turned to the director.

"There was an attempt upon the General's life," Blanche-Aster said.

"A terrible tragedy. Air Marshal Ulrich became unbalanced."

"Why do you suppose that happened?"

"Madam, the military clique is rife with non-socialist behavior that the rest of us find quite inexplicable."

"Ah, yes. Your latest witch-hunt is called the Anti-Rightist Movement."

"The Highborn rebellion proves the thesis, Madam. The Military is a seedbed for rightist tendencies. PHC works hard to root out this madness."

"To bring *unity* to society?" asked Blanche-Aster.

Yezhov stiffened, and he now spoke with a nasal quality. "Director Blanche-Aster, PHC will mercilessly destroy *any* rightist who dares sabotage Social Unity. High or low, we will root them out."

The one hundred and sixty-two-year-old director leaned forward, pulling the many medical tubes with her. "You dare hint that I'm unorthodox. You dare this here?" The physical effort cost the ancient Blanche-Aster. She fell back into her padded rest.

Yezhov seemed to remember where "here" was. "Madam, I assure you your ideology is not in question."

"I've long served the people and kept them safe from class-enemy exploiters and profit-imperialists. Before you ever memorized the social crèche credo—
"

"We are all tiny cogs in the machine of State service," Yezhov quoted. He stretched his lips in an imitation of a smile. "The Air Marshal's strange behavior proves that we are on the correct path. The Rightist Movement must be stamped out. I'm sure you agree that at this time we cannot tolerate any deviancy in the upper echelons of Social Unity. The ripple effect the billion casualties had on the rest of the populace has left us little room to maneuver."

She stared at the Chief of PHC. "Do you know that the Military found six members of your shock squads in the Joho Park, slain by the General's bodyguard?"

Yezhov shrugged. "Foul slander, Madam."

"I've seen the pictures."

Yezhov shook his head. "Crude plants to throw the blame of this assassination attempt onto PHC."

There was wonder in Blanche-Aster's tone. "Can you be this certain about your position?"

215

"I don't understand."

"You're playing a dangerous game, Yezhov."

"Game, Madam?"

"We suffered brutal losses on May 10. But because of General Hawthorne we inflicted great pain and injury on the Highborn."

"Excuse me, Madam, but several thousand enemy dead, a couple of hundred destroyed orbital fighters and a nearly crippled Doom Star... Those can't compare to a billion deaths."

"I didn't say that. However, those Highborn losses are the best Social Unity has been able to achieve, at least until the *Bangladesh* struck. Both times the tactics that enabled it were the brainchild of General James Hawthorne."

"Any general could have supplied similar tactics."

"Oh, there you are badly mistaken, Yezhov. He is a genius, at least in the venue of military movements."

Yezhov's smile turned sardonic. "Madam...perhaps you place too much faith in this general."

"Oh?"

"He refuses to recombine the Fleet and attack the enemy, to hit him hard, to disrupt the Highborn in their free space movements."

"The *Bangladesh*—"

Yezhov interrupted with a snort. "This one attack, which he yearns to break off. Isn't it obvious? General Hawthorne has no stomach for a stand-up fight. Maybe he pulled a stunt on May 10, but the ferociousness of that battle scarred him. He's terrified of the Highborn, overcome by their style of warfare."

"Hard words, Yezhov. They may come to rebound upon you."

"They are words of truth, Madam. Look how the islands of Earth fell one after the other. And what did the General boast as his major achievement? That he slipped a few troops out of the cauldron."

"Three-quarters of a million trained soldiers," said Blanche-Aster.

"Bah! Men that are trained in running, in hiding, in fleeing from the enemy."

"You could do better?" asked Blanche-Aster.

Yezhov squinted. "I have a plan, yes."

"Go on."

"I will kill the Highborn and their highest-ranking FEC traitors."

"How would you do it?"

"Assassination teams."

Madam Director Blanche-Aster raised her old eyebrows. "How will get past their security?"

"Notice."

Yezhov moved his fingers into a unique pattern. Before he could take aim, however, a door burst open. Behind it stood General Hawthorne and a team of his bionics. The general had waited for this precise moment. As Yezhov's hand rose, Hawthorne stepped through, his short-barrel .44 in hand. He fired three times, driving Chief Yezhov against the wall, chunks of his flesh exploding at each hit. The bionics beside him held their fire, calculating that more bullets were unnecessary.

It took the ancient Blanche-Aster time to regain her composure. "What… What is the meaning of this?"

"Check him," said Hawthorne.

The door swished and bionic men rushed in. They began searching the slain Yezhov.

"Check him?" she asked.

"His fingers," said Captain Mune.

A moment later, a bionic warrior looked up. "Street tech, all right."

"What?" said Blanche-Aster.

"Each finger is a one-shot gun," the bionic man said.

Blanche-Aster wheeled around to face Hawthorne. "How did you know he was going to try to kill me?"

The General shrugged.

Before she could ask again, the Madam Director's chrome desk chimed.

"May I answer it?" she asked Hawthorne.

"Certainly."

She wheeled her chair there and turned on the screen. Her jaw sagged.

"What is it?" said Hawthorne.

"The Chief of PHC wishes to speak with you," she whispered.

General Hawthorne scowled. "But that's impossible. Yezhov lies dead on the floor. Wait! Who is it, you say?"

"It's the real Yezhov," she said. "He wants to make a deal."

Shock Troopers

1.

Admiral Rica Sioux leaned forward in her command chair, with her right hand pressed against the comlink embedded in her ear. Her ancient face was lined with concentration.

General Hawthorne's plan was complex. Three days ago, he had sent a message, ordering them to break off their proton beam attack on the Sun Works Factory. Their destination was now Mars, to try to awe the rebels there and then get re-supplied. But in order to get the *Bangladesh* to Mars in one piece... The Supreme Commander played an interesting game with the Highborn.

What was that old saying? A picture was worth a thousand words. Admiral Sioux shut her right eye, the better to view the VR-monocle in her left, and then she twitched her left hand, the one gloved to the computer.

A small model of the inner solar system leaped onto her virtual reality monocle. The Sun blazed at one end, Mercury orbiting around it, then Venus, the Earth and Mars.

All the solar system's planets orbited in the same direction. If one looked down from the Sun's North Pole, they moved counter-clockwise. Also, all the planets orbited on nearly the same plane, or ecliptic. The ecliptic was inclined 7 degrees from the plane of the Sun's equator, although the plane of the Earth's orbit defined the ecliptic of all the other planets. Even in 2350, humanity kept its Earth-centric outlook on the universe. Far-off Pluto had the greatest inclination, 17 degrees, and it had the most eccentric of all the orbits.

Compared to the Outer Planets, the four Inner Planets hugged the Sun. If one changed the millions of kilometers to mere steps, the relationship became more easily understood. Admiral Rica Sioux recalled her grade school science class and the teacher who had actually made the subject enjoyable. From the Sun to Mercury would be one step. To Venus would be one more step or two steps from the Sun. To the Earth would be another step and Mars one more or four steps away from the Sun. But to go from Mars to Jupiter took nine more steps or a total of thirteen steps from the Sun. Saturn would be 25 steps from the Sun, Uranus 50 steps, Neptune 78 and Pluto 103 steps. The nearest star, Alpha Centauri, would take 200 miles worth of stepping using this model, while the distance between the Earth and the Moon would be the width of a person's little finger.

The planets, naturally, didn't all orbit around the Sun in unison, with each one perfectly lined up behind the other. Each circled Sol at different speeds and as a matter of course, some had farther to travel than others. Mercury took 88 days to complete one circuit around the Sun. Venus, 225 days; Earth, one year or 365.26 days, and Mars took 687 days to travel one complete circuit around the Sun.

Such were the major terrain features of the inner system, with each planet tugging with its gravity, although none pulled upon objects like the monstrous Sun. Each planet and their moons, and of course the Sun, created gravity wells, deep holes in terms of escape velocities needed to climb out of, and they also created gravity centers that bent light and thus laser beams that sped past them and they also affected missiles in flight. It was always much easier to shoot objects like missiles or asteroids down into, or around gravity wells than up from them. Minor terrain features like the magnetic belts, such as the Earth's Van Allen Belt, and the solar wind also had to be taken into account by targeting computers and ship's AI.

The *Bangladesh* sped past Mercury as the planet continued its endless journey around Sol. Much farther ahead of Mercury in its own counter-clockwise orbit was the Earth, almost out of the line of sight of someone on the surface of Mercury. If they were out of the line of sight, then direct laser-link communications would be impossible, as the Sun would block such a beam. Given time, Mercury would lap the Earth, but by then it wouldn't matter to the *Bangladesh*. Venus was farther behind Mercury but not by as much as the Earth was ahead. Mars, in its much slower circuit around the Sun, was presently between Venus and Mercury in terms of lines of sight.

Admiral Rica Sioux studied the four planets and their relative positions because of General Hawthorne's complex fleet maneuvering.

The *Bangladesh*, as it passed Mercury, had changed heading so that given time she would reach Mars. Meanwhile, three SU missileships from two very different locations sped up to match the beamship. They would all join a little beyond Venus's orbital path. Two battleships, two cruisers and a missileship also built up speed to join them, but they wouldn't link up until near the Earth's orbital path.

Once all together they would be the strongest SU Fleet Flotilla formed. Still, any of the Doom Stars could beat them, expect perhaps for the badly damaged *Genghis Khan*.

The Highborn, damn them, hadn't been idle while all this took place. The Doom Star in orbit around Venus had left the planetary system and now gave chase, building up speed at sixteen Gs acceleration. The *Gustavus Adolphus* Doom Star that normally circled Mercury also chased after. The goal of two such super-ships would usually be to bracket an enemy ship, although with the *Bangladesh's* head start, and the two Doom Stars' starting locations, that wasn't going to be possible.

Even so, General Hawthorne had anticipated the Venus maneuver. He'd sent two SU battleships and six cruisers at Venus. They came from seven different places in the voids of Inner Planets.

To Admiral Sioux and probably to the Highborn as well, it looked as if the General had finally given up his game. Either that or he was trying to keep the Highborn honest and force them to keep their Doom Stars around each of the planets.

221

Venus only had the one. So if Venus's Doom Star traveled very far and built up too much speed, it wouldn't be able to turn around in time to stop the two SU battleships and six SU cruisers that headed to Venus. That force could probably take on the HB laser stations in orbit around Venus and whatever orbital fighters they had. But if the Doom Star returned to Venus, those ships would have to alter course and flee. So it wouldn't do for them to get to Venus too soon.

Fleet maneuvering in space was an intricate business, a complex management of speed and heading and fuel and armor and missiles and lasers and re-supplies. Each side depended heavily upon its predictive software and AIs. Even Highborn minds couldn't cope with the bewildering amount of data and spatial decisions.

Admiral Sioux twitched off the VR-monocle. In her gut, she wanted to gather all the SU spacecraft and try to hit one lone Doom Star. Look at what the *Bangladesh* had done to the Sun Works Factory. The Highborn weren't invincible.

This called to mind that strange call five days ago from a Director Gannel, asking her opinion about gathering the Fleet. She'd decided to play it safe and had wanted to know what the Supreme Commander thought.

"Never mind that, Admiral. We want your opinion."

"Who are we?"

"I speak for the Directorate of all Inner Planets."

Arrogant politician, she hated their power games. She had not been able to avoid such games on her way to the top, but hated them all the same.

"I would of course obey a more aggressive policy," she'd finally said.

"I'm not asking you about your loyalty, Admiral. I want to know what you think about hitting the Highborn harder."

"If the correct safeguards are taken, it could be very beneficial to Social Unity."

There had been a pause, much longer than the transmission time. Then he'd said, "I'd thought better of you, Admiral."

And that had been the end of that. It meant a power struggle was going on, she was certain of it. But of whom and over what she didn't know. When General Hawthorne had beamed his message he'd said nothing about new policies, but he had ordered this gathering. What did it mean?

She frowned. Better to concentrate on matters at hand, on things she could actually affect.

"Tracking," she called.

"Yes, Admiral," said the officer in the Tracking module.

"How soon until the HB missiles reach beam range?"

She wanted to know how soon until the enemy jinking and ECM drones wouldn't so adversely affect the proton beam that it wouldn't be worth firing. Usually that began anywhere from 100,000 to 80,000 kilometers for a moving target, depending of the intricacy of the enemy's electronics.

The Tracking Officer studied her board, studied the HB mass of missiles that had converged toward them, closing day by day, hour by hour.

"Soon now, Admiral. Say, two hundred and fifty minutes."

Admiral Sioux rose and walked carefully toward the tracking module. They fled from Mercury, building up speed at one and one-half gravities, which played havoc with her knees if she moved around too much. They had burned at eight Gs for several hours, with everyone in the acceleration couches, but now they slowed and jinked. Zigzag jerks and starts and slowdowns and sudden accelerations were a matter of course during combat flight.

The *Gustavus Adolphus* had given chase ever since the Doom Star had dumped masses of lead-impregnated aerogel and prismatic crystals near the Sun Works Factory. Social Unity had discovered this with an optic observer carefully hidden these several months between Mercury and Venus. The small ship with its powerful telescopes was sheathed in the latest stealth technology. The *Gustavus Adolphus* had no chance of hitting them at this range, but with those masses of missiles fast approaching, the *Bangladesh's* choices had been narrowed. Its cones of probability weren't as large as before.

The Tracking Officer sucked in her breath.

"What's wrong?" asked Admiral Sioux.

"This can't be right," said the Tracking Officer. "It must be Highborn ECM playing tricks on us."

Admiral Sioux hurried to the module, a bad mistake. She had to step down to reach it. The one and one-half Gs caused her to twist her leg and put too much force on her left knee. She hissed, and collapsed as pain shot up her thigh.

"Admiral!" shouted the First Gunner, shucking off his VR-gloves and moving out of his module to assist her.

"Never mind me," she said, using the tracking module to help her stand. Then she groaned. She couldn't put any weight on her left knee.

The Tracking Officer looked pale as she kept rechecking her board.

"What is it?" said the Admiral, as she peered into the module.

"The missiles," said the Tracking Officer, shaking her head.

"What about them?" They were small red blips on the officer's VR-screen.

The Tracking Officer looked up, her thin lips trembling. "They just began hard deceleration. And I count twice as many missiles as before."

Shock swept through Admiral Sioux. Twice as many missiles as before? The idea made her dizzy. Then she shouted, "Battle stations!" She shoved the First Gunner's hands off her—he tried to help her to the command chair. "To your post, mister," she said. Then she threatened to twist her right knee too, by hopping on her good leg back to the command chair. With a groan, she sank into the cushions.

"Admiral!" shouted the Shield Officer.

"Calmly," said the Admiral. "I can hear you quite well, thank you."

The Shield Officer stared at her, nodding a moment later. "Yes, Admiral," he said in a quieter, more professional tone. "Ship's AI suggests that we get into the acceleration couches."

She checked her own compulink to the AI. Hmm.

Several seconds later, she opened intra-ship communications. "Attention crew, this is the Admiral speaking. Prepare for extended acceleration. I repeat, extended acceleration."

2.

Needles stabbed. An, awful, smothering feeling threatened Marten's sanity. It made him recall a story of his mother's, the way they say a dying man sees his life flash before his eyes. She'd been a strong-willed woman of faith, a Bible reader, and she'd often spoken about this passage.

Marten recalled the story of Jonah and the whale and he felt like Jonah right now diving into the depths. The pressure, oh it was awful, compressing and mind destroying. He moaned as he heard Vip raving over the comlink, and as their Storm Assault Missile began hard deceleration.

Vip's screams broke through to Marten. The small man's cries were hoarse and wild, desperate beyond dementia.

"Vip!" shouted Marten. "Listen to me, Vip!"

More screaming and sobbing.

"We're going to make them pay, Vip. Hang on. Fight it. Resist. I promise you we're going to make the HBs pay as they've never believed possible. So we're the subhumans, eh? We're nothing but dung beneath their feet? Their lord highnesses, Highborn, lofty ones, arrogant bastards! We are men! Do you hear me, Vip? You and I are men. Omi, Lance and Kang are men. The shock troopers are men. Hang on, Vip. Because once we have that beamship... oh Vip, we're going to surprise them. Ha! Surprise, Vip. A really big surprise is what the HBs will get when we subhumans take over the *Bangladesh.*"

Kang hissed, "You're raving." Then the maniple leader groaned in misery and could say no more.

"Not raving, Kang," whispered Marten. "I'm promising. Do you hear me? Promising!"

The crushing pain, the nausea and Vip's screams became too much. Like a dumb beast, Marten endured the horrible deceleration.

3.

The HB missile barrage didn't intersect the *Bangladesh* in one vast clot. They came from around a 60-degree arc, from all their various original cones of probability. Nor did they all fly at the same speed. Some had been programmed to travel faster, to reach the target sooner.

In front sped ECM drones: electronic countermeasure missiles. They scrambled and jammed the *Bangladesh's* radar. They had kept secret the true number of missiles, hiding and halving the actual amount. Now they created electronic ghost images. They sprayed aerogel with lead additives, shot packets of reflective chaff and they worked around the clock to break the beamship's ECM. AIs, ran the drones. Predictive software, battle-comps and probability equations gave them a seeming life of their own. One thing the drones didn't have was biocomps like the New Baghdad cybertanks. The Highborn loathed biocomps. They felt such things to be unholy and monstrous. Life shouldn't be mated to a machine, not in such a way—although they found nothing hypocritical about hooking the shock troopers to the G-suits and packing them into the missiles as biological bullets.

The masses of cocooned space-warriors suffered in the crushing grip of deceleration. Many screamed. Some stared dully. Others wept. A few laughed. Only thirty-nine died from heart failure, strokes and panic seizures. The rest simply longed for an end to their agony. The entire time, the missiles remorselessly closed as the *Bangladesh* fled.

At 80,000 kilometers separation their quarry's proton beam stabbed into the eternal night. It slashed through a ghost image. Immediately HB radar and optics detected the beam, the fact of its existence and that the enemy had at last tried to hit them. Most of the incoming missiles decelerated hard. Twenty others seemed to leap ahead because they decelerated less. Each of those mounted a single laser. In three seconds, they were pumped and ready to hotshot, a special process that burnt out the tubes faster but delivered a stronger initial punch. ECM drones locked on target and fed the battle data to the missiles. Twenty lasers flashed at the *Bangladesh*.

4.

Everyone aboard the *Bangladesh* lay on acceleration couches or were assigned to damage control parties, where they piloted special repair vehicles that could move about under eight Gs. VR-goggles supplied information, although ship's AI made the majority of the decisions while the *Bangladesh* was under eight gravities acceleration.

In the armored command capsule, hidden deep within the beamship, Admiral Rica Sioux presided over her officers via comlink.

"Particle Screen 1 is degrading," said the Shield Officer.

Outside the beamship, sixteen enemy lasers burned into the 600-meter-thick rock-shield. The hotshotted lasers chewed deeper and deeper into the mass. If they broke through and breached the Bangladesh's inner armor the battle would quickly be over.

Ship's AI aimed giant spray-tubes and pumped an aerosol cloud to blunt the effect of the beams. At the same moment, the *Bangladesh's* mighty engines quit. The enemy beams slewed ahead relative to the ship. Six seconds later the beams retargeted and burned through the aerosol cloud. More aerosols flowed out, tons of it. The engines reengaged, turned off, restarted over and over, slewing the beamship randomly tiny fractions of arcs.

"Deploy mines in the seventh quadrant," ordered Admiral Sioux, who had carefully studied the incoming missiles. Overlaying her view of the battle on her VR-goggles was a grid pattern to help her better understand locations, vectors and distances.

Giant rotary launchers poked out the *Bangladesh* and aimed between the interstices of two nearly joined particle shields. They spewed mines the size of barrels, firing them by magnetic impulse. Every fifth round was a radar mine. Every tenth contained chaff. The rotary cannons fired continuously. A vast minefield grew in the path of the oncoming missiles.

"I have lock-on," said the Targeting Officer.

"Proton beam charged," said the First Gunner.

"Fire," said Admiral Sioux.

5.

The distances closed rapidly. From their 60-degree arc, the HB missiles swarmed toward the *Bangladesh*.

Flashes winked in space as the proton beam destroyed HB laser missiles. One after the other they ceased to exist. By firing, the missiles had made themselves vulnerable to targeting. With cold calculation, the HB probability equators had accepted that. Most of the surviving missiles now decelerated. Those didn't decelerate moved ahead of the mass.

Twenty new lasers stabbed at the *Bangladesh*.

HB optic and radar missiles recorded the breaching of the first particle shield. Behind a cloud of instant aerosols, that shield rotated away and a new one moved into place.

In quadrant seven, as viewed from the *Bangladesh*, the HB missiles entered the minefield. A signal pulsed from the beamship's AI, activating the radar mines. Mass and velocity was almost instantly verified. The radar mines screamed on their high-band frequency. Thousands of other mines within listening range detonated. They strewed depleted uranium shrapnel into the path of the oncoming missiles. The missiles' speed made such particles deadly. When they met, the shrapnel smashed through the missile's ceramic-ultraluminum armor. Ten HB laser missiles disintegrated, as did several ECM drones and five Storm Assaults missiles, loaded with their biological cargo. Twenty-five shock troopers perished. Their remains became just another part of the debris of space junk.

Ten EMP Blasters now leapt forward. Meanwhile, the bulk of the Storm Assaults dropped to one-G deceleration. And within them, or those that still worked, the three atmospheres of pressurized glop drained into space as needles and special drugs normalized the shock troops.

The EMP Blasters inched toward the *Bangladesh*, closing the distance, closing—

One vaporized, the proton beam catching it perfectly.

Nine others exploded, sending a nuclear fireball that arced toward the beamship. As planned, they were closer to the ship and farther away from the missile barrage. Heat and blast damage had no effect at these distances in vacuum. In this initial phase of the attack, the nuclear explosions had only one purpose: a focused electromagnetic pulse, the EMP. It traveled toward and soon washed over the beamship, destroying any unshielded electronics and played havoc with the rest.

More lasers then stabbed at the new particle shield the ship had rolled into place, burning into it.

6.

"They're too many of them!" shouted a SU officer. "The missiles closed too rapidly."

"Kill them one at a time," said Admiral Sioux, her voice as relaxed as if she sipped coffee.

"Rotating Shield Three into position," said the Shield Officer.

"Spreading the minefield to quadrant nine."

"Launch anti-missile torps," said the Admiral.

"Firing," said the Launch Officer. "Admiral! Tubes three through eight aren't responding."

"Reroute those torpedoes to the working tubes," said the Admiral.

"What are those missiles to the rear of their formation?" asked the Tracking Officer. "I don't recognize the type." "Their ECM drones are fantastic. How could there be twice as many missiles as we suspected?"

"Tubes four, five and six won't respond," the Launch Officer said.

"Damage control," said the Admiral. "Check torpedo tubes four, five and six."

"Roger, Admiral."

"How are we supposed to beat off all those missiles? They're too many of them!"

"Switch offline, mister, if all you spout is defeatist garbage," said the Admiral.

"Admiral!" said the Targeting Officer. "Look at those."

"Re-target the proton beam," said the Admiral. "Don't let—"

Flashes showed on their VR-images as enemy missiles fired lasers.

Admiral Rica Sioux clenched her teeth. She suddenly had the gut feeling that maybe it wasn't possible to beat the Highborn, that the HBs truly were superior in every conceivable way. What a horrible feeling that was. She fought off the feeling and tried to think of a way to defeat these masses of clever missiles.

7.

Ten minutes after the molasses-like glop drained into space, water sprayed into the SA missile compartment. Soon the water also swirled out.

Hiss—pop!

The first G-suit cracked open.

Pop!

Pop!

Pop!

The others did likewise.

More buckles snapped. A seam in a suit appeared. Someone groaned. Then a hand, smooth and naked, without any artificial protection, slipped out of the seam and pried at the suit.

"Six minutes to combat acceleration," crackled an automated voice.

Weak-voiced curses were the only reply, although new hands appeared at the seams of the other suits. Slowly, the shock troopers struggled out of their cocoons.

Marten broke free first. He wrestled through the tangled tubes attached to his suit and dropped heavily to the wet floor. On his hands and knees he panted, naked and trembling, his hair damp and a scraggly growth of beard on his face.

At the sound of hoarse breathing and desperate struggling, he looked up. Vip, his face bone-white and sweaty, his eyes wide and pupils jittering like rubber balls, fought against the masses of tubes around his suit.

Marten forced himself up. He trembled, but he locked his knees. Willing himself to stand, he lurched to Vip's suit.

"Vip." Marten's voice was scratchy. He cleared it. "Vip."

The small man stopped what he was doing and stared without recognition.

Lance tumbled out of his suit, to lie gasping on the floor.

Marten grabbed two tubes, yanking them out of Vip's way. Vip continued to stare.

"Leave him there," Kang said.

Vip's eyes widened in fright.

Marten turned. The massive Mongol, as naked as himself, stood to his left.

"You can't stay in there," Marten told Vip. "You gotta come out and help me kill HBs."

Kang elbowed him in the side. "Shut up. I said leave him."

Marten ignored Kang as he helped Vip. Soon, Vip plopped to the floor as he made retching sounds.

Marten knelt by him. "You're okay, now, do you hear? You're out of that thing forever."

"I can't do that again," whispered Vip.

"I know."

"I'd go crazy."

"We're all crazy," said Lance, kneeling on the other side.

Then the hatch cracked open as Kang twisted the wheel. "We got four minutes," he told them, "and then it's more acceleration."

Vip looked up, sick fear giving his skin a greenish tinge.

"Let's get dressed," Marten said, helping him by the elbow.

They filed out of the dreadful compartment and entered the other one. There they donned brown jumpsuits and climbed into the battlesuits. Marten still had the shakes, so he activated the suit's medikit. It diagnosed him and shot him with a pneumospray hypo.

In their battlesuits, they looked like mechanical gorillas, huge beasts with exoskeleton power and dinylon armor. They screwed on the helmets with the names KANG, LANCE, OMI, MARTEN and VIP, and they strapped on thruster packs. Oxygen tanks were already part of the battlesuits, while laser rifles and breach-bombs had been packed away for them in the

236

separate torpedoes. For tiptoeing inside here, the servomotors were geared way down to minimum.

"No neurostims until we're outside," Marten said, speaking to them by helmet communicator.

"I'm the maniple leader," Kang said.

"You're third in command of the entire mission," Marten said. "You don't have time to lead our maniple as well."

"Don't think I've forgotten about your treachery," Kang said.

"We're all gonna be killed," said Lance, "and you're worried about a few wrong words spoken during the hell-ride here?"

"No defeatist talk from you either," warned Kang.

"Relax, okay," Marten said.

"I'm the maniple leader," Kang said. "Training Master Lycon must've known you were a turncoat. So he put someone reliable in charge."

"Why don't you shoot me now then?" Marten said, disgusted with the whole conversation. "You're so ready to be their butt-boy, maybe that'll earn you points."

Kang balled his exoskeleton fists. The suit's engine whined as he revved it for combat power.

"Don't be an idiot," said Lance.

The five, battlesuited shock troopers faced each other, their suits purring.

"We're gonna need everyone we have in order to fight into the *Bangladesh*," said Lance.

"And we only have two minutes to enter the torps," Omi said.

"And in the suits, you're no stronger than we are," Martin grated.

The battlesuit with KANG on the helmet turned away first. He opened the hatch to a long torpedo. The others hurried to theirs. Each climbed into the torpedo's mini-cockpit. They buckled themselves into the seats and flipped a switch.

Slam, slam, slam, went the hatches, and the forward compartment of the Storm Assault Missile was devoid of men. Five sleek torpedoes, like bullets in a cartridge, waited near the firing chamber.

Thirty seconds later the SA missile leapt forward at eight Gs.

"Here we go again," Marten said, via comlink. This time, however, he had a little display screen in front of him. He would have minimal control in the torpedo, once it was fired. But having just that little bit gave him a needed psychological boost.

"Next stop, outer space," said Lance.

"Where we'll be as free as eagles," Marten said.

"Yeah. Sure."

8.

"What are those missiles in the rear of their formation?" asked the Tracking Officer. "Why haven't they *done* anything yet?"

"Good question," said Admiral Sioux. She'd been wondering that herself.

"Particle Shield 5 rotated aft," said the Shield Officer. "Shield 6 in place."

"Fire minefields at will," said the Admiral.

On the screens nearby flashes told of more enemy EMP Blasters igniting.

"Rotary cannons down," the First Gunner said.

"Only launch tubes one and twelve are in working order," the Second Gunner said.

"Fire!" said the Admiral. "Fire everything we have before it's too late."

"Aerosol levels in the red, Admiral."

Outside the beamship, HB lasers almost stabbed through Particle Shield 6.

"Get ready to re-deploy Particle Shield 1," the Admiral said."

"It can't take more than ten seconds of those lasers," said the Shield Officer.

"Get it ready," the Admiral said.

"There are just too many of them," an officer said with a sigh. "They are like a pack of dogs pulling down a lion."

"Those missiles in back are moving up," the Tracking Officer said.

"Particle Shield 6 rotated away. Shield 1 re-deployed into primary position."

"The aerosol tanks are empty, Admiral." A heavy sigh. "That's it then."

Admiral Sioux understood. The aerosol clouds kept the lasers at bay while they rotated particle shields. Without the aerosols, those lasers would probably breach the ship's inner skin before the shreds of another particle shield could be put between the *Bangladesh* and the hated beams.

She squinted at the VR-images in her goggles. They had destroyed an amazing number of enemy missiles, fully three-quarters of them. She ground her false teeth together. She wasn't dead yet, so defeatist thinking was senseless. "Keep firing the proton beam," she said.

"Next target acquired," said the First Gunner.

Outside the beamship was a mass of confusion with beams and missiles and EMP pulses and torpedoes and exploding mines with depleted uranium shrapnel and wisps of aerosols.

"Point defense cannons ready," the Second Gunner said.

"What are those missiles?" the Tracking Officer asked. "What is their function?"

"They almost look like ships."

"Are they orbital carriers?"

"What does Analysis make of them?" the Admiral asked.

"In this mess?" asked the Tracking Officer.

"Admiral!" said the Shield Officer.

"Is Particle Shield 1 gone already?" asked Admiral Sioux, a hint of resignation in her voice.

"Yes. No. I mean—"

"Talk to me, mister."

"The HB lasers stopped just before the particle shield was breached."

"Have we beaten them?" the First Gunner asked. "Have we actually held out long enough and taken all they can give?" He laughed in disbelief.

"I don't think so," said the Tracking Officer. "Here come those mystery missiles. There're a lot of them, too."

"But why did the lasers stop?" asked the Admiral. "Are they out of juice?"

Just then the lasers re-energized, all the beams lancing at the proton beam cannon.

"This is it!" someone shouted.

"Long live Social Unity!"

But the lasers snapped off again.

There was a moment of silence.

"It's like they're trying to disarm us," the Admiral said.

"Why would they do that?" asked the First Gunner.

"I bet we'll know in a minute," said the Tracking Officer. "I'm picking up activity from those mystery missiles."

"What do we have left to fight with?" asked the Admiral.

"A few point defense cannons," someone said. "Maybe in time damage control could get one of the launch tubes fixed."

"Hold the PD cannons. Don't fire just yet," the Admiral said. "And get me an open launch tube!"

"What is it?" asked the First Gunner. "What do you know?"

"Is it a hunch, Admiral?" the Tracking Officer asked.

"They're playing their mystery card," the Admiral said. "I just want to have something left in case…"

"In case what, Admiral?"

"We're not defeated until we're dead," said Admiral Sioux. "Remember that. All of you."

There was silence again as they waited for the mystery to unfold.

9.

The 101st Maniple's Storm Assault Missile nosed toward the mighty *Bangladesh* like a hound sniffing at the carcass of a bull elephant. Beside that missile sniffed other SAs. A hatch blew off the nose of the 101st's missile, revealing a torpedo launch tube.

Inside the missile, the firing chamber opened. Like a shotgun shell, the first torpedo slid into the breech. The chamber clanged shut, and the entire missile shuddered. Within the torpedo, Marten Kluge clenched his teeth. He knew the SA missile would launch his friends, one after another.

Open, slide, fire!

Open, slide, fire!

An invisible hand fired the SA like a hunter shooting a rifle.

Despite the intense Gs, with the battlesuit's servomotors it was possible for Marten to lift his hand. He flicked on the torpedo's screen. The huge *Bangladesh* leaped into view. The massive beamship was his world. Bright stars surrounded the ship, while the flame of the *Bangladesh's* engines showed him that it still tried to run away.

Good.

Shredded particle shields hung around the vast beamship. Black holes showed where the lasers had pitted the rock.

He rode a rocket sled toward the *Bangladesh*. He tried his comlink, but only got crackling static. ECM jamming filled the ether, making communication impossible at this point.

He was the leader in the sense that he'd been fired first. He aimed at the nearest particle shield. Despite his speed, it seemed that he only inched toward it. This was the most dangerous time. Almost anything could destroy the torpedo. It had only been built to withstand the shock of impact and burrow deep. It had no other shielding. A ship's primary lasers would crisp it in a second. Maybe it could shrug off a few point-defense rounds, but military spacecraft usually spewed thousands of such rounds a second.

Something blossomed brightly to his left.

He hoped it wasn't anyone he knew.

Then more blossoms flickered all around him.

He cursed the Highborn, for having put him in this position.

Pinprick flares dotted the *Bangladesh*. He was certain it was point defense cannons firing at them.

Chaff would have been fired from some of the SAs, he knew. Radar jammers were blaring. EMP blasts hopefully had made the beamship stupid. And HB lasers—even to his untrained eye the massive beamship looked badly scarred. So why did he feel so naked? He shivered in dread. He wanted to live. To really live! To run again, to eat steak while sitting at a table, to read a book and to kiss a girl. Maybe he should have slept with Nadia when he had the chance what seemed eons ago. Was it reactionary to want to marry a woman before you slept with her? That's what Social Unity taught, that his ways were old fashioned and out of style. He flinched as a blossom closer than the others flared beside him. He swore he could feel the torpedo shudder—although he knew that was impossible, unless something actually hit his torp. Then he would be dead, not thinking anymore.

He shouted in an effort to release his stress. The sound was loud in his helmet. He felt naked and vulnerable. He wanted to smash his screen. Instead, he chinned his suit for neurostim. The hypo hissed. Ah! Beautiful.

Chemically induced anger washed over him. It covered his feeling of nakedness. Now he wanted to kill.

He veered more sharply for the pitted particle shield.

The rocket-ride was almost over. The pitted particle shield grew dramatically in front of him. He roared and raved, and at the last minute, he remembered to clench his teeth together. During practice runs, shock troopers had bitten off their tongues. The shock could click one's teeth together like a guillotine.

The pitted particle shield grew mammoth-sized. Then it was all he could see. Blackness! Shock! Then he knew nothing more as he passed out.

10.

"They aren't exploding!" shouted the Shield Officer.

"I don't understand," Admiral Sioux said.

"This doesn't make sense."

"Admiral," said the Tracking Officer.

"What?"

"I..."

"Do you know what those torpedoes are?" asked Admiral Sioux. "What they do?"

"I'm picking up life readings."

"Are you sure?" asked the Admiral. "Command told us that the HBs hate biocomps."

"Not that kind of life readings, Admiral. Men."

"Men? Do you mean like us?"

"Yes, Admiral. Men, humans—soldiers, I should think."

"They fired soldiers at us?" Admiral Sioux asked in disbelief.

"How could regular men withstand twenty-five gravities acceleration?" asked the Shield Officer. "The say the Highborn can take sixteen. But twenty-five! That's impossible for anybody."

"They're there," the Tracking Officer said.

"Are you certain the ECM blasts didn't distort your sensors?" asked Admiral Sioux.

"I've picked up life readings, Admiral, of Homo sapiens. And there's nothing wrong with the sensors. I already ran two diagnostic checks."

"So what are soldiers doing on the particle shield?" asked the First Gunner.

Admiral Sioux's old eyes suddenly widened. Her heart beat hard. "They're trying to capture my ship."

"Admiral?"

She scowled, and she repeated, louder. "They're trying to capture MY SHIP!"

"The soldiers are boarding us?" the First Gunner asked. "Like pirates?"

"But…"

"Does that mean we can surrender?" asked a suddenly hopeful officer.

"Who said that?" snapped Admiral Sioux.

No one volunteered to say.

"We're not surrendering," Admiral Sioux said. "We're fighting to the last round, to the last bullet."

"Bullet, Admiral?"

"I'll blow the *Bangladesh* before I let the HBs get their hands on her."

The sudden and profound silence around Admiral Sioux made her wonder if the beamship's officers would let her carry out such a threat.

"Here comes another volley," the Tracking Officer said.

"Damage control!" shouted Admiral Sioux. "Get me a working launch tube."

"We're trying, Admiral."

"Then try harder, dammit!"

"Look at that," said the Tracking Officer.

Admiral Sioux looked. It made her snarl. They weren't going to get her ship. No, sir. That wasn't going to happen.

11.

Pain throbbed in his head. Marten tasted blood in his mouth. He smacked his lips as klaxons wailed for his attention. *Kill, kill, kill,* in time with his heart beat somewhere deep within him. He stirred. Then he blinked. His eyelids felt gluey, almost stuck together. He wondered if he had a concussion. Then the fog over his thoughts lifted and he knew that his torpedo had burrowed into the particle shield. Marten Kluge slapped the torp's ejection button.

His seat moved backward, picking up speed as it slid out the rear of the torpedo. Buckles unsnapped and the battlesuit's servomotors roared into life. Eight Gs of the *Bangladesh's* acceleration still pulled at him. But the battlesuit had exoskeleton power. He used his muscles and the suit amplified it many times over. With such suits on Earth, the Highborn could make 100-meter leaps. Here it allowed him to crawl out the hole made by the torpedo.

Over his gloves, he wore special pads. Every time he put his palm down, twenty-centimeter curved spikes thrust out and held on tight. Little barbs jutted out of the nails, helping the spikes hold onto the particle shield rock. He had the spikes in his boot-toes as well. To withdraw them he had to chin a switch in his helmet. It was hard getting the hang of it. Slap your hand down, *slam,* the spikes thrust into the rock like explosive pitons, and then out shot the barbs. Chin for the left hand to pull in the barbs and then the claws, lift up the hand, move it, thrust in those spikes again, chin for the right hand, move it, thrust down, chin for the left foot. It was slow work climbing out this hole. He felt the *Bangladesh's* high acceleration tugging at him the whole time. He decided to take his time and do it right.

Soon, like some bizarre space gopher, he popped his head out of the hole that the missile had burrowed. The pitted particle shield spread in all directions. Motion caught his eye. Out of a nearby hole, as if shot by cannon, a shock trooper flew away. The man's arms flailed in a tragic-comic way, as if he could climb back to the particle shield with an invisible rope.

That man hadn't been careful enough. The Gs had ripped him off the rock and hurled him into space.

Marten swallowed hard.

The shock trooper shrank to a dot and disappeared into space. His oxygen would last several hours, several lonely hours with absolutely no hope of rescue.

What would he think about?

Marten shook his head, trying to drive away the thought, but it hung there, taunting him, frightening him, reminding him that failure to take the beamship meant death.

He chinned his suit so it glowed with a bright blue color. Then he crawled out the hole, pressing his body against the rock as if he loved it. So very carefully, he moved one hand or foot at a time, crawling across the particle shield, making sure those deeply curved spikes had driven in as far as possible. Other shock troopers did likewise.

Meanwhile, the *Bangladesh* continued to flee from Mercury.

Marten glanced back over his battlesuit's shoulder. An HB missile moved up. It terrified him. A red laser flashed out its cone. Marten shouted hoarsely. Then something exploded, a flash and then nothing, darkness. Other movement caught his eye. More torpedoes coming. Two blossomed in space, hit by point defense before they could burrow to safety. Marten groaned. Bile rose in his throat. That could have been him. He didn't know why he was the lucky one. Then more surviving torps smashed into the particle shield that he was on. The shield shook, and that threatened to loosen his grip.

"No, please, no," he whispered, as his right hand slipped up and then whipped off the rock, the curved claws showing with

248

their little barbs. His servomotors whined as he hammered the spikes back into the rock. Motion in the corner of his visor caused him to look to his left. Another shock trooper had lost his grip and shot outward into space.

"Help me, God," Marten whispered. "Please don't let me die like that."

His helmet crackled. Garbled, static, scratchy voices sounded. For a brief, insane second he thought it might be God answering. The reality of where he was took over. He squeezed his eyes shut, trying to make out the words.

"One hundred and twenty-fourth Maniple, report."

More static, then little tinny voices tried to respond.

"Basil here, Maniple Leader."

Marten dared look around again. He saw blue-glowing shock troopers clinging to the particle shield as he did. A few had green-glowing numbers.

Right, right, he chinned his suit, turning all its colors on. A big green 101 would now be on his back and helmet. And that action seemed to let him think again. He dared dial himself another shot of neurostim. Riding the particle shield with one tiny wrong move that would lead to a lonely, terror-filled death by suffocation was simply too debilitating for normal thought. As the drug pumped into him, more anger, rage, washed through him. It made him angry that he was scared. Then he really got pissed.

He started crawling—carefully! Yeah, yeah, he wasn't *that* mad.

He avoided a huge laser-blast hole. It was deep and big. He glanced around. A lot of those holes dotted the shield. He bet some went almost all the way through.

Marten tried the comlink. It crackled horribly, and he heard many tinny voices.

"One-oh-one, report," he said. He repeated it several times.

"Marten!"

"Here, Lance."

"Where?"

Marten wasn't about to raise an arm.

"Look around. Do you see any one-oh-one's glowing?" he said.

"Oh, right," said Lance. "We're supposed to chin on the numbers. Just a minute."

Marten swiveled his helmeted head. He saw a green 101 pop on thirty meters from him, on the other side of a laser pit.

"I see you," Marten said. "Look across the pit."

"Gotcha. Oh, yeah, there you are."

"Let's meet halfway," Marten said. He started crawling.

Other maniples called in and now more of the shock troopers showed their numbers. A few of the battlesuits didn't move. Maybe their owners were too terrified. Most of the men crawled toward their maniple leaders.

As he crawled, Marten noticed how shot up the particle shield really was. It could break apart at any moment. That meant they had to get off it fast.

"Wu, here," called a man. He was the mission's second in charge.

"Kang, here, Wu."

As the dreadful fear of the shield breaking up caused him to crawl faster, Marten also counted battlesuits. Maybe a hundred shock troopers had landed on this broken, battered particle shield. They all had to get off. A hundred was too many to lose. He dared lifted his hand and point his maniple where to go. He did it as he slid his right hand forward to crawl another inch.

No, they weren't his maniple anymore. They were Kang's. He laughed harshly. "Screw you, Lycon," he said.

The others, close now, crawling together, peered at him. He'd had his comlink open when he'd said that. He could see their questioning eyes.

"We gotta move!" Marten said. "We gotta get off this particle shield."

"Wu gives the orders," Kang said.

"Neurostim yourselves," Marten said. "From here on in you'll need anger, lots of it, to drown out the fear."

"Don't listen to him," Kang said. "I'm in charge of the one-oh-one."

"Stay if you want, Kang." To the others Marten said, "Follow me. The particle shield could break up at any time."

"Wu," Kang said via comlink.

Wu didn't answer. Maybe he was out of range, maybe he had other things on his mind.

"The particle shield could break up?" asked Lance.

"Have you taken a good look at the shield?" Marten asked. "There are too many laser holes for my tastes. What if one section of the shield crumbles?"

Vip cursed in fear.

"Neurostim yourselves to a two-dose level," Marten said.

"No," Kang said. "Only one dose, as per HB orders."

Marten hissed, "You're a stupid idiot, Kang. It's time to get mad. We gotta hustle off."

"Three-oh-ninth leader here, Marten," said a shock trooper. "What's this about a crumbling shield?"

Marten told him. He told someone else. And so the word spread.

Marten, getting the hang of it now, crawled faster than before. The horrible tug always dragged at him, threatening to tear him off for good. But like a big mechanical baby, he had learned the crawling trick and had almost perfected it.

"Come back here," Kang said.

"Everyone else is following me, Kang," Marten said between gasps. Even with the battlesuit, it was hard moving fast under eight Gs. "I suggest you do likewise."

Kang growled, but he started after them.

In time, Marten reached the edge of the particle shield. He poked his head between the gap of this shield and the one beside it. What if the people in the ship pressed the two shields together? Hamburger shock troopers, that's what. He couldn't see down to the ship. Six hundred meters, if he recalled this beamship's specs right, that was the depth of the shields. He swallowed, and then he started "down." Only it felt like "up." One wrong move and they would fall down the cliff and out into space. It felt safer here, but that was an illusion he knew. If he lost his grip, the eight Gs would simply rip him away and maybe knock others off as well.

What a way to make a living.

His rage against the HBs grew. But he was getting tired, too. All those days locked up in the G-suit without exercise was having its effect.

251

Keep moving, boy.

"Uh, oh," said Lance.

"What is it?" Marten said.

"We lost another one."

Marten said a short prayer for the hapless victim. Then, "Is everyone else following?"

"Seems like," said Lance. "Omi, can you see?"

"They're coming."

Down or up, toward the ship Marten crawled. His breathing was harsh in his ears. Then he reached the inner edge of the particle shield. He checked his HUD radar, and saw giant pivoting struts attached to the inner beamship's skin. He crawled under the shield, and now he could move faster because the Gs pushed him against the shield, like a sloping floor. Soon he reached the nearest metal strut, a vast girder that moved the particle shield around to wherever it was needed.

Spikes wouldn't work on the girder.

Marten cudgeled his wits, trying to think of something.

Suddenly a man screamed. That cut through the static all right.

"PD cannon," growled a shock trooper.

Marten peered at the inner armored surface. There! A cannon poked out the skin like an ancient pirate's cannon on those old wooden ships. Balls of orange plasma from several battle-suits' plasma cannon roiled toward the PD cannon that was shooting.

A moment later, the plasma washed over and melted the cannon.

"Ten dead," said a shock trooper.

"Keep your eyes open for more PDs."

"They know we're here," Marten said. Then he knew what he had to do. "Once you reach the girders put away your spikes."

"Are you crazy?"

"Maybe," Marten said.

He put one spike-pad away. Then he reached out. With full exoskeleton power, he clutched hold of the girder. His power-gloves dented the metal. It would leave a handprint, all right. He moved his left hand, and as he tried to slip off the spike-pad, it flew away. He sighed, and then he grabbed the girder with his left. He shimmied up the giant strut, wrapping his battlesuited legs around part of it.

"Marten's a monkey," Vip said.

"Just make sure you follow me," Marten said.

A man cursed as two more PDs popped out and fired. Plasma rolled at them, but not before five more shock troopers died.

"Bastards!" cried a man.

We all are, Marten decided. *Them and us, maybe everybody in the solar system.*

Soon others crawled behind him and up the girder. Attached to their battlesuits were breach-bombs and plasma cannons, while hooked to their arms were laser tubes.

"This is thirsty work," said Lance. He tried for levity. He sounded as frightened as Marten felt. Neurostim didn't seem to last long while they were doing this.

Marten concentrated on crawling. His skin itched. He wanted more neurostim. *No, no, keep your head clear now, Marten, my man. Just enough neurostim to dull the fear. Or maybe just enough to mask it.*

The fear, dread, anger and hard work made him sweat. He chinned for a drink of water. But finally, Marten reached the end of the giant strut. The inner armored skin of the *Bangladesh* had countless crisscrossing tracks, deep grooves. It was how they moved the shields around, he guessed. He licked his lips. He didn't know if this would work. If it didn't…the Gs would hurl him back "down," against the underbelly of the particle shield. If he landed on his feet, he might not die on the spot. Maybe crush his bones, though. He shook his head. This was all insane. They shimmied up a giant strut while the *Bangladesh* sped through space. Suddenly the strut vibrated.

"What was that?" Omi said.

"Why is it shaking?" whined Vip.

"Hurry!" shouted Marten.

"Use yours thrusters?" Vip said.

"No!" shouted Marten. "Don't be a fool. The beamship's fleeing at full acceleration."

"If you use your thrusters," said Lance, "you'll barely crawl at one G, but the ship will move at eight."

"Then it's bye, bye," Kang said.

Marten reached for the beamship's inner armor above his head. He turned on the battlesuit's magnetic-clamps at full power. His hand attached to the ship's armor. The clamps were also on his elbows, belt, knee and toes. Like a fly, he attached himself to the beamship. Slowly, with a clang, clang, clang he crawled along the surface.

"Move," he said to the others.

The ship underneath him shuddered. Marten looked over his shoulder. The struts trembled. Then his eyes opened wide. The struts, the giant girders, blew off and out of the ship's grooves. The particle shield detached, and it was snatched away at 8 Gs, maybe more as the *Bangladesh* shed the huge weight. Over the comlink, shock troopers screamed in rage and fear. Some tried to jump, their thrusters burning hard, spewing out hydrogen particles. For a second a man actually crossed the meter of distance he needed to go. Then he seemed to stop and flipped back hard into space as the huge ship accelerated away from him.

In silence, the handful of shock troopers on the beamship's armored skin watched their comrades recede into space. As the particle shield rotated, they saw other shock troopers leap off the shield as their thrusters burned. It was a pitiful sight. Hydrogen spray spewed out the packs, but it was far too little. They dropped farther and farther behind as the *Bangladesh* continued its acceleration at eight gravities.

"Poor bastards," said Lance.

"What's going to happen to them?" asked Vip.

"What do you think?" snarled Omi.

Then Kang reached them. His normally slit-shut eyes were as wide open as theirs. Through his helmet visor, he looked terrified.

"Wu is gone," Marten said. "So now you're second in command."

"If Mad Vlad still lives, that is," said Lance. "If he's dead then you're the mission commander."

"What do we do now, Kang?" asked Marten.

Kang licked his lips. He peered at the tumbling particle shield. Soon he faced Marten. "You got any ideas?"

12.

Cheers and wild whooping filled the *Bangladesh's* command capsule.

"Ha-ha, look at them go!" shouted the Pakistani First Gunner. "Bye, bye, you traitorous scum."

"I love it. They're trying to jetpack their way to us."

"Good luck," said the Tracking Officer.

"Enough of that," Admiral Sioux said.

"What's wrong, Admiral?" asked the Second Gunner.

"They're soldiers just like us," Admiral Sioux said. "We defeated that batch. And I'm glad for it. But let's not mock brave soldiers."

"They're the enemy," the First Gunner said.

"Traitors to Social Unity," said someone else.

"Admiral, I detect enemy on the inner armored skin."

"See," the First Gunner said. "They're still going to kill us."

"Or they're going to try," said the Tracking Officer.

"That's what I meant," the First Gunner said. "I hate traitors. If we defeat them, I plan to cheer while Security teams hold them down and slit their throats."

"What about re-education?" asked the Tracking Officer.

"Not for traitors," said the First Gunner.

Admiral Sioux only half-listened. She couldn't find it in herself to hate the enemy soldiers. She studied the situation through her VR-goggles. Some of the HB missiles had passed the *Bangladesh*. They rotated and watched, but didn't fire the lasers. Why?

"Launch Tube Twelve in operative condition, Admiral," a damage control officer said.

"Here come another swarm of missiles," the Tracking Officer said.

The First Gunner swore in frustration. "Slitting their throats would be too good. Torture them first."

"Better hope they don't play back the bridge vid," the Second Gunner said.

"Belay that sort of talk, mister," the Admiral said. "No one is taking my ship."

"Yes, Admiral. I'm sorry, sir."

Admiral Sioux suddenly thought she understood the enemy's plan. The HB lasers and other missiles weren't firing because these soldiers were on the beamship. Not very many were on, but as long as the soldiers tried to breach the *Bangladesh*, it was safe from HB missile attacks.

"Pilot," the Admiral said. "Get ready to rotate the *Bangladesh* one hundred and eighty degrees."

"Admiral?"

"Do it at my command," said Admiral Sioux.

"What are you planning, Admiral?" the Tracking Officer asked.

"How much fuel do you think those missiles have left?"

"Not much," the Tracking Officer said. "But what does it matter? It was enough to reach us."

"Ready," the Pilot said.

"Now," said Admiral Sioux.

The *Bangladesh's* mighty engines turned off. Attitude jets fired. The massive beamship rotated ponderously in space. Soon the front of the Bangladesh was aimed where the engines had been burning these many days. They were pointing toward the Sun. Then the huge engines engaged again, generating eight gravities as the beamship braked hard.

The HB missiles coming up on the *Bangladesh* sped that much more quickly toward the beamship.

"Enemy torpedoes are firing like before," said the Tracking Officer.

"PD cannons ready," said the First Gunner.

"Don't fire!" shouted Admiral Sioux. "Let the enemy torps hit us."

"There are fifty torpedoes, Admiral," the First Gunner said.

"I can count, mister. Just make certain you don't fire. Shield Officer, seal the shields together. Don't leave any gaps between them."

"Yes, Admiral."

The huge beamship shuddered as the majority of the torpedoes slammed into Particle Shield 4, or what was left of it.

"They've landed," said the Tracking Officer.

"Yes, thank you," said Admiral Sioux. "Pilot, rotate us ninety degrees."

"Rotating."

The beamship's main engines quit again. Attitude jets fired. Ponderously, the mighty *Bangladesh* rotated ninety degrees.

"Detach Shield 4," ordered Admiral Sioux.

"Detaching," said the Shield Officer.

On their VR goggles, they watched the huge hunk of rock blow off the *Bangladesh* and tumble slowly away, although not very far. Some enemy soldiers leaped off the particle shield and jetted for the beamship. Both the shield and the beamship kept relative speeds.

"PD cannons fire at will," the Admiral said.

"Firing," growled the First Gunner.

All along the *Bangladesh's* side spat PD cannons. Shock trooper plasma globs rolled at them, together with battlesuit rifle lasers. The PD cannons shrugged off the small lasers. The superheated plasma was another matter. It took out cannon after cannon. But not fast enough. Soon all the soldiers were dead, blown apart by point defense weapons.

"Do we brake or flee?" asked the Pilot.

"Tracking?" asked the Admiral.

"One last spread of missiles is approaching fast, Admiral," the Tracking Officer said.

"Let's use the launch tube," said Admiral Sioux.

"The lasers will take it out," the Tracking Officer said.

"Belay that order," said Admiral Sioux. "Yes, you're right," she told the Tracking Officer. "Pilot, aim a particle shield at the incoming enemy. We'll let them come in unharmed."

"They might not fall for the same trick twice," the Tracking Officer said.

"Admiral!" cried a damage control party leader.

"Report," said Admiral Sioux.

"Enemy soldiers have breached the *Bangladesh*. What are your orders?"

"Security Chief," said Admiral Sioux, "I hope you're online and listening."

"I'm listening," the Security Chief said, a gruff-sounding man. He'd killed the mutinous ringleaders while they'd orbited the Sun those long months waiting. He had few qualms when it came to killing. He now said, "If you accelerate faster than two Gs we can't fight. But keep us one-G or less and we'll take them."

"How many have breached?" the Admiral asked.

"I'd say ten soldiers," the damage control officer said. "But they're wearing high-tech fighting suits. Just like Highborn use."

"Incoming missiles," said the Tracking Officer. "Their last batch, I think."

"HB torpedoes are launching!" shouted the First Gunner. "Let me PD them, Admiral."

"Not as long as they have laser missiles on this side of us," said Admiral Sioux.

"But there are fifty to sixty more torpedoes, Admiral."

"Turn the ship aft," said Admiral Sioux, hoping to increase the distance between the incoming torps.

Attitude jets burned again. But the shock troop torpedoes proved as maneuverable as the vast ship. The fifty-plus torps came at the beamship on an unprotected side.

"Fire the PDs," said Admiral Sioux.

Those fired for three seconds. Then HB lasers melted them. In the meantime, five shock trooper torps exploded.

"Good work, mister," said Admiral Sioux. "Launch our torpedoes."

On their VR goggles, they saw it for the futility it was. Three torps made it out. Then lasers destroyed them and the tube. Soon thereafter, the HB missiles flew past that part of the *Bangladesh*. The mighty beamship shuddered as the surviving HB torpedoes slammed into the ship.

"Those are all now aboard the *Bangladesh*," the Tracking Officer said.

"Thank you," said Admiral Sioux. "That makes sixty to seventy enemy soldiers. What do you think, Chief? Can Security take them?"

"Depends on how good those soldiers are."

"That's the wrong answer, Chief."

"We can take them, although I'll need damage control to pitch in."

"Pilot, one-G acceleration until otherwise ordered."

"In what direction, Admiral?"

"Where else?" asked Admiral Sioux, "toward our rendezvous with the flotilla."

13.

Nadia Pravda hesitated as she stood before the stealth pod's airlock.

For seemingly endless days after she'd left the Mercury System she had slept, watched videos and thought deeply about her life. When she'd noticed she was putting on weight she had exercised religiously and tried to eat less. Finally, the boredom had overwhelmed her. So she'd broken open a baggie of dream dust, snorted, and fantasized until she had come down days later, dehydrated, ravenous and the baggie empty. So she had drunk water until she'd been ready to vomit. Then she had eaten and for several hours just gazed at the stars. Slowly the desire to return to her fantasies had come upon her. It had been then that the realization that she was about to commit suicide jerked her upright in the pilot's chair. She had paced in the light gravity until she found herself in front of the airlock.

If she broke open another baggie, she would doubtlessly snort dust until she died. Maybe that wasn't a bad way to go. The truth, however, was that she didn't want to die. She wanted to live. But the boredom was so awful. Maybe it would have been better to have Hansen and Ervil aboard. No way.

She drank water and like a zombie found herself approaching the stored dream dust. She stared at it for a long, long time. This was her stake in the new world. Without it, she would be without credits, valueless in the cold calculations of the habitats. But if she kept it, she would use it, and if she used it, she was dead.

Slowly, hesitating often and with many doubts, she put baggie after baggie into the airlock. Finally, all the pod's drugs were piled in the pressure chamber. She closed the inner hatch, rested her forehead on it for fifteen minutes and then activated the outer hatch. She gave the pod a tiny jolt with an attitude jet, enough to send the drugs out of the airlock.

She went to a side port and watched the powder drift into space. She cried afterward. Then she went to sleep. When she woke up, she was bored. "But I'm alive," she whispered. And in a year, she should reach the Jupiter System. So she did two hundred jumping jacks and settled into the pilot's chair for another movie.

14.

Ten trolls prowled through the *Bangladesh*. At least that's what they looked like to Marten. Attached to the gorilla-sized battlesuits was the mission's complement of munitions, all they had to take over the beamship. Extra laser-juice, more plasma coils and batteries, oxygen rechargers, suit-fluids and rations and more neurostims, Suspend and Tempo.

The beamship's corridors were dark. It didn't matter, though. The battlesuits turned radar and motion scans into VR-images on each of the shock troopers' HUD. Visual information, a grid and targeting crosshairs were all shown holographically on the inner surface of each helmet visor. To the left side of a visor was a grid map of the beamship. It showed their position. The *Bangladesh* had a similar configuration to a Zukov-class battleship, although there were differences, and sometimes those differences had surprised them.

After the initial breach and slaughter of some unarmed ship's personnel, the outer portion of the beamship seemed to have been evacuated. Thus, they tramped down long, empty corridors, crossed various rooms and blasted booby-traps and door-locks.

"Tank coming at three o'clock," Vip said, who had point in the latest corridor.

"They've recovered from their initial shock," Marten said. "Stay alert. We're finally going to see what they have."

"What the—Gas!" Lance said.

"Where?" Marten asked. They were in a recreation area with tables, chairs and a music unit.

"It's coming through the vents."

"What kind of gas?"

"It's not combustible or corrosive," said Lance. "My guess is it is knockout gas."

"There are guys behind that tank," warned Vip.

"Wernher, set up the cannon," Marten said.

"Roger," said Wernher, who followed close behind Vip.

"Kang, Conway, watch the rear," Marten said.

Kang grunted. He'd given tactical command to Marten while he considered strategy.

"The tank stopped," Vip said. "It's launching grenades!"

"Omi, Lance, burn through the right walls and flank them," Marten said.

The two shock troopers attached a breach bomb to the wall and stepped back as Omi activated it. The shaped charge blast disintegrated a portion of wall. They bounded through the smoking hole.

The sound let Marten know that this section of ship still had an atmosphere. He switched to Omi's HUD, putting it on his. They used another breach-bomb to tear through another wall, watching the ship's blueprint on their HUD to see where they had to go to flank Vip's tank. HB tactics stressed surprise and doing the unexpected. Fighting through the laid-down corridors, which the defenders would always know better than the invaders, would give the tactical advantage to ship's personnel. Creating new corridors and bursting through walls to attack would heavily favor the side that had the ordnance to do so. And that was how they had practiced.

Marten checked Vip's HUD. The tank had stopped at an intersection of corridors. He studied it. It wasn't really a tank. He flicked through an itemized list of known SU ship equipment. Ah. The 'tank' was a damage control vehicle normally used when the beamship was under eight-G acceleration. The grenade tube attached to it was no doubt a jury-rigged device. That told Marten somebody on their side was thinking fast and turning decisions into commands.

"The tank's coming forward again," Vip said. "There are at least ten people behind it."

"Back up," Marten said. "Wernher, get ready with the cannon."

"Should I leave them any surprises?" asked Vip.

"Negative," Marten said. "Just back up to Wernher."

The seconds ticked by.

"Ambush!" said Lance. "Omi's taking hits."

"Coming," Marten said. He mentally berated himself for getting sloppy. Somebody on the other side definitely thought on their feet and had already incorporated the wall-breaking tactic into their battle considerations and was using it to ambush them!

Marten ran though the wall openings that Lance and Omi had made, with two other shock troopers following him. They were the reaction team. He read Lance's HUD. Omi lay on the floor, a gaping hole in his battlesuit. Lance crouched behind a bulky unit of unknown nature. He fired at the enemy, his heavy laser burning holes in the walls and through personal body-armor. Then Lance dove aside as a plasma glob touched and vaporized the unit he'd been hiding behind. Marten hoped superheated plasma wasn't what had hit Omi. He sprinted down a different hall with the long glide they had been taught to use in ship corridors. He checked the blueprint grid and slapped a breach-bomb to a wall. Seconds later, he and his two mates burst through the wall and behind the enemy. In two heartbeats of glaring red lasers, all the enemy jerked, screamed and curled like burning leaves. Then it was over. Marten's battlecomp counted ten corpses, three of them suited with SU security gear.

"We keep going and flank the tank," Marten said. "Lance, check Omi. Close his battlesuit with construction foam."

BLAM, BLAM, BLAM. The reaction team burst through three more walls and came upon the damage control vehicle with its jury-rigged grenade launcher and the fifteen people crab-walking behind it. Laser beams and several grenades took them down before the enemy even knew they had been flanked. This wasn't a battle, it was butchery.

As he stood over the dead SU remains—a hulking mechanical troll in the guts of the *Bangladesh*—Marten finally allowed himself to worry about his friend. "Report," he said.

"Omi is out," said Lance.

Marten hesitated, part of him terrified to ask more. He had to, though. "Is he dead?"

"I shot him with Suspend," said Lance.

Marten couldn't breathe. He didn't dare close his eyes even to mourn his friend. This was just one more mark against the HBs. No. It was more than that. He tasted his sweaty battlesuit air before he asked, "Was he dead when you did it?"

"No," said Lance. "But is chest is badly burned."

Why Omi? Why not Kang? Marten forced himself to hang onto the fact that Omi wasn't dead. But a plasma burn and with no medical facilities for millions of kilometers—

"Bring him along," he said.

"We don't have the luxury to carry our dead. ...To take anyone who's out," Lance finished lamely.

"You carry him," Marten said.

"Maniple Leader—"

"Do it!" Marten said. "That's an order. We'll all carry each other. No shock trooper leaves another behind. We're all we have in this lousy universe."

"Roger," said Lance.

Marten didn't want to think about Omi, his one true friend, his only friend ever since Nadia had been torn from him. He switched to the command channel. "What do you think, Kang? Do we continue to lunge at the command capsule or do we go for the engines?"

"Highborn battle-tactics always say to lop off the brain first," Kang said.

"True. But what's in our best interest?" Marten asked.

"Meaning what?"

"Have you contacted any more shock troopers?"

"I would have told you if I had," Kang said. "But they're jamming pretty heavy down here. So how can we know or not?"

"We can't know," Marten said. "So we have to assume the worst. With nine of us the best we can do is bargain."

"With these pansies?" Kang said. "You're kidding, right? We're slaughtering them."

"Omi is out," Marten said. "What does the *Bangladesh* hold, two thousand personnel? We can't afford to keep trading losses at the present ratio and win."

"Then we're dead," Kang said. "We might as well shoot ourselves and save them the trouble."

"Why do you figure that?" Marten said. "We take over the engines and make a deal."

"What kind of deal?" Kang asked.

"They take us to the Jupiter System where we all get off."

Kang laughed harshly.

"Isn't that better than dying?"

Kang was silent. "What if more shock troopers show up?"

"They haven't so far. But if they do... why not talk them into the same deal? What's the use of working for the HBs when nine out of five hundred make it to the target?"

"I'll think about it."

"Listen to me, Kang. The enemy will expect us to go for the command capsule. With nine men, we have to do the unexpected. It's our only chance for victory."

Kang was silent for several seconds. "You have a point. But HB battle-tactics say—"

"Screw the HBs! We're on our own, Kang. Nine of us! You gotta think like a gang leader again, like a Red Blade in the heart of Sydney's slums."

More silence, then Kang said, "Yeah. We'll do it your way."

Marten switched to open channels. "We have a little change in plans."

15.

Admiral Rica Sioux made a fist and kept tapping the arm of her command chair with it. The *Bangladesh* accelerated at one G for rendezvous with the flotilla of spacecraft that would all join up near Venus' orbital path. Of course, the planet wouldn't be there. It was over sixty days from reaching that point in its orbit. The HB missiles had all passed the beamship or had been destroyed. One Doom Star accelerated toward them, although it no longer fired its long-range lasers. It would take several weeks for that enemy to reach them. The other Doom Star had turned back for Venus. General Hawthorne's ploy of feinting battleships at Venus had worked to pull that Doom Star off them.

Despite all this good news, Admiral Sioux scowled. Her officers huddled by the Tracking Officer's module. They whispered among themselves and kept glancing at her. She hadn't given them the arms-locker key yet. It rested in the middle of her fist, the one that tap, tap, tapped her armrest. Enemy soldiers were on her beamship. They were few in numbers: less than one hundred versus her two thousand ship's personnel. That was twenty to one odds. It shouldn't be a problem defeating these few. But to use all two thousand personnel meant she would have to give up the code to the weapons bins. Her officers would also demand to be armed. Some might even want to leave the armored command capsule in order to help fight the invaders. But once they were armed— could the *Bangladesh's* two thousand stop the enemy space marines? Because if they couldn't... once her people were armed, she didn't think the officers would let her blow the beamship. Yet if she didn't arm ship's personnel would her Security teams be able to defeat the enemy?

Her chair's speaker unit blinked. She opened the comlink channel.

"Security Chief here, Admiral. I'm ready to attack the smaller concentration."

A sinking feeling filled her. "I thought by now you would have slain those few."

"They're a tough bunch, Admiral, and very clever. They slaughtered those I sent to keep them busy. Now I've left a covering force to slow down the bigger concentration. I want to wipe out these few first so they can't do anything cute while I turn and overwhelm the bigger concentration with everything we have."

Her chest constricted and she found breathing difficult. She was the Admiral, the one in charge. She had to make the decisions. Yet space combat was so different from infantry action. She wasn't sure what to do. "Should I arm everyone, Security Chief?"

He didn't answer immediately. "Some of the lowerdeck personnel might have long memories, Admiral."

"You mean when we liquidated the mutinous ringleaders while we were in near-Sun orbit?"

"Right," he said.

"Maybe they will have long memories, Chief. But I'm sure they won't remember until after the enemy is slain."

"You're probably right."

"So what's your recommendation?"

"I'd arm everyone and use them. These space marines are tough and obviously highly trained and armored for exactly this type of fight."

Admiral Rica Sioux massaged her ancient chest. Nothing was guaranteed. "No one is taking my beamship," she whispered.

"Admiral?"

She punched a sequence of buttons on her armrest panel. "I'm releasing the locker codes now." She pressed the last button, blowing the locks on the weapons bins in the outer beamship.

"Very good, Admiral," said the Security Chief. "I'll swamp this smaller concentration and wheel and hit the bigger one. Out."

She sagged in her chair, forcing air into her lungs. Slowly the constriction in her chest eased, although now her bad knee started throbbing. She noticed the First Gunner approaching her.

"Yes, First Gunner?" she said.

"Shouldn't we open our own gun-locker?" he asked.

"Do you want to join the Security Chief?"

The First Gunner stiffened. He wore his tan uniform and hat, a lean Pakistani with deep brown eyes. "I'm not ground-troop trained, Admiral."

"Ah."

"But if something should happen," he said. "It seems the height of reason that we be armed."

The others now edged toward her. A determined look had settled upon them. Always command, the Admiral knew.

"Tracking Officer," she said.

"Admiral," the officer said, saluting.

"Open the gun-locker and pass out ordnance." She threw the key to the Tracking Officer, who snatched it out of the air and turned smartly toward the locker beside the outer door. Then Admiral Sioux slumped in her chair. It was two thousand or so against seventy-odd enemy. They should easily win. She wondered then why she felt so gloomy about the prospects.

16.

"Let's take a breather," Marten said. "Vip, Wernher, stand guard at either end of the corridor. Everyone else, re-supply yourselves."

"They're hot on us," said Lance.

"We've got thirty seconds, the way I time it," Marten said. They were in a wide corridor, a service ramp. Whenever the beamship entered space-dock, vehicles would use this ramp to bring in heavy equipment and supplies.

Marten knelt on an armored knee, reached back and unclipped a laser pack. He powered his heavy laser-tubes with the old pack, pumped the rest of the juice into recycling and then detached the drained pack, slapping the fresh one into place. He rolled ten grenades at his feet and inserted a fresh tube into his launchers. Lastly, he relieved himself, letting his battlesuit take care of wastes, gulped some concentrates and drank a lot of water. While he did that he made two bomb-clusters with the grenades, looked around and rigged one to the pipes overhead, tacking on a motion sensor with a forty-second delay so they could get away. The other cluster he stuck to the corridor wall, timing it to blast in sixty seconds. As Lance had said, the enemy was hot on them.

"See anything, Vip?"

"I killed three scouts while you all lounged around. There are a lot of others working up their nerve in the room just behind those three. Most are armed with las-rifles, useless against our armor."

"Don't get cocky, Vip," warned Lance.

271

"I hear you," Vip said. "And I ain't."

"Is everyone ready?" asked Marten.

They said they were.

Marten scanned their surroundings, checked the ship's blueprint and said, "Through the six o'clock wall. Go, go, go!"

BLAM, the hole was made and they charged off the service ramp.

"They coming!" Vip said, who stood guard in the corridor.

"Go!" Marten said. "Run!"

"Relax, Maniple Leader," Vip said. "I'm slaughtering them. None of them have any armor and like I said, all this bunch has is las-rifles."

"They're throwing fodder at you," Kang said, "to make you overconfident."

"I rigged the corridor to blow," Marten said. "Retreat, Vip! Do it now!"

"Roger," Vip said. "I'm on my way."

Marten kept blowing through corridor walls and then using a corridor for a two-hundred-meter stretch. He kept switching methods to keep the enemy off balance and guessing. They entered a large engineering section, with plenty of floor space and big domed generators with panels attached. According to specs, the generators charged the proton beam, or at least they started the process here.

"This is perfect ambush territory," said Lance.

"So perfect that even they would realize it," Marten said. "Keep going."

Nine shock troopers in battlesuits charged past the many-domed generators. Their radar pinged and the motion-detectors scanned.

"Should we booby-trap anything?" asked Lance.

"Negative," Marten said. "Let them get mad at themselves for being too cautious. Then they'll start getting cocky again and that's then we'll hit them. That will turn them even more cautious later on."

They exited the huge engineering area. A few stray las-rifle shots hissed near as the boldest SU soldiers entered the generating room.

"Here's our spot," Marten said a minute later. It was an intersection of corridors, one going straight up, with ladders and float rails. "Wernher, set up the cannon and melt a clot when they show themselves."

"Roger," said Wernher. He put a bulky plasma cannon onto its tripod holder and adjusted the settings. An orange light winked, meaning it was charged and ready. It took ten seconds between shots for the cannon to recharge.

"They might start blowing walls like we do," Lance said. "Making new ways to move and then surround us."

"Our sensors will detect them if they try that," Marten said. "Then we'll show them another trick about wall busting."

"Here they come," said Wernher.

"Wait until the last moment," Marten said.

"Hey, I'm the cannon king," said Wernher. The plasma cannon was slaved to his HUD. He hunched over it, adjusting another setting.

Then SU fodder leap-frogged into the corridor. They didn't wear any suits but had screwed up, terrified faces, with breathing masks over their mouths. Those wouldn't be much help in vacuum, but with all the fumes from the lasers and plasma cannon it wasn't a bad idea. They fired as they advanced—running, crouching and lifting their las-rifles. Las-bolts hit walls and corridor equipment. Oily smoke billowed. Despite their breathing masks men coughed. They were brave enough, poor sods. They didn't stand a chance. Several las-bolts glanced off a battlesuit, turned by the reflective microcoating. Wernher chuckled over the comlink. With a sizzling sound, the cannon belched an orange glob that boiled into a horrified mass of men. Some melted, showing bones and spilling guts. Others vanished in the superheated plasma charge. For a few of them, there was enough time for a microsecond scream. One man actually tore off his breather. Then an awful odor of death filled the corridor and dark, greasy smoke and fumes. Lance, Vip and Marten glided forward, firing red laser light into the shocked survivors.

"Advance," Marten said.

"What for?" Kang asked. "You said we should go to the engines first."

"We're fighting our way to the proton generating room," Marten said. "My guess is that right about now their commander has sent his good troops around in order to ambush us. These poor sods were acting too much like they were trying to herd us forward."

There was some muttering, but they listened to him.

So for the next several minutes they advanced according to HB tactics. They blew out walls, ambushed many and lobbed light grenades to blind and then fragmentation grenades to kill. It was murderous work. Over fifty enemy corpses lay burned and blown in the corridors. Then they broke into the generating section using breach bombs. Wernher set the plasma cannon and slaughtered another group. Then an enemy grenade caught him at just the wrong angle. A depleted uranium grenade-shard sliced through his helmet and lodged in Wernher's brain, splattering the inside of the helmet with gore.

"Another one down," Marten said. "Conway, take the cannon."

"What about Wernher?" asked Lance. "Do we take him too like we did Omi?"

"Kang, carry him," Marten said.

"He's worthless!" Kang said.

"He's full of munitions," Marten said.

Kang grunted and picked up the dead shock trooper.

"We're taking a different route," Marten said. "Nine o'clock and through the wall. Go, go, go!"

17.

"Security Chief here, Admiral."

Admiral Rica Sioux hunched over the armrest. Her confidence had waned as she listened to the combat chatter on the net, to the constant screams of their dying. Her old lined faced betrayed her worry. *I have to set an example. Show your confidence.* So she sat up, adjusted her cap and straightened her uniform.

"Things are starting to fall apart," the Security Chief said.

"I've been listening to your communications net," said Admiral Sioux. "The enemy is good."

"Good? The smaller concentration is a pack of devils, Admiral. They keep retreating, pulling my people farther and farther away from the main group. And they slaughtered... This is butchery, Admiral. Why don't we have space marines like this?"

"We did," said Admiral Sioux. "Now they call themselves the Highborn. I wonder what these marines call themselves?"

"We're badly out of position, Admiral. So I'm calling off the chase of the smaller group and throwing everything at the larger one. We've had better luck with them."

"How can that be?" asked Admiral Sioux. "The larger group is marching straight here and there are over fifty of them left."

"That's true. But we've killed more of them, Admiral. Their tactics aren't as innovative as the smaller group. Whoever's leading the main concentration—he's not like the leader of the smaller group, Admiral. That man is uncanny."

"Can we stop them? Is there any hope?"

"If I can get my Security teams back there in time, Admiral, yes. Every time I tried to trap the smaller group, they avoided a stand up fight. But I'm certain that if I can get my best people into position, then we have a chance at stopping the bigger group. All they've been facing are unarmored men with las-rifles, yet still we've taken out about ten to fifteen of them."

"Hit the larger group with your Security teams. They're the real danger anyway. And hurry, Chief."

"I'm on my way," said the Security Chief.

18.

The shock troopers led by Marten broke into the main engine control room. It was a vast area crowded with generator domes, comps, consoles and repair vehicles presently secured and locked-down. Engine personnel had been waiting, sprinkled with a handful of Security people. Marten butchered them too, although a shock trooper named Gerard died when a main vent blew superheated coolant on him.

After Marten and Lance shut off the main valve and the others rigged the corridors leaning into the Engine Room, they huddled together by the lifts that led into the guts of the actual engines, where the Fusion Drive expelled the hot gases that propelled the beamship. There they discussed their next move.

"We control the engines and from here we can destroy them," Marten said.

"How do we do that?" asked Kang.

"Breach bombs should do it," Marten said, "but I'm sure once we've downloaded the specs we can do it from these control boards."

"We'll give you that for the sake of argument," said Lance. "My question is: so what?"

"So now we make our pitch," Marten said.

They glanced nervously at one another. They knew about fighting. It's what they did. But this idea of fleeing to the Jupiter System, that meant bucking the Highborn. They had been re-educated by the HBs more than once. First, to get into the FEC Army each of them had passed through brutal training that had taught them the superiority of the Highborn and that

277

one must always obey members of the Master Race. Then they had fought in the Japan Campaign, a murderous affair where thousands of FEC soldiers had died hideously. There the Highborn had once more shown their superiority, that no one in the end could win against them. In a sense, they hadn't known anything yet, not compared to shock trooper training. Perhaps the trip here had been rough and many had cursed the Highborn, but to go directly against HB wishes... They knew what happened to those who had tried in the past—they were all dead.

"Uh, look, Marten," Vip said uneasily. "Maybe the HBs are already on their way here. We would look pretty silly sipping tea with the enemy. It would mean the pain booth, maybe a lot worse."

"All life is a gamble," Marten said. "We all know that. But what kind of gamble is worth it when nine out of five hundred make it?" He looked around and through their faceplates. They were scared. "Sure this pitch to the enemy is a gamble. But it will get us out of this crazy war. We all survived the Japan Campaign. Now we've survived being shot to the *Bangladesh*. We're the ones who made it. Omi, Wernher and Gerard made it here too but died anyway. How much more luck do you think the rest of us have left?"

"Yeah," agreed Lance. "We've all used up our luck. But if the HBs are about to land it's all moot."

"How do you figure they're about to land?" asked Marten. "They shot us here as a gamble. Now is the moment to take over and run, but we don't have the numbers to take over. So we gotta deal. Okay, it might be true the HBs are coming. That's just another part of the percentages. After today, though, I don't ever want to count on my luck. I've used it all up."

"Kang?" asked Conway. "You're officially in charge. What do you think?"

"The HBs put him in charge," Vip said. "Marten is the one who got us here. If we're leaving it doesn't matter who the HBs selected."

"Do what you want," Kang told them. "But my vote is against it."

Marten eyed the others. Most of them looked dubious, but they no longer seemed ready to grab their weapons and stop him. So he found a comlink and opened channels. "This is the leader of the shock troopers speaking," he said. "I think it's time the *Bangladesh's* Captain and us talked."

Nothing happened.

"It's no good," Kang said. "That's just what I thought would happen."

A few of the others shifted nervously.

Marten pressed the comlink again. "I'll blow the engines unless you talk. We want to make a deal. So I suggest you don't be stubborn and kill us all." The seconds ticked by. Marten felt more nervous now than at any time during the battle. His armpits grew slick and his stomach churned.

"Listen up," Kang said.

Just then, a voice spoke out of the comlink: "What kind of deal?"

19.

The command capsule was filled with arguments and loud noise. Finally, Admiral Sioux stood and shouted, "Quiet! I can't talk to him if I can't think."

That settled down the officers. The First Gunner studied the others—several of them nodded encouragement—then he faced the Admiral and cleared his throat. Admiral Sioux waved him down as she re-opened the comlink.

"What kind of deal?" she asked.

"We want to go to the Jupiter System."

Several of the officers nodded as if that made perfect sense.

"At least trick him," whispered the Tracking Officer.

"Why do you want to go there?" asked Admiral Sioux.

"Why else?" said the enemy space marine. "We want to get out of this war."

"Just a minute," said Admiral Sioux. "I have to see what my chief officers think." She switched his link onto standby and opened the comlink with the Security Chief. "You heard him. What do you think?"

"See if speaks for all of them," said the Security Chief. "This bigger group is slaughtering our people, although the lower deck personnel are holding. Some of them are a lot tougher than I thought. If I can get all my Security teams together in one place, with a few of them circled around behind the bigger group, then we might still win. What I need, though, is time."

"You're suggesting we trick them?" asked the Admiral.

"Yes! Yes!" said the Security Chief. "All war is deception. We didn't call up the Highborn and tell them we were going to beam their Sun Works Factory did we? Any subterfuge is allowed during war. By all means, trick them."

Admiral Sioux reopened channels with Marten. "Do you speak for all of your troops?"

"Yes," Marten said. "We're all agreed to this."

"I'll need a few minutes to talk it over with my officers, to see if they can convince their people."

"By all means," Marten said. "But don't take too long."

Admiral Sioux switched channels to the Security Chief. "He agrees to a temporary truce while I consider it."

"Perfect," said the Security Chief. "I'll pull back the lower deck personnel and regroup to a better defense position. All I need is about five minutes. Then we'll have them."

Admiral Sioux sat up, gazing at her officers. "It was all a matter of will," she said. "Despite their training and effectiveness, the enemy's spirit was lacking. That is why Social Unity will win in the end."

Several officers nodded.

Encouraged, Admiral Sioux sermonized some more, warming up to her theme. She finally ended with, "Now, we should lock up the weapons."

"Your line is blinking," said the First Gunner.

"Let the enemy wait," said Admiral Sioux. "Let his uncertainty unnerve him."

"No, the Security Chief is calling."

Admiral Sioux saw that he was right and opened channels.

"It was a trick!" shouted the Security Chief. "I started pulling back the lower deck personnel and they hit us with everything at that exact minute."

"But how could they have known what we planned?" shouted Admiral Sioux.

"They must have tapped our communications."

Admiral Sioux slammed on the comlink to the space marine that she'd spoken with. "You lied to us!" she shouted.

"How have I lied?" He even managed to sound genuinely surprised.

"The others attacked when you said that you would give us several minutes to think it over," said Admiral Sioux.

"What others?" he asked.

"The others on the A-deck!" she shouted.

"They are more shock troopers here?" she heard a different man say.

Admiral Sioux blinked, and then she bowed her head. It hit her then that this smaller group hadn't known about the larger one. It seemed that the *Bangladesh's* jamming was the one thing that had worked. What was that name the man had said: shock troopers?

"The deal's off," said this different man. He sounded brutal, speaking with a slum accent.

20.

"Why did you tell her that for?" shouted Marten.

The shock troopers crowded around the comlink.

Through his helmet's faceplate peered Kang's wide, emotionless face with its almost slit-shut eyes. "You heard her," Kang said. "Others of us made it aboard the beamship. And I bet HBs are on their way here, almost aboard ship by now."

Marten stubbornly shook his head.

Kang regarded the anxious shock troopers. "Think about that. The HBs are almost here and we've captured an important part of the ship. But once the HBs learn what Marten tried to do they'll kill him for sure. And they'll kill anybody who helped him."

"This isn't the time to lose your nerve," Marten said.

"That's right," Kang said. "It's time to make sure we keep the Highborn happy. Conway, Higgens, grab him!"

The shock troopers regarded Marten, who stepped back and lifted his arm with the attached laser-tube, although he didn't directly aim it at anyone. "You can't possibly know that the HBs are coming."

The words worked like magic, but not in the way Marten wanted. Conway and Higgens suddenly lunged for him, trying to grab his arms. Marten jumped back and aimed the laser-tube at the nearest, Conway. "You'd better rethink that," he said, already angry with himself for having stepped back the first time. He should have tried to bluff, but he hadn't trusted Kang so near to him.

Lance, who had stepped to the side, now came up behind Marten and yanked back the arm. "We gotta put to this to a vote, Marten."

"Let go!" shouted Marten.

Servomotors whined as their exoskeleton powered battlesuits wrestled.

"This isn't personal!" shouted Lance. "I just don't want to fry in some HB horror chamber."

Marten noticed Conway and Higgens creeping closer. So he relaxed, letting Lance jerk back his arm. "Listen to me," he said, with all the earnestness he could muster. He even twisted his head to peer at Lance, who frowned and then nodded, relaxing his hold. Marten shifted sharply, throwing Lance off balance. He then grabbed Lance by the shoulders and shoved him into Conway and Higgens. With a metallic CLANG, the three fell into a mechanical heap.

Kang clanked forward with an override unit—each of the top three mission officers had been given one. He tried to slap the unit onto Marten's suit. Marten jumped backward, slamming into a lift, crumpling the thin metal door.

"What are you gonna do to him?" Vip said, an edge to his voice.

"I'm going to let the HBs deal with him," Kang said, hopping forward, the override unit almost touching Marten.

Marten got an armored foot on Kang's chest-plate, and he kicked, hurling Kang's half-ton battlesuit against the nearest wall. Then Marten righted himself as Lance, Conway and Higgens also rose to their feet.

"Are you siding with Kang?" shouted Marten.

"I don't want the HBs killing me," said Lance. "So you gotta forget this Jupiter nonsense."

Marten glanced at the others. They peered at Kang, who roared curses as he aimed his heavy laser.

Marten ducked, turned and leaped deeper into the huge engine room.

"Traitorous scum!" roared Kang, a red laser beam lashing out after Marten.

Then Vip said, "If you fire again I'll kill you." He aimed his laser at Kang.

Marten glided behind another lift, shifted around and then entered it. Over the still-open comlink, he heard Kang and Vip argue.

"You're helping the traitor!"

"That's what *you* call him."

"That's what I'll tell the HBs."

"So I'd better burn you where you stand, that's what you're telling me."

"Why are you aiming a laser at me if you're not helping him?"

"Who's aiming anything at you?"

"Now he's gone, you idiot."

"Where's he gonna run to, Kang? Think about it."

"To the enemy, you dolt."

"I don't think so," Vip said "Besides, Marten got us here. I sure don't wanna see you burn him down. Because he helped you survive too. You want to hunt for him later that's your problem. Right now, we gotta secure the *Bangladesh*."

Kang grunted angrily.

Marten's lift opened two levels down and he moved down a different corridor. He'd made his move and lost. Now he had only one option left. Get aboard an escape pod and leave before the HBs arrived. But he left his comlink on receive, turning off the transmitter. Maybe they would forget he could listen.

21.

Admiral Rica Sioux slipped a tight wrap around her bad knee. She'd already had the medic shoot it with painkiller. Meanwhile the Tracking Officer brought body armor and a las-rifle and laid it beside the command chair.

"Admiral!" said the First Gunner. "This is madness. We must all make a run for the escape pods."

Admiral Sioux ignored him. At her age, she had learned when not to argue. He spoke for the rank and file, nothing more. Around her, the command team watched the VR-screens in dismay. The HB-trained soldiers were uncanny. The larger group was smashing straight toward the bridge. The smaller group had six active members left, hitting and running wherever they weren't expected.

An armrest button flashed.

"Security Chief, here. It's no good, Admiral. Now they're slaughtering my Security teams one by one. If only I could have used everybody together, I could have beaten them. It was a mistake to chase the smaller group."

"I'll be down to join you for the final assault," said Admiral Sioux.

"Admiral, I must protest."

"Noted. Now no more arguments, please. My mind is made up."

"Aye-aye, Admiral. But you'd better hurry if you want to fight with us."

Admiral Sioux motioned the Tracking Officer to help her put on the armor. As she did, the Admiral said, "You and the others will head to the escape pods, just like the First Gunner suggests."

"We want to fight with you," the Tracking Officer said.

"Senseless. Live to fight another day."

"Then you're not blowing the *Bangladesh*?" whispered the Tracking Officer.

Admiral Sioux knew that several officers watched her closely as they fingered their weapons. She had no doubt they would kill her if they suspected she would use the destruction code. The enemy's swift success had broken their last scruples—or so Admiral Sioux suspected. The destruct procedure was complicated, so she couldn't hide it from them.

The last buckles of the body-armor snapped closed. She put on her helmet and slid open the visor. Settling back into the command chair, she put a call through to General Hawthorne on Earth. Those in the command capsule continued to watch.

"General Hawthorne," she said, "enemy soldiers called shock troops have boarded the *Bangladesh*. We're fighting desperately. I am about to go down and join the Security Chief. Here are the specs of the enemy battle tactics." She pressed transmit, sending a data dump of everything they knew. At least he would have the information to formulate new tactics. Then she rose from her chair and her eyes swept her command team.

"I am proud to have served with you. I wish you luck getting through to the escape pods."

"Join us, Admiral," said the First Gunner.

"I am too old to run." Admiral Sioux hefted her las-rifle. "But not too old to aim and fire."

She limped to the sealed door, voice-keyed the lock and watched it slide open. From deep inside the *Bangladesh* came the screech of combat. "Is anyone joining me?"

None of her officers dared look her in the eye.

She nodded and limped into the dark corridor of her beamship.

22.

Earth—New Baghdad

General Hawthorne cleared his throat, nodded to the holo-director that signaled him and peered into the camera. He sat at a desk, with small SU flags on either side of him. Behind him was a representation of the four Inner Planets, with the Social Unity Logo of four hands one atop the other interposed as background. His military hat was cocked at the angle he felt portrayed confidence and a dash of genius. His bony fingers were folded atop the desk.

A recorded voice spoke: "Citizens of the Four Planets, of Mars, Earth, Venus and Mercury, I give you Social Unity's Supreme Commander, General James Hawthorne." Martial music played.

As the music wound down, Hawthorne nodded at the camera as he saw the red recording light blink. "Good evening, fellow citizens. It is with a heavy heart that I come to you tonight. Let me add that not with a heart bowed with defeat or despair. Rather, I wish to… clarify some of the words spoken to you earlier this year. This has been a year of great tragedy, as I know that you are all aware. The Highborn have brutally invaded the Four Planets and slain many that otherwise would have lived long and useful lives. The words that must be explained are those in the past year spoken in haste and fear. Namely, that this will be is a short war.

"In their love for the people of the Four Planets the former Directors believed the ugliest assessments should remain hidden. They felt it was better to forge the tools to defeat the enemy and let you go on with your lives in peace. But the Highborn are not easily beaten. They are vicious, merciless and savage, and let me add, brilliant soldiers who make well-laid plans. The Directors of many years gone designed the Highborn to be such soldiers. Alas, treachery infected the Highborn and they turned on us all."

"As Supreme Commander I have led the fight against the traitorous Highborn. I have witnessed both defeat and victory against our wily foe. I know what many of you don't. That despite our various defeats victory is inevitable. But victory will not come cheaply or quickly. Knowing this, my heart was still troubled because I saw that many of the Directors lacked faith in you, the people of Social Unity. So I came to New Baghdad to speak with Madam Director Blanche-Aster. Her nobility encouraged me to speak plainly with her, even as I saw that the many burdens had worn her down to a shell of her former greatness. She agreed with me and suggested that in this dark hour that I take the reins of authority and guide the Four Planets."

"I refused. I am a fighting man, not a politician. But she argued that now is the not the time for politics but for rolling up our sleeves, picking up our guns and fighting. 'Guide us,' she pleaded. 'Help me show the other Directors that we must go to the people and tell them the bitter truth.' I finally agreed, with the proviso that she would remain by my side to help me. She reluctantly agreed, as age has stolen so much of her vigor. Yet I am grateful for as much help as she can give."

"This is why I have come to you tonight, my brave and loyal citizens. As Supreme Commander, I beg for your help and your understanding. In the coming days we will continue to take heavy losses. The Highborn are too powerful for it to be otherwise and their treachery has infected too many who should have known better. Yet Social Unity is stronger than mere fighting prowess and without a doubt stronger than base treachery. Our great hearts beat too purely for it to be otherwise. Millions of you will enlist in the armies that push the invaders from Earth. Others will join Space Defense to find and destroy the Doom Stars in our new and improved battleships and beamships, while many millions will work overtime in order to build the weapons we need to defeat the so-called Supremacists."

"Citizens of the Four Planets, not all my news is gloomy, or about the hardships to come. The Highborn are dangerous but they are not invincible. As Supreme Commander, I ordered a space attack on the Sun Works Factory around Mercury. The Ring-factory has become Highborn's home base, their processing plant and manufacturing yard. We hit it savagely with our latest beamship, the *Bangladesh*, a breakthrough design that has challenged all the old methods of space war."

"Many of you have been heard to ask: 'Where are our space fleets?' I shall tell you where: Hitting the enemy even now! Striking him ruthlessly and making him quake with fear! We will go on hitting him until he is defeated. We shall never surrender. Not as long as your hearts are true and as you realize that together, in our complete unity, that we shall overcome."

"Thank you, my dear citizens, my fellow cardholders, good night, and may the creative force of our wills continue to shine."

General Hawthorne peered straight at the camera until the holo-director said, "Cut. That was excellent, General. A fine speech."

Hawthorne nodded as he rose and strode to the door. Yezhov congratulated him, shaking hands. "Wonderful, General. A splendid speech. The masses will be hardened in their resolve and flood into the recruiting stations."

Hawthorne nodded, and he shook more hands as he listened to more effusive praise. The Chief of PHC worked for him now, although Hawthorne would never trust Yezhov until the man was incinerated and his ashes thrown down a deep-core mine. The Bionic, Captain Mune stood behind the secret police chief, ready to kill him at the first hint of betrayal.

"I was hoping you could check my latest list," said Yezhov, edging forward.

"Assassination teams that are to be slipped onto the orbital farm habs?" asked Hawthorne.

290

Yezhov winced and glanced around, lowering his voice. "Please, General, this is a sensitive project. Its success hinges on the fact that it remains secret."

Only those screened by Hawthorne's MI teams were allowed in his presence, and his bionic men watched those closely. A glance around showed him seven bulky bionics. They held gyroc rifles and continually scanned the crowd, making everyone nervous. Good! Let them all quake at the thought of treachery.

He and Yezhov had made a deal. Slippery Yezhov, the sly and cunning chief of Political Harmony Corps. During his coup attempt, Hawthorne hadn't the strength to beat PHC in a straight shooting match. So he'd made the deal and now worked to chip away at their power, just as they tried to chip away at his. All the directors had been replaced except for Blanche-Aster on his side, and Gannel on Yezhov's. The others were nonentities. So in a sense the tripod of power in Social Unity had been reduced to a bipod, a balance: the Military and the Secret Police.

To wait until the Cyborgs arrive was Hawthorne's policy. He wasn't sure what Yezhov's plan was. These assassination teams were part of it, maybe the core. Yet the secret police chief's plan was ingenious and bold. The assassination teams would infiltrate Highborn areas and kill them. Just like PHC had infiltrated the Joho Command Center and almost kidnapped him. He needed to keep reminding himself how close PHC had come to victory.

A door opened and Madam Blanche-Aster rolled in on her bulky medical unit. Behind her followed her guard-clone, unarmed these days. Neither the clone nor the director looked happy. Hawthorne excused himself and greeted the Madam Director. He inclined his head, even as he heard Captain Mune walk up behind him.

"A fine speech, General," said Blanche-Aster, only a hint of sarcasm in her voice.

"Thank you, Madam Director."

"I'm afraid I have some bad news."

"Can't it wait?" asked Hawthorne. "I need to meet with the new directors and—"

"It's about the *Bangladesh*," she said.

His eyes narrowed. "Yes?"

"It's been captured."

"What?"

People turned and stared.

Hawthorne noticed. He lowered his voice and said, "Come with me."

23.

Hawthorne clicked off Admiral Sioux's recorded message and with his bony fingers, he massaged the side of his head.

"It doesn't appear as if the Highborn themselves stormed aboard," said Blanche-Aster. She scanned a readout-slate hooked to her chair. "Normal men did this. Which is amazing. According to the Admiral's report, seventy to eighty space marines captured the *Bangladesh*. Actually, amazing is probably the wrong word. Treachery is more like it. How can seventy to eighty space marines capture a beamship the size of the *Bangladesh*?"

Hawthorne sat behind his desk, shaking his head and with his shoulders hunched. Captain Mune stood at attention behind him. The Director's guard-clone kept her gloved hands on the handles of Blanche-Aster's medical unit.

"The Admiral called these space marines shock troopers," said Hawthorne.

"Does that mean anything?"

"It must signify something. Perhaps these shock troopers are like our good Captain Mune."

Blanche-Aster wouldn't look at the hulking bionic soldier. "I'm sorry, but I don't think even seventy Captain Munes could capture the *Bangladesh*."

"I strongly disagree," said Hawthorne.

"I imply no disrespect to these mechanically enhanced warriors of yours, General. But to me treachery seems like the more probable answer."

"Seventy bionic soldiers could capture the *Bangladesh*—quite handily in fact," said Hawthorne. "But I don't believe that the Highborn have modified people in such a fashion. Their psychology dictates against it." Hawthorne pursed his lips. "Shock trooper is an interesting term. The same philosopher, Nietzsche, influenced both the ancient Nazis and the Highborn. He espoused the doctrines of the superman and the will to power. Perhaps the Highborn have combed the FEC ranks for superior soldiers and trained them in space marine tactics. And they had powered armor."

"That's all very interesting," said Blanche-Aster. "But normal men can't accelerate at twenty-five Gs."

"You're missing the point, Director. Why are the Highborn training regular men to fight in space? Have they run low of Highborn personnel?"

"I would think so," said Blanche-Aster. "And if so, then Yezhov's plan becomes even more essential."

Hawthorne regarded the Madam Director. "A momentous decision rests on us."

Blanche-Aster looked away, troubled.

"I think Admiral Sioux knew that when she sent the message."

"I don't understand why she didn't self-destruct the ship," said Blanche-Aster. "That she didn't validates my theory that treachery, not some new combat species, lost the beamship."

"Circumstances may have warranted against self-destruction."

"You saw the Admiral as she dictated the message. She wore armor and held a las-rifle. Her officers surrounded her and they stood in the command capsule. Unless… do you think these shock troopers had broken the destruct-link?"

"Who can know," said Hawthorne. "Perhaps not enough of the officers had agreed to self-destruct."

"I realize that too much emphasis on training the intellect and not enough on social responsibility has left much of our military weakened. But these officers were our best, the elite. When the moment came that the *Bangladesh* fell into enemy hands they should have pleaded with the Admiral to destroy it. At the very best, the Highborn will break them in reeducation camps. They gutted sections of the Sun Works Factory. The Highborn will savage them. No. It makes no sense to wish to live through that. Treason, General, if you had all the facts you would see that treachery overcame the *Bangladesh*."

Hawthorne appeared thoughtful. "Maybe the enemy offered them generous terms. They have after all become adept at turning captured soldiers into their own creatures."

"That's what I'm saying. How could an officer steeped in social responsibility possibly consider surviving the capture of his ship?"

"The will to live is strong," Hawthorne said philosophically. "It may be that not all the officers were up to the task."

"Treachery piled upon treason. This is a terrible blow, unfathomable, mysterious and sinister. We can't allow the Highborn to tow the *Bangladesh* to the Sun Works Factory."

Hawthorne began to pace. "If you'll excuse me, Madam Director, I must see the new Space Commander and get his recommendations on how to achieve our goal."

Blanche-Aster motioned to her guard-clone. "I'm sorry to have brought this news, General. My recommendation is to look into each of the officer's records. Somewhere is the clue as to who sold his comrades to the Highborn." The guard-clone wheeled the Madam Director away.

Hawthorne turned to Captain Mune.

For the first time during the conversation, the hulking bionic soldier seemed otherwise than a statue. His steely eyes flickered over the hunch-shouldered General. "It has to be done, sir."

"You're right, Captain. But it's a filthy business." Hawthorne knew he had to order the *Bangladesh* destroyed, to kill his own people, those who had survived the storm assault.

"That's why they pay us, sir, to do the dirty work the civilians won't."

Hawthorne smiled painfully, putting his hand on Captain Mune's shoulder. "Let's get this over with, shall we."

"Yes, sir."

The two men headed down the corridor to Space Command.

24.

With his battlesuit powered down low Marten crept through a corridor.

For 72 hours, he had survived the cat and mouse chase. First, he'd modified his battlesuit, removing its electronic ID tag and switching the setting of his Friend or Foe selector. Then he'd jury-rigged *Bangladesh* damage control crawlers, setting them on automated search and repair. The massive inner destruction to the beamship kept them busy. They thus constantly moved, which showed up on the *Bangladesh's* motion detectors. Those detectors Marten destroyed with religious fervor, along with deactivating ship's cameras. Then a coded command—preset by Admiral Sioux—shut down the beamship's computers and engines. From their comlink chatter Marten learned that the shock troops gave first priority to restarting the engines, then to hunting him, and finally to trying to override the computers.

For the past 72 hours, Marten had lived on stims, Tempo and water. He had debated about walking up to a group of his old comrades and explaining reality to them. They could listen or gun him down. He'd abandoned the idea when he couldn't think around the fact that they would simply capture him and leave him for the HBs. Then in a recreation room he'd run across several recorders. He climbed outside the ship through a damaged section, and carefully thought out his options. After a half hour, he recorded a message. It went like this:

"I've given this a lot of thought, more than probably any of you realize. The Highborn mean to rule us, the premen herds.

296

They won't stop with the premen herds of Earth or Venus; they will go on to the Jupiter, Saturn, Neptune and Uranus herds. At least that's how they think of us, as cattle. If Omi were awake, he'd confirm their plan to geld us. Think about that: cutting off your balls to make you more docile. That's what Training Master Lycon said. I heard it and so did Omi. Sure, we're the shock troopers, the elite, the purebreds, they say. But what kind of future is it if we're the premen, the Pre-Men?"

He switched the recorder off and thought more. Finally:

"Kang and others will tell you it is the best deal we can get. They're probably right. The HBs won't give you a better deal than what you already have. The truth is I'm not promising you anything new, except you get to keep your manhood. What I'm suggesting is to use it, to make your manhood count. Stand up like a man and take action. Or play it safe and remain a slave as you are. I heard Omi say a few weeks ago that we're like nothing more than those oversized fighting fish at the Pleasure Palace. If that's all you want to be, then you deserve castration. Only I don't think that's true, either. No one deserves that. So that's what I think, I, Marten Kluge the Man. What do you think?"

Marten turned off the recorders and played back the message. Maybe he could refine later it to something perfect, but it said what he felt. When he returned to the inside of the ship, he left the recorders in various open spots he knew the shock troopers would come through. He hoped it would sway them, but he didn't think it would. He just wanted somebody to know what he thought. Besides, it felt good to speak his mind.

Now, after 72 hours, he realized that as good as he was he couldn't keep ahead of thirty or so shock troopers forever. That's how many they kept in rotation hunting him. It was a big ship with kilometers of open corridors and spaces, but they were good and learning fast. So as little as he had in way of supplies and without Omi, he crept for the escape pods. Earlier there had been too much fighting around them. Now some escape pods would be rigged, he knew, but he had to get off the ship while there was still time. He paused, extreme fatigue pulling at his eyelids. Every part of his body ached. At times he found himself blinking, wondering how he'd walked so far. He realized he was falling asleep on his feet. Soon he'd simply keel over. Then he'd probably wake up with Kang holding a vibroknife under his chin.

The corridor was dark. Blasted utility units lay like junk on the floor. Dried blood was smeared everywhere. The corpses had been removed, whether by busy damage control vehicles or shock troopers, he didn't know or really care. To activate his radar might give away his position, so his visor was up and he washed the corridor with a helmet-lamp on low.

The *Bangladesh's* air was a cocktail of strange odors. He picked out blood, the stench of laser-burns, plasma and hot grease. The tread of his half-ton battlesuit was loud, the servomotors a constant reminder that eventually his suit would break down.

A loud *click* made him freeze. It came from around the corner.

He switched off the helmet-lamp and waited in darkness. No one washed radar over him and no motion detector could see what didn't move. His eyes couldn't adjust to complete darkness, but his fatigue caused splotches and imaginary images to dance before him. He finally turned his beam back on. The weariness made his skin sag and his limbs tremble.

On ultra-low power, he shuffled toward the corner. He listened, but all he heard was his suit's whine. Finally, he snarled to himself and bounded around the corner, to see two shock troopers aim heavy lasers at him.

When they didn't fire, he shined his headlight on their helmets. Stenciled on the foreheads was LANCE, VIP.

Vip's visor opened, although Lance's remained shut.

Marten wanted to tramp the last few meters between them and hug the rat-faced little Vip. The crazy eyes jittered and the mashed nose was the same. Vip even managed a grin.

"Hey, Maniple Leader."

"Hey, Vip."

"I listened to your tape. Made some sense."

"What about Lance? What does he think?"

"He thinks you're crazy."

"Is he going to shoot me?" asked Marten.

"I don't think he's made up his mind."

"Where are the others?"

"Around."

"How come you're here, Vip?"

"Doesn't this seem like the obvious place for you come?"

"Yeah, I suppose it does. So why isn't everyone here?"

"They're not as patient as me."

Marten smiled.

"But you're also out of luck," Vip said.

"Why is that?"

"The other shock troops launched escape pods whenever they came upon them so the Social Unitarians couldn't use them. Once Kang linked up with them and we took control of the ship, they launched the rest. I think maybe one got away with SU people aboard."

Marten swayed as he felt his resolve beginning to crumble.

"Maybe that's why some of the others didn't stake out this area. They knew the pods were gone, so why should you try for them?"

"Yeah," Marten said.

"So you're out of luck."

Marten nodded.

"If you want to come with me I'll see that they treat you right."

"Until the HBs show up."

"You've burned your bridges, Maniple Leader. Which isn't like you. Usually you have two plans going at once."

"I'm a soldier. It's what I'm supposed do."

"Yeah," Vip said. They looked at each other. "What should I tell Lance?"

Marten glanced at the dark visor, at the laser-tube aimed at his chest. That wasn't a little las-rifle but the heavy-duty beamer that could penetrate battlesuit armor.

"Ask Lance if he wants it on his conscience that he's the one who captured me so the HBs could put me in a pain booth."

"I can answer that for him. It would bug him."

"That's it?" Marten said. "Just bug him?"

"Yeah. Lance is pretty set on making it out alive."

Marten nodded. He was so tired. He wanted to quit now anyway. Instead: "I'm leaving, Vip."

"Where can you go?"

"I don't know. But I haven't given up yet."

Vip chuckled.

"If Lance wants to shoot me, now is the time."

Vip glanced at Lance, and it seemed as if Vip listened. Then Vip grinned again. "Good-bye, Maniple Leader."

"Good-bye, Vip. And Vip?"

"Yeah?"

"Why don't you leave Omi somewhere I can pick him up?"

"Maniple Leader... it's over, finished. You're a dead man. Do you really want to take Omi down with you?"

Marten considered that. He finally nodded. "Omi would want me to."

"Okay. I'll think about it." Vip cocked his head. "You'd better go if you want to stay free for a while longer."

Marten hesitated, and then he stood at attention and saluted Vip and Lance. When Lance saluted back, Marten hurried away into the darkness.

25.

A 623 Prowler Repair pod scanned the inner ring of the Sun Works Factory. Expelled hydrogen particles propelled it across the metallic surface, a man-sized globe with a small radar packet and searchlight that swept back and forth. It cut a twenty-meter swath as it first went fifteen kilometers one way and then turned around and traveled fifteen kilometers the other way. Twenty meters at time, searching, scanning, the white light washing over the station for signs of breach or meteor damage.

Then it found something. Its searchlight washed over a large hole. The tiny pod computer beamed a message to the main station comp. As it waited, the red strobe light atop it winked at ten second intervals. A message returned.

The Prowler pod acknowledged and logged the command, and then so very gently it applied thrust as it entered the gaping hole. The white light washed over a large cavity and over what appeared to be ship locks and oxygen pumps. Then two floating objects, highly reflective, man-shaped and secured by lines to the farthest reaches of the cave came to light. The Prowler pod paused, rotated and slowly withdrew from the gaping indentation. All the while, it broadcast an emergency code for the two life forms it had found outside the livable portion of the station.

26.

Anxiety on one hand, and boredom on the other, had turned Training Master Lycon irritable. He sat in front of a computer screen and checked report after report. He rubbed his eyes and leaned back in his chair. Outside his cubicle marched a platoon of monitors, barking orders and promising dire wrath to anyone that slacked off.

The anxiety came because too few shock troopers had made it aboard the beamship. The skill of the enemy in repelling so many space marines had surprised the Top Ranked Highborn and even more surprised Lycon. It was another dreaded indication that not everything went according to the great master plan. That in turn had weakened the Grand Admiral's position—and that hurt Lycon because the Grand Admiral was his sponsor. The *Bangladesh's* surprise proton-beam attack had already dealt the Grand Admiral a severe blow. That a premen spacecraft had been able to cause so much damage and thereby throw the Highborn into such a crisis meant that someone had erred. Premen were inferior, a fact that no one could deny. Inferior beings do not deal superior beings such reverses unless those in charge are reckless or careless. Logic dictated as much. And since the Grand Admiral was ultimately in charge of all Highborn activity, this crisis threatened his exalted position.

Even worse than the weakening to the Grand Admiral's position—in Lycon's view and to his goal—was that because of the *Bangladesh's* success the Sun Works premen had become restless. They stirred with the beginnings of rebellion.

And the scandal with the Chief Monitors, that they had been practicing drug lords, had hurt, too. Their daring was amazing and disconcerting to the Top Ranked. How Hansen and his chief aide had escaped was still a mystery. That there had been corruption among the most trusted premen and now with these hints of rebellion had proved to the Top Ranked that premen could never be trusted. That severely weakened the validity of the shock troops in space. In other words, the Praetor's philosophy and those who held it had gained ascendancy. Drug lords working under the Praetor's administration undermined his authority. He thus drove all Sun Works personnel to acts of precision and relentless activity.

That meant the Training Master and his marshals helped suppress preman thoughts of rebellion. Thus he and the other four "beta" Highborn, Lycon's training team, oversaw monitors who made sure premen repair teams did their utmost.

Lycon read more reports. A few minutes later, a cough interrupted him. He scowled at a monitor, a lean man who stared at the floor.

"Yes?" asked Lycon.

"Highborn, there is a report that might interest you."

"Yes, yes," said Lycon.

Without looking up, the monitor held out a paper.

For reasons he couldn't explain Lycon hesitated. Then he snatched the paper. "A pod found two premen, so what?"

"The pickup ship did a bioscan, Highborn."

Lycon's eyes dropped to the paper:

Bioscan: Heydrich Hansen, Ervil Haldeman

"Is this certain?" asked Lycon.

"Yes, Highborn. My team awaits your orders to bring them around or not."

"Meaning what?"

"They've been given Suspend, Highborn. Both are very much alive."

Lycon wondered what this meant to him. Maybe nothing at all or maybe— He nodded. "Yes, revive them and let me know when they come around."

"Yes, Highborn." The monitor saluted and marched away.

Lycon thoughtfully rubbed his jaw and then he turned back to the reports and kept on reading.

***

An hour later Lycon stood in a sterile medical center. A gnome-like doctor in a green gown stared meekly at the floor while nurses hurried by. One level down was the Neutraloid surgery room. This level saw to burn and revival victims.

"Are they both lucid?" asked Lycon.

"Yes, Highborn," said the doctor, a wizened old woman with bad breath.

"Have either made any statements?"

"Both were cautious, Highborn, and were clearly terrified. They raved, in fact, one of them trying to break free to kill the other. At my orders, both were been given tranquilizers. They are heavily sedated."

"I'll see them anyway."

"Yes, Highborn." The old doctor opened the nearest door.

The room was small, with two steel-lined beds, each holding a white paper-clothed occupant. Short, broad-shouldered Ervil lay strapped to his bed. He stared at the ceiling with blank eyes. Hansen kept testing his straps, until he noticed Lycon. He paled considerably.

"You may leave," Lycon told the doctor.

"Yes, Highborn." She hurried out.

Hansen managed to pry open his lips. "You-you-you…"

Lycon cocked his head. As a former Chief Monitor, Hansen should know better than to speak first; even drugged he should know. Why was it that both the Praetor's chief monitors lacked proper protocol?

"You are an odd species," said Lycon, moving closer, putting his hands on the bed's stainless steel railing. "Given rank and trust you turn around and practice the worst kind of deceit. Whatever motivated you to manufacture dream dust?"

"Motivated me?" croaked Hansen. "What about you?"

Lycon shook his head. Hopelessly deranged, this one. He had scanned the report of the 623 Prowler's find. It had been a hanger of some kind, and by the particle traces in the hanger, a spacecraft had left within the past few weeks. These two had probably planned to escape and been double-crossed and left behind. As Chief Monitor Hansen had an enviable life ahead of him, Lycon couldn't understand why he would make drugs and then try to flee to who-knew-where?

Hansen drooled and spoke in sly undertones. "You killed Bock for a reason. I know that much."

"Highborn," corrected Lycon. "When you speak to your superiors you must use the correct protocol procedures."

Hansen blinked several times before he asked, "If you're so high-born how come everyone's been able to trick you so easily?"

"Explain."

Hansen's head lolled back and forth across his pillow. "No, no, no. Nothing for nothing is my motto. If you wanna know then you gotta promise to help me."

"Don't trust him," warned Ervil.

Lycon was surprised that Ervil meant the warning for him. "Why shouldn't I trust Hansen?" he asked, bemused by these two.

"Because he's a double-dealing bastard. I'll kill him when I get the chance."

"Be quiet, Ervil," slurred Hansen. "We gotta get Lycon to help us." With his long, sly face, Hansen regarded Lycon. "You'd better deal with me. It would be in your long term interest."

Lycon snorted at their audacity. Two hopeless buffoons that had no idea of the danger they were in. The best way to use them was as a lever on the Praetor. It seemed incredible that these two had been the masterminds behind the dream dust operation.

"So do we have a deal?" asked Hansen.

For their lack of proper protocol, he should discipline the premen. But what was the use? Lycon strode from the room and found the wizened old doctor.

"Yes, Highborn?"

"Transfer those two downstairs," he said.

"To the Neutraloid section, Highborn?"

He checked his chronometer. "Do it immediately and inform me when the operations are complete. Tell no one about this, not even the Praetor's people. I want to surprise him."

"Yes, Highborn, it shall be as you say."

27.

The cell door slid open and a shock trooper shoved Admiral Rica Sioux in. She staggered and collapsed in a heap, the front of her dress uniform spotted with blood. She'd been captured during the fighting and later had the privilege of watching the shock troopers break her officers. A brutish monster named Kang had laughed as he'd used a shock rod on the First and Second Gunner. Both had died honorably under the shock trooper's caresses, revealing nothing about the beamship's functions. The Pilot however had broken after the third shock-rod stroke.

With that information, the enemy had been able to turn the *Bangladesh* and now braked at two-Gs. Kang had continued to torture the others for further information, turning the command-capsule into an abattoir.

"Are you all right, Admiral?" asked the Tracking Officer. They were in a security cell, six of them packed in a room built for two.

Rica Sioux spit blood from her mouth. They had knocked out her false teeth and had given her drugs to keep her tripping heart from quitting. Her chest thudded, and it made breathing a dreadful chore. She knew that at best she only a few hours left.

"They're monsters," said the Tracking Officer, as she knelt over the Admiral and carefully blotted blood with a dirty rag.

"It doesn't matter," whispered Rica Sioux."

"Yes, it matters," said the Tracking Officer.

Rica Sioux closed her eyes. The *Bangladesh* was doomed. The monster in the command capsule was doomed. Sadly, so were the last of her officers. She'd seen the dead shock troopers laying in their battlesuits. Too bad, they hadn't been able to kill all the enemy space marines. She'd asked to speak with the cunning leader who had foiled them, the one who had called her and had led the smaller team. None of the enemy had looked at her then. That's when her beatings had really started. So she'd asked only once more, and Kang had knocked her implants out one by one, telling her to mind her own business.

"What do you mean it doesn't matter?" asked the Tracking Officer.

Rica Sioux opened her eyes and closed them again. The Tracking Officer was a blur to her. Anyway, it hurt her head too much trying to see. She wouldn't say why it didn't matter because she was afraid the officers had all turned. They knew she planned something, and they no doubt worked for that monster in her command capsule. The Highborn had trained him well. That monster, Kang, he was much more clever than he looked. He understood about breaking people. It was an art he knew well. Her officers should have let her blow the ship.

"Admiral!"

"Leave me alone," whispered Rica Sioux.

"She's dying," said someone.

"Better tell Kang."

Rica Sioux smiled. There! Now she knew they had been turned.

"Admiral!"

"Good-bye," said Rica Sioux. Her old heart defeated the drugs trying to keep it going. The ancient organ quit and Admiral Sioux stopped breathing.

28.

Marten woke up outside the beamship, secured to the underside of a blasted particle shield. He'd slept nineteen hours. It didn't completely dispel his extreme exhaustion, but he'd woken with an idea. That's how it usually went with him. He had a problem. He wrestled with it and then he went to sleep. When he woke up or during his morning shower, the answer just popped into his head.

He could use a shower now. His jumpsuit was grimy and he itched all over. As he sipped water from his tube, he relieved himself. A battlesuit's waste-disposal system regressed a shock trooper back into a baby with diapers. He went in his suit and the battlesuit recycled the body wastes for him. A handy feature, Marten supposed, but he always felt strange using it. He slurped concentrates and began the journey back into the beamship.

Once aboard he used a comlink to check various damage control crawlers that had been under his command nineteen hours ago. Six of them had been shut down. He checked his own motion detectors that he'd been setting up the entire time and saw that six battlesuits roved the engine room looking for him.

They had probably grown tired of searching for the unfindable, the reason only six did it and not the usual thirty. Anyway, he finally had the answer to his problem. The question was, could he implement the answer before the HBs arrived? Leaning his half-ton battlesuit against a wall and switching off, he began the three-minute procedure that took him out of it.

He felt naked stepping out the suit in his bare feet. The two Gs of braking pulled hard at his muscles, but it felt wonderful to scratch his chest and legs and a spot on his back. Then he put on a special cup around his genitals. Two Gs could do the nastiest things. Finally, putting on combat boots, he prowled the corridors until he came upon one of the shut-down damage control crawlers.

He manually opened a hatch, slipped into the cushioned seat and checked the HUD controls. Soon he revved the crawler into life and peeled out, traveling down the long, empty corridors. He sped toward a specially-selected missile locker. It took him an hour to crawl past all the battle damage and take two detours from prowling shock troopers. Finally, he entered a huge storage area, devoid of light. With the crawler's beam, he viewed the huge missiles that still hung from their racks. Using the vehicle's mechanical arms, he hauled two of the missiles from their racks to a nearby firing tube. Unfortunately, the firing tube was blasted wreckage.

He checked the time and decided to leave on the double. Too long in one place was asking for bad luck. As he drove, he pulled a detonator out of his pocket and pressed several buttons. The *Bangladesh* shuddered so he knew that several of his pre-positioned bombs had gone off. Just as importantly, the two Gs of braking quit and he felt the zero G. The automatic engaging of the crawler's magnetic locks told him that.

He grinned. That should keep the others busy fixing the engines. The damage shouldn't be too great. Enough to temporarily stop the engines but not enough so they would throw up their hands and hunt him in vengeance. Still, this would make them angry and search harder. So he headed for his battlesuit. It was time to go outside again.

***

From outside the *Bangladesh* he worked to clear his chosen firing tube. He'd found several Zero-G Worksuits and had torn them apart, taking a welder arm and work laser. As he clung like a fly to the vast beamship, he used both tools on the tube, cutting a bigger opening. The glare of the welder and the laser caused his visor to polarize.

"Marten!" suddenly blared in his headphones. It was Kang.

Marten shut off the work laser, hooking it to his battlesuit. Magnetic clamps kept him attached to the *Bangladesh*. Around him shone millions of stars. The particle shield behind him kept the blazing Sun from cooking him.

"I know you can hear me, Marten. And I know that you're too scared to answer. But here's my deal. We'll stop hunting for you if you promise not to blow any more bombs. The men agreed to let the HBs do their own dirty work. You were a shock trooper once and you did help some of us enter the beamship. Vip says you want Omi. So we're leaving him in the Deck 15 Recreation Room. I know you know the ship's layout like the back of your hand. You can pick Omi up if you want. We won't stop you. And I'll give you this, Marten. You're a tough bastard. Kang, out."

Marten managed a chuckle. A neat little trap old Kang had set. Could he trust him? He would continue to work on a war footing. Then he reconsidered. This might mean that the HBs were almost here.

Marten swore, turned up his air-conditioner unit, detached the work-laser from his suit and with its beam began to cut through more armor plating.

29.

Lycon stood in the Game Room, as it had come to be called. Sage-dotted dunes rolled under a holo-simulated, sun-bright sky. A machine-made breeze blew past tall cacti while somewhere an eagle screeched.

Lycon wore his blue dress uniform with crisscrossing white straps, with a blaster on his hip and his Magnetic Star First Class on his chest. A wall panel slid up and the huge form of the Praetor strode in. He too wore his uniform, brown with green stripes on the sleeves. His pink eyes glittered and his frown gave him a dreadful presence. Lycon noticed that he carried a folder in his enormous hands.

"Greetings, Praetor."

"Training Master."

"I request an intersystem shuttle so I may head to the *Bangladesh*."

"You have requested such a spacecraft earlier and I denied it. What has now caused you to think that I'll change my mind?"

"Your generosity, Praetor."

If anything, the Praetor seemed to become more dangerous. The inhuman angles to his face tightened and the bristles atop his head seemed to stand that much stiffer. "I am generous to those who help me, Training Master. Once I offered you a position. You refused. Thus I too must refuse this request."

"As you know I am not fond of the Neutraloids. Ideas, not chemicals, are the method to controlling premen."

"I am aware of your position." The Praetor held up his folder. "This will considerably weaken it."

Frowning, Lycon took the proffered folder and paged through it. Space photos, mostly, little specks against the backdrop of the black void. "I don't understand."

"Flip to the back and read the charts."

Lycon did. Missiles, it said. Then he noticed that sweat stung his eyes. He used his sleeve to wipe the sweat. Suddenly he felt weary. Handing back the folder, he asked, "What about the *Gustavus Adolphus*, can't it intercept them?"

"If you would have read a little farther you would have seen that several attempts have been made. The *Gustavus Adolphus* is now headed here. The second Doom Star headed back to Venus quite a bit earlier."

Lycon knew that the Venus Doom Star headed back in order to intercept SU battleships that had sped for Venus as soon as the Doom Star had left the system. Fleet maneuvering was such an intricate game. He shook his head. Infantry tactics is what he knew.

Lycon asked, "Did the *Gustavus Adolphus* try to intercept with battle lasers?"

The Praetor nodded. "Enemy jamming is effective, and of course they jink enough to cause misses."

"What about anti-missile torps?"

"Did you read the distance spreads?"

Lycon shook his head.

"The *Gustavus Adolphus* is still too far out, much too far away to be able to affect the battle. Perhaps battle is the wrong word. Annihilation is more appropriate. The *Bangladesh* is doomed."

Lycon suddenly hated how the Praetor loomed over him. He hated the arrogance in the pink eyes that blazed with the accusation that he was only beta, an original, an inferior Highborn who couldn't think through elementary facts.

"There will be no more shock troops," the Praetor said. "Long-range capture assaults are meaningless when the enemy simply destroys the prize ships."

"Perhaps you are right," said Lycon, desperately trying to control his temper. "Still, I must try to achieve in the manner I think best."

"Your sponsor, the Grand Admiral, has lost face."

"But he hasn't lost rank."

"No," said the Praetor, "not yet."

For a moment, they listened to the holo-simulated eagle screech. Lycon marshalled his thoughts, mastered his anger and spoke in an even tone.

"I say this without rancor, Praetor, but you too have lost face."

The nine-foot tall Highborn grew very still. Lycon felt the hostility, the emanating rage.

"Is this how you would move me to give you a shuttle?" the Praetor asked softly.

"I appeal rather to your logic."

"I see no such appeal."

Lycon detached a small capsule from his belt. He handed it to the Praetor, who merely eyed him with a strange, pink-eyed suspicion.

"There is a button on this capsule. When you press it four Neutraloids will be released into the Game Room."

The Praetor shrugged.

"The names of the Neutraloids might interest you."

"What possible interest could such names contain for me?"

"Dalt and Methlen are two of them. Ervil and former Chief Monitor Hansen are the others."

A strange ecstasy twisted the Praetor's features. In a husky voice he asked, "Is this true?"

"It is true."

The Praetor reached for the capsule and hesitated. "Once news of their capture spreads it will strengthen my position."

"Yes, Praetor, this I realize."

"Changing them into Neutraloids will also prove that traitorous premen can be rehabilitated through my procedure."

"Agreed."

"It would seem I owe you a favor."

"My only desire is to serve."

314

The Praetor nodded. "I order you to the *Bangladesh*, Training Master. Take your training marshals and do what you can for your doomed shock troops."

"As you command, Praetor." Lycon clicked his heels and dropped the capsule into the Superior's huge hand.

The Praetor closed his fingers around it, an awful smile on his pearl-white face. "I'll wait until you've cleared the room."

"Thank you, Praetor." Lycon strode quickly, and once over the first set of dunes he began to jog. After the third set of dunes, he passed two cages. One held three Neutraloids, savage beings, their muscles quivering, stark and tattooed a deep blue color. They snarled at the fourth Neutraloid, one alone in its own cage. He was thinner, with white bushy eyebrows and a long face. His muscles also quivered and hate blazed from his eyes. He held onto the bars of his cage, watching Lycon as he passed, never taking his eyes from him.

Lycon felt uncomfortable being the object of such hatred. How the Praetor hoped to use these creatures was beyond him. They were brutes, nothing more, berserk killers, unusable in any but the most artificial circumstances.

"Hansen!" snarled one of the Neutraloids, the shortest of the caged three, he with extra-broad shoulders. "We're gonna skin you alive, Hansen!"

"Eat you!" shouted another, straining, reaching between two bars as if he could clutch the one he hated.

"Kill you, you bastard!" howled the third, rattling his cage as hard as he could.

Hansen shuddered, but he didn't take his eyes off Lycon.

Then, thankfully, Lycon topped the last set of dunes and hurried for the exit.

30.

Marten waited until the end to get Omi. He didn't trust Kang. But he figured the others had spoken honestly. He probably would never have been able to build his jury-rigged craft if they had kept after him.

His ship amounted to two missiles, minus the warheads he'd detached from them. He'd welded several damage control vehicles to the missiles. Those he had cut apart and re-welded, gutting some to make room for a medical unit, supplies, computers, radar equipment and the like. What his ship amounted to was a seat and toilet for him and a medical rack for Omi, who would remain in his Suspend condition. Unfortunately, Suspend wasn't cryogenic sleep. It was meant for temporary suspension of cell death until a doctor could repair massive bodily damage. The longest anyone dosed with Suspend had been kept under and brought back to normal was about three months. Marten figured his trip would take at least a year, and that would merely bring them to far Earth orbit. From there...

He refused to think about then. One problem at a time was all he could deal with. A year sitting in one spot—He blanked that out too. Survival, the refusal to quit was what drove him. Social Unity hadn't broken him. He wasn't going to let the Highborn kill him.

The time finally came to get Omi. He used an engine core-lift with detachable controls, normally used to go into the Fusion Drive and repair damage. From outside the beamship he controlled the core-lift, which drove to where they had put

Omi. Under Marten's guidance, the vehicle picked up the motionless Korean and carried him to an outer lock. There the core-lift deposited Omi, who still wore his battlesuit and helmet. The inner lock closed and the outer one opened ten seconds later. Marten couldn't know it, but Vip had removed the bug that Kang had put on Omi as well as shut off the alarm rigged to him.

After a long wait, Marten picked up Omi and carried him to his ship, which was clamped like a lamprey to the side of the *Bangladesh*. His craft's airlock took up half the free space of the escape vehicle. Inside the ship, he pried Omi out of the battlesuit and hooked him to the medical unit. The battlesuit he stored in the same locker where he'd put his own. Then he settled into his chair and activated the bombs that he'd put on this particle shield's struts. They blew, and the busted shield detached and floated away from the *Bangladesh*. Marten flipped switches and released his ship's magnetic locks. He too floated away from the beamship.

The *Bangladesh* braked at two Gs, although such was its velocity that it still moved farther from the Sun.

Marten used the hydrogen burners he'd taken off several zero-G Worksuits and welded to his makeshift capsule. Slowly, he moved toward the floating particle shield and then up and over it and then behind it. From there Omi and he were shielded from the *Bangladesh*.

Marten stared at the stars. One year sitting in this seat beside his only friend in the medical unit was going to be a long time.

"Here goes," whispered Marten. He fired the first missile, and was slammed back into his chair as the rocket burned and accelerated them.

31.

Marten traveled five hundred kilometers from the *Bangladesh* when the missiles launched by General Hawthorne's orders slammed into the vast beamship. The missiles had been fired from the missileships that the experimental beamship had been en route to meet—from the flotilla the beamship was to lead to Mars. The nuclear explosions vaporized much of the mighty structure and irradiated everything else. More missiles arrived and detonated, chewing up the mass into finer debris.

Marten had fled far enough so that the heat and blast from the explosions had no effect upon him or his ship. The electromagnetic pulse, however, blew his main controls, prematurely detaching the living quarters from the two missiles. Marten and Omi tumbled end over end as the welded missiles sped in the direction of where Earth would be in a year.

Openmouthed, shocked and uncomprehending Marten stared at the spinning stars. Finally, numbly, he used the hydrogen burners to stop their endless spinning. He wanted to scream, to rave at the injustice and futility of life. Yet he wasn't vanquished. He refused to surrender. They still had air and could survive for a long, long time.

So that he wouldn't cry or go berserk, he began to sing the songs his mother had taught him in the Sun Works Factory. *A Mighty Fortress is Our God* by an ancient called Martin Luther was the song he remembered best. He sang until his throat went raw, then like a lunatic absorbed in his dull witlessness, he stared at the vast star-field the entire time.

32.

Sometime later Lycon's intersystem shuttle sniffed through the *Bangladesh's* debris, which maintained its velocity and heading. Scanners searched the junk for signs of life.

Lycon had studied the shock trooper transmissions sent from the *Bangladesh* before it had been destroyed. Those who had stormed aboard the beamship had clearly taken heavy losses. Highborn training had given them strict procedures for dead or dying shock troopers. Such individuals were to be injected with Suspend and battlesuited with fully charged tanks and their vents opened to ship air. When the beamship had been destroyed, the air vents would have automatically closed and the battlesuit would have switched to tank air. Those suits were the best in the Solar System, able to take incredible damage. Lycon's hope was that a few such premen had survived the nuclear explosions. He needed live shock troopers as examples of the success of his idea.

A day's search garnered exactly nothing.

To go home empty-handed meant at the very best that he would become a trainer of the Neutraloids. Lycon loathed the idea. "Increase the range of our sweeps," he ordered.

"At once," said the training marshal acting as pilot.

They searched a second day and then a third. On the fourth day, the pilot turned to Lycon.

"I'm picking up a distress call."

Lycon lurched to the com-board.

"I can't make anything out of it," said the pilot.

"Go there," said Lycon.

"Are you certain?"

Lycon laughed harshly. "I grasp at straws because we have nothing else."

The pilot set course for the weak distress call.

33.

First, Marten saw the braking jets, a bright smear in the darkness of space. Then he watched the shuttle visibly grow from a dot to that of a discernible spacecraft.

A beard covered his face and his muscles had already grown slack. He couldn't describe his emotions. Birth was indescribable. To float alone in space, drifting, hopeless, repeatedly rethinking conversations and actions was a hellish experience. He shuddered and made a croaking sound after crying for a long, long time. He believed he would walk again, talk to people, eat, think, and have plans, hopes and dreams, and fight.

He tried to concentrate. Training Master Lycon had come. Lycon was Highborn. The last time they had spoken Lycon had been unhappy with him. Marten couldn't concentrate. Instead, he wiped tears from his cheeks. Oh how he wanted to live.

"But not on their terms," he croaked.

He sipped water from his bottle and shook his head. The stirrings of hatred returned. To be born afresh, that's what he experienced. Life! What an incredible word it was. What a gift to breathe, play, eat, and meet women. Life!

"Hurry up," he whispered, his heart beginning to race.

34.

The shuttle eased beside the tiny life-pod, dwarfing it, belittling its crudeness. An emergency tube of flexible plastic snaked from the shuttle and sealed over the pod's airlock. Soon air was pumped into the tube. After a time the pod's hatch slid up and Marten Kluge pushed an inert Omi toward the shuttle.

Marten peered at the vastness of space surrounding him. He used the plastic railing attached to the inner tube, pushing Omi and pulling himself. The shuttle airlock opened and Lycon waited at the end, his angular face impassive, but his strange energetic eyes filled with questions, and it seemed to Marten, traces of wonder.

As Marten pushed Omi to Lycon, the powerful Highborn nodded. Marten nodded back as one would to an equal. They entered the shuttle's airlock. As the inner hatch opened, Lycon removed his vacc helmet.

"He has a plasma burn on his chest," Marten told a waiting Highborn, a seven-foot fellow with a medical tag on his shirt. "If you have any medical facilities—"

"We do," said Lycon.

"Good," Marten said. He took Omi from Lycon and pushed him to the other Highborn. "Let's get him hooked in and brought around."

The two Highborn exchanged glances. "Yes, a good idea," Lycon said a moment later. Together the three of them floated Omi to the medical center. There the second Highborn took over, stripping Omi of his filthy clothes, tsking at the sight of the ugly plasma burn across his chest and then securing him into the medical cradle. Drugs, blood and special concentrates surged through the attached tubes and for the first time in weeks Omi's body quivered with life.

The other Highborn checked his medscanner. Then he turned it on Marten, sweeping it over him. To Lycon he said, "He should shower, change into clean clothes and take an injection I'll prepare."

Lycon turned to Marten.

"I heard him," Marten said. "Just point the way."

Lycon hesitated, nonplussed, before pointing toward a hatch.

***

Apparent gravity returned to the shuttle as it accelerated at one-G for Earth. Marten relaxed in a chair, sipping coffee. He wore a clean jumpsuit with the shock trooper skull-patch on his right pectoral and left shoulder. The beard was gone and his blond hair was cut short. He was thinner, his cheeks gaunt. His eyes had changed. They were hooded, guarded, wary. It seemed too as if part of him still floated alone in space, as if not all of him had returned to the land of the living.

The exercise room had padded walls and ceiling and several isometric machines. Lycon sat across from Marten. The seven-foot Highborn, with his legs crossed, doodled with a stylus on a portable comp-screen.

A door opened and the Highborn acting as medical officer poked his head in and reported to Lycon. "It looks like it will be a full recovery."

"When can I talk to him?" asked Marten.

The Highborn scowled, although he said, "Two days, two and a half at the most."

"Thanks. I appreciate what you've done."

The Highborn lifted his eyebrows before he withdrew, closing the hatch behind him.

"Your experience was no doubt horrifying," said Lycon. "But you must use correct protocol procedures when addressing us."

Marten smiled, but more the way a gang leader would to a cop than with any genuine pleasure. "Yes, Highborn," he said, saluting him with the coffee cup.

Lycon frowned. Then he sat a little straighter and tapped the tip of the stylus on the portable comp-screen. "I'm curious how Omi and you found yourself in such a makeshift escape pod."

Marten crossed his legs and leaned back in his chair. He didn't stare at the Highborn. Rather, he picked a point on the wall to examine.

"The *Bangladesh's* pods had already been jettisoned, Highborn."

"Yes. But how did you come to make your spacecraft?"

"From an intense desire to leave the beamship, Highborn."

"You knew that the missiles were coming?"

"To my knowledge, Highborn, the shock troops never fixed the beamship's radar pods. Yet the enemy missiles did seem like a logical move on Social Unity's part. Logic then demands one find a way to avoid the missiles."

"Your craft only has what appear to be hydrogen burners taken off zero-G Worksuits."

"The EMP blast from the enemy missiles wreaked havoc on my controls, Highborn. Because of mixed signals the missiles I'd attached to my pod dropped off and rocketed away."

"Your heading appears to have been toward Venus or Earth."

"To Earth, Highborn."

"Shock troop headquarters is on the Sun Works Factory."

"The Sun is also much hotter there, Highborn. Among other things I feared radiation poisoning."

"What did the others think about your escape plan?"

"I didn't ask all of them, Highborn."

"They didn't try to stop you?"

"For awhile they did, Highborn. Then they said they wouldn't try to stop me anymore."

"What convinced them that what you did was correct?"

"I worked hard to persuade them, Highborn. I can only think they finally fell to the force of my arguments"

"Your answers are evasive, Marten. Why is that?"

"I'm merely stating facts, Highborn."

325

Lycon tapped the stylus once again. "Facts as you deem them or the truth?"

"Highborn... You consider me a preman. How am I supposed to discover truth?"

"You *are* a preman, Marten."

Marten remained silent.

"Ah. You don't believe that, is that it?"

"I fought in the FEC ranks, Highborn, and was among the first to storm the merculite missile battery in Tokyo. Because of it, I received a medal and entrance into the shock troops. As such, I led the experimental assault upon the *Bangladesh*. We conquered the beamship as ordered, but it was destroyed. Omi and I are the only survivors, at least as far as I know. Given these facts it is difficult for me to think of myself as just a preman."

"You have done well," Lycon said, "and you are a gifted tactician. Sometimes I wonder about your loyalty, but as you say, you have worked hard in the service of the Highborn. Such hard service brings rank, as you have learned. The facts also show that you are superior among premen. Who else among the shock troops escaped the *Bangladesh*? That is why as Training Master of the shock troopers I am recommending that you receive the 'Hammer of Thor' medal for excellence in combat."

Marten sat up. "You honor me, Highborn."

"The Grand Admiral himself will pin you with the Hammer of Thor and Omi with the Crossed Swords."

"We head to Earth, Highborn?"

"We do. And the shock troopers are to be reborn."

"But... The beamship was destroyed, Highborn."

"The Grand Admiral has a different use for you, one in orbital Earth. You and Omi will each be a commander of an assault force. They will be named Assault Force Marten and Assault Force Omi."

"You're making us into heroes?"

"You will be models of what one can achieve if he labors hard in the service of the Highborn."

"I... I don't know what to say."

"Highborn," corrected Lycon.

326

Slowly, Marten said, "Yes, Highborn."

Lycon rose. "Excellence brings rank, Marten. Ponder that." He strode out of the room.

Marten did ponder it. A hero for the beings he hated. They had once thought to castrate him. What was to stop other Highborn from doing it? They had loaded the shock troopers into missiles, as living ammunition. They treated him as an inferior, as a trained animal. These medals were pats on the head. Now they planned to do it again.

Marten squinted. He was on a shuttle, a spaceship. Only three Highborn were aboard. If the Highborn died... he would finally own his own spacecraft.

Marten's heartbeat quickened as he began to make plans.

35.

It was dark in the shuttle as Marten crept to the medical unit. The ship was under one G of acceleration. Using the glow of the life-support monitor, he examined Omi lying in the clear cylinder. Tubes were attached to the Korean's flesh. His chest rose and fell with each breath.

Marten studied the cylinder. It was airtight. He pressed a switch. There was a beep as a small red light blinked. Clamps appeared, securing the medical unit for emergency ship maneuvers.

Marten exited the chamber. His features were stern and his heart hammered. Any number of things could go wrong. He knew Highborn arrogance had given him this chance. Surely, they couldn't believe they were in danger from a lone preman.

The hatch to Lycon's sleep cubicle was open. This evening, all the hatches were open. Marten had made sure.

He eased onto his stomach and slithered past the hatch. On his feet again and in another section of the shuttle, he used a stolen electronic key, opening the suit locker. With practiced speed, he donned his old vacc suit. He tried to be quiet, but there were clunks and clatters. Finally, he sealed his helmet and shuffled to the airlock.

A fierce grin spread across his face. The Highborn had been careless. He was only a preman. What could he do to them?

Marten produced an override unit, one he'd tampered with the past few hours. He licked his lips and entered his code. Then he engaged the manual override. Numbers flashed on the unit. A klaxon should have sounded, but Marten had overridden it with his stolen unit.

There was a hiss as the inner hatch slid open. Marten worked feverishly, applying clamps, making sure it was impossible for the inner hatch to close. With the last clamp in place, he stepped into the airlock. He switched on the vacc suit's magnetic hooks to full power, securing himself to the wall. Then he manually opened the outer hatch.

Immediately, air hissed past as it rushed out into the vacuum of space. Then the airlock was open all the way and the sound became a gale-force shriek.

A stylus with a purple tip shot past Marten. Then cups and cutlery flew past as they tumbled into the cold of space.

Marten heard screaming. Almost too fast to notice, the Highborn pilot flew past him. Marten resisted the impulse to lean out and watch. Instead, he remembered how shock troopers had tumbled off the *Bangladesh's* particle shields. Now their arrogant, uncaring commanders would pay.

The medical Highborn flew outside next.

Then Lycon the Training Master appeared. The seven-foot Highborn managed to latch his fingers onto the hatch clamps. He strained to hang on, his massive body inches from Marten. In a feat of amazing strength, Lycon tore off a clamp. With desperate will, he began to work on the second.

Then the rapidly dropping air pressure began to tell on Lycon. His body and face began to bloat as his blood and other bodily fluids began to turn into water vapor and form in his soft tissues. The embollism occurred even more strongly in his lungs. The escaping water vapor cooled around his open mouth and nostrils, creating frost.

Then, as he was magnetically secured, Marten began raining body blows against Lycon's horizontal and now grotesquely swollen torso.

With the last of the ship's air shrieking past his bloated face and whipping his hair, Lycon peered blindly at Marten. The Highborn must have realized he was dying. Maybe he wanted to take Marten with him. Bare fingers reached for Marten. Marten desperately slapped the freakishly large hand. Lycon's frost-covered lips moved soundlessly. Then the huge Highborn lost his grip and he shot out into space. Marten leaned out and watched the Training Master tumble away into the void.

Marten closed the outer hatch. Next, while breathing hard, he turned off his magnetic hooks. Then he removed the clamps and let the inner hatch hiss shut. The shuttle immediately began to pressurize.

A terrifying laugh escaped Marten as he removed his helmet. He owned a spaceship and he was free!

The End

Made in the USA
San Bernardino, CA
05 December 2017